Season On the Brink

by

Rich Maclone

ISBN: 9781070181882

Any reference to historical events, real people, or real places are used fictitiously. Names, characters, and places are products of the author's imagination.

First printing edition 2019.

www.RichMaclone.com

For Owen and James, and

The Fellowship

The Roster

Wes Garrett – Forward, Eastport hockey (Injured)
Craig Bishop – Lineman, Eastport football; Forward, Eastport hockey
Collin "OB" O'Brien – Linebacker, Eastport football; Def., Eastport hockey
Danny Stone – Forward, Eastport hockey
Josh Hutchinson – QB, Eastport football; Forward, Eastport hockey
Cyrus Carpenter – Captain, Eastport hockey
Billy Walker – Captain, Eastport hockey
Scott Frazier – Defense, Wellington Academy hockey
Emily Brown – Captain, Eastport lacrosse
Melissa Johnson – Defense, Eastport lacrosse
John Scadorski – Head Coach, Eastport hockey
Tom Henry – Assistant Coach, Eastport hockey
Harry Burnette – Athletic Director, Eastport High School
Mac Richardson – Sports Reporter, Eastport Enquisitor

1

"You know why I love cooking bacon so much?"

Everyone in the room cringed. They knew the punchline. They'd heard it countless times, and there was nothing they could do to prevent their friend from completing his corny joke.

"Because it sounds like it's cheering for me while I cook it."

Craig Bishop smiled to himself. He knew that the joke, which he'd stolen from Jim Gaffigan's Netflix special, wasn't very funny. Without turning around he could see that his friends were shaking their heads and covering their eyes. It didn't matter, he always told that joke when he cooked pregame breakfast, and that wasn't about to change now.

"That joke isn't getting any funnier, dude," shouted Collin O'Brien from the big chair in the adjoining living room. "You need some new material."

O'Brien returned his attention to the new material he was working on as he strummed away at his guitar. The acoustic six-string looked tiny in comparison to his massive frame, almost like a ukulele would in anyone else's. No matter how hard he tried, he just couldn't get the opening to "Wish You Were Here" down pat. The hammer-ons just weren't right. It was frustrating the 17-year-old immensely.

Josh Hutchinson, Danny Stone and Wes Garrett laughed to themselves, spreading their attention between their friend's typical banter and their iPhones. In most respects, it was just another Saturday morning, like so many before it. In reality, it was different than any they'd experienced before. This one preceded the biggest event of their young lives.

With mischief on his mind, Hutchinson set down the screen in his hand and began to needle O'Brien instead.

"Man, I hope you block better today than you play that guitar. If you don't, I'm going to spend a lot of time on my ass," he said.

O'Brien smiled, removed his left hand from the strings and extended his middle finger toward the kitchen island where his friends sat.

"Keep it up and you'll know exactly what all of the stadium lights look like from a prone position," O'Brien said.

Before the banter could become mean-spirited, Stone changed the subject. "Hey Bish, when's that food going to be ready? I'm starving over here."

The chef grabbed a plate of pancakes piled 18 inches high and spun around. "Someone grab the juice out of the fridge," he said.

Like malnourished animals, the boys grabbed for the pancakes with their bare hands and piled them on their plates. Bishop had made enough food to feed twice as many normal people as were in the room, which still might not be enough for his buddies. He'd fried up two pounds of bacon, cut up a half-dozen apples and emptied two jugs of OJ. It was nice that his grandmother didn't mind the boys emptying her cupboards and freezer every week. It was also smart that she shopped at the warehouse club because this crew ate in bulk.

The boys were too busy filling their plates and stuffing their faces to grab the orange juice. Bishop did it himself. He turned around and was instantly horrified.

"Really, one pancake? I cook for an hour for your dumb asses and you save me one damn pancake?"

"Don't worry, I got you, Bish," Danny said, tossing a pancake from his plate over to his friend.

"Yeah, me too, I got you," Wes said, adding another one to his friend's small pile with his good hand.

That was just how it always was with "the Boys." They'd grown up in the seaside town of Eastport together and had played Little League, Pop Warner and youth hockey together. When O'Brien discovered naked girls on the internet, it wasn't a full day before the rest got their first glimpses of what lay beneath a bra. When Wes had busted up his hand, it was Danny who drove him to the hospital. When he left the exam room the others were in the waiting room. Craig's grandmother, Cookie, liked to say that she felt bad for the girls they were going to marry because they'd have to

7

book flights for all of them to the honeymoon.

The broken hand was still a sore subject for Wes Garrett. His now ex-girlfriend had told him she didn't think they should see each other any more. Someone sent him a message on Twitter saying that it sucked that she'd broken up with him, and then the kids from Hyannis High – Eastport's rival – caught wind of what had happened and decided to have some mean-spirited fun at his expense.

The trolling had been vicious. Pictures from Garrett's Instagram feed, and from the newspaper of him playing baseball, were photoshopped and turned into memes. All of them were sent to him and got meaner and more disgusting as the days passed. The last one he bothered to look at was the straw that broke the camel's back and the picture that eventually broke the linebacker's hand.

The original photo had the happy couple with their arms around one another. Her eyes were drawn to something off-camera, and she had a huge smile on her face. In the moment, on July fourth at a cookout, she was smiling at her five-year-old cousin, who was running through a sprinkler and screaming his head off. In the photoshopped version, she was smiling because someone's junk was coming toward her face. The caption "onto BIGGER things" was beneath the two teenagers.

Wes balled up his right fist and tried to put it through the wall. Had the punch landed a couple of inches to the right or the left, he simply would have had to learn to fix a hole in drywall. He wasn't that lucky, though. Beneath that drywall were two 2x4 studs nailed together, serving as the frame to his bedroom. The drywall caved in some, but the pressure-treated wood beneath did not yield and the knuckles on his middle and ring fingers were busted.

No football at all, a late start to hockey season, and learning to take notes for classes with his left hand were what he had in store for the upcoming months. Not playing football was tough. He knew that with or without him, the Cannons were going to be fantastic. Garrett played all three sports that his buddies played – football, hockey and baseball. His productivity in those sports was inverse. On the football team, he was second string. On the hockey team, he had been a third line forward. Baseball, though, that's where he made his bones. Wes could hit, and that earned him a spot in the lineup. Baseball was a long way away, though, so his only athletic endeavors over the next few months would be skating circles at captain's practices until the cast finally came off.

"We did save you some apples, though," Garrett giggled as he stuffed an entire pancake in his mouth.

"How ya like them apples?" Hutchinson chimed in, reciting everyone's favorite line from the old Matt Damon classic "Good Will Hunting." Bish smiled but wasn't all that amused.

Craig stuffed an entire pancake into his mouth and then spoke while chewing.

"You know, I'm going to be chasing the quarterback tomorrow. If I run out of gas in the fourth quarter, I'm blaming you guys."

They all knew he wouldn't be blaming anyone. Craig Bishop never ran out of gas. He played every game at full speed no matter what. When everyone needed a lift on the field, Craig was the one that provided it. On the field, his energy was boundless. That was a stark contrast to his off the field persona.

When Bish wasn't playing sports he was chill. He rarely shaved or cut his brown hair and loved stoner rock from the 1970s. When it was his turn to choose the music, it was almost always Pink Floyd, and usually "The Dark Side of the Moon" that played.

"The Boys" were always impressed by their laid-back buddy's luck with the ladies. He didn't struggle to connect with them, nor did he seem to be afraid to talk to them at all. In groups, they marveled at the ease he had at wiggling into a conversation and inserting himself seamlessly. It didn't usually take long before Craig had them asking to run their fingers through his long, brown locks.

Craig never shared his secret with his friends because it wasn't something he could put into words. Actually, his use of words, or lack of it, was the big mystery he kept to himself. Rather than try to steal the show and impress

9

them, he simply entered a group, said "hello" and listened. He sidled up next to the group and let them carry the dialogue. He nodded at the appropriate times and laughed at the jokes. Before he knew it, two of the prettiest girls had tapped their cell numbers into his phone and began texting him regularly.

He hadn't even reached his 16th birthday and the popular girls at school were going out of their way to include him in plans. The dudes in the senior class could have easily shunned the youngster, but they couldn't help but be impressed. In reality, he was just a kid who had been a little shy in the moment, but that had opened doors he was more than happy to walk through. "The Boys" were more than happy to ride his coattails into the high school upper echelon with him.

As seniors now, they didn't need anyone to usher them into the limelight. This was their time to shine, and that's what they planned to do. It was time to make a memory that would live on forever. Their senior year had started out fantastically, and the next day they were going to try to do something that no one from their town had ever done before.

2

Collin O'Brien and Craig Bishop sat side-by-side on the cramped vinyl seats of the school bus just like they had hundreds of times over the last 12 years. The first time they'd shared a seat on a bus they'd been destined for the first day of first grade. Their feet didn't touch the ground then, and they could have easily fit another friend on the bench. O'Brien proudly wore a fluorescent John Cena T-shirt and a pair of jeans that his older brother, Roman, had worn five years earlier on his first day of school. Bishop had been dressed in a collared shirt and khaki pants, an outfit painstakingly chosen by his doting mother, who had to make sure everything on her boy looked perfect.

Happenstance landed them in the same seat. Craig had been one of the first ones on the bus that fateful morning, walked to the middle of the bus and carefully selected a seat on the left side. His older cousin had told him never to sit in the front because the driver could hear everything you said. He'd also said not to sit in the very back, because they'd assume you were a bad kid. That left the middle, and little Craig Bishop, with his politician's haircut, went right for the middle.

Over the next 15 minutes, the bus had made several stops. Each time the boys and girls would bypass sitting with Craig in favor of an empty spot, or one next to a friend that they already knew. Then the bus stopped at the corner of Carriage House Road and Tee Time Drive. Collin O'Brien strutted onto the bus, looked around and hopped onto the same seat as Bish. By the time the bus had reached the school, a friendship had been born.

The two boys were disappointed to discover that they were not headed to the same classroom that day, but it was probably for the best. Even as a seven-year-old O'Brien's personality filled the room, and everything he did made Craig laugh loudly. If they'd been in the same class all day neither one of them would have ever learned a thing. During recess, they were attached at the hip, and there was not a bus ride over the next dozen years, with the exception of the occasional sick day, where the two did not ride side-by-side in the fourth seat on the left.

A dozen years later the duo was in the middle of the bus and on the left again. They had graduated from the constant chatter of youth long ago. Well, Bishop had, O'Brien never would. Collin had a million things he wanted to say to his best friend, but Craig was in dreamland. Adrenaline coursed through the veins of the 17-year-old, and his best friend was missing everything.

"Dude, would you please wake up," O'Brien pleaded. "We're almost there."

The wheels on the bus had gone round and round for a little over an hour before turning off of Route 495 and onto exit 14, toward Foxborough. Car dealerships, gas stations and motels blurred by. Suddenly the bus slowed as it neared the final destination.

"OB, I've been awake the whole time," Bishop said groggily to his oldest friend. He wasn't completely lying, he had found a happy place between awake and asleep, relaxing and meditating on what was to come in the next few hours as Pink Floyd weaved some psychedelic riffs in his headphones. "Just thinking, getting ready."

Bishop squinted his eyes against the early December sunshine. He and the other 53 football players from Eastport High School all saw Gillette Stadium's exterior at the same time. A hush came over the bus.

Collin broke it.

"There it is boys, that's our house today."

The Eastport Cannons cheered in unison. For the first time in school history the football team was playing in the state championship game, and they'd be doing it on the same field that Tom Brady used to abuse NFL defenses for the past 15 years.

The Cannons were exactly where they'd hoped to be back in August when they had begun training for the season. Coach Kevin Anderson's team had played 12 games so far, and they'd won all 12. Most had been blowout wins. In fact, over the course of the 12 games, the Cannons had only trailed for a grand total of 73 seconds.

During the second quarter of the state semifinal game, a week earlier, the Cannons committed a rare turnover. One of the running backs put the ball on the ground and the defense picked the ball up at the 11-yard line. Three plays later they punched it in from the two and went up by a 13-12 score.

Some teams would have panicked after having been so dominant for the entire year only to have someone punch them back. The Cannons weren't built that way, though. This year they'd blown out just about everyone and were one of the best teams in the state. However, the year before they'd played a ton of close games, so this wasn't uncharted territory. Coach Anderson had warned that they'd have to deal with adversity at some point. He'd said that championships did not come easily and that they'd have to earn it.

It turned out he knew what he was talking about.

They did earn it. First, Matt Lawless ran the kickoff back 65 yards down to the other team's 30. He then turned a carry upfield for nine yards on first down. Then, on second and one, Josh Hutchinson looked off the safety and hit a perfect pass down the seam to Javy Martinez to give the Cannons the lead back. They never trailed after that and ended up winning 27-20, which landed them in Foxboro to play Swampscott High for the Division 2 state championship.

The initial buzz subsided as the bus wheeled behind the stadium and to an adjoining parking lot. The hydraulic doors hissed open and the players stood as one and reached for the ceiling, stretching their bodies after the long ride. As they exited the bus the junior varsity kids grabbed the equipment bags and the players jogged to a pair of big, blue metal doors emblazoned with the New England Patriots logo.

Game time was still about two hours away, and the Cannons walked into the practice bubble like they owned the place. Hutchinson threw his bag up against the wall and noticed an abandoned football a few yards away. The quarterback scooped it up, squeezed it and then rolled the leather National Football League game ball between his palms. Upon closer inspection, he saw a small Patriots logo on the side opposite the large NFL shield. A smile hit his face. For a moment he was 10-years old again ready to scream "I'm

Tom Brady" on the field at recess.

Not that he'd ever identified himself as such, but Josh Hutchinson was the Alpha athlete at Eastport High School. He was one of the best quarterbacks in Massachusetts and a great hockey player. Baseball, though, was where his star shined brightest. He would actually be throwing baseballs in college and not pigskins. Josh spotted his buddy Collin O'Brien about 10-yards away and had to share his find. "OB, heads up," he said before zipping a spiral right into Collin's stomach.

The lineman turned around just in time to have the wind knocked out of him. An audible, "Oooph," escaped his mouth as the ball bounced off his gut. It didn't hit the ground, though. With his right hand, he tipped the rebound off of his body up into the air and then squeezed the ball tight between both of his big paws.

Unphased by his friend's joke, OB inspected the ball. "This is an NFL game ball," he said. "That's so cool."

The boys tossed the pro ball around for a moment before being called into their respective group huddles to begin their stretching drills. Hutchinson put the ball back up against the wall and made his way to the QB coach who would put him through his paces for the next 45 minutes.

Shortly after the Cannons had entered the practice bubble, the Swampscott Sailors joined them. Eastport set up shop on the far side of the warehouse-sized space, and Swampscott used the side nearest the doors. Having gotten there first, Eastport chose the side away from the draft. The pregame preparations were similar for both sides. The teams stretched and ran through some plays, and the players patted each other on the helmets and psyched each other up.

"Let's go!"

"I got you! You got me!"

"You ready for this?"

"Our time, boys, our time."

Coach Anderson put his index fingers together and pierced the murmur with a loud whistle. The Cannons snapped to attention and gathered around their coach.

"Time to line it up, boys. We're walking into that stadium like we've done everything since August, together, side by side. You've got two minutes, gather up your stuff, get it to the managers and they'll get it on the bus. No goofing off, do not waste time. Remember, this isn't a vacation. You are on a business trip, and we're here to do what?"

All 53 boys screamed in unison, "Work!"

Ryan Matthews then took center stage. The heart of the offensive line, the center, he wasn't just in charge of starting every play. He was the man who started the team's motor every game with the opening prayer. It was a responsibility that had been handed down to him from his predecessor, Alberto Sanchez, the year before. Bert had gotten the prayer from the guy that was center before him, Harry Pires, and he had gotten it from the center before him, Mitchell Rainnie, and so on and so forth. Who started it? No one really knew, but they did know that the starting center was responsible for turning that key by reciting those words, and Matthews was the man who was in charge of doing it this year. This was the final time he'd have the privilege to deliver it.

He'd worried about this all week long. *What if I tear up and can't get the words out*, he pondered. He'd cried when he saw "Inside Out," and that was just some stupid Pixar movie. What would happen when he had to give the prayer for the last time?

Coach ceded the center of the circle and stepped out of it. Ryan took a deep breath and limped into it. He'd been playing the last month with a crack in his ankle that he refused to have X-rayed because he knew that the doctor would hold him out. He closed his eyes and silently asked, "God, get me through this."

Sometimes he screamed the words. Sometimes he just spoke them. This time, it was almost a song that left his lips. It had never come so easily, with so much love.

"Boys, repeat after me."

"Dear Lord above, as we go through life..."

They roared back his words.

"We ask in our prayer for strength and health..."

"If we should win, let it be by the code with faith and heads held high..."

"If we should lose, let us stand by the road and cheer as the winners go by..."

"It's game time..."

"We can't be beat..." Matthews continued, dragging out each syllable, stressing each one.

"Won't...Be...Beat!

"Eastport Cannons rule the day!"

The team did not repeat the final phrase. They ended with a loud and boisterous, "Amen!"

The goosebumps stood tall all over his body as if someone had dropped the thermostat 40 degrees. He'd nailed it. Damn, that felt good. Now he just had to keep Josh from getting knocked down for the next four quarters, then he could think about getting his foot checked out.

Coach Anderson spun his finger in the air and then pointed it toward the door. "Grab your stuff, and let's go win us a championship, fellas."

Hutchinson, Matthews, OB, and Bishop had all put their bags alongside one another on the wall. They grabbed them and brought them to the managers. At the last minute, OB turned around, bag in hand, and hustled back.

"Almost forgot something."

3

The click-clack of 53 pairs of cleats echoed through the tunnel leading to the field. They halted when they reached a pair of security guards wearing blinding neon green jackets, who put up their arms and instructed the Cannons to "wait here until your music hits."

What had been a march became a nervous bouncing of 53 pairs of football shoes. The butterflies in their stomachs were now the size of birds, and the adrenaline in their blood was boiling.

Josh Hutchinson had never felt more alive in his life. Baseball and his scholarship were the furthest things from his mind. Right then, all that mattered was the next couple of hours on this chilly December day. At that moment it seemed ridiculous that he had had to argue with his father back in August about actually returning for his senior season on the gridiron.

His father's concerns were valid. What would they do if some jerk decided to plant him on his right shoulder and tore up his potential moneymaker in the third quarter of a meaningless blowout win? He told his dad he couldn't worry about what-ifs by creating a bigger one.

"What if I don't play this year and we don't go all the way? How would I live with that? How would I look my friends in the eyes knowing that if I had played they would have had a chance to go to Gillette?"

Having played high school football himself, his dad got it, and he conceded. That would be a difficult burden to carry around. "Just be careful. I understand that you don't want that regret in your life, but you also don't want the regret of missing out on a baseball scholarship."

Josh was snapped back to the here and now when Angus Young's opening solo to "Thunderstruck" began blaring over the loudspeakers. As soon as the music started the security guys put their arms out and said, "Good luck, Eastport." With that, they hauled ass toward the middle of the field.

As soon as they left the tunnel they felt the electricity. A roar rose up from the sections of seats directly behind their bench. It looked like the entire town of Eastport, all 33,000 year-round residents, had traveled the 68 miles to Foxboro and shelled out the $15 ticket price to watch them play. Parents, brothers, sisters, girlfriends, friends and classmates were all there wearing the school colors, maroon and white. The soccer team wore maroon too, but theirs was painted on. The shirtless boys had painted "Eastport Cannons" spelled out in individual letters across their chests.

All of the football players joined up right atop the Patriots logo at midfield and began to bounce up and down. Hutchinson was dead center, the leader of the team. "Time to go to work boys, punch those time cards."

Hutchinson, Matthews and O'Brien were the captains and called out for the coin flip. As the visiting team for the day, Eastport was charged with calling heads or tails, and Coach Anderson had told Hutchinson to call heads, as they had every time they'd had the choice this year. They weren't about to change anything at this point.

The referee rested a quarter on his thumb and demanded that Eastport "call it in the air."

"Heads," Hutchinson said.

The coin hit the artificial playing surface, bounced one time and settled flat. The referee bent over, scooped his change and said, "Heads it is..."

Before he could finish the rest of the instructions, all three Eastport boys shouted, "We want the ball!"

Swampscott chose to defend the end zone with the lighthouse behind it so that they'd have the wind at their backs. The ref put the captains in position and went through his arm signals as he informed the crowd that the Cannons got the ball and that the Sailors would be defending the east end zone. He wished the teams luck and the captains began their walk back to their teammates before the opening kickoff.

Looking around the stadium and into the stands, the moment sunk in for Hutchinson. "Ryan, this is pretty awesome!" he screamed to his center.

"Amen, Hutch, Amen. Let's do this."

"I got you, brother, I got you!" Josh shouted over the noise.

The Cannons' date with destiny was about to begin.

4

One hundred and twenty-five miles away, Scott Frazier rushed up two flights of stairs, fished out his key and worked the lock on room 311 at Ferreira Hall. Hockey practice had ended 35 minutes earlier, and he'd had just enough time to sprint to the dining hall, throw down two turkey and cheese sandwiches and a side helping of mashed potatoes and drink a glass of milk. He flipped open his laptop and navigated to Twitter, where he sent a direct message to Mac Richardson, the sports beat reporter for the *Eastport Enquisitor*.

"Hey Mac, where can I find the game online?"

He then tapped his fingers impatiently, waiting for the longtime sports guy from his hometown to get back to him. He would, Frazier knew, he was good like that.

As he fingered through his Instagram feed on his iPhone, an alert tone signaled a new message. "Massachusetts High School Athletics home page has a stream. How's Wellness School?"

Mr. Richardson loved to bust balls. He knew the name of the private school where Frazier was. He had warned him that the grass wasn't always greener elsewhere. Mr. Richardson said that Scott would miss playing his senior year with his buddies, even if Wellington Academy had offered him a huge scholarship to come play at their little hockey factory in the woods of southern Vermont.

"I'm doing fine, the hockey's good. We should have a good team. Thanks for the hookup," he typed and sent to the sports reporter.

Most of that was true. The hockey here was good. Really good, actually. It was the first time as a hockey player that Scott could remember where he wasn't the best player on his team. He was the second-best, but the best was a post-grad player that had a chance to be drafted in the NHL Draft that June, so Scott wasn't too jealous of his place on the team's totem pole. And, as he said, the team was going to be pretty good. He'd yet to skate in a game yet — the season was supposed to start in two weeks — but he could tell that these guys were solid. The fourth line guys would have been starters back home.

And, they were good enough guys. Scott hadn't really had any problems with any of them since getting here. They were cool. They just weren't his brothers. They weren't "the Boys."

The "I'm doing fine" part of the message to Richardson had been the untruth he'd relayed. Hockey was going fine, classes weren't that bad, but something didn't seem right. At night he stared at the ceiling for hours sometimes, listening to the trees rustling outside his window and wondering, "Why am I here?"

Truth be told, Scott never really wanted to come to Wellington. He'd have preferred to stay at Eastport, play football and hockey and baseball like he had the year before, and then go off to do a post-grad year somewhere, or play junior hockey before college.

His mother, though, had wanted to ship him out of town. Dottie Frazier believed he might make it to the NHL one day and that to make that happen that he needed to get out of town. When Wellington had offered to pay $47,000 of the $52,000 tuition for them, she'd signed the papers and sent them in before he'd had a chance to process what had just happened. She signed him up in July, and he hadn't even told his friends, or coaches, that he was leaving until the first week of August, just two weeks before he had to be on campus.

As the days of summer neared an end, his sense of dread grew. His mom kept telling him, "You've got to do this, it's what's best for you." He wasn't sure he believed that, but he soldiered on.

He'd tried to confide in his older brother that he was thinking about asking out of it in the days leading up to the trip north. Teddy, who was currently hoping to get picked up by a Division 3 college team after two years of junior hockey, was no help. He may have had the same opportunities had he been more concerned with protecting the puck than taking cheap shots. "Stop being soft. You're better than this place. I wish I could have played at Wellington."

Everyone had said this place was going to be awesome. Scott kept waiting for the awesome to begin. It was okay, but it wasn't where he thought he belonged. It wasn't home.

Where he belonged was lining up with his buddies at Gillette Stadium for the opening kickoff. He probably would have been a primary blocker on the kickoff team and a starting linebacker on defense.

Rather than wearing a helmet and pads, he was trying to get comfortable on an old folding chair in front of a computer screen. The announcer talked about how Eastport had gone 12-0 and was considered the favorite today as they looked for their first-ever state championship in football. Scott closed his eyes tight and wished he was there.

"Come on boys. Can't be beat, won't be beat."

5

All week long during practice Coach Anderson had stressed one thing with his offense. "We've got to start fast, guys. Don't let them believe that they can play with us. We need to hang points on the board and make them chase us."

After taking the opening kickoff back to the 43, just seven yards short of midfield, the Cannons set about doing exactly what their coach had prescribed. Lawless ran for 12 on the first play of the game, and would have gone all the way had a diving linebacker not got a piece of his left foot as he tried to break away. He then broke a 20-yard run right up the middle of the field on second down.

Martinez came off the sideline and jogged into the huddle with the call for the third play of the game. Hutchinson heard the call and glanced sideways at his favorite receiver.

"Already?" he asked.

"Yup, lay it up nice for me, Hutch."

"Don't worry about that, I got you," Josh stated.

Coach Anderson was the son of a coach. He'd been a standout high school player and a decent small time college player. As soon as he left college he'd become one of his father's assistants, teaching the offense the same plays he'd mastered back in the day. Eastport ran a variation of that offense, and over 90 percent of the time one of those guys, or the quarterback himself, would run the ball. The quarterback's job was to recognize what the defense was likely to do and decide which of the running backs should get the ball.

Some days Lawless ran all over teams like it looked like he might do today. Other days it was Stevie Fillion, the other tailback, or one of the fullbacks. Other days it was Hutchinson himself who diced the defense. Because the Cannons had such versatile threats, they were nearly impossible to stop

23

when they ran the ball, which made their passing attack an afterthought for most defenses.

Swampscott had shown on the first two plays that they planned on selling out to stop the run. They weren't worried about the passing game, which made some sense since Hutchinson had averaged just seven pass attempts per game all season long. That number was skewed, though, because the Cannons had been blowing people out all year long. There usually wasn't much need to put the ball in the air.

Eastport broke their huddle with a reminder that the snap count was on two and a joint clap. Hutchinson took his spot behind Matthews and began to bark out his cadence.

"Boston... Boston... hut... hut."

Josh's left foot stepped back and to the left. As Lawless circled toward the line of scrimmage, the quarterback put two hands under the ball and feigned a pitch to the corner. The Swampscott defense bought hard on the fake. Most importantly, the free safety, whose job was to protect the middle of the field, found himself nearly at the line of scrimmage by the time Hutchinson had delivered the fake toss. After the fake, he stepped further back into the pocket while bringing his money-making right arm back, cocked and loaded.

While all that was going on, Martinez did what he did best: run really, really fast down the sideline. The left cornerback stumbled on the stop-and-go move, and could only watch in horror as Hutchinson lofted a tight spiral ball down the middle of the field to the wide-open receiver.

Javy watched the picture perfect pass fall from the heavens right into his waiting arms. He caught the ball at the eight-yard line and could have crawled into the end zone from there. The play was perfection, a 25-yard strike for a touchdown that gave the Cannons the early lead, just one minute and 27 seconds into the state championship game.

The receiver stopped in the end zone, spiked the ball and then pointed to his hometown crowd before being tackled to the artificial turf by Hutchinson, who chased his throw to the end zone, knowing it was good for a touchdown as soon as he put the ball in the air.

"How's that one!" Hutchinson screamed excitedly. "Told you, I got you."

"You laid that one up nice, Joshy boy, really nice."

Eastport was feeling great about itself. It was a good start, but there was still plenty of football left to play.

6

With points on the board early in the game, the Cannons were flying high. The defense, behind the strength of O'Brien and Bishop, got the ball right back for the team. Hutchinson led another touchdown drive, with Lawless and Fillion trading runs until Lawless punched one in from six yards away to make it 14-0.

Swampscott's sideline was in disarray. The coaches were yelling into their headsets, profanities flying, as they tried to wrap their heads around what was happening to them. The Sailors believed that they had a great plan to stifle Eastport's running game. They had analyzed Eastport's previous games and believed that they understood what their foes wanted to do and how to counter it.

The famous boxer Mike Tyson once said that "everyone's got a plan until they get punched in the mouth." The Cannons packed a wallop, and Swampscott was out on its feet by the time the second quarter rolled around and Eastport added another touchdown to go up by 21 points at halftime.

Everyone on the Eastport team seemed to play one of their best games of the season on the biggest stage of their lives. O'Brien had seven tackles, and Bishop had four. They combined for a beautiful sack in the third quarter. Hutchinson threw two touchdowns and ran for another. Matthews didn't miss a block.

With about two minutes left to play in the game, the Cannons defense stopped a run on fourth-and-three that all but ended the game. O'Brien had jumped into the fray to make sure no one made any further progress, as he always did, and Bishop extended his hand to help his lifelong friend up off of the Gillette Stadium turf.

"I told you we'd do this," O'Brien said as he popped up off the ground with his buddy's assistance.

"You were right, the Boys never lose," Bishop said as he jogged to the sideline, exchanging a high-five with Hutchinson as he took to the field.

Hutchinson jogged over from the sideline to finish the game. He entered the huddle and said, "Look around, soak it in. Enjoy this moment, boys. We earned it. Champions for life."

He scanned from left to right, and saw nothing but smiles from the 10 other teenagers that had sweat, bled and won with him for the last four months.

"Real simple, victory formation on one. Don't be stupid, let's knee this out and party," he finished.

The first kneel down wound the clock under a minute. The second one served as the last play of the game. Josh went back on his knee and then sprung up toward the sky. The first person to greet him was Coach Anderson. The two approached one another with their arms wide. As they embraced they were soaked to the bone as the second team defense unloaded the contents of the Gatorade bucket over their two leaders.

Pandemonium followed. Every Cannon was either bouncing or hugging someone.

Craig stole a second to himself, put his arms behind his neck and looked up to the sky. He thought briefly about his mother and wished she could have seen this. He was glad that his grandparents had witnessed it, though. What a moment for him and the Boys. They'd done it. They'd actually done it. They'd talked about this exact thing for four years. "Imagine if we won a state championship. Imagine how cool that would be." When they'd talked about it as freshmen, it seemed like a pipe dream, like a six-year-old telling his teacher he was going to be a ninja astronaut. Now, it was real. It was *really real*.

The lights and sounds of the stadium seemed far away as he thought *Thanks, God, and give mom a hug for me.*

A backslap from OB snapped him out of his daze.

"Attaboy Bish, love you man, great job," his buddy bellowed.

"Love you too, man!"

A reporter stuck a microphone between the boys.

"Craig, great job. The play of the defensive line was a big factor tonight. Can you tell me how you guys were able to slow down their run game?"

When you're a senior and a captain, you've got to speak for everyone. How had they done it? The game was such a blur right now. He knew that they'd won, and they'd earned every bit of the trophy that they'd be presented with in a moment, but the game itself seemed long ago and far away at that moment.

He improvised and used cliches. Coach had always said to never be interesting when talking to the press.

"It was just everybody. We all came together and played... great. It was awesome. This is awesome. This is something we talked about since we were freshmen, and to have it come to reality is unbelievable. I don't know what to say. I'm just so happy, and I love these guys, every one of them. Nobody wins on their own, but together we made this happen. No matter what happens, for the rest of our lives, we are champions and no one can take that away."

The reporter seemed satisfied, nodded his head, and went to grab Josh, who was better at these things anyway.

The Cannons all met in the middle of the field for a photograph. "The Boys" were all down front, holding the state championship banner. There were so many cell phones and cameras that everyone seemed to be looking in a different direction. Every guy in the frame looked like it was Christmas morning and Santa had brought everything they could ever want. That picture ran in the next day's newspapers and later was hung on the wall at the school. The Cannons had never been happier.

Walking off the field together, Collin, Craig and Josh spotted their friends in the stands. Wes and Danny leaned over the barrier and yelled to them. The three football players sprinted over and jumped into the crowd. "Champs, baby!" Wes yelled as he and Craig hugged one another tightly.

"Dude, this is the best feeling in the world!" Craig screamed to his buddy. "I wish it could last forever!"

7

The ride back home to the Cape was far removed from what the players thought it might be. There wasn't much hooting or hollering. Once they'd settled in, the guys all relaxed and fell into a steady quiet buzz. Stories were whispered of the individual glories on the field that day, and the occasional chuckle could be heard, but the moment was pretty subdued.

So much energy had gone into the game that everyone's batteries were drained. It wasn't just this game, it was an entire season's worth of effort that had been expended and now all they wanted to do was eat and sleep, not necessarily in that order.

"Bish, are you awake?" O'Brien whispered.

"A little."

"What do you want to do when we get back tonight? Where are we all going?"

"I don't know, it's too cold to go anywhere outside. Let's figure that out at the team dinner. Someone will have a basement we can chill in."

O'Brien nodded his acceptance to the non-answer and decided to check his iPhone to see what the world was saying about what they'd done. He powered up the phone and was blown away by the number of notifications he had. Since he'd last checked his phone he had received 57 text messages. His mom, brother and sister had all wished him luck before the game. Wes had too, but with far more colorful language. The in-game messages made him laugh.

"Attaboy OB, Beast Mode fo sho. You killin dem, way to get it," was his favorite. It was from Wes. Man, Wes should have been out there on the field with the rest of them.

Next, he opened Twitter and saw that he had 99-plus mentions, most of them by Mac Richardson about hits he'd made, and then a lot of favorites of those tweets. He then switched over to Richardson' feed and favorited nearly every tweet that the local writer made that day.

"Great day to be at Gillette for some football...

"Cannons look fired up as they take the field...

"Wow, big hit block by O'Brien opens the lane for Lawless to get a first down...

"Touchdown Cannons..."

On and on it went as O'Brien re-lived his experience through the descriptions. Reading through the timeline it was evident just how good the team had been in the game.

The time spent captivated by his phone had made the 75-minute bus ride home go by quickly. He barely noticed the cars driving beside the bus honking their horns, and didn't look up until they reached the Bourne Bridge for the final miles home.

"Are we getting pulled over?" asked one of the sophomores riding up front. "Yo, there are four cop cars with their lights on."

The police were not there to apprehend anyone on the bus. Four Eastport police cruisers had left their jurisdiction to escort the football team home. The cops led the way, and then a firetruck slipped in behind the bus and turned on its lights as well. The inside of the bus looked like a nightclub. Someone fired up some house music on their phone and the party that O'Brien expected the bus ride home to be finally began. All that was missing were some beverages that weren't Gatorade or water and some girls. Girls would have definitely made it better.

Wes had gotten back from Foxboro before the bus. After dropping Danny off at home he headed to the school and waited in the parking lot with the engine running and the heat blasting. He still couldn't believe how awesome his Boys had played. They'd actually done it. "They're the state champions, just like we talked about as freshmen," he said out loud in the empty car.

His phone chimed and it was Bish finally getting back to him. Knowing his best friend, he'd probably dozed off on the ride home.

"Almost back 2 The Port. Will pull in to the school in 5 mins or so. U back to town yet?"

"Yup, waiting in the lot for U."

"Cool, gotta shower quick, and then we're having a team dinner in the gym. Pizza 4 days. Come get in on it. Coach won't care."

Coach Anderson had been pissed at Wes after he'd broken his hand. He'd said that the six foot, one inch, 210-pound kid was going to be a big part of his defensive scheme. He was going to play a lot of weak side linebacker and was going to be in the running for a starting job. His punch to the wall had ended all of that. After a few weeks, Coach simmered down, probably because the defense had been doing so well. "You should be on the sidelines, you're a part of this team," Coach had said in an attempt to bring Wesley back into the fold.

The extended olive branch was nice and all, but Wes did not want to be a glorified water boy for his senior season. Rather than watch from the sidelines and do nothing, he had decided to become the team's biggest cheerleader. He painted his body up as the 'E' in Eastport for all of the home games, with the rest of the letters being repped by either soccer or hockey players. He got kicked out of a road game for making fun of the other team's cheerleaders and then had to write an apology letter to the South Yarmouth Athletic Director and was put on probation by the Eastport High AD, Harry Burnette. They made him stay away from the next game, but thankfully it was a meaningless game in Forestdale against a school that really sucked. It rained hard that night anyway. Eastport led 42-0 at halftime. If there was a game to miss, that was the one.

Being a spectator for a season had actually been a lot of fun. He'd hung out a lot with kids he hadn't known that well before, sidled up to some ladies and experienced high school football as a fan.

The police escort pulled into the parking lot, which woke Wes up out of his daze. As soon as the bus door hissed open he got out of the car to go greet his victorious friends. He fist-bumped the JV kids and then started getting hugs from his former teammates. OB and Bish walked out one after the other, and the three longtime friends squeezed one another tight.

"You should have been out there, man, it was awesome," OB said as he hugged his friend.

"I was, you guys played it for me," he said, "and you did it a lot better than I would have."

"Yeah, we did. Told ya, I got you," Bishop said with a smile.

The three friends laughed and then Josh jumped into the pile for hugs with Wes. Someone snapped a pic, and then the players went into the locker room to shower and change. Wes followed them but stopped at the entrance to the sanctuary.

"Don't take all night in there getting pretty, it won't help," he said.

Coach came around the corner and Wes offered his hand. Coach accepted it and pulled him in for a hug. "Now you go get your title on the ice," he whispered into Wes's ear.

"I'll try, Coach, I'll try."

8

John Scadorski had been at Gillette Stadium over the weekend and beamed with pride as he watched several of his high school hockey players capture the state football championship. Scads, as he had been known for as long as he could remember, was overjoyed as the boys waved to him in the stands, pointing at the trophy they'd won.

That team had done it the right way. They'd set a goal early on and accomplished it by following the game plan. He'd been impressed by Coach Anderson's attention to detail, but most of all the leadership roles that the older kids on the team had taken stood out to the Cannons' hockey mentor.

Scadorski knew what it took to win at the high school level. Thirty-five years earlier he'd helped the same maroon and white-wearing school to the 1981 state championship. He was the top defenseman on a team that gave up only about a goal per game over the course of their 20 regular season games and had even scored a rare goal – just his third of the year – in the state semifinals.

College hockey followed with a good career at the University of Vermont. He'd done enough for the Catamounts during his time in Burlington to get drafted in the fifth round of the NHL draft by the Pittsburgh Penguins. He rode minor league buses for four seasons before a shoulder injury took too much away from his slapshot. Just like that he had to accept that he was not going to make it all the way to the Igloo in Pittsburgh and returned home to the Cape.

A heady player throughout his days on the ice, Scadorski knew the ins and outs of hockey better than most of his coaches did coming up through youth hockey and into high school. His acumen for the game had not gone unnoticed. When his old high school coach heard that Scads was coming home he quickly offered him a job as an assistant coach.

Scads began coaching the defense for the Cannons in 1990 and helped the team win another state championship in 1996. He settled down, married his high school sweetheart, opened a used car dealership and fathered three kids. He'd had two girls and a boy. Junior played hockey, like dad, but despite inheriting his father's size and quickness, he never developed the elite skills that his old man had. After high school, he'd skate around the bogs with his buddies during winter visits home from trading bonds in Manhattan.

Scadorski served as an assistant coach for more than two decades, patiently waiting for his mentor to decide to turn things over to his protege. Finally, after waiting all those years, it was his turn. His mentor decided it was time to step aside, and within a few weeks of that Scadorski was hired to take on the job.

Over the next three years, the program had been steady but was yet to have a breakout season. They'd won just one state tournament game over that time. The first year was a transition from one style to another. With better goaltending, the team did pretty well and won its first-round game in the state tournament before running into the eventual regional champion in round two.

Year two saw a talented group of sophomores fill up a good portion of the roster, and they showed promise. They were also too young to compete against the best in the state, and another year finished in the first round. A year later expectations were high, but key injuries proved to be too much to overcome. The Cannons limped into the postseason as one of the last teams to make the tournament and were bounced in the first round.

If ever the Cannons were going to make a run, this upcoming season was the year. With nine seniors on the roster, at least of three of whom could really put the puck in the net, Eastport had a chance to go after the state title for the first time in two decades. Scadorski had been around for each of the last 19 seasons, and he could not wait for the first official day of ice hockey practice to commence on the Monday after Thanksgiving.

High School sports seasons start on predetermined dates that are decided upon by the state athletic association and pretty much run right into the next one. In Massachusetts, football teams were allowed to begin their practices two weeks before classes began. The other fall programs started four days later.

All of the other sports finished their seasons no later than the middle of November. Soccer players that happened to also be hockey or basketball players had a good three weeks of rest before having to be ready to go. Football players, though, did not get any downtime between seasons. Because the Cannons had gone to the state championship, the players that were also going to be on the hardwood or ice were a week behind practice-wise.

Scadorski's first practice of the season went well, but it was obvious to him that the missing pieces were big ones. O'Brien was a starting defenseman and his team's enforcer. Bishop was his grinding right wing on the first line. He did the dirty work so that the 'skilled' forwards could get the glory by scoring goals. Garrett would not be cleared to play for a few weeks but should be back by Christmas time to play on a wing where he would definitely help, playing a similar style as his buddy O'Brien, but up front. Two more forwards that had a chance to do some good things, and one more defenseman, were also still wearing football pads when practices had begun.

Mac Richardson waited for about 10 minutes outside the locker room after practice for Coach Scads on the Friday before the state championship football game before knocking on the door to the coaches' office.

"Hey Mac, how's life?" Scadorski asked the local scribe. The two had a good relationship – as good as any coach and journalist could. Richardson seemed to know every little thing that happened in town, but never painted the team or the kids in a negative light, even though he knew most of the dirty secrets. He was the rare reporter who actually loved what he did, and still had a passion for sports.

"Good Scads, good. So, kind of tough to run a practice with a glorified JV team out there, huh?" the reporter asked while extending his iPhone to record the conversation.

"Yeah, it's tough to get ready to go when you're missing the pieces we are. But, those guys are playing for a state championship on Saturday and we can't wait to watch them go out and win it. The way I see it, that experience is going to benefit this team in the long run. Those guys are going to be big leaders for us on the ice, and they know what it takes to get to the promised land. It's win-win for us, even if we are a little behind schedule right now."

"It'd be a little easier if Frazier was still here," Richardson said, referring to the star defenseman who had defected to private school for his senior year rather than remain home, where many – including Richardson and Scadorski – thought he should have stayed.

"Yeah, but we can only worry about the guys that are here in this locker room. Scotty is a huge loss, there's really no replacing a talent like that. He would have been the best player in the league. Heck, he would have been one of the best players in the state. I think that even without him, though, that this team has more than enough talent to get to where we want to be."

"Have you decided on a goalie yet?" Richardson asked.

Scadorski paused. With a good goaltender, there was no doubt that the Cannons would be a top contender for the title. Unfortunately, they did not have one of those.

One senior up for the job, Jimmy Martinage, was extremely nearsighted, which was certainly an issue when your job depended on excellent hand-eye and leg-eye coordination. The floppy-haired 18-year-old wore lenses as thick as old-school soda bottles in everyday life, but on the ice, he donned simple athletic goggles. He claimed the prescription was good enough, but anything shot from beyond the circles was an adventure.

Martinage had won a couple of big games during the previous season, mostly against teams that had not figured out his fatal flaw. Against opponents who learned that shooting from the perimeter was the way to go, he struggled and cost them dearly. The Cannons lost a number of games Coach Scads believed they should have won, including the team's first-round loss in the state tournament.

The game was close after one period, tied at 1-1. The Cannons were flying on the ice, and a goal by Bishop had tied the score with three minutes to go in the opening frame. The final two periods were horrific for Eastport. Martinage coughed up four goals in five minutes in the second. All of the fire and grit the maroon and white had felt in the first period evaporated. In the end, the Cannons were bumped from the postseason with a 7-2 loss. It was disheartening, and it had stuck with Martinage for the past nine months.

Eastport's other two candidates for the keeper spot could see better, but not necessarily stop the puck any better. Marc Rollins was a senior who hadn't been good enough to beat out a legally blind competitor the year before. Rollins flummoxed the coaching staff. In practice, he looked amazing and stopped nearly everything fired his way. When it was game time, though, he was mediocre on his good days. Sophomore Keegan Doogle was nicknamed "Doggy" by his teammates. He played into the moniker by wearing an odd jersey number for a goalie, a 9. He was K-9. He oozed potential but had yet to prove anything when it mattered.

"The goalie situation will work itself out," Scadorski said. "It's an open competition, and one of them will have to take the bull by the horns and earn the starting job. I have full confidence that we will be better between the pipes this year."

The coach believed every word he'd just uttered, even the last part. He figured they couldn't be any worse.

Richardson had done a variation of the same interview every year for the past 19. He knew the truth that Eastport's goaltending was problematic, and ultimately it would probably cost them when it mattered, just like last year. The thing is when you write for a town newspaper it isn't the same thing as covering a professional team. In the big city, the readers want the dirt. They want to know how the coaches really feel about the players, and which players can't stand the coach. Infighting and problems sell newspapers and equal internet clicks.

Richardson could have filled a book with all of the behind the scenes intrigue he'd gleaned over the years. The best nuggets only would have served in getting the players suspended by their high school, which would have hurt the product on the fields of play. Everyone would have blamed the newspaper for the losses, the coaches would stop giving him info he needed for stories, and life, in general, would be tough. Dirty looks and whispers would follow him everywhere. There's a definite difference between the big time and the small towns.

Fifteen minutes later the coach and reporter had discussed potential line combinations and defensive pairings. Everything was technically still up in the air since the football players were not ready to practice yet with the hockey team. The dynamic today was far different from what it would be in a few days. Scadorski couldn't wait for that day to arrive.

9

Monday morning came fast. Saturday had been the big game, with two parties following the monumental victory that evening. The first was an official team gathering. Pizza was eaten, coaches gave speeches and hugs were doled out liberally throughout the gym. The players were dismissed around 10 PM and scattered.

Most of the seniors found their way to O'Brien's basement for a few hours. A bucket rested at the bottom of the stairs with a sign demanding that everyone leave their cell phones in it. The request was not a way to make the millennials actually interact with one another, but a brilliant idea Garrett had concocted. A tennis player at EHS had been suspended for a quarter of his team's season last year after the prom because someone had posted a photo of him taking a pull on a bottle of booze at a party. That photo eventually was seen by the athletic director, who was quick to send him to the sidelines for violating the school's code of conduct for athletes.

That code of conduct had been a point of contention for athletes for years. Students who did not play on a sports team suffered no repercussions at school whatsoever if they were found to be in the possession of or to have used drugs or alcohol off campus. If you played a sport, though, you missed a quarter of a season for your first violation, half for the second. Three strikes and you were out, done for the year as an athlete.

Wes had seen a documentary in school about World War II and had learned the slogan, "Loose lips sink ships." Knowing so many of his contemporaries documented their every exploit at parties, he thought it would be a great idea to take away the temptation.

Eastport's Code of Conduct was violated by just about everyone in attendance. The celebration went into the morning, with the majority of the attendees sleeping on the hardwood floors O'Brien's father had installed two summers ago as part of his basement renovation. There were plenty of stiff backs on Sunday morning, but no one had been pulled over and issued a DUI, so it was a good trade-off.

Still groggy on Monday morning, Bishop flipped a couple of fried eggs and grabbed four pieces of wheat bread out of the toaster. Two he buttered liberally, and on the other two, he slapped heaping portions of peanut butter.

Pouring two cups of coffee, he turned to see Wes Garrett walk through the door at the same time he did every day, 7:11 AM. Craig wasn't sure if his friend was simply an extreme creature of habit, paying homage to the convenience store downtown, or just oddly consistent. Regardless, he knew when he'd be there, and put the two plates of food on the table. They sat down for a quick bite before the duo had to rush out the door to make their first classes at 7:45.

"You taking the day off, or skating at practice?" Garrett asked between bites of egg.

"Coach said we could skip today, but I'm gonna go. I haven't skated full speed in months, gotta work the kinks out. Plus, I don't need some freshman or sophomore taking my spot."

"No one's taking your spot. Me, on the other hand, I'm going to have work to do when I get back. I can't believe the doctor won't let me on the ice for another month. I'm going to miss like seven games."

"Hey, you'll be back for Hyannis."

"Yup, back to rip the anus."

Both boys giggled at the old joke that had been told countless times by Eastport athletes.

"And on that note, we've got to run or we're going to be late," Garrett said. He grabbed his peanut butter toast, wrapped it in a paper towel and chugged his last swig of coffee before heading to the door. Bishop threw his backpack over his shoulder, muscled on a jean jacket and popped a Patriots winter hat on his head as they hustled out to the red Jeep Cherokee in the driveway.

Garrett's ride was older than both young men. It had been new 19 years and 201,165 miles ago. He bought it before the start of the school year off of a friend's dad for $1,200. It was a great deal, as the Kelly Blue Book value had it listed at about $3,100 despite the age and wear.

The sport utility vehicle had been well taken care of by its previous owners and had just a few minor scratches and a little rust creeping in around the left headlight. The radio had been upgraded by the Boys, an all-day project undertaken one Saturday afternoon in October. The guy on YouTube had said it was an easy job and should take no longer than a half-hour to complete. The guy on YouTube was a liar. It was tricky as hell and had taken closer to four hours to complete. When it was said and done the new head unit allowed for cell phones to be plugged in and used over the speakers, which was far better than just having the original AM/FM tape deck.

Craig said he was sad to see the tape deck go. He liked retro things and had even bought half of Pink Floyd's library on cassette for the Jeep after finding a great deal on eBay.

Garrett's iPhone 5 with the cracked screen was plugged in with a USB cable and his best friend pulled up Spotify. Their favorite playlist was the classic rock one, and they were pleased when The Who's Baba O'Riley led off the drive to school. The boys sang the chorus at the top of their lungs as they turned on to Work Horse Lane for the last leg before the Eastport High School parking lot.

"Teenage wasteland, it's only teenage wasteland ... we're all wasted!"

10

Danny Stone took a left turn into the Eastport Technology Park, which was the home of the three-year-old Eastport Ice House. The home rink for the Cannons was a state of the art facility, with an NHL-sized rink, as well as a half-sheet for skills improvement and the little ones to skate on. Danny pulled his aging Ford pickup into a vacant parking spot and hopped out of the driver's seat quickly.

The 18-year-old hauled his hockey bag out of the back of the truck, gingerly slung it over his surgically repaired right collarbone and double-timed it into the rink where he was hit in the face with his favorite smell, fresh cookies baking at The Snack Shack.

Danny waved a greeting to the girl behind the counter, took a hard left toward the half sheet of ice, and then a right toward the NHL rink. Around the far corner boards was the Eastport locker room. The senior went in and found that he was one of the first ones to make it in for the day's session. Danny had come straight over from school, and there was still 45 minutes remaining before he and his teammates had to be on the ice.

He began to undress and put on his hockey gear. He popped his left arm out of his Toronto Maple Leafs t-shirt and then eased his right one out before lifting the shirt over his head.

"Dude, is that arm still bothering you?" The question came from Assistant Coach Tom Henry, a monster of a man who had played high-level hockey until topping out in the American Hockey League, one stop short of the big time.

Stone ran his fingers over the two-inch scar above his clavicle.

"I'm fine, it's just a little stiff. Still getting back into hockey shape, it's been a while."

It had been roughly 19 months since Danny Stone had played in a real game for the Eastport Cannons. As a sophomore he was the biggest surprise on the team, scoring five goals on the third line that year while playing with reckless abandon, especially for someone who was built like a flagpole. In the penultimate game of that season, the confident youngster chased a puck into the corner, with plans to backhand a pass to the slot for his streaking linemate Cyrus Carpenter. The pass found the mark, but the shot missed the net.

What did not miss the mark was the late hit that came from the defenseman. The check turned 16-year-old Danny into a pretzel. He heard the collarbone snap like a dry twig. The bone did not protrude out of his skin but pushed up against it. It looked like a finger was trying to push out of his upper chest from inside.

Danny had hoped to be back as a junior for the Cannons, but a setback cost him the whole season. Doctors had cleared him to play, but a hit from a teammate – a light one at that – during a preseason practice re-broke the bone. The injury was not nearly as bad, but his parents and doctors both agreed he should not play at all that season.

Being held off the ice for an entire campaign made for a pretty awful year for Danny. He spent all of the season watching his teammates play and wishing he was out on the ice with them. He easily would have been on the second line and played a big role for the club.

Rather than score goals and dole out assists, he videotaped the games. He sat next to Mac Richardson in the press box and worked the camera so that the coaching staff could break down the games and use them during film sessions at practice.

Danny was not the greatest cameraman of all time. He missed plays from time to time because he was too caught up in the action. However, he was a huge hit with his teammates because of his running commentary during games. He had not figured out how to switch off the microphone on the camera. During film sessions he could be heard cheering on his teammates, jeering at their mistakes and adding his take on what they should have done instead of what they did do on the ice.

This year, though, he would no longer be serving as the team's play-by-play and camera operator. This year he would be the one on those tapes, and he could not wait for the season to begin. Since there was a chance that another hit could re-break his clavicle, he planned on going all-out all the time. Stone would not be playing in college, except for maybe intramurals. He would never play in any games that mattered as much as the ones that the Cannons would play this year. If his senior year was a basket, all of his eggs were in it, and he just hoped that his shells did not crack again.

As Danny wiggled into his pads, his teammates started to make their way into the room. Carpenter entered with O'Brien and they were involved in a heated exchange.

"Carp, you've got to chill out. It's not that big of a deal."

"It is a big deal! All fall I had to put together captain's practices. I had to make sure everyone was on the same page. He's the co-captain, and he hasn't done a damn thing he's supposed to. I'm sick of it! Captains are supposed to be leaders, and he's just doing his own thing!"

Cyrus Carpenter was pissed off at his teammate and fellow co-captain, Billy Walker. The two had once been best of friends, having spent season after season as the top two forwards on every youth team Eastport had as they came up through the ranks. Carpenter was the set-up guy, and Walker the goal-scorer, though each was more than capable of doing both things. With Bishop as their right wing, pounding on the defense and setting the tone, the trio was expected to be one of the premier goal-scoring lines in the state. That depended on them being on the same page, though.

Right now, the chemistry was toxic. Carpenter was right, Walker had eschewed most of his responsibilities throughout the offseason. He rarely made appearances at the "optional" practices, which the captains were supposed to set up. He did not respond to text messages from his former best friend. He had isolated himself from the group in many ways, and that was a problem and becoming a bigger one by the day.

"I'll talk to him," O'Brien offered.

"What good will that do? He'll say 'don't worry about it.' Then he isn't gonna do a damn thing. Look around the locker room. Everyone is here, right? Except one guy, the other supposed captain."

44

As if on cue, Walker sauntered through the door with a baseball cap on backward covering up his shoulder-length brown hair.

"What's going on boys?" he said to no one in particular.

No one in the room responded.

"What's up? I don't know, we're getting ready to go on the ice. What's up with you?" Carpenter glowered.

"What's your problem?" Walker retorted with a disinterested shrug.

Cyrus tried to settle the bile rising in his stomach and approach things diplomatically. "My problem? Oh, I don't know, maybe that we are supposed to be co-captains and you haven't done anything to help this team get ready for the season," he said, his volume increasing with each word. "We play our first game next week. Just because you score every now and then, you think you don't have to do anything off the ice. Must be nice. This is a team, Walker."

Walker pushed past his old friend. Cyrus had done a good job keeping his cool to that point, but Billy's blow-off was too much. He reached out and grabbed Billy by the shoulder, spun him around and shoved him squarely in the chest. He was ready to have it out then and there. Thankfully O'Brien and Bishop stepped into the fray. OB grabbed Cy's cocked right hand, hooked his arm under it and hugged him with the left, around the waist, and pulled back. Bishop snuck in behind Walker and pulled him out of reach of any potential swings.

"Calm down boys, no reason to get so heated," Bishop offered up. A beast on the ice, and a butterfly off of it, the multi-sport star hoped to return the locker room to a more chill atmosphere. That wasn't going to work today.

Walker eased out of his teammates' grasp and said, "Bish, I got this. Don't worry, I'm not going to throw fists with him."

He then turned his attention to Carpenter.

"You need to relax, dude. First off, neither one of us would be a captain if Frazier were here. Secondly, you aren't in charge, so back off."

Coach Scads flew through the door, his eyes scanning the area. O'Brien and

Bishop backed away from their fellow seniors and faded back to the corners of the room, leaving Carpenter and Walker face to face with their coach.

"What the hell is going on here?"

Both boys raised their shoulders and were about to say something, but Scadorski put up a hand and muted them.

"I don't care. You two are supposed to be captains, and this team is supposed to be on the ice in five minutes. From the looks of it, everyone except for the captains are ready to go. If you're not all out there at go-time, there will be no pucks on the ice today, all skating. Do you understand me?"

"Yessir," echoed through the locker room.

The door slammed, leaving the room full of maple locker stalls and maroon walls eerily silent.

Carpenter sliced the quiet.

"You heard the man, five minutes. Let's go, boys," he said with a clap, pretending everything was just fine.

"Yeah, let's go, boys," Walker said to himself.

Billy Walker did not need this drama. He had enough of that in his life at home with his sober-some-of-the-times mother. Maybe life would be better if he just walked out the locker room door and drove away from hockey, his lush mom and all of this drama.

11

Deciding he didn't need to add to the drama, Billy hastily donned his practice jersey, pads and skates, and barely made it onto the ice before his coach's deadline. Hockey season was just a little over a week old and already he felt pretty much over it. This used to be his favorite thing in the world to do. Now, it was like going to work. It used to be his escape from everything.

Billy Walker once scored seven goals in a Pee Wee game against a pretty good team from Medfield. He had four in the first period and then two more in the second. The coaches didn't want to run the score up so they moved him back to play defense in the third period. He still managed to hammer in a slap shot from the blue line for his seventh goal. Playing in 44 games that winter Billy scored 103 goals and also had 26 assists.

The year prior to his big breakout he'd had a respectable 29 goals, but that was before he grew four inches and gained 20 pounds of muscle over a span of just a few months. Usually, when puberty strikes it comes at the cost of dexterity and coordination, but Billy's ability to weave through defenses and see the ice had actually gotten better.

At 12 years old Billy had a vague idea of what a scholarship was. It had something to do with college and his dad wanted him to get one. Only the best players got them, and they meant you were probably going pro. "You get a scholarship and it'll make up for all of the child support I've had to shell out," his father would say when the subject came up. Maybe it was a joke. Billy wasn't sure.

Those ideas were refined over the next several years. During that time his desire to get an actual scholarship rose dramatically, not because he had a strong desire for an education, but because it was how the best players seemed to keep score against one another.

His body didn't seem to be as invested in the idea of going to college for free nearly as much as his parents were, though. By his senior year, he

47

stood at an incredibly average five feet, 11 inches tall, and weighed just 175 pounds.

Billy was still the best goal-scorer on this team, and he skated at an elite level. He was frustratingly good enough to get noticed, but not special enough to get offers. At the end of his junior year, Billy had come to the realization that he probably wasn't going to go to college to play pucks. His dad had accepted that fact far earlier and had been trying to explain to him for the last couple of years just how unlikely that prospect really was. Billy heard the message but misinterpreted it. He had confused dad's words as motivation to get bigger and better, to work harder, but now he realized that his father was simply trying to soften the blow for when reality reared its head.

With a shake of his head, Billy took a few strides along the slick ice and snared a loose puck from behind the near goal. He left the puck behind, kicked it with his left foot back to his right and then wove it between his legs, back and forth, with his stick blade. In one motion he spun 180 degrees and went through the same routine while skating backward. He then spun back to forward, repeating the process in a circuit around the rink before stopping in front of the Cannons bench where he began to stretch.

Immediately to his left was Danny Stone. They acknowledged one another with a nod.

"Don't worry about Cy, he's just wound up. Coach is riding him hard. You know how it is," Danny said.

"Whatever," was the only response Billy could muster.

Scadorski whistled the practice into session and began to issue orders. With the return of the football players, he hoped the intensity level would rise. The guys that had returned were obviously enthused, but they did not have their legs under them just yet. Halfway through their first practice, it looked as if O'Brien might lose his lunch, and his fellow footballers were equally drained.

OB's chest heaved with every stride. He was just two days removed from crushing bodies at Gillette Stadium, but football shape and hockey shape

48

were two very different things. Each play in football requires a player to go full speed for five to 10 seconds, resulting in a pileup and then some time to recover before repeating the process.

In hockey, the plays can be continuous for 45 to 60 seconds, sometimes even longer. When you play defense, especially in high school, your recovery time on the bench is usually only about as long as the time you were out on the ice. When you're a top guy, sometimes it's even less.

O'Brien's quads were barking at him. He had entered football season convinced he was in the best shape of his life. He was probably going to be named to the football all-state team and several small colleges were after him. He'd miraculously gotten through the entire season with no injury worse than a sprained finger. He thought he'd fall right back into hockey with no problems at all.

Boy, was he wrong.

Bishop was in the same boat. Coach had offered to let the football players have a few days to recover, and with 20 minutes still to go in their first practice of the year, he was wishing he could still take the offer. During a water break some of the hydration came back up on him, and he spit it out on his jersey. Thankfully no one had really noticed. If they had, they didn't say anything.

Mercifully, the practice finally ended. Carpenter and Walker begrudgingly lined up opposite one another at the door as the players exited the ice, patting them on the back for their efforts. The duo was just four feet apart, but neither made eye contact.

As the last player cleared the ice and the Zamboni machine inched out to do its job, Carpenter stepped off, leaving Walker by himself. Billy glanced around the rink, wondering if he'd be back tomorrow.

12

At almost the same time in Vermont, Scott Frazier removed his helmet, wiped his sweaty brow and left the ice at his team's rink. Breathing heavily, he looked around and wished practice could go all night. He was dog tired after a rigorous practice had run the Wellington team ragged for 90 minutes, but he'd happily trade burning muscles for a spinning head.

Every time he had called home over the past few weeks, his mother had assured him that sticking it out was the best choice and that things would improve over time. Time kept going by, but things weren't getting any better. Scott had not grown any closer to his teammates. He would fight for them on the ice because that's what you were supposed to do, but there was no bond like he had with the guys back home. In Eastport if one of his teammates got cheap-shotted, Scott was always the first to race to his side and happy to take a penalty to protect one of his brothers. Here at Wellington, if one of his teammates got run, he'd put himself into the fray, but it just wasn't the same.

He just couldn't fight the feeling that he did not belong there. Statistically, he was having a great season. Wellington had played five games so far, and he had already scored three goals and six assists, the second-most points on the team.

As usual, Scott was the last one out of the locker room that night. He stood under the stream of hot water in the shower stall for 20 minutes before finally twisting the handle and grabbing a towel. He mopped off his shoulder-length black hair, wrapped himself in a towel and walked into an already vacant locker room. He was alone, again.

The walk from the rink to his dormitory was roughly a half-mile over the campus. He could easily jog the distance in three or four minutes. A brisk walk would put him out the front door of the rink and to the front door of his dorm in exactly nine minutes. With three hours of calculus, history and Latin ahead, he was in no hurry.

It took him 22 minutes to get to his room.

Facing the inevitable, Scott cracked open his calculus book and called up the class syllabus on his iPad. His professor had just introduced infinite limits to the class. Getting through the work before tomorrow's class would probably take an infinite amount of time.

Ten minutes of rereading the same problem over and over resulted in a few scribbled lines. How in God's name was he ever going to get through this?

At Eastport, there had never been a question in his mind that he'd graduate. His guidance counselor understood Scott was a standout on the ice, but average – at best – in the classroom. His schedule had been structured in a way that he took classes he was equipped to pass. With a built-in study period at the end of his junior year schedule, Scott rarely had homework and managed a B-minus average. It had been his best year grade-wise in three years of high school, and he was on track to get through the NCAA clearinghouse and have no eligibility issues to worry about.

Ironically, doing as well as he had last year was a big reason he was in his current mess. Had he finished the school year with just a C-plus average, he would not have qualified to get into Wellington in the first place. But, with the B-minus, he just barely reached the minimum requirement for entry.

After deep-diving YouTube tutorials and Googling numerous topics in an effort to figure out just what the hell the calculus assignment was all about, he did something he had never done in a game. He gave up.

Glancing at his iPhone, he saw it was now past midnight. He'd accomplished nothing in over two hours of study time. He'd forgotten to take the phone off of silent mode after practice and missed a call from his brother and several text messages.

"Hey Scotty, it's Ted," his one-year-older brother said. "Just figured I'd see how things were going. Give me a call."

He had three text messages from his boys back home. Cyrus wanted to talk about the ongoing Billy issues, Wes just texted, "waddup" and Danny had said, "hit me up."

Scott began to respond to Cyrus's message but deleted the message instead. He hated seeing his old friends and teammates were having a hard time figuring things out without him around. His absence was a big part of the reason they were squabbling. If he'd been there, he would have set Billy Walker straight and that would have been that.

The hardest part about leaving Eastport behind had been bailing on his teammates. He had been one of the only juniors in the history of the program to wear an assistant captain's 'A' on his sweater the year before. At the team party after the end of the season, Coach Scads had pulled him aside and told him he would be the captain for next year. Not one of the captains, but *the captain*. "I think we're going to do big things next year. You lead the way, and they'll follow," the coach had said.

He'd left that behind. And for what?

13

Collin O'Brien hated being late to anything. He was always in a hurry. Maybe that was why he'd had so many quarterback sacks during his high school career. He had to be the first one to arrive for everything.

He hated getting out of bed even more than being late, though. Having overslept by 15 minutes, his chances of making it to school before the start of the first period were almost nil. He lived exactly 4.2 miles from Eastport High School, a twisting and convoluted 4.2 miles.

With two PowerBars and a can of Red Bull in his hand as he sprinted out the door, the three-sport star athlete flung himself behind the wheel of his 2005 Toyota Corolla. Collin paid just four grand for the car, using the money he'd earned the last few summers working as a busboy at The Fiesta Ristorante. The car had been in perfect working condition, with the exception of needing a bumper, which he'd been able to get at a salvage yard for 20 bucks.

With Kayne spitting fire on the sound system, he set out to break his record for those 4.2 miles. Collin took a quick right out of his road, then skidded to a halt at the stop sign up the street and spun his tires as he took a left onto Stage Coach Road before coming to yet another annoying stop sign. Three minutes into his sprint he slipped into traffic on the busy Forestdale Road and rode the Mercedes' bumper in front of him to the next light before a right onto Wood Stove Street.

Knowing that a cop loved to prey on speeders by lying in wait at the Knights of Columbus Hall halfway down the road, he kept it at 40 miles per hour until he reached that spot. Technically that was speeding since the limit was 35 on that road, but no cop was ever going to pull you over for five miles an hour over.

The cop wasn't in the parking lot waiting to nail anyone because he already had found his victim. About a 100 yards past the K of C Hall a red Mazda was pulled over, and a gorgeous 20-something was searching for her registration. Collin put the pedal down to 60 as he passed by, which got him to the lights at Grews Pond Road exactly two minutes before the start of school, and into a parking spot as the starting bell was about to chime.

Slamming the car into park, Collin flung his backpack over his shoulder, took one last swig on his Red Bull and sprinted to the side door just as the EHS Security Guard was about to lock it.

"Cutting it close again, Mr. O'Brien," the guard said as Collin slipped by him and began climbing the stairs to his first-period class, leaping them two at a time.

"Had it all the way," he called over his shoulder.

While Collin had made it into the building in time to avoid being marked tardy, which would have earned him extra sprints at practice later that day, he did not beat the closing of the door for his first-period class, Environmental Science. Mr. Cory opened his textbook and then made Collin wait a few moments before cracking the door.

"Mr. OBrien, how nice of you to join us today," the bearded and balding science teacher said. "Since you're making such a pronounced entrance, I wonder if you could add to this excellent moment by telling the class one of the biggest impacts to the upper atmosphere the earth has endured since the start of the 21st century?"

"Besides the increase in Sharknados?" quipped the senior.

Some teachers would have sent him directly to the principal's office after that remark. Mr. Cory, though, was known to be an uber nerd. The shelf behind his desk was full of Stars Wars figures and old Transformers, and he had the SyFy channel bookmarked on his remote control. The teacher laughed out loud and conceded the point to the star athlete.

Collin made it to English on time and then had no trouble in the third period, where he enjoyed the easiest internship he could have hoped for. He was the third period assistant to the athletic director's secretary, meaning he'd usually just have to double check which teams traveling on that day were assigned to which bus, what time that bus was supposed to leave, and from where. He'd type that information up and spend the rest of the period looking at his phone. The fourth period was gym class, which was a weightlifting class this quarter. Having gone hard in practice the night before, he did mostly stretching and some biceps curls, doing three sets of 10 with 25-pound dumbbells on both arms.

Lunch was next. Having left the house so quickly, Collin had forgotten to grab his midday meal out of the fridge. His mother had packed him up with three grilled chicken breasts, a small garden salad, an avocado, an apple, a banana and three chocolate chip cookies. Other than the cookies, he ate as healthy as could be on most days to turn that protein into muscle.

Cafeteria food, even in this day and age, was pretty much garbage. With no better options, he spent five bucks on two pieces of overcooked cheese pizza and figured he could forage through his friends' meals for stuff that bordered on healthy the rest of the time block.

He sat down at a round table in the caf where Craig, Wes, Josh, Melissa and Emily had selected. Wes had found a way to steal the seat next to Melissa, someone whose attention he'd been trying to gain for the past few weeks.

"You guys going right to the rink after school?" Collin asked his friends.

"Yeah, we all have to get our skates sharpened at the pro shop," Wes said, "so we're heading down in my car."

"Bish, either you or Josh want to ride down with me?" Collin asked.

The two boys paused. They loved their buddy, but they did not love getting into a car with him. He drove his Toyota like it was a performance racing machine and liked to show off behind the wheel. Any time any of them had said anything, he'd laugh and tell them to, "grow a set," or, "Calm down, Mommy."

"Nah, I think we're good with Wes," Craig said.

Collin wasn't pleased that his friends were all blowing him off like that. *What was the deal with that?*

14

"Dude, you can't just ask for cash for Christmas," Wes Garrett said while eyeing his buddy Josh Hutchinson through the rearview mirror.

"Why not? I don't need any clothes. I don't need any computer stuff. Obviously, I don't want school stuff. Cash rules. I'd rather find a bag of fifty dollar bills under the tree than a new pair of headphones," he said.

"First of all, your parents don't have a bag of fifties to give you. If they did your dad would drive a newer truck. Second, parents like to give things. They aren't going to take a picture on Christmas morning with you holding a wad of cash," Bish added.

"You asked what I wanted for Christmas. That's what I want. If I get money, I can buy my own presents," Hutchinson retorted. "Besides, what are you asking for?"

"I haven't really asked for anything. I just want to get this cast off. Unfortunately, Santa isn't going to be able to speed that up. I don't know, a new iPad or laptop would be cool," Garrett said.

"Dude, you should ask for a toothbrush. What the hell did you have for lunch?" Bishop said to his best friend with a smirk.

"Umm, tuna sandwich. And, screw you. You're lucky I can't punch you with this hand," Garrett said through a clenched smile.

With the three boys lost in conversation, Garrett was meandering down the road that they'd driven hundreds of times to and from the Eastport rink. Pickerel Pond Road could be just as slippery as the toothy fish it was named after, twisting through a sparsely populated area of town toward the technology park where the hockey rink was located.

After coming around a bend, the road straightened out for about 200 yards before rolling back to the left past the road's namesake. With his attention on the road in front of him and his conversation about the upcoming holiday, he did not spot the Toyota Corolla that was speeding up behind him. He nearly wet himself when the silver mid-sized family car pulled alongside him, matching his speed momentarily.

"Holy crap!" Garrett exclaimed.

Collin O'Brien rested his left hand on the Toyota's steering wheel, turned his gaze toward his friends in the red SUV and raised his middle finger in their direction before putting the accelerator on the floor and speeding away.

"He's crazy," Hutchinson said. "He's gonna get himself killed driving like that."

"Scared the crap out of me," Garrett said.

"OB being OB," Bishop said with a sigh. "That's why I'm in this car."

Three minutes later the three boys pulled into their usual parking spot under the snow canopy, which had a light layer of ice atop it, and were greeted by their friend. The chest beneath his maroon Under Armour sweatshirt was puffed out further than usual and he laughed at his friends.

"Man, you guys never saw me coming," he giggled. "That was great."

"It's not gonna be so great when you total your car," Garrett said.

"Dude, not cool," added Bishop. "Not cool at all."

O'Brien shook off the rebuke and switched modes quickly.

"Coach Scads should have the lines today. I think he's gonna pair me up with Moxon," the experienced defenseman said.

"Doesn't matter to me. I'm just going to be listed on the DL," Garrett sighed. "I am getting pretty good with the camera, though. Maybe I can get a job at ESPN someday."

The boys shuffled off toward the locker room and spied the sheet of paper hung by a strip of hockey tape next to the door. O'Brien's premonition of his spot had been correct. However, the top two lines were shuffled and not what had been expected.

"Dude, he has Cy and Billy skating together on the first line. How's that going to work?" wondered Garrett. "They can't stand each other."

57

"They can't stand each other this week," Bishop said. "They'll figure it out. Besides, I'm riding the wing. They're just going to be feeding me for snipes anyway. What's the school record for goals in a season?"

Craig's friends laughed at that comment. The mop-haired lover of classic rock was old school when it came to hockey too. His goal was to get at least one good hit on an opponent on every shift. He thrived along the boards and in the corners, where you had to be brave to wander. When he scored goals, they were usually the ugly ones, popping a rebound or deflecting a shot from the outside. The season before he'd been freed for five breakaways in 21 games. He scored on one. The goalie stopped his shot, but the rebound had hit his skate and trickled in.

"Me, Danny and Davey on line two," Hutchinson said, perking up that he was centering the second unit. "That's going to be fun."

"A pitcher, a cripple and a rookie. Sounds like money to me," O'Brien said while putting an elbow in his friend's ribs.

"That kid's going to be really good," Hutchinson said, referring to sophomore Davey Gaudreau.

Since day one of practice, it had been obvious that Gaudreau was going to make the varsity team, despite being just 15 years old and weighing in at 110 pounds on a good day. One of the team managers, Coach Henry's son who was in the eighth grade, was bigger and stronger than Gaudreau. Though the sophomore was not big, his speed and skill made up for his lack of size.

"I just hope that the little guy can make it through the season. You know someone's going to take a cheap shot at him at some point. He might break in half," Hutchinson said, with genuine concern.

"Let them try," O'Brien said. "He's so quick, he'll have the puck in the net before they turn back around. And if they do get him, then I'm getting them."

The corners of Collin's mouth rose at the thought of mixing it up with someone who would try to bully his teammate. OB wasn't about to let anyone mess with his teammates as long as he was around.

15

Practice for the next three days had its ups and downs. Everyone wondered how the team's two captains, Cyrus Carpenter and Billy Walker, would coexist on the same line. Each thought he was the Alpha. Both boys preferred playing center, and it was the fiery Carpenter who was given that spot, with Walker on the left and Bishop on the right. The sibling-like rivalry led to inspired play at times, but also mistakes.

Sweat-drenched and drained, the varsity squad heeded the screech of Coach Scadorski's whistle and formed a semi-circle around the bench. The coach clapped his hands together and motioned for everyone to take a knee. Helmets popped off, and players squirted themselves with water bottles and caught their breath after a grueling 60 minutes of work.

"Good work today boys," the coach began.

"Tomorrow it's for real. Game one, of 20. It's a long season. We're probably not going to win every one of them, but we're capable of it. This team has talent. I look around and I see as much skill as we've had in a long time.

"Skill doesn't win games, though. Hard work, discipline, sticking up for each other, being willing to give that little something extra when your tank is empty, that's what wins games. It wins championships. Just ask OB, Josh, Bish, and the rest of the guys who played on that football team. That was a long freakin' season. They started in August and just finished up. Now they're here, and I know each and every one of them would love to get that feeling again. Bish, tell them what it's like."

Bishop looked up from his water bottle and scanned his teammates.

"Amazing. There's no other word, it's amazing. Best feeling I've ever had," the starting right winger said.

"Better than sex," O'Brien said with a laugh.

The coach again motioned his hands downward, settling his players and quieting them back down after the group guffaw.

"Amazing … better than sex. Sounds pretty great to me. It's been a long time since the Eastport Cannons put a state championship banner on that wall behind us. The girls did it two years ago, you were all there to watch it, and I don't know about you but every time I look at it I get jealous. I want one of our own. There's only one way to get one. They don't give those things away. You earn championships," Scadorski proclaimed.

"I come from a small family. It was me, my parents and my brother. We were a tight-knit unit, and Dad was tough. He coached me at the old rink, and he told me something I never forgot. If you've played on the varsity you've heard this before, but it's just as meaningful now as it was then. You guys on the ice right now, we are a family. These are your brothers. The next three months can be some of the best of your life, but you've got to put the effort in. When you're tired, you go through the wall for your brother. When the team is down, you make a play for your brothers. That's what it is all about, gentlemen. Do those things, and in March, whether we hang one of those flags, or are still jealous of the ones that are up there, you'll have your brothers."

The coach motioned his hands to the middle, and everyone huddled together. Carpenter counted them down, "1-2-3, Eastport," the boys yelled in unison.

As they left the practice ice, the boys were reminded to wear shirts and ties for the next day's game and to be at the rink no later than 5:30 PM for the 7 PM contest. They rushed off to shower and change before dispersing to their homes for dinner. The team's curfew was 11 o'clock the night before a game, so getting ready quickly was paramount for those who hoped to make it to an early movie or date.

Garrett was waiting at his locker stall for his friends to finish up. The jerseys had been hung up during practice and he looked at his white home sweater with the number 22 stitched on the back. He'd wear it the next night but over a shirt and tie. Waiting for his broken hand to heal was difficult, but it was just a few more weeks before he'd be able to practice again. He ran his fingers over the large block 'E' on the front of the sweater.

"Daydreaming again?" Bishop quipped, snapping his friend back to reality.

"Yeah, it's killing me to have to sit out tomorrow. Opening night and I'm running the camera. This sucks."

"Don't worry about it, you'll be back on the ice in no time. Besides, there's always ESPN. See if you can get my goals on SportsCenter tomorrow."

Wes laughed at his friend's joke, but inside it wasn't very funny. He longed to get back out on the ice. Sooner or later he was going to get his chance to make a difference for this team.

16

In Vermont, it wasn't Opening Night. It was just another afternoon game in front of a mostly empty hockey rink for Scott Frazier at Wellington Academy. He went through the motions and had another strong game, picking up two assists as his team won 3-1. The only goal St. Anthony's Prep had scored in the game was when he was on the bench.

After the game, a coach from Framingham State that had waited around to talk to Scott congratulated him on his efforts earlier in the day. The coach then went about selling the greatness of the school he coached at. "You'd be a perfect fit for us on the blue line," the coach promised. "You'd probably start all four years for us, and I'm pretty sure the financial aid package we can put together would work well for your family."

Frazier had heard it all before. Salem State, Nicholls State, the University of New England and a couple of others had all gotten themselves some post-game face time with the defenseman after games this season. They'd all said pretty much the same things. They all promised they'd help make his future great and that he'd fit in perfectly at their place.

He doubted it. He didn't seem to fit in anywhere right now. Here at Wellington he just couldn't get comfortable. At home, he didn't fit in anymore, either. How could he? He'd abandoned his buddies — his home — because that's what "was best for his future." He couldn't help but wonder why it seemed that the future was always more important than the present. *Was it worth it to be miserable day after day for the possibility of maybe being happy later on?* It didn't make a whole lot of sense.

Scott again was the last one to leave the locker room and make his way back to his dorm. In his rush to get to the rink, he'd forgotten to grab his phone. He picked it up to see that Cyrus had called 15 minutes earlier and left a voicemail.

"Yo, Scotty, it's Cy. Saw the box score, nice game dude. We got our opener tonight, was wondering if you were coming down for the rest of the weekend. Give me a call."

The excitement in Cyrus's voice was obvious. Opening night was special at home. The rink would be packed, at least 1,000 strong. He got goosebumps just thinking about the opening chords of "Thunderstruck" blaring over the sound system while boys' skates hit the ice and they circled the zone in front of their bench. He was jealous. He hadn't played to an excited crowd since his last game as a Cannon back in March. If he'd known then that it was his last game with his boys he would have taken the time to soak it in.

Scott fingered through his contact list and decided to send a text to Cyrus rather than call him back. The last thing he wanted to do was bum out his buddy before game one and he didn't have the energy to fake it.

"Thanks for the message, bro. Kick ass tonight! Call me after u win."

The little gray dots appeared on his iMessage app, meaning his friend had received the message and was responding. After about 20 seconds the phone chimed. "Will do. Gonna put a hurting on Wrentham tonight."

Scott had considered going home for the rest of the weekend. He had the rest of the day free and there were no scheduled team activities again until Monday afternoon. Seeing his friends take on Wrentham would have been fun, but he couldn't bring himself to ask anyone to come all the way up to pick up him and then bring him back the next night. His older brother Teddy probably would have done it for him if he didn't have to work.

He could have asked his mother, but the idea of being grilled about how things were going at Wellington was enough to make him puke. He hated lying to her, but he'd learned after a few weeks that no matter how much he told her he disliked where he was she would tell him, "It'll all work out, you just have to give it a chance," and, "You are in the best possible place that you can be. It's so good for you, and you'll grow so much."

Half the school year was over and he'd given it a chance, and "the best possible place" just resembled a hellhole to Scott. As for personal growth, he didn't care. No progress was going to be made on that front anytime soon, so rather than ask her to make the drive he would just order a pizza and follow the game on the computer.

17

"Why can't I ever seem to get the length right?" Craig complained while his fingers contorted around the tie he wore for every game.

"Probably because you weren't meant to wear nice clothes," Wes Garrett replied. "It doesn't have to look right, it just has to be around your neck. There are no bonus points for looking dapper."

Garrett looked rakish in his beach sand-colored khakis, baby blue button-up and matching tie with whales all over it. His hair was gelled and combed to perfection, and with a sweet pullover sweater to complete the look, he was sure to look great while working the camera from the press box.

"Easy for you to say. You look like an ad for Vineyard Vines."

Bishop had a similar outfit, but none of the tight creases or flair that accompanied it. The left side of his shirt had already come un-tucked, and he was on his fourth try to get the front of the tie to actually hang lower than the back of it. He hadn't bothered with any product for his hair, he'd simply combed it straight back upon exiting the shower. He'd be wearing a helmet over it in a few hours anyway.

Craig took a look at himself in the mirror and shrugged. "That's about as good as it's going to get."

"Whatever, dude. Let's get going, we can catch the first period of the JV game if we head out now. We wait much longer and you're going to be sitting out the first period for being late," Garrett said.

The two boys exited Craig's bedroom and headed downstairs to the kitchen. Bishop grabbed two bottles of water, tossing one to his friend before twisting the cap off of his own. His grandmother had been waiting for their appearance and was not going to allow them to leave without making a fuss.

"Don't you boys look handsome," she said. "You are not walking out that door without taking a picture."

The two teenagers hated having their momentum halted, but knew better than to bicker with Cookie Foley. She'd taken Craig into her home when his mom, a single mother, had died unexpectedly a little more than five years earlier. Along with her husband Carl, Cookie did her best to keep up with the active boy and had given him a life that was more than he, or his mother, could have asked for. His grandmother was not a replacement for his mother — no one could ever be that — but she made sure Craig had every advantage in life.

Hiding their annoyance, Craig and Wes stood shoulder to shoulder and attempted to look happy to be taking the photo.

"Now Wes, be a sweetie and take one of me, Craig and Carl together," Cookie said sweetly.

Wes accepted the cell phone from his surrogate grandmother, aimed it at the three family members and said, "Say cheese." Cookie and Carl both followed the order, while Craig shook his head and laughed at his friend.

"Good luck boys, see you at the rink," Carl said as Cookie planted a kiss on her grandson's cheek and then did the same to Wes.

Jogging out the door, the boys scurried into Garrett's Jeep and clicked on their seat belts. Wes put the SUV into reverse while Bish texted Collin O'Brien, "On our way. Be there in 10."

The ride to the rink was silent for the first few minutes, both boys lost in their thoughts. Craig finally broke the silence as the boys turned onto Pickerel Pond Road.

He blew out a sigh and said, "I wish I had a better feeling about tonight."

"What do you mean?" Wes asked while turning his eyes toward his best friend.

"Something's off. We should be awesome this year, but I'm not feeling it. Our lines aren't clicking and Cy and Billy just can't get on the same page. This is our senior year, I really don't want to suck."

Wes paused. He couldn't attest to the overall cohesion of the lines because he wasn't out on the ice yet, but what he saw didn't look great. He looked down at his casted hand with disgust for the millionth time since he stupidly hurt himself and pondered what to say.

"Well, you can't help that you suck. That's how God made you," he said through a smile.

"Thanks."

"You, sir, are welcome. No, seriously, I think it will be fine. Once you hit the ice for real, it'll come together. Even if it isn't tonight, we are too good to suck."

"I hope you're right," Craig said. "I hope you're right."

Collin O'Brien stood outside the locker room, dressed from the waist down. He had on his hockey pants, pads, socks, skates, and shoulder pads. He gripped a football and tossed it to Danny Stone, who was also standing outside the door to the locker room, which opened to the main rink. The boys lobbed the pigskin back and forth while watching the junior varsity team skate against that night's opponent.

Mac Richardson made his way around the boards toward where the boys were standing and knocked on the coach's room door. He waited a few moments, but no one answered. Rather than make his way up to the press box, he engaged the two players in conversation.

"Hey boys, any idea who's starting in net tonight? I wanted to ask Coach Scads, but he's not around."

"He's probably out in the lobby," Stone said. "I saw him earlier."

"They haven't told us yet," O'Brien said. "He said at practice yesterday that he was still thinking about it."

"Okay," Richardson said, gesturing for the football. O'Brien fulfilled the request, lobbing a tight spiral into the sportswriter's waiting grasp.

Richardson eyed the football, turning it over in his hands. The leather was broken in perfectly, the laces tight. It was a great football. Then he noticed the Patriots logo embossed into the side.

66

"This is nice. Did you get it at Gillette?" he asked.

"Yup, stole it from Tom Brady," O'Brien said with a laugh.

"No, seriously, how'd you get it?" Richardson queried.

"We were in the Pats' practice bubble and me and the guys found it. We were tossing it around and when we finished warming up for the game I threw it in my bag. I didn't think that one football was going to kill the budget."

Richardson laughed at the audaciousness of the high school senior.

"Well, I guess even if you'd lost you would've had a helluva nice souvenir of the game," the reporter said.

"I wouldn't have kept it if we'd lost," O'Brien said matter-of-factly.

"Come on," Richardson retorted. "That's too cool not to keep."

"If we'd have lost I would have punted it over the stadium," O'Brien said seriously. "I wouldn't have wanted to look at it again. We won, though, so I keep it in my bag. It's a good luck charm. Worked really well once."

Richardson tossed the ball back to O'Brien, nodded his head to Stone and wished the boys luck as Coach Scadorski came around the corner, opened his door and waved the reporter over.

Entering the coach's retreat, Richardson leaned up against the wall and grabbed his notebook out of his backpack. The coach grabbed a seat and said, "What's up, Mac?"

"Just wondering who's starting in net tonight and what your lines looked like."

"Who do you think should start in net?" Scadorski asked, sounding serious.

"Well, I haven't seen too many practices, but I'd guess one of the seniors, probably Martinage, I guess since he started the most last year, but you could tell me any of the three and I wouldn't be surprised."

"That's the problem. It could be any of the three. None of them have really stepped up yet. They've all looked awesome at times, and horrible. Yeah, I think we're going to let Martinage go and see what happens from there. It's his job to lose, but I wouldn't be surprised if Doogle takes it by the end of the year. Who knows."

"So I can Tweet out that it's Martinage?"

"Yeah, at least for the first period," the coach said with a chuckle. "You could see all three tonight."

"And the lines?" the reporter asked.

"First two are what you'd expect. Carpenter with Walker and Bishop; Hutchinson with Stone and Gaudreau. Third line will be mix and match until something sticks."

"Alright. You must be excited. Game one of 20. Opening night," the reporter said enthusiastically.

"Mac, this group is hard to figure out. We could win 16, 17 games easy. We could miss the playoffs. It's all on them. They need to come together as a group and they haven't. I can't put my finger on it, but something is off. There's so much talent out there, every coach I talk to thinks we're going to compete for the state title, but they're not at practice. There's a disconnect, and we have to figure it out or it's going to be a long year."

Scadorski had no idea how prophetic he was at that moment.

18

The lights dimmed, a spotlight shone toward the Cannons' entrance and the music hit. Jimmy Martinage skated onto the ice first. That meant he was going to be the starting goalie, and he was followed by his teammates, hopping one-by-one onto the ice and speeding off to circle the rink. The captains, Carpenter and Walker, high-fived and glove-tapped the Cannons as they followed the keeper out onto the ice, repeating, "Let's go, boys, get it... Come on guys, let's do this."

The final Cannon in line was O'Brien. He removed his right glove and shook hands, first with Carpenter, who was on the left and then Walker. He uttered, "I got you," to both and then made his way out to the playing surface. The two captains followed suit, shaking hands with one another before heading on themselves. Behind them, Garrett slammed the door shut before shuffling off to the press box.

After the pregame warm-up, the public address announcer communicated the starting lineups. He started with Wrentham and the riled-up Eastport crowd turned its collective back on the Rough Riders as the list was read. Each name was followed up with, "Sucks!"

The young fans hadn't gotten through the forward line before the AD, Harry Burnette, came over to tell them to stop, threatening to kick out the next person to violate the code of conduct. The 300 or so students in the stands looked at him as if he was obviously angry with someone else, but lowered the volume on their heckling until the game actually began.

Next, the Cannons names were read and the building got loud. Each name was greeted with an ovation. While the starters' names were announced, the rest of the team stood along the blue line, shuffling back and forth on their blades. First game jitters were evident as the boys could not sit still.

Danny Stone might have felt the most butterflies flying around in his stomach. It had been nearly two years since he'd played in a game for his team. The waiting had nearly driven him mad at times. Sleep had not come easily last night.

As the starters skated out to their positions, the rest of the team made its way to the bench. Stone sat on the bench with his stick between his knees and stared straight ahead. Danny was next to Josh Hutchinson and maybe the only other person as nervous as he was, Davey Gaudreau, who was about to play his first game in a varsity uniform.

As the puck dropped, the players leaned over the edge of the boards to watch the action. Carpenter won the drawback to Alex Gossard, who flung a pass up the wing for Bishop. The grinder for the Cannons sent the puck deep into the zone and chased it. Wrentham came away with the puck, eventually got it across the red line and sent it to the corner, where another battle ensued.

Eastport reclaimed the puck as Billy Walker skated across the red line. His two linemates circled back to the bench. Carpenter left the ice and Hutchinson hopped on to replace him. Bishop entered through the door, and Gaudreau hopped over the boards and sprinted into the zone.

"Come on Walker, get a change, get a change," Stone mumbled to himself, dying to get into the game.

Walker didn't get a change, though. As the new forwards came onto the ice, the starting left wing and co-captain tried to make something happen at the top of the left circle. He tried a head fake to get a shot off, but the defense poked the puck free. A Wrentham player took away the puck and went the other way.

A pass, a fake, a shot. Martinage bought the fake and was too late to recover for the shot. Wrentham had a goal, just 57 seconds into the season. The Rough Riders were up 1-0 before the crowd had finished finding their seats.

As the visiting team celebrated, Danny Stone replaced Billy Walker on the ice. Walker slinked back to the bench, greeted by a cold stare from Coach Scads.

"Hey, if the shot's not there, pass it or get it deep. Don't try to do it all on your own. That one's on you, go get it back," the coach said.

Walker thought about making an excuse. *What could he say though?*

Stone's return to the ice for the first time in 22 months was uneventful. His linemates had already skated about 10 seconds without him, the time it took for Walker to cough up the puck for the breakaway. He didn't touch the puck on that first shift. Playing the left wing, the action was tilted to the right for the next 32 seconds. Before he even got close to the puck he heard Coach Scads whistle calling them back for the third line.

Danny was the first back to the door and as he grabbed his seat he watched third line player Cam Roget hop on. Hutchinson was next, and he slid in tight, followed by Gaudreau.

"Good shift boys," Hutchinson said to his linemates. "We're into the game now, let's go get one. We've got this. I got you."

Danny caught his breath and watched the action unfold. The rest of the period was unremarkable. On his fourth shift of the day, he took his first shot of the year, but it missed the net a little to the right. He'd tried to pick the corner, but let it go a little early. Carpenter came close to scoring for the team with three minutes to go in the first, but the Wrentham goalie did a great job of moving laterally and got his pads to the post for the denial.

Fifteen minutes of hockey had taken about 28 minutes to play. To the 20 kids on the Cannons bench, it felt like two minutes. Before they knew it, the horn sounded and they were back in their locker room for the first intermission.

Inside the Eastport locker room chests heaved while orange slices were sucked on and water was guzzled. Everyone muttered something along the lines of either, "Let's go," or, "We got this."

Scadorski pushed through the door to rally his troops two minutes before they were due back on the ice. "Not a bad period. You made one mistake and it cost us. No selfish plays, move the puck, be a team. You're better than they are, and they know it. Get out on the forecheck and pick up the tempo. Let's go!"

Scadorski was wrong. Wrentham did not think that Eastport was better. Taking a lead into the break, the visiting team believed that it was the

71

superior team, and played like it in the second period. The Cannons didn't know what hit them.

Three minutes into the period Martinage waved at a wrist shot from high in the zone and missed. Two minutes after that Carpenter wound up for a slap shot from the high slot and it was blocked. Fast break the other way and 3-0.

The nail in the Cannons' coffin came with a minute to play in the second period. Looking to lift his team's energy, Collin O'Brien lined up a hit and stapled one of the Wrentham players into the boards from behind. He was called for boarding and sent to the penalty box. He watched in horror as Alex Gossard tripped over a stick while trying to kill the penalty and Wrentham exploited the hole. Their power play goal made it 4-0 at the end of the second period.

Leaving the ice O'Brien snapped his stick over the boards. In the stands, his mother looked mortified. She was upset that her son had acted out – and knew doing so would result in a third-period benching – but she was also upset about the $275 price tag for a new stick. Collin's tantrum would prove expensive.

"He's paying for that himself," Mrs. O'Brien said to no one in particular.

Scadorski stormed into the locker room on the heels of his players. Typically the head coach and his assistant spent a few minutes analyzing the previous period before talking to the players. The Cannons were still finding their seats at their lockers when the tirade began.

"Are you kidding me? Is this how it's going to be? Carpenter, Walker, you are allowed to pass the puck to one another you know. Stop this dangling garbage. Pass it or get it deep, this isn't some video game. And O'Brien, what the hell was that? You're lucky the ref didn't throw you out of the game for that garbage. Do you want a suspension, because if you get called for a misconduct – and you should have gotten one – you sit the next two. You're not playing the rest of this game. You're a senior, you know better," Scadorski screamed.

Silence overtook the room, except for the coach's accelerated breathing. No one dared make a sound for fear that they'd be the next target in his crosshairs. Pacing from the front of the room to the rear and back, Scadorski wrung the life out of a lineup card that had been pristine an hour earlier but now was a crumpled mess.

"Get it together gentlemen. You've got one period and a big hole to climb out of," he bellowed before pointing at his team's seventh defenseman. "You take O'Brien's shifts this period."

The coach turned on his heel, flung open the door and exited, slamming it shut behind him. The parents and friends in the stands turned in unison at the sound of the portal crashing into the frame on the other side of the rink.

Inside the locker room, the silence did not cease. The first two periods, coupled with Coach Scadorski's tongue lashing, had left the Cannons stunned.

Sweat dripped down Craig's brow. The senior lifted his head, flung his mop of brown hair back and stood up. He looked around the room.

"Forget the score guys. Unless we go out and get three quick ones it's probably over. That doesn't matter. Let's go out and win the period. Hit 'em every time you can and shoot the puck. Let's just play some hockey. We don't suck... at least not this bad."

The last statement broke the tension, at least a little bit. Several players audibly exhaled and others rose to their feet.

Hutchinson started on one side of the room and made it around, tapping every Cannon on the head. "Let's go," he repeated over and over. "Get a hit, get a shot."

Though they intended to adhere to the coach's wishes in the third period, the Cannons continued to play poorly. Wrentham scored again early in the third to make it 5-0 before Eastport finally ended the onslaught with a goal that came with six minutes left in the game. Hutchinson followed his own advice, getting a hit on a defenseman to free the puck, and then a shot from just above the right faceoff circle. The goalie stopped the bid, but the senior crashed to the net and was able to tip in his own rebound.

For the first time all season the loudspeakers blared the goal horn and

"Zombie Nation" played loudly. None of the usual celebrations followed the goal, though. It changed the score, but not the outcome. Josh received some half-hearted hugs and pats on the back, but it didn't change a thing.

Shortly after, the horn sounded the game's end. Eastport shuffled through the handshake line, with most of the Cannons staring down at their skates while they touched gloves with the Rough Riders, all of whom seemed very satisfied with themselves. After getting through the lineup the downtrodden boys made quick turns toward the locker room.

Coach Scadorski was quick with his postgame comments to his players.

"We have to do better. You know it, I know it. That team is not better than you. They sure as hell aren't 5-1 better than you. I want you to think about how you played tonight – you – and what you need to do to be better. That's it."

Scadorski and his assistant coach left the locker room and entered his office. The two men each grabbed a seat. Tom Henry was the first to find the words.

"We sucked," the big man said while unzipping his warm-up jacket. "I mean, we saw signs in practice that this might happen, but man did we suck."

Scadorski loosened his tie and ran his hands through his thinning hair, threatening to tear out what was left of his once-flowing mane. He rubbed his eyes and then lifted his gaze toward the ceiling.

"I'm at a loss. A couple more of those stink bombs and we're on a collision course with a lost season, a lost year. This team is supposed to be our contender," Scads whispered. "I just don't get it. These kids have been playing together for years. They looked like strangers out there."

The assistant agreed.

"What do we do on Monday? I got a feeling it's gonna get worse before it gets any better," Scardorski said. "If it gets better," he added under his breath.

19

Wes Garrett waited impatiently in the lobby for his teammates. Having not played in the game, he had no reason to bother with a post-game shower. He'd listened to Coach Scads' comments and quickly made for the door. As soon as he'd reached the large common area in the front of the rink he found himself engulfed by his mom, Darlene, and Craig's grandmother, Cookie, along with several other moms who all wore big metal buttons with their respective player's face on it. He answered a few questions about his hand and tried to feign interest in their thoughts about the game.

Finally, after 15 minutes, the other Cannons began appearing in the lobby. Martinage was first to come through and did not even pause for his parents. He charged through the room and into the cold night air. His mom and dad shared a look of concern and followed their goaltender toward the parking lot.

Cyrus Carpenter followed, his arm around Davey Gaudreau. The sophomore looked upset and Carpenter was offering him some kind words.

"It's one game man, you've got something like a 100 more to go here. Don't worry about it," the co-captain whispered to the rookie.

"Yeah, but I only got one shot on net, didn't score, and I turned the puck over. I was awful. He's probably going to send me down to JV on Monday," the youngster retorted.

"No, he won't. You played defense, which is more than I can say for a lot of the guys tonight. You're good, you're going to be fine. Try not to think about it. Go home and play some video games, forget about it," Carpenter advised.

The senior patted his young friend on the back and headed over to his father, who threw his arm around his son and gave a squeeze.

"Well, that happened," the elder Carpenter said.

"Yup, that happened," muttered the son.

Bishop and O'Brien were next to materialize and they too went right to their families.

"Did you remember to tell Coach Scadorski you won't be at practice the next few days or at the next game?" Cookie Foley asked, kissing her grandson on the cheek.

Both O'Brien and Garrett looked quizzically at their friend.

"What?" Garrett said.

"You got somewhere better to be?" O'Brien asked.

"Yeah, um, I forgot to tell you guys. I'm heading to the Carolinas with Gram for a couple of days. We're going to look at a couple of schools. I set up a meeting with the baseball coach at East Carolina and we're going to look at a few others too," Bishop said, adjusting his untucked shirttails.

Garrett perked up.

"Can I come?" he asked, only sort of kidding.

"Sorry Wesley, while you are my favorite surrogate grandchild – no offense Collin – we already have flights booked and an itinerary. You will just have to manage a few days without your friend."

Coach Scadorski had found out his first liner would be missing for the second game of the season on the first day of practice when Cookie Bishop had pulled him aside, unbeknownst to her grandson, and informed the coach that she was taking him away for a few days during the season. Vacations in-season were a no-no and usually resulted in a suspension. The coach was not going to enforce that rule in this case. Bishop was not going on a holiday to work on his tan. He was legitimately looking to further his education, which was something, considering how little he had cared about such things when he started high school.

Bishop nearly failed off of the JV team as a freshman. A lecture from Scadorski and a kind English teacher who allowed him to hand in some extra credit work to get his grade up to a C, had kept him eligible. That lecture kick-started a turnaround. Craig was hardly in the running to be the valedictorian for the senior class, but his grades were good enough to get him into college. In the big picture, missing one game wasn't that big of a deal.

"You riding with me or your grandmother?" Garrett asked.

"I'm going home with her. I haven't packed yet and we have to get up at like 4AM to hit the road," Bishop said.

The friends parted ways and weren't all in the same place again until Friday morning. Wes, with O'Brien riding shotgun, pulled in to pick up Bishop for school. Collin had wanted to skip the day, but if he didn't go to school he wouldn't be allowed to practice. If he didn't practice, Coach wouldn't let him play the next night.

Since Wes had had to run by OB's house to pick his other friend up that day, he simply honked the Cherokee's horn and sat idling in the driveway. Cookie Foley opened the door, waved to the two boys and put up a single finger, telling them that Craig would be along in a minute.

As usual, Bish was a bit disheveled as he sprinted out, and was surprised to see his other friend riding shotgun, occupying his usual spot in the Jeep.

"Dude, you're in my seat," he said.

"Get in the back, world traveler, I get shotgun today," O'Brien said with a smirk.

Craig was not used to sitting in the backseat of Wes's ride. He could count on one hand the times he'd been downgraded to the rear of the vehicle and those times had all been because girls were present and required the front seat next to Wes. Those times were understandable. This was less so.

"So, you guys want to explain to me how you lost to St. Luke's 11-0? I know they're good, but 11-0. What the hell?" Bishop was going to ease into that conversation, but his plan changed when he'd been relegated to the backseat. "And how come you're not in your car, OB?"

"I hit a pothole yesterday pretty hard and messed up the suspension. I have to drop it off after school to get it worked on. It's going to cost me like 500 bucks to get fixed. It's gonna wipe out my bank account. I'm bitter," O'Brien said.

"I'm more bitter about St. Luke's," Garrett said. "They just killed us. We played all the goalies, didn't matter. It was like they were playing the NHL video game on rookie level. Every shot went in. And, they were so freaking fast."

"Yeah, you've heard about that kid they have, the one who already signed at BU," O'Brien said.

"Yeah, he's supposed to be nasty," Craig said.

"You have no idea. That dude came down the wing, and I had him lined up dead to rights. It's still the first period, just like 1-0 at the time."

"It was 2-0," Garrett corrected.

"Would you let me tell the story? Okay, 2-0, anyways he comes down the wing and I'm about to lay him out flat. So I step up, and just as I do, he headfakes me to the inside, and I bite – hard – and the next thing I know he puts the puck between my legs and goes around me on the other side. It's just him and Martinage, and that did not end well. He bears down hard, puts on the breaks and one-hand flicks it under the bar."

"Richardson almost fell out of the press box when he saw that," Garrett said. "His coffee shot out his nose. It was pretty funny."

"So that made it 3-0 and they got two more before the end of the first. It was eight at the end of two. We sucked," O'Brien continued.

Bishop just shook his head. He hated not being there for his brothers, though he knew his presence would not have changed the outcome.

"Well, that sucks. I'll tell you what did not suck, though, East Carolina. I'm applying, and I think I will get in," Bishop said.

"Cool," O'Brien said. "What was it like?"

"Campus was nice, we got a tour. Freshman dorms were decent and the baseball facility was just so sweet. I met with the coach – I'd sent him my highlight reel – and he said I could try to walk on to the team during fall ball. If my grades are good enough, and I can hit a bit, I have what he called a 'preferred walk-on spot.' Basically, I'll get a spot on the team, but no scholarship freshman year. If I do well, I can earn one for sophomore year. Hell, he said he has connections up here, and if I crack the starting lineup I could play in the Cape League."

"That's unreal," Garrett said as he pulled into the high school parking lot. "That's pretty much what they told Hutchinson – except he's already got a scholarship. Can you imagine, you could face him in a Cape League game. How cool would that be?"

Craig thought it would be amazing to play with or against his friend in the Cape Cod Baseball League, the best summer college league in the country. His focus at the moment, though, was helping his teammates fix what was wrong on the ice. Leaning back, he promised himself the Cannons would be better. He'd make sure of it.

20

"So I hear you're going to take me deep in the Cape League in two years. We'll see about that. Gonna be hard to get a piece of one I put in your ear," Josh Hutchinson said while taking his skates off following one of the first productive practices the Cannons had experienced in a while.

"Dude, one thing at a time," Craig retorted. "I was just told I could walk on and that I had a chance to make the team at ECU. The Cape League's a long way off. Besides, they'd probably put us both on the same team anyways, here in town, so they don't have to worry about housing us."

"That'd be even better," Hutchinson said. "Congrats, though, that's awesome. Imagine that, the two of us are both going to play D1 ball. Who would've thought that back in Little League?"

"When you two are done stroking your egos can we discuss what we're doing tonight?" Collin O'Brien said as he entered the locker room with a towel around his waist. "There are skirts to be chased and beers to be drank."

"Can't tonight," Hutchinson said. "I've got a workout session at 8 for baseball and then I'm calling it a night."

"Sorry OB, but me and Wes are out too," Bishop piped in. "We already told the girls we'd go to the movies with them."

"You guys suck. Can I tag along?"

"If you've got a girl to go with, sure," Wes said.

Collin did not have a date that night. He enjoyed hooking up with new girls whenever he could, but steady girlfriends weren't his thing.

"I'm having a few of the boys over for pizza and Call of Duty," chimed in Danny Stone from the corner of the room. "If you can promise you won't rage on us when you get killed, you can join in."

"Who's going?" queried O'Brien.

Joey Moxon raised his hand. Cyrus Carpenter said, "I'm in."

Alex Gossard shrugged his shoulders and Marc Rollins perked up as well.

"What about you, Walker?" O'Brien asked the enigmatic team co-captain. "You up to get blown up tonight?"

"I don't know," Billy Walker said.

"Yeah, well what are your plans?" Carpenter asked.

"Nothing really, just chillin', watch a movie I guess," he said.

"Dude, you're coming to Stone's. I'll pick you up," Carpenter said, extending an olive branch. "I'll grab Baby Gaudreau and you."

"Whoa, how did this become a party?" Stone asked.

"Not a party, a team bonding session. We ought to force Bish and Garrett to ditch their chicks, make it mandatory. Get the whole unit out there," Collin announced.

With that a few of the others who had not yet been included in the video game night balked, claiming their own plans with girlfriends, other friends or family. Stone did not show it outwardly, but he was relieved. His basement was going to be cramped as it was, and he still had to explain to his parents that what had been two or three guys coming over to hang out had just become something far larger and louder.

"I guess I can swing by after baseball," Hutchinson said. "I can't stay too late. I've got stuff to do in the morning."

"I'm not bailing on Emily," Craig said. "She'd kill me after being away. But me and Wes will text you guys after the movies. Maybe we will stop in for a quick game."

"We could do that," Garrett added.

Stone wrote down pizza preferences and took donations to the food fund. He collected $27 from the boys, which would hardly cover the costs. Rather than complain about his teammates' cheapness, he opted for a smarter option.

During the fall Danny had played on the school's golf team along with a couple of his hockey teammates. The game frustrated the hell out of him, mostly because he could not hit anything longer than a seven iron straight. However, one of his best friends on the team used to play hockey until it became clear after his sophomore season that he would never see any substantial playing time at the varsity level. Mitchell Ehrhardt wasn't much of a winger, but he was a good dude and his dad owned a pizza shop on Main Street.

Danny left the locker room and entered his car. He fingered through his contacts and called Ehrhardt.

"Hey Mitch, I've got a problem and I need a hand. Somehow I ended up with most of the team coming over to play video games tonight, and they want pizza, but the cheap bastards only gave me 27 bucks. Any chance you might be able to hook something up with your old man? I can probably do about 50 bucks," Danny said with the hopes he could beg his parents to not only open their home to most of the team but also foot some of the bill.

"Stoney you're killing me, you know it's Friday night, right? I've got like a hundred other orders - from paying customers," Mitch said.

"I'll owe you one. You should come over, too. I mean it's gonna be all dudes, but it should be fun," Stone said, hoping the invitation might swing things positively.

"I'm stuck behind the counter until 10, which sucks for me but works for you. What do you need?"

Thankfully the orders from the guys had been pretty simple, two pepperoni, two meatball, one cheese and one request for a Hawaiian. Mitchell said he couldn't send out a delivery guy, but to have someone drop in to pick them up at 7 and he'd figure a way to keep the price under $50.

"Dude, you're the best," Danny said, relieved that his friend had come through for him.

While the Cannons were finishing up their practice, Scott Frazier was lacing his skates up for his last game before Christmas break. It was December 20 and Wellington was playing Rye Preparatory School. Both teams would have two weeks away from campus following the game.

Scott had run back from his final class of the day to pack up his room. It had taken some effort to get everything into the suitcase he had, but all of the clothes had to go home. He hadn't done any laundry in a few weeks and couldn't wait to hand it over to his mom and let her deal with it. He also pined for his own bed. The one in his dormitory was standard issue for a place like this. He guessed that at least 15 other people had owned it in the past and the springs did not support his chiseled frame very well. He'd tried flipping it, turning it, putting a pad under it. None of that made any difference, though putting a couple of old books under the box spring had at least leveled out his feet and made it so that he didn't feel like he was sliding to the floor each night.

That night Frazier played like a man possessed. Knowing he had a vacation on the horizon, he was invigorated and had his best game yet in a Wellington uniform. In the first period, he clapped in a shot from the high slot, beating the goalie over his right leg pad. He set up a goal in the second period and assisted on two in the third. Wellington won 5-2 and Frazier had four points for the night. He'd noticed a couple of notebooks out behind the goals, and familiar faces scribbling in them, during the game. Afterward, the scouts approached him to pitch a junior program, a Division 3 college team and a low tier Division 1 team. This was becoming the norm: play a game, have someone try to recruit him. The ones he would love to hear from: Boston College, Boston University, Northeastern, UMass, Merrimack - the Hockey East schools - still weren't showing up, though.

"Whatever," he said to himself in the shower. "It's time to go home."

21

After promising his parents that he and his friends would gladly shovel out the driveway the next time it snowed, talking $40 out of his dad's wallet to add to the kitty, Danny drove down to the Eastport Plaza. He went into LeMoine's Market and filled a cart with bottled water, Coke and Mountain Dew. That left him a little over $50 for the pizza, which he hoped would be enough.

Dan popped open the trunk, put in the beverages and then walked across the plaza to the pizza shop, hoping to draw zero attention as he made his way to the side of the counter to talk to his friend. Those hopes were dashed, though, when Mr. Ehrhardt eyed him opening the door. Mitch's dad was bigger than the pizza oven, all six feet, five inches and 350 pounds of him. A black man who had played college football 25 years ago, his expressive face always told the story. With his ball cap backward and eyes shooting daggers, Danny feared death was imminent.

"I hear you're having a little party tonight and I'm providing the food for the hockey team at a substantial discount. How am I supposed to stay in business giving away pizzas, Danny Stone? How exactly does that work?"

Danny stopped dead in his tracks and felt the blood rushing to his face. His ears were on fire from the embarrassment. For a second he contemplated aborting the mission altogether and retreating to the parking lot.

"Umm, well, I mean if it's a problem, Mr. E, I understand. I didn't mean to..."

As soon as Stone began to stammer, Henry Ehrhardt cracked. His flat-lined mouth turned into a huge smile and his t-shirt exposed the bottom of his belly as he laughed.

"I told you I'd make him piss himself," Ehrhardt said to his son, who had hidden in the back of the room so he didn't ruin the prank. "Your friend looks like he's seen a ghost. Grab this boy his pizzas and a rag to clean up the front of his jeans."

84

Mitchell grabbed six boxes stacked on top of one another and then motioned to Stone to grab the pile of four next to them. "Hey, give me a hand with these."

"Dude, that's 10 pizzas, I only ordered six. How much do I owe you?" Danny asked. "I've got $50 bucks."

"Danny Stone, that's $145 worth of pies right there," Mr. Ehrhardt bellowed. "Keep your money. Let's call it a donation to the Eastport Hockey program. You guys go out and win tomorrow, and then make sure you tell the newspapers it was because of Port-A-Pizza. I want a quote Stone. I want to see it, and you'd better get me a goal."

"I promise," Danny said, thankful that the team was scheduled to play the worst team in the league tomorrow night, Eastham High. He'd have a good chance to fulfill that promise. "I'll do my best, and thanks. I owe you one."

Danny and Mitchell walked to the car and Stone pushed the key fob to unlock the doors. They stacked six of the pizzas on the passenger side floor and the other four on the seat. He thought about trying to belt the pizzas in but was afraid that could lead to disaster if he took too sharp a corner.

Danny reached into his pocket. "I know your dad won't take the money, but throw this into the tip jar or something."

Mitchell stiff-armed the attempt. "Nope, Dad said donation, it's a donation. Besides, I haven't hung out with all those guys in forever. This is going to be a good night. I'll see you in a couple hours."

While Danny drove home with the pizzas, Wes and Craig were pulling down the long driveway that led to Emily Brown's house to pick up the girls. Each boy had on his nicest pair of jeans. Wes had opted for a red Vineyard Vines golf polo and had styled his hair nicely for his first official date with the captain of the Eastport High School girls' lacrosse team, Melissa Johnson, who just happened to be close friends with Craig's girlfriend Emily. Bish, not trying nearly as hard to impress his lady on their hundredth or so date, had opted for a Rolling Stones 1988 tour t-shirt he'd found on eBay a few weeks earlier. The vintage clothing had only cost him $12 and it was a find he was very proud of. His long brown hair was combed back but threatened to cover his eyes with each turn of his head.

"Calm down Wes, you've hung out with Mel before, this is just a movie. No big deal. Don't make it out to be something massive, we're just going to see Star Wars," Craig said.

It was actually the second time the boys had been to the newest Star Wars movie. They'd made a point of getting to the earliest screening a week earlier when the movie had been released. Growing up the two of them had watched all of the Star Wars movies over and over. Not many of their friends knew just how nerdy Wes and Craig actually were.

The boys exited the Jeep Cherokee and went to the front door. As Craig drew his right hand back to knock on the door, it flew open and in the doorway stood the figure of Walter Brown, Emily's father. "Go away, you've got the wrong house."

Emily rushed around the corner to the rescue. "Dad, stop trying to be funny, it's not working," she scolded, reaching around her father to grab her boyfriend by the hand and pull him into the living room.

Emily, wearing a red cardigan over a white t-shirt and ripped jeans, pushed up on her toes and kissed her boyfriend on the cheek, leaving a slight ring of lipstick on his cheek. "Hello, Craig," she said. "We are just about ready to go. Melissa is finishing up her braid."

At the mention of his date's name, Wes shifted on his feet and tried to peer through the walls to see how things were progressing. Emily noticed the nervousness of her boyfriend's best friend and smiled. She'd been the one to suggest this possible match and had finally weaved it together after dropping countless hints to both parties.

Melissa entered the room and all five heads in the room turned. She'd spent the better part of the last two days trying to figure out exactly what to wear for this "casual" date. In the end, she and Emily had figured out the perfect compromise of dressing to impress without trying too hard by pairing a sundress with black leggings and a little white sweater. She knew she'd nailed it from the smile on Wes's face as she entered the room. That smile grew wider when she tacked on a peppy, "Hi, guys."

Seeing his date enter the room, Wes excitedly began to shuffle in her direction to greet her. She looked awesome, and he had to say so. The toe

86

of his sneakers caught the edge of an expensive Oriental rug and down he went, taking his date to the floor with him.

"Are you okay?" he asked.

Melissa brushed her bright red – some would call it orange – hair away from her face, collected herself and burst into laughter.

"I'm fine," she said, holding back tears of laughter. "That's one way to make an entrance."

With a beet red face, Wes hopped up quickly. He offered his non-casted left hand and pulled his date to her feet. She popped right up, showing off just a small portion of the athleticism that had her on the wish list for several college field hockey programs around New England, though she was leaning toward eschewing the game in college to go south, preferably the University of South Carolina, to be an engineering student.

"So, Star Wars?" Melissa queried Wes, trying her best to put him at ease.

"Umm, yeah, if that's okay. We thought it would be fun."

"I don't know, I've got a bad feeling about this," she said, searching Wes's face for a reaction.

It took him a second but then recognized that Melissa had just recited one of the most famous lines from the Star Wars franchise, one that had appeared at least once in every one of the films thus far.

"It's going to be fun, search your feelings, you know it to be true," he countered.

"If you two would stop nerding out with one another we could get to the theater and see the movie unless you two would rather just put on a performance of the saga for us," Emily said to her two friends while buzzing from the connection that they'd obviously made.

"Let's go," Wes said.

"And may the force be with us," Craig added.

Emily playfully punched him in the arm. This was a double date she'd been looking forward to for a long time.

22

Scott spent his weekend doing a whole lot of nothing. His friends didn't know he'd already come home from Wellington and he kept a low profile for the weekend. His mother had picked him up at school and given him a sideways look when she saw just how much stuff he had to bring home in their four-door sedan.

"Good thing your father had to work tonight. There wouldn't have been enough room for all of us. You know that they let you keep things in your room over the break," she had said humorlessly.

"I know. I've got a lot of dirty laundry, I guess," he shrugged.

For five hours they rode side by side but said little. Mrs. Frazier had attempted to make small talk a few times, but Scott replied with quick, short answers, content to watch trees and rest stops blur by out the passenger side window. Mom stopped for coffee and a snack north of Boston at one of the state's countless Dunkin' Donuts. Scott chose a bottle of water out of the cooler and an almost ripe banana off the counter.

As the radio played songs from his mother's youth he stared blankly out the window as the miles passed. Finally, after 279 tedious minutes, the car meandered through a slow highway bend to reveal the first thing that felt like home. Rising in the distance was the top of the Bourne Bridge and below it, cut into some evergreen bushes were the words 'Cape Cod.'

"Almost home," Mrs. Frazier said, as she did every time the family crossed the bridge.

Scott smiled. "Yup, almost home."

From there it had taken another 20 minutes to make it their humble three bedroom ranch in North Eastport. Scott flung a duffle bag over one shoulder and rolled a suitcase through the doors. His father was asleep on the couch. His brother was out.

Scott kissed his mother's cheek and thanked her for the ride. "I'm going to crash, I'm exhausted," he said before trudging up the stairs. He flung open his door to find the bedroom exactly as he'd left it four months earlier, except the sheets had been changed and the bed had been made. Digging through the duffle bag, he found his toiletries and entered the bathroom where he relieved himself, brushed his teeth and washed his face. The washcloth had left the front of his hair looking like he'd just stepped off the ice.

Scott slid under the covers and slept better than he had in a long, long time.

When he finally awoke Scott was a bit discombobulated. He'd left his iPhone in the bathroom and with no other clock in the bedroom, had no idea what time it was. His brother had always been jealous of the fact that the sun rose on the other side of the house, meaning that the harsh morning rays never disturbed the younger brother. Scott didn't want to get up, but Mother Nature forced him to rise and go the bathroom.

"Hey Siri, what time is it?" he asked, standing in front of the toilet.

"It's 1:17 PM," chirped the digital assistant.

"Whoa, really?" he replied. Siri did not respond.

Scott headed downstairs to attack the refrigerator. He scrambled half a dozen eggs and melted cheese on top. While the eggs cooked and a bagel toasted, he downed a large glass of orange juice.

It took him 10 minutes to inhale the food. He then realized the house was empty. No parents, no brother, no noise. Having gotten about 14 hours of rest, Scott thought about going out for a run, but balked when he asked Siri what the temperature was outside and she said, "Brrrr, it's 26 degrees."

He opted instead for a long shower and then tossed on sweats. With no one to bother him, Scott decided that he owed himself a little relaxation and plopped on the couch. He remained there, watching a marathon of Harry Potter movies until his brother got home several hours later.

"Hey man, welcome home," Teddy Frazier said as he walked into the living room. "When did you finally get up?"

"Around 1," Scott said.

"Wow, good for you. I had practice this morning and then put in a few hours at the hardware store. I'm thinking about heading over to the Eastport game. Ya wanna come?"

Scott definitely wanted to go to the rink to watch his boys play and win. It was the questions from his friends following the games he wanted no part of.

It would also be painful to watch the guys skate and compete without him for the first time. He decided he would wait another couple of days before heading over to the Eastport Ice Arena. He could binge some more TV today, watch the Patriots tomorrow and tell the boys he was back on Monday.

23

Coach Scadorski noticed the difference in the mood the second he got to the rink. Several of the Cannons were in the corner kicking a soccer ball as a Pee Wee game wound down. They were all smiling and laughing.

Something was in the air. Something positive.

As the minutes counted down to the drop of the puck, and game three of the season, the mood around the team had seemed to change to something far more positive. Maybe it was the confidence of knowing that the junior varsity team could probably win the day's game, but the Cannons were showing a side of their collective personality they hadn't all year. Coach Scadorski was pleased.

Carpenter exited the locker room in full battle dress, methodically wrapping maroon tape around his stick blade. He then switched to white tape for the grip and brought it down all the way to the bottom of the shaft, candy cane like. As the captain finished his art project, the coach ambled over.

"Carpy, what did you guys do last night? The team seems looser."

"Pizza, game night over at Stone's house. We put down 16 pizzas, it was crazy. We scarfed 10 in like a half hour, then a bunch of other guys came by – Garrett, Hutchinson, Bish – and then Mitch Ehrhardt showed up with another six pizzas. It was pretty awesome. Heck, I even got Walker to come out. He even laughed a little."

"Good work. That's leadership," the coach said with pride.

"Wasn't me, wish I could take the credit. Stoney put it together, kind of on accident. Mr. Ehrhardt donated all of the pizzas for free. We just paid for the soda. I made sure everyone was on the road by 11 so no one missed curfew and I drove baby Gaudreau home myself."

"Sometimes all it takes is a little bonding to get it going," the coach said.

The bonds showed on the ice from the start. In the first period, things began to click as Carpenter scored early and then Walker followed it up with one of his own. Inside of five minutes, it was 2-0. Bishop popped in a rebound of an O'Brien clapper late in the period for a three-goal lead. The second period was more of the same. Walker got a second, and so did Carpenter. Gossard made it 6-0 for the Cannons.

Scadorski called off the dogs against the overmatched Eastham team in the third period. He started the third line, rolled out the fourth after that and sparingly played his top two tandems.

Both Carpenter and Walker needed one goal for a hat trick, and each would have loved to have had it. If Eastham had shown any signs of life they could have gotten away with adding one more in the flow of the game, but the visitors couldn't get out of their own way. Not wanting to rub it in on the Cape Cod Athletic League foes, Coach Scadorski ordered his top two lines to dump the puck to the corners and retreat. "No shots from you guys, it's unnecessary. Dump it and get out."

On their final shift of the game the first line had a chance at a sure thing breakaway. A shot from Eastham hit Bishop in the skates and ricocheted right to the waiting stick of Carpenter. Walker had flown up the ice as soon as the shot was taken and was unmarked at the opposite blue line. He tapped his stick repeatedly on the ice, letting his teammate know that he was open.

Carpenter looked up, saw the chance and ignored it. Coach Scadorski had said no shots. Carpenter skated up to the red line, flipped the puck to the far corner and switched out as the game clock rolled under a minute left to play.

Walker couldn't believe it. There he was, all alone, and Carpenter froze him out of the play. The senior co-captain slammed his stick to the ice, breaking it right at the heel, and moped back to the bench.

"What the hell was that?" Walker said. "I was open."

"Coach said no shots, so I dumped it," Carpenter responded. "Sorry, man."

"The hell you are," Walker responded, slapping his teammate upside the head.

Carpenter spun to face his linemate. "Don't touch me, Walker."

Before the situation could escalate any further, Assistant Coach Tom Henry intervened. "You two knuckleheads knock it off."

The boys shut their traps and knew anything that was said in anger was sure to get back to Coach Scads. Before the situation could develop further the final horn sounded on an 8-0 Eastport victory. The offense clicked and the defense thrived, allowing just five shots on goal in the game. Jimmy Martinage played the first two periods in net and Keegan Doogle finished it up.

Leaving the ice, the coaching staff took a hard turn into their office. Normally they'd be pumping fists and excited beyond belief to get the first win under their belts, but the late game situation with Carpenter and Walker had soured the moment. The two captains hoped Scadorski had not noticed their altercation, but he had. It was not sitting well with him.

"Selfish, just plain selfish," the coach bellowed. "How am I going to get through to that kid? I've had it."

"I can only think of one thing, and it'll send a message, but I don't know if you're gonna like it," Tom Henry whispered.

"What's that?" the coach asked.

"Take away his 'C'."

"Ya think?" Scadorski asked, rubbing his temples.

"It sends a clear message. Let's be honest, he's only a captain because Frazier isn't here and he's a goal-scorer. He hasn't brought any leadership to the table. Carpenter has done okay, but you've got kids in that locker room who deserve a captaincy a whole lot more than Walker does, a whole helluva lot more."

Scadorski paced the room. "Let me think about it. It's on the table. We need to go give them the attaboy talk before they leave."

Loud hip-hop boomed throughout the Cannons locker room as the players milled about, giving high-fives as they stripped off their sweaty uniforms before filing into the shower stalls. The coaches entered the room to find the majority of the team reveling in its first success of the season, while Walker sat at his stall, still in full uniform.

As the coaches entered, someone spun the volume knob down to nothing, which cued silence to the rest of the Cannons. Everyone stopped and found their seats in front of their lockers, still riding the adrenaline of the past two hours.

"Good job boys. That's how we do it," Scadorski said. Clapping and hoots followed.

"Settle down. For the most part, that was great. You moved the puck, you found the open man. Defense, nice job keeping the play in front of you and forcing things wide. That's one, we need at least nine more, but that's the first one. Tell Mr. Ehrhardt he has to fill you up with pizza before every game," the coach said with a laugh.

"No practice tomorrow, film session on Monday at 3:30 before we hit the ice. Carpenter and Walker, come by the office together after you get cleaned up."

Cyrus Carpenter changed back into his civilian clothes within 15 minutes. He stood by the door of the locker room, hair still dripping, and congratulated his teammates as they left. The second to last to leave was Joey Moxon, who had a bit of a limp after having taken a shot off the knee.

"Get some ice on that thing, Mox," Carpenter said. "If it's still stiff tomorrow set up some PT for Monday."

"That's the plan, Cy," the defenseman said as he left. "Good game buddy, nice goals."

With the locker room empty, Carpenter shouted back to the showers.

"Hey Walker, let's go, man, I don't have all night."

The other senior came out of the showers a minute later, a white towel wrapped around his skinny waist. He pulled on his boxers, then a T-shirt, khakis and slowly buttoned up a dress shirt that still had the tie around the neck. Walker ran the towel over his head one last time, looked at

Carpenter and spoke for the first time since arguing with him during the game.

"Let's get this over with."

24

"You want to explain to me what that was all about at the end of the game?" Coach John Scadorski calmly asked his two captains.

Neither boy said a thing. Scads waited a full 60 seconds, which felt 10 times as long, and still, no words were exchanged. Finally, he spoke.

"What we saw was one player acting selfishly. Carp, you played it right. We're up eight goals, game's over, you dumped it and got off. That's what I want there. If it was closer, different story, but you both know that.

"Walker, from where we're standing, we saw you cherry-picking, looking for a hat trick. Seriously, what does a hat trick matter when you're up by eight? Can you explain that? Get a hat trick against someone good and we can talk, but against those guys, who cares? It's meaningless. You got anything to say?"

The senior looked up and shook his head.

"I didn't think so. So here's what's going to happen. You just lost your 'C.' I haven't decided if it's permanent or not. Letters on uniforms are for leaders and you haven't acted like one. It's been all about Billy Walker getting goals and Billy Walker getting ice time. Leaders look out for their teammates first," Scadorski said. There was no vitriol in his voice; it was matter-of-fact. "Tell me I'm wrong."

"You're not wrong," Walker said.

Carpenter couldn't believe his ears. He never, in a million years, thought the coach would demote Walker. Sure, he deserved it, but he never thought they'd pull the trigger. And Walker agreed that they were right. What was going on?

"If you want it back, you have to play like it. You have to act like it, on and off the ice. Show me some leadership, show me some character, and we will talk."

Walker moved his chin up and down slowly. "Okay," was all he mustered.

"That's it. You two are dismissed. Have a good Sunday, see you on Monday."

The players left the room. Carpenter was about to offer his condolences to Walker, but the boy walked out the door and straight to the parking lot, never looking back.

Dumbfounded by what had just transpired, Cyrus stood frozen outside the coaches' office. After a moment he knocked on the door and stuck his head back in.

"Got a minute, Coach?"

Scadorski nodded and the lone captain for the Eastport Cannons reentered the room.

"I'm a little confused by what just happened. Am I the only captain now?" he asked.

"For now, yes. On Monday, we will have a meeting to discuss things before watching film. I have a few ideas, I need to talk them over with Coach Henry. We'll let you all know what's going on then."

Carpenter nodded and left the room. He walked through the lobby, which had emptied out with the exception of one of the arena staff, who pushed a broom aimlessly along the rubber floor. Putting one Timberland in front of the other, he left through the front door into the frigid December air as a snow flurry blew in. The team's foundation had just shifted, for good or for bad.

25

Cyrus got into his car and powered up his iPhone. Immediately it chimed with text messages and voicemails. He touched the VM button and saw his mom had called, as well as several teammates.

Mom's voice asked, "Wondering if you wanted me to heat up some food. Let me know, great game honey."

Gaudreau's tiny voice was next. "Hey Cy, just wondered what the meeting was all about."

Several teammates had the same question. The most recent one was OB, "Dude, it's OB, call me. Just want to get caught up on what's going on. Nice game brother."

As the car reached a comfortable temperature he called his mom and asked her to heat something up, anything but pizza after having gorged himself the night before. He then called O'Brien, put the phone on speaker and eased out of his parking space.

"Hey, there you are. What was up with Coach?" his friend wondered.

"You aren't going to believe it. He took away Walker's 'C,' said he wasn't acting like a captain and that he needed to earn it back. It was intense."

"Whoa, what did Walker say?"

Cyrus paused and thought about it. *What had Walker said*?

If Coach had taken away his captaincy he'd have blown a gasket and thrown things. Being captain of the Cannons meant the world to Cyrus Carpenter. He'd just been happy to be on the varsity as a sophomore, but then last year he'd realized what he was capable of. He'd started sharing the puck, making sure his teammates were involved. Walker had been a huge beneficiary of Carpenter's unselfish play. Being a captain was everything to Cyrus. Shouldn't it mean the same to Billy?

"He didn't say much, honestly. He kind of just accepted it."

"Weird... that's just weird. Think I should call him?"

"You can try. He won't really talk to me these days, but he *was* pretty cool at Stone's house yesterday, started to feel like the old Billy."

O'Brien agreed. "Yeah, he's been weird since the season started. I didn't get to spend much time with him during the fall because of football, but he hasn't been Billy. He's kind of gone emo on us."

For the first time since the meeting, Cyrus smiled and almost laughed. "Check at practice to make sure he's not wearing black guy-liner under his helmet," he deadpanned.

"You know, I did notice his eyes were really popping," O'Brien retorted. "I'll be in touch, I'm gonna give him a ring."

Collin O'Brien had sped home to feast on his mother's shepherd's pie after the game. He sat on his couch watching college football highlights with the sound off while shoveling the food in. After hanging up with Cyrus he called Walker, but it went to voicemail.

"Hey Bill, I know you're home. Don't send me to voicemail. I'm coming over and will be there in 10 minutes."

He then texted Walker. "Coming over right now. Be there in 10."

O'Brien grabbed his jacket off the hook and told his sister, Samantha, that he was heading over to Billy's place for a few minutes. "Tell Mom I won't be long."

The flurry that had begun earlier had coated the roads with a layer of white. It looked like he was driving on top of a birthday cake. The conditions made Collin drive much slower than he liked to, but Cape Cod roads in the winter can be slippery, so the 10-minute drive took more like 20. He pulled up to the Walker's beautiful golf course-abutting home around 11:15 PM and parked directly behind Mrs. Walker's Audi SUV.

Before Collin could ring the doorbell Billy opened the front door. He didn't say anything. He just allowed his friend in.

"Hey, man, you okay?"

Walker shrugged.

99

"You want to talk about it? Or… we can just not talk about it."

Walker reached into his pockets and inspected the floor. He seemed poised to say something but stopped short.

"Hey, we can just chill if you want. You got Netflix?"

Walker laughed. "Great OB, you come over here to take advantage of me? I know what Netflix and chill means."

"Yup, bring that fine body over here," Collin said, lunging at his friend.

The two laughed, crashed on the couch and fired up the TV. They stopped on "Die Hard" and took turns quoting Bruce Willis's lines.

As John McClane tried to save Nakatomi Tower, Billy finally broke his silence.

"Dude, what's wrong with me? Seriously, tell me, what's wrong with me?"

"Besides your face, I'm not sure," Collin said.

"Seriously OB, I knew exactly what I was doing in the third period. I knew I was being stupid and I kept being stupid. It's like since hockey started I can't act like a normal person, and I don't really care all that much about it all. It's messed up," he said, his voice breaking. "Coach took away the 'C' tonight. I didn't even argue with him."

"Yeah, Carp told me. We both thought it was kind of weird," O'Brien admitted.

"It is weird. I wasn't surprised. I saw the writing on the wall, I'm a sucky captain. I wish I wasn't, but I am. Carpenter lives for that stuff. I just don't. To be honest with you, there have been plenty of days where I was on the way to the rink and thought about just turning around and going home."

"If it makes you feel any better, I'm glad you didn't. We kind of need you. You are pretty good."

"I know, I'm not going to quit. Not this year. I think I'm done after high school, though. I've got some D3 schools that I could go play at, but I don't want to go to them. To be honest, I kind of want to leave Cape Cod behind and go south. I need a change."

"Dude, no offense, but you sound like an idiot right now. You're Billy Freaking Walker. You could play D1 in a heartbeat. You need to quit it with this 'I'm not good enough' crap. You and I both know you are," Collin said.

"According to my dad, I'm not big enough, fast enough, or skilled enough. I'm never enough," he said, choking up. "If I'm not good enough, why chase a dream that's never going to come true? I might as well just pack away the skates and start thinking about which college I am going to spend the next four years drinking at."

"Arizona State has hot chicks, all the Florida schools pretty much do too. Oh, and South Carolina. You ever see the stands at a football game at South Carolina? Hoooo-leeee crap. Now that you mention it, I think I'm going with you."

That finally did it for Billy Walker. He could not help himself, he cracked up laughing. His diaphragm ached from it.

Collin O'Brien had done what he had set out to do. OB sat up straighter and looked his friend straight in the eyes.

"Listen brother, I get it. I've had to live up to the memory of the almighty Roman O'Brien. He played D1 football and played pro in Canada. I almost didn't play football because everyone always asked me, 'you going to be as good as Roman?'" O'Brien confided. "One day I just realized it wasn't about what everyone else thought of me, or what they wanted for me. I love playing football, hockey and baseball, so I play. I'm with my boys every day and it's the best thing in the world."

Pacing the living room, Collin picked up an old team photo that sat framed on the mantle. They were all 12 years old and beamed with pride. In the middle of the picture were Billy and Cyrus holding up the trophy that they'd just won at some random tournament in New Hampshire. He handed the photo over to Billy and laughed.

"Two seasons, that's what we've got left. Then we all go our separate ways. I don't know about you, but I don't want to waste that time. Every game, every practice, I'm gonna enjoy them, have fun. I want to win another title before we leave Eastport in the rearview. Dude, you are going to be on that ride with us. You're a reason, maybe the biggest reason, we could get to the Garden."

The boys sat in silence. Billy studied the photo intently. He then patted his friend on the shoulder, stood up as if to make a formal announcement, and spoke.

"I'm in. You're right. We've got 17 games left, we are 1-2, and I don't want to lose another game. If this is our last ride together, we're going all-out," Walker said, enthusiasm behind every word.

"Attaboy," O'Brien whooped. "All aboard for the last ride."

26

Billy was the first one at the rink Monday afternoon. He'd driven alone right after school and asked the rink staff to open up the locker room for him. It had been a long time since he'd been excited to lace up his skates and practice. School had been painful to get through as the clock ticked in slow motion all day long. It was the last few days before Christmas vacation, which already made the days drag, but hockey was once again pounding in his heart. He wanted to feel his blades cut the ice and work the puck on his stick.

He'd played coy with his teammates all day. As far as they knew, he was still in the doldrums of having lost his captaincy and getting chewed out by Coach Scads following the game. Rather than tell them all he was reinvigorated – thanks in large part to OB's impromptu visit – he wanted to show them. Proving it meant a lot more than saying it.

Bill was all set to go before anyone else had shown up. He looked at the clock on the wall and saw that it was already 3:35. He'd spent nearly an hour getting his head on straight, and his practice gear on, and hadn't noticed that he was by himself. Where the heck was everyone?

"Oh shoot, it's Monday. Film study."

Realizing he was already five minutes late, Bill untied his skates, left them in front of his locker and sprinted out the door, through the lobby and around the back end of the building to the film room. He exploded through the door to find his teammates and the coaching staff in a darkened room watching a 10 x 8-foot projection of his first goal from the other night.

Twenty-two heads spun in unison to see the interruption. Walker's face turned nearly the same color as his maroon practice sweater. He tiptoed to the back of the room in his socks and found an empty chair.

"Walker, you're 10 minutes late," Coach Scadorski announced.

"I know Coach, I'm sorry."

"You're also a little overdressed for film study."

Billy stood up, his profile illuminated by the video projector. He inhaled deeply.

"Coach, guys, I've been a jerk. Coach, you were right to take away my letter. Hell, you should probably take away my jersey. I'm late because I forgot it was a film day, and I was in the locker room getting dressed for practice. I couldn't wait to get on the ice. I'm sorry for being selfish. That's what it comes down to. This team means a lot to me and somehow I forgot that. I'm all-in, from today on, I'm all-in."

The monologue felt like a scene out of a movie, except the team did not begin a slow clap and put their former captain on their shoulders. He was not carried out onto the ice where he put on a display of awesomeness for all to admire.

There was a lot of skepticism in the room. Coach Scadorski took a deep breath but showed no emotion. The leader of the program had heard it all before. He needed to see it to believe it.

"That's nice Walker, but you've got a room full of guys that were already all-in. They've been all-in since day one. You've got a lot of catching up to do. You're left wing on the third line today, second and third wings from Saturday night, you guys move up one. Every spot on this team is earned, you want that top line spot back, show me."

Billy sat back down. He stared straight ahead at the screen. "I will."

After breaking down game film for an hour the team hit the ice. Practice was filled with more enthusiasm than it had been in a long time. Walker was engaged from the moment the team stepped on the ice and it was clear that he'd meant what he'd said. His head was up every time he had the puck and he zipped passes to his linemates. More often than not the puck exploded off of their sticks. They were younger players and not acclimated to playing with a linemate who could deliver the pellet with the accuracy and velocity that Walker could. Billy adjusted. He took a little off of his passes and the third line began to find its rhythm.

"Maybe he meant it," Scadorski said to his assistant coach.

As practice finished up, O'Brien skated up behind his friend and threw his arm around his shoulder. "Damn, where has that Billy Walker been?"

"I don't know OB, but I'm glad you found him, dude."

"Yeah, me too. He's not much to look at, but he sure can shoot the puck."

Walker entered the room and slapped hands with half the team, lifted his jersey off his sweaty body and fell into his stall, feeling exhausted in the best possible way. Sitting to his left, with a smile on his face, was Craig Bishop, who wore a goofy grin as he took in the scene.

"Do me a favor, Bill."

"Yeah?"

"Keep that up. I want our line back together. You, me, Cy, that's how I want to roll."

"Me too. It'll be soon, I promise."

With a fist bump, the two returned to removing their gear. They loosened up their laces just as Coach Scadorski entered the room.

"Nice practice, boys. As you know, we had a bit of a shuffle with our captains."

Walker looked his coach in the eyes and did not break contact. There was no ill will exchanged. He'd lost his 'C' on his own. He planned to earn it back.

"With that said, I've given a lot of thought to what to do. Cyrus is going to remain our only captain going forward. He's shown a lot of leadership and he's steering your ship. However, I do want to single out two guys who have also stepped up and they will be wearing assistant captain 'A's' on their jerseys."

Heads looked left and right. Standing in the corner, Wes Garrett knew it wasn't him because you can't lead when you're not playing. He had a good idea who might be getting one, though.

"The first one is Danny Stone."

Sandy brown hair whipped up and over Stone's eyes, which could not hide his surprise. Danny stood and met his coach halfway across the room, reaching out to take the three-inch cloth square with a white 'A' outlined in maroon.

"Thank you, Coach."

Scadorski smiled. The room broke into congratulations, led by Walker.

"You've earned it, Stoner."

Scadorski waved the room quiet.

"Settle down. Alright, the next one I think most of you guys can guess. Honestly, you knuckleheads should have voted this guy a captain to begin with. Bish, come up and get your letter."

Bishop raised his head and his smile widened. To be made an assistant captain was something he'd cherish forever.

"Yeah, what were you guys thinking? He's right, I should've already been a captain. Get your asses on the ice and give me 50 push-ups."

Craig pushed his hair out of his eyes, accepted the letter from his coach and went back to his seat. He could not take his eyes off the patch and ran his fingers around the outline. Christmas had come a few days early.

"Okay, Stone, Bish, make sure those are sewn on to your home jerseys before Wednesday night's game. I will have the ones for your road jerseys taken care of but get your moms, or grandmother, or girlfriend or whoever to get that ready for Wednesday night.

"The rest of you, practice tomorrow on the ice at 4:15. We've got a big game with Lakeville High on Wednesday. Win that one, we're back to .500 and right back in the mix of things. They beat us last year, time to return the favor."

The coach exited the locker room, leaving the players to finish changing out of their practice gear and to head home for the night. Most of the younger players headed right for the showers, while the seniors gathered around Bishop and Stone to discuss what had just happened.

"Just remember, I'm still the captain," Carpenter said with a chuckle. "I'm happy for you guys, that's pretty awesome. I gotta be honest, though, I thought maybe Hutchinson would get one."

"Nah, I've had my turn with football, and I got voted captain for baseball. The right guys got the letters. Bish, Stoner, let's do this."

"What the hell, I deserved it more than either of you guys," Collin O'Brien said, punching each of his teammates in the arm. The swing at his lifelong friend Bishop had a little extra on it. "I'm going to march right into Scadorski's office and demand that you both be stripped of those on the account of the fact that you're both wimps."

"Thanks, OB, I love you, too," Stone said with a smile.

"You can sew it on my shirt if you want, Collin," Bishop said gleefully.

Wes had stood on the outside of the circle with a smile on his face. Finally, he patted Danny on the shoulder and then did the same to Craig.

"Mr. Assistant Captain, if you wouldn't mind getting changed so we can head out. I've got a ton of homework tonight and as much as I would love to revel in all of your glory, I also would like to pass English."

27

Wes didn't just want to pass English class. He wanted to ace it. During his first two years of high school, he had done just enough to keep his mother off of his back, with plenty of Cs and C-pluses to his credit. His grade point average allowed him to keep him playing sports but wasn't anything to be proud of.

At the end of his sophomore year, though, he had a revelation thanks to YouTube. He'd been clicking through videos, watching trick shots. After watching a dude knock a chip shot from the top of a football stadium into a coffee mug the next video was a motivational speaker. He was ready to start looking for more fun stuff in the search bar when the man shouted through the computer at him.

"You're probably not man enough to keep watching this video."

That challenge kept him staring at the screen for a moment longer.

"You're coasting through your high school classes, just getting by, thinking it's good enough. Maybe you can dunk a basketball, or throw the football 75 yards on a dime or hit a baseball 500 feet. That don't matter. If your grades suck, you'll be the best player on the playground, but you won't be playing in college. Guys that don't play in college don't make the pros. It's that simple. Unless you're the one percent of the one-percent in hockey or baseball, you have to go to college to continue playing at a high level. I'm not making this up."

Wesley Garrett watched the next 15 minutes of the video intently. He searched the speaker out on Twitter and followed him. The realization hit him like a slapshot on the shin, he'd been slacking and it might cost him.

He spent the summer cutting lawns and riding his bike to the beach to watch bikinis with the Boys. He'd almost forgotten about his big breakthrough, but another message from the speaker on Twitter caught his attention two days before the start of the school year.

"Start strong, finish stronger. Lead, don't follow."

On the other side of the country that motivational speaker was just trying to stay on message and keep his brand going strong with a daily Tweet to his 233,908 followers. He'd gotten through to at least one because Wes Garrett was determined to do exactly those things.

The results did not come automatically. He made some progress in the first quarter, but a concussion in October – thanks to a blindside hit on the football field – had slowed him down. By November the headaches were gone, and his grades rose steadily. When report cards came out in the second quarter he'd done something he'd never done before: earned a spot on the honor roll. The third term was the same, and in the fourth, he'd nearly made high honors. Algebra II had kept that from happening, but he'd gotten a solid B there.

As far as colleges were concerned, getting his act together as a junior was massive. His guidance counselor had made it clear to him when he was a dumb sophomore that if he didn't make positive progress as a junior he'd be lucky to get into a community college. That had shaken him. He'd had nightmares of working behind the counter at the gas station up the road, with his high-paid friends coming in and laughing at him as they filled up their sports cars.

That one year of A's and B's wasn't going to be enough to get him into Harvard, but it was going to help him avoid the night shift at the Quickie Mart. Wes wasn't sure where life was going to take him, but he was pretty sure he'd done enough to avoid handing out lottery tickets and figuring out what would remove the smell of petrol from his jeans.

Wes's mother, Darlene, sat at the dining room table with a glass of red wine to her left and a copy of the *Eastport Inquisitor* open to the right. She skimmed through the police reports, wondering which of the local felons had been arrested this week.

"Do you remember the weirdo that used to ride around town on his bike with the cat on his shoulder?" she asked.

"Yeah, he treated it like it was a parrot. We used to call him the 'Feline Pirate.'"

"He got picked up for intent to distribute a Class B substance, resisting arrest and criminal mischief."

"Gonna be tough to beat the mischief charge," Wes said with a laugh.

"Speaking of mischief, you're late. Your dinner's in the oven, it's probably dried out by now. I made a roast."

"Okay, sounds good. I'm gonna take it to my room if that's okay. I'm supposed to read the first four chapters of 'Great Expectations' tonight and write a synopsis of it by Wednesday. Then I have to read the next four and have a synopsis of that by Friday."

"I love that you're reading the classics. Have you started it yet?"

"Nope, but I'm planning on blasting through it over the next hour or so. It'd be a lot easier if I could just watch the movie, but Mrs. Huff is pretty smart, that's what the synopsis is all about. You can't really get the details from the movie. I might look for a copy online after I finish, though, if I like it."

"Well, it's probably a whole lot more edifying than the police briefs, maybe even more entertaining. Do you know what it's about?"

"Basically, a dude falls in love with a rich girl and spends his life trying to impress her."

"Hmm, sound familiar?"

"First off, Mother, I'm hardly in love. Melissa and I have been on one date. She's cool, and ummm, attractive, but don't think about wedding plans. I don't know that I'd call her rich, either. Her dad's got a good job, but it's not like she drives a sports car and rocks Gucci every day. They're well off."

Darlene Garrett simply smiled at her son as he piled baby carrots and spinach on his plate next to a huge slab of meat. She knew teenage love when she saw it. Her Wesley had come home from that first date walking on air. He was smitten, even if he didn't realize it yet.

"Just make sure you don't leave any of those dishes in your room. It already smells like a locker room, we don't need it smelling like a dumpster."

Wes said he'd take care of that and hustled off to his room to hit the books. He just hoped he'd be able to concentrate on his work now that his mother had thoughts of Melissa running through his head again and when they'd get to spend some quality time together. He had an idea, but the guys might not like it.

28

Tuesday at school was a rare treat for Craig Bishop. It flew by. None of his teachers had hassled him to remove his backward baseball cap, which was a necessity on this day because his hair simply refused to stay out of his eyes without it. None of his teachers had dropped a surprise quiz and there was no drama to speak of with any of his friends or teammates.

He'd spent his study hour working on his application essay for East Carolina University. The prompt was to write about the most difficult obstacle he'd ever overcome. The answer had been simple. His mom had died when he was young. Not a day went by that he didn't think about her. His pen had flown across the paper and the words had come easily. By the time that period ended he'd nearly finished his rough draft. He'd have Emily give it a read before he typed it up and sent it in.

The bell rang to signal the end of the day. With homework in just one subject, math, he only needed to stuff one book into his backpack before heading out to the car to meet up with Wes. Collin stood outside the Jeep, leaning up against the door, and was clearly not in as good a mood as he was.

"Hey, Bish, would you please tell our buddy here that he is not going to ditch us on Friday to go shopping with Melissa instead of us. Tradition is tradition and he is not allowed to bag on us to shop with her instead."

"Whoa, whoa, whoa. Slow down. This is the first I'm hearing about this. Wes, what's the deal?"

"Melissa asked me if I could give her a ride to the mall so she could grab some presents for her brother and parents on Friday morning. I totally forgot that *we* were supposed to go shopping, so I said 'yes.'"

"Easy enough, tell her you screwed up and you can't flake on the Boys. Tradition is tradition," Craig said.

"Tradition is tradition," OB echoed.

112

The tradition of going together for last minute Christmas shopping had begun when the Boys were 11 years old. They'd gotten their parents to drop them off at the Cape Cod Mall with a few dollars each. The boys found joy in picking out the dumbest, and most useless, presents for their siblings, while slyly trying to get actual worthwhile stuff for their parents. Craig, the lone only child in the group, loved to help find the stupidest stuff.

The best part of the game was that none of the siblings were in on the joke. They were left thinking that their brothers were all supremely out of touch and daft.

To make it even more entertaining, the Boys had started to shoot video of their brothers and sisters opening the presents. After all of the Christmas festivities were finished they would all gather at Craig's that night to laugh their asses off at the expressions that their brothers and sisters had to their gifts.

Josh Hutchinson had won the previous year's competition by getting his older brother Matt a copy of "Hair Metal Hits of the '80s on cassette tape. Matthew Hutchinson was a connoisseur of hip-hop, especially the feel-good stuff from the 1990s. He tore the wrapping paper off of the box, looked at it and said, "What the hell is this?"

The video went from funny to hysterical when Mrs. Hutchinson yelled, "Matthew, what is wrong with you? That is no way to react to a heartfelt gift." Josh posted it to his Twitter feed and the video got over 5,000 likes. Matt was not pleased about becoming internet famous and had begged his brother to take the video down. Josh resisted but lost the battle when he forgot to log out of his account one afternoon that spring. Matt deleted the post from Josh's feed.

Realizing he was never going to win this battle with his friends, Wes changed tactics.

"What if, I mean, how about, we invite the girls to go with us and we turn it into a bigger group."

Collin and Craig both sighed.

"No, no, no, this will be good. We can make them do it, too. We'll make them buy something stupid for someone and have to videotape it."

"Can we make Melissa buy a marital aid for her mother?" Collin asked with a smirk.

"I tell you what, you ask her to do it yourself," Wes said.

"You can ask Emily to do it," Craig said with a smirk. "I'd enjoy watching her smack you upside the head. You know she's a lot stronger than she looks."

Craig powered open the creaky old door to Wes's Cherokee and pulled himself up into the passenger seat. Removing his old Red Sox cap, he shook out his mop of hair and then returned the hat to its proper spot, resting backward on his head.

"Captain, my captain, straight to the rink?" Wes asked.

"Umm, that's Mr. Assistant Captain, actually, and no, can we stop over at 7-11 first? I forgot my PowerBars this morning, and I could use a Gatorade for after practice."

"Sure, I wouldn't mind grabbing a candy bar. Oh yeah, don't forget, I can't drive you home from practice on Thursday. I've got my appointment at the orthopedic guy's office at 4:30. If everything goes well the cast is coming off, and I'll be suiting up by New Year's Day."

"Alright, I'll grab a ride from someone. How's the wrist feel?"

"Honestly, it's hard to tell. It's been in a cast for so long that I'm not sure. I just can't wait for them to cut the thing off. My forearm is probably thinner than a pencil right now."

"You mean thinner than your..."

"Shut up. Anyways, there's a chance that they won't let me play for even longer. I might need to do occupational rehab first."

"What does work have to do with it?"

"How are you passing your classes? Occupational rehab is stuff they do to make sure you can do everyday type of stuff. They make you pick things up and test that you can use it like you did before."

"How long will that take?"

114

"Depends, I guess. I might not need it. I'm not sure. I just want to get back on the ice."

"Yeah, well, more importantly, you need to be able to swing a bat, man. You're okay at hockey, but you're a helluva hitter. You've got to be ready to go for baseball season and summer ball."

"And hopefully college next year, yeah, I know. But watching you guys struggle has been awful. I want to get back out there. I want to put someone on his ass. I want to play against Hyannis with all those people going crazy in the stands. I miss it, Bish. I mean, I really, really miss it."

"I get that. We miss having you out there with us, although you are really good at videotaping. Coach Scads may just keep you up there in the press box with Mac when you're cleared. You're going to be tough to replace."

"I hate you."

"I love you too, man."

The buddies laughed as they pulled into the 7-11 parking lot. Craig grabbed three PowerBars and two bottles of orange Gatorade. Wes picked out a giant-sized Twix and a liter of water. They both smiled at the gorgeous Jamaican girl behind the counter who greeted them with a smile that sparkled like the August sun.

"How are you boys this great day on Cape Cod?" she said while adjusting the bookwormish frames resting on her nose.

"Not as great as you are," Craig said impishly.

"Oh, you boys, always trying to charm me. That will be $9.55, please, sir."

"Can you throw his stuff on there too, please?" Craig asked, turning his head to Wes. He added, "I haven't given you any gas money this week."

"Thanks, buddy," Wes said, happy he didn't have to break the last 20 dollar bill he had in his wallet.

"Okay, Mr. Big Spender, that is $12.33 then."

Craig handed over his debit card. His summer money earned teaching kids how to properly navigate a kayak around the harbor at the yacht club had run out weeks earlier. That was hardly a worry, though. His grandmother regularly put a couple hundred dollars in his account so that his "day to day expenses," as she put it, were taken care of. She'd made a boatload of money as a high-priced real estate lawyer and had retired to the Cape with more money than she could ever spend. She loved to spoil her grandson. With that card, Wes's Cherokee was almost always topped off, and Craig was able to look gentlemanly when he and Emily went to the movies or dinner.

"Must be nice to have cash for days. What are you going to do when you have to actually get a real job, Bish?" Wes said.

"I'll figure something out," Craig said with a smile. "Besides, Emily's got great earning potential. I can just let her be my sugar momma and I can bask in luxury while she brings home the bacon. You know I love the sound of bacon, right?"

29

John Scadorski gripped an erasable black marker in his right hand and pointed to the 22 boys seated in the Cannons' locker room. He needed to select one of them to write the message for the night on the dry erase board. So far the game day ritual had not provided the desired result.

Leaning on his captains, he'd chosen Billy Walker for game one. Walker scribbled down, "Go hard" on the board. The team had played soft.

Before traveling for their second game, Scadorski chose the other captain, Cyrus Carpenter. Carp had written, "NO REGRETS," all in caps, for emphasis. Everyone regretted the ass-kicking they'd suffered through that evening.

For game three he had stuck with his seniors and went with Collin O'Brien. The big defenseman had chosen the simple, "win." They did, easily, but it was against a cupcake. He could have written down "gobbledygook" and the team was going to skate away with a win that night.

Tonight was a huge game, though. Silent Lake High School was a big regional school with almost 2,000 students. They were one of the teams that everyone had slated for the Super-8 tournament, the tourney for the best of the best high school teams in the state. This was not a game that Eastport had to win, but they needed to play well. If they did, Scadorski was positive the team could gain momentum and become legitimate playoff contenders. If they got toasted like they had a week ago, who knows where things were going.

Surveying the room again, the coach noticed Craig Bishop smoothing out the newly earned 'A' on his jersey. He'd made the kid a part of the team's leadership, might as well put him in the spotlight and see what happened.

"Bish, you're up. What's the motto tonight."

Startled, Craig looked up at his coach and smiled. He placed his sweater back in his locker stall, stood up and drew groans from the rest of the room.

Craig had not yet finished dressing. He had a threadbare "Dark Side of the Moon" T-shirt on along with his jock strap and nothing else.

Mooning his teammates, Craig stared at the blank dry erase board with dark brown eyes, studying the empty space intently. The canvas showed smudges of previously drawn letters that had been wiped away.

The suspense grew as Craig stood there, marker in his hand, unmoving and half nude. Just as the silence became uncomfortable, his right hand began to move. He swept the black ink up, down, across, down, sideways and so on. Dramatically, he capped the marker, tossed it back to his coach and sat back down.

"H-E-A-R-T."

"Okay, heart, I like it. What's it mean, Bish?"

"Every shot, every shift, every check, every second, play with heart. Play like you love it!"

"There you go, boys. That's what it's all about. Tonight, we play with heart."

A knock came on the door and Coach Scadorski opened it a crack. "Two minutes, we'll be right out."

"Captains, I need you dressed ASAP. You've got two minutes."

Cyrus Carpenter was already dressed and ready for action. Danny Stone was most of the way there and threw his white home jersey over his head to complete the job. Bish had to kick things into high gear. Underwear, shoulder pads, T-shirt, pants and then finally he pulled his sweater over his head and ran his hand through his hair.

The three boys exited the locker room together, with Carpenter leading the way out the door. They were greeted by their coach and Mac Richardson, who had a Canon camera slung over his shoulder. The reporter ran a side business taking photographs of youth sports teams in town and also did work for the high school's athletic program. He'd taken the team photo a few weeks earlier when Bish was down south and still had to grab a headshot of him for the team's yearbook. They planned on taking that same image and photoshopping him into the team photo as well. Richardson had left a space in the top row of the pose where he'd be able to insert the team's resident goofball once he'd finally snapped his photo.

"Guys, Mac needs to grab a picture of the new captains for the yearbook."

Richardson snapped a picture, fiddled with a few buttons and then directed the three players to look at the lens again.

"Guys, look right at the lens. Smile, no really, smile, your mothers are going to see these and they don't want to see you pretending you're tough. I've known you all since you were Mites, none of you are really tough."

The boys all laughed at that and Richardson got the picture he wanted. Satisfied, he dismissed Stone and Carpenter.

"Bish, I need to grab a quick one of you for the program."

Mac posed Craig and straightened his shoulder pads. The photographer gently pinched the edges of the jersey to pull it up so that the letters would sit straight, looked down at the new assistant captain's 'A' on the jersey and began laughing.

"What?" Bish asked sheepishly.

"Dude, did you use stick tape to stick that letter onto your sweater?"

"Yeah, don't tell Coach. I forgot to have my grandmother do it. I got to the rink and Danny asked me how my letter looked stitched on. I panicked. Coach will kill me if he finds out. Don't say anything."

"I won't, but promise me you'll remember to bring it home with you and get it taken care of. You know that's pretty ridiculous, right?" Richardson said as he pointed the camera and snapped two quick headshots of the high school senior.

"Hey, Mac," Craig whispered. "Thanks."

He pointed into the camera with a big smile on his face, the part in his long hair forming a 'V' right in the middle of his forehead.

"Great, you look beautiful, Bish. You'd better hope that that thing doesn't fall off during the game."

30

Silent Lake High School lined up on the blue line for the National Anthem and the entire roster seemed to pick out his counterpart on the Eastport side and issue a death stare across the ice. The Lakers had hate in their eyes and bad intentions, that much was clear from the first shift of the game. Bishop got off the ice after his third turn to skate and looked over his shoulder in the direction of their trainer.

"Got a Band-aid?" he asked the team's medic.

An adhesive bandage appeared over Craig's shoulder. He popped the helmet off of his head and was about to apply the bandage to his chin. He'd been on the business end of a hard check into the corner that had opened up a gash that trickled crimson down the front of his shirt.

"Hold on tough guy, let me see that first," the trainer barked. "Meh, it's not too bad. I don't think you're gonna need stitches. We'll put another one on it after the period. Try not to open it up any worse."

"No promises," Bishop said with a laugh.

Just as he finished applying the bandage to his chin he looked up to see Silent Lake take the lead. A stumble in the corner by Alex Gossard had left the right wing open. A pass from high in the zone found the unmarked man and he rung a shot in off the far pipe, out of the reach of Jimmy Martinage to make it 1-0.

The score stayed the same until the end of the first period. Bishop's bleeding had stopped and he did not miss a shift. The Cannons had taken the printed word of the new assistant captain seriously because they were playing with vigor every second, but they still weren't scoring. Walker, who was still with the third line, almost tied it himself early in the second period with a nice backhander, but it clanged off the iron. Joey Moxon and Collin O'Brien both hit hard slap shots that the Lakers goalie had kicked out. Eastport was not giving up any ground, but they weren't making it up either.

After two periods the score was still 1-0. Coach Scadorski came into the locker room five minutes before the team was supposed to be back out for the last period and kept it simple.

"Remember what it says on the board. Play with heart. You've done that for two periods, but find some more in the third. Whatever you've got, use it."

O'Brien shouted, "We've got this, boys. Let's go take it."

One reason Collin O'Brien preferred football to hockey was that there were no penalties for getting in someone's way. It was encouraged. You were allowed to manhandle opponents. On the ice, he had to take care not to hit anyone who did not have the puck, or make sure they saw him coming before putting them on their butt. In football, as an outside linebacker, his job was simply to find the guy with the ball and do everything short of decapitate him to stop his progress.

But when opponents had the puck, he *could* be physical. If he was a little faster on his skates he'd have been really dangerous, but even though he was just average in the speed department there was usually at least one play every game where he was able to line a guy up and wait for the crowd to react with an audible, "Ooooohhh." Getting the crowd to make that noise was his favorite part of playing.

Early in the third period, one of those "ooooohhh" moments led to the second best noise in hockey, as far as he was concerned: the crowd roaring its appreciation for a goal, followed by the fog horn and more cheering.

Skating backward toward his defensive blue line, Collin had his head on a swivel. He was focused on the center, who skated fast over the red line with his head up, looking for an outlet to pass to. On the football field, he loved to lock eyes with a QB and figure out where the ball was going just before the ball would be thrown. That allowed him to sometimes grab an interception, but more often to crack a tackle through a running back. Twice during the run to the Super Bowl, he'd laid dudes out, looked down into their helmets and seen blank stares looking back at him. The lights were on, but no one was home.

121

On the ice, those times were fewer and far between, but on this shift, he saw it. The Lakers' center looked to his right, then left, but then came back to the left again. As the eyes returned to the original target, Collin noticed the center cock his hands back in preparation for a hard pass to the winger that was directed toward his side of the ice.

The puck left the center's blade and Collin put on the brakes. He watched as the puck slid toward its target. At the same moment that it met the winger, Collin exploded through him, accelerating through the point of impact.

A tingling elation came over the Eastport defender, but it was very quick. Not only had he destroyed the Silent Lake winger, but he also created a turnover. The puck was inches from his stick, and he snared it up and saw his good friend Craig fly out of the zone on the other side, skating by himself. OB flung the puck diagonally up that side of the ice.

Bish couldn't believe the hit OB had laid on that poor kid from Silent Lake. Not only would that kid have to get checked for a concussion, but OB was sure to retell this story for the rest of the winter. "Remember that time I wrecked that dude from Silent Lake?" he'd remind them daily. There was no time to worry about that right now, though. Not only had OB destroyed a guy, but he'd also just sent a perfect pass to Bish.

With his stick blade pointing straight ahead, Bishop settled the pass down and crossed over the blue line, skating right through the faceoff circle and preparing to shoot the puck.

Scoring goals is hard. The shooter has a nanosecond to decide where he's going with the puck. If he guesses right, it's party time, if he guesses wrong, he's swearing at himself.

Craig guessed wrong, and right, at the same time. He snapped off a shot for the near side post, but the goalie got his big leather pads down in time to stop the bid. However, he did not control the puck, and the rebound popped off of those pads and sat just beyond the crease for what seemed like an eternity.

That eternity was probably a half second in reality, but that was all Cyrus Carpenter needed. Carpenter had exited the defensive zone just after

Bishop, and like his linemate, he was off a step quicker than the Silent Lake defense. Unlike his linemate, Cyrus was legitimately fast and much more skilled with the puck. Those attributes enabled Cyrus to tip the puck a foot to the left and then poke it into the empty far side of the net to tie the score at 1-1 with nine minutes and seven seconds left in the game.

"Hell yeah, woooooo!" Cyrus exulted just before he was mobbed by the other four skaters on the ice. Bishop and Danny Stone circled toward him and flung their arms around their friend. O'Brien followed, leaping onto the pile and then Moxon.

Tie game, just like that.

"Way to bring the heart boys, way to bring the heart," Scadorski said from the bench.

The first-liners turned things over to the second line after that, who failed to build on the momentum that they'd just acquired. The third line also did not score. Silent Lake tried as well, but the two teams weren't able to get that one big opportunity to break the tie until the last few minutes.

Eastport had done everything it had set out to, except for score more goals. After 42 of the game's 45 minutes, each side had struck once. A tie would have been somewhat unrewarding for both, but preferable to a loss.

Eastport would have taken a tie, that was for sure.

The losing goal came jarringly after what looked like an uneventful sequence of events. Silent Lake fired the puck into the zone and it went into the corner. Two Cannons and two Lakers met in that rounded off back section of the playing surface and kicked and poked at the puck until it was jarred loose. One of the Lakers swung his foot again at the puck, soccer style, and sent it right out to the front. Jimmy Martinage scrambled to get on top of it, but it slid under his glove and out the back side. More sticks crashed down on the vulcanized rubber, with one catching just enough to send it on edge and over the goal line. One of the refs pointed at the back of the net and blew his whistle. The Lakers jumped for joy. The Cannons could not believe their misfortune.

The rest of the time played out the way they often do in games like that.

Eastport made a push up the ice and had Martinage leave the ice with 90 seconds left in a mad attempt to tie the score with an extra attacker on. Silent Lake got it out and wristed a shot into the empty goal with 35 seconds remaining. That was it, 3-1 Lakers.

Eastport showed the heart that they needed, it just wasn't enough that night. As lousy as the loss was, the Cannons' bad week was only just beginning.

31

"Son of a bitch," swore Scott Frazier when the puck trickled past Martinage. After hiding from his buddies for a few days, he'd finally worked up the courage to go back to the rink Wednesday night. He'd shaken hands with the dads in the crowds, been kissed on the cheek by the moms, and – the best part – gotten hugs from the girls. He'd chosen to stand with the boys' basketball team during the game and had cheered like a rowdy fan. When OB had laid out that guy, he'd let out a whoop. When Cyrus scored seconds later, he pumped his fists. It was the first time in a long time he'd actually gotten to watch, rather than play, a hockey game.

The experience was better than he would have thought, except for the outcome. He had to admit, the defense didn't look all that bad, but he knew – deep in his heart – things would have been different if he was wearing an Eastport uniform.

"Dammit, I should be out there," he muttered to himself.

"Yeah you should," one of the basketball players said. "Why'd you leave anyway? Is Wellington any good?"

Scott just shrugged. But he'd been asking himself that same question for months. Why had he left? More importantly, could he come back? Was there any way, or had that ship sailed?

As the crowd began to dissipate, Scott pulled his sweatshirt's hood over his head, buttoned his coat and began to head to the exit when an arm swooped around him, grabbing him into an embrace.

"Scotty, dude, I didn't know you were back. What's up? Man, we've missed you."

Wes Garrett was excited to see his friend. They had not spoken since August, just before Frazier had left. They'd been teammates since they were kids, and good, but not the closest, friends.

"Yeah, just got back, figured I'd surprise you guys."

"Oh man, they'll be happy to see you."

"Don't know how happy anyone in that locker room is right now."

"Yeah, it sucks. We're 1-3 now. Whatever, we'll turn it around. Come on, let's go down to the locker room."

"I don't know."

"Are you kidding, come on. Coach will be happy to see you. Who knows, maybe you can get these guys motivated."

Reluctantly, Scott joined Wes as they wove against the outgoing crowd and made their way to the locker room. They paused at the door, to make sure no one inside was being yelled at, and cracked the door open to a silent gathering of hockey players. Melancholy filled the musty room, with most of the heads staring straight at the ground.

"Look what I found in the crowd," Wes announced cheerily, hoping to jar his friends out of their stupor.

It worked.

"Scotty, hey, what's up," Billy Walker said, leading the welcoming committee. All of the veterans in the room, the boys who had gone to war with Scott Frazier the year before, stood to greet their former teammate.

"Dude, I didn't know you were home," Collin O'Brien said.

"Yeah, you could have told me you were back. I would've stopped by," Cyrus Carpenter added.

"Sorry guys, I should've said something, figured I'd surprise you tonight."

Coach Scadorski burst into the room to see what the commotion was all about.

"What are you guys all blathering about over here?" the coach asked before seeing his former star standing in the middle of the circle.

"Oh, Frazier... good to see you kid. Coulda used you out on the blue line tonight," the coach said, joking, but not really.

"Yeah, wish I could've been out there," Scott said.

126

Scadorski smiled, knowing the sentiment was true. He could see it in Scott Frazier's body language, he had buyer's remorse when it came to private school. Some kids went away and flourished, others found that the grass was not truly greener on the other side. It was really a case by case basis, but in the case of Scott Frazier, it was clear he was beyond having second thoughts.

The coach scanned the room. "Boys, I'm proud of the effort tonight. Losing sucks, but that was everything we need to be successful."

He pointed at the board. "You played with heart. Keep giving those kinds of efforts and we're going to start winning games, we're going to be alright. But, it takes *those types* of games. Nothing less, maybe even more," he said, pausing briefly.

"Practice tomorrow, on the ice at four o'clock here. You've got Friday and Saturday off, to be with family, and Sunday is Christmas. Next practice after that is Monday and we play on Tuesday and Thursday. Now listen, tomorrow come ready to work. We're going to do some breakout, passing drills, the whole shebang. Your vacation doesn't start until the end of practice, so I want your heads in the game."

The players all nodded.

"Frazier, you bring your equipment home?"

"Yeah, Coach," he said. "It's at the house."

"Wanna skate tomorrow with us? I'm sure the Wellington guys want you to stay sharp."

"Umm, yeah, that'd be great. I'll be here, on time."

"You'd better be. You don't want to be skating extra laps with Walker."

Billy Walker looked at his coach with a good-natured 'who me' stare. The rest of the boys laughed, even Scott Frazier. He felt like he was home. He felt like he belonged again.

32

Setting his text tone sound like the Boston Bruins' goal horn had seemed like a good idea a few weeks ago. Being away from his friends on a day-to-day basis had led to fewer and fewer texts for Scott. He was out of sight, so obviously he'd also been out of mind. Now that they'd seen his face he had returned to their thoughts and for two straight hours, the phone sounded like the B's were turning some poor goalie into a sieve at the Garden. Finally, he had to put the iPhone on vibrate.

Near midnight, he felt the phone vibrate on his desk again. This time, though, it continued to buzz. Collin O'Brien was calling him.

"Hey OB, what's up?"

"Nothing, I've been sitting here feeling like a jerk. I wanted to apologize to you."

"Apologize? For what? Last time I checked, we were cool unless you've got something you want to tell me."

"Nah, man, nothing like that. It's just that I feel like a dick. I haven't called you or texted much since you left. When I saw you in the locker room I realized that, and I've been sitting here thinking about it. I'm sorry. I mean, I would've lost my mind being away from everyone for that long. I don't know how you did it."

"No big deal. I get it, you're here and I was there, and people are busy. When was the last time you talked to your older brother?"

Collin paused to think about that.

"You know what, I don't think we've talked since October. He came down for Columbus Day weekend with his girlfriend."

"See, that's your brother. It's all good, seriously."

"I know, but you're my brother too, dude."

This time it was Scott's turn to pause. That's exactly how he felt about his closest friends. He'd missed Cy and Bill and Danny and Josh and Collin, and even Wes, terribly. He missed the teasing, and the jokes, and being teammates, being brothers.

"I know what you mean, man. I've got to be honest, I kind of hate it up there," Scott said, telling someone else his secret for the first time. "I really freakin' hate it. That place sucks. None of the guys matter to me. The team is okay, but I don't care if we win or lose that much. Remember when we were kids at CCD and they told us about purgatory? That's kind of how I feel about Wellington, like I'm stuck between worlds."

"So leave, what's keeping you there? If you hate it just come back."

"It's not that simple, you know that. I've got a scholarship, and what would the scouts think if I bailed?"

"Screw that. You and I both know you can play D1 if you want to. Worst case you play a year of juniors next year and then go. It's not like they're paying you to be there. The scholarship isn't worth anything if you hate being there. You can always come back here. You should. You can graduate with your boys and then we can all worry about our big bad futures in the summer. Don't stay just to stay."

"Yeah, but if I came back I can't play on the team here. It's too late, the season's already started. They're not going to let me join after playing in the private school league."

"Hey, you never know. Maybe Coach can get a waiver. And, if you can't play, he'd still let you skate at practice, and you can find a junior team to finish the season on. Life's too short to be miserable, man. That's what I think, at least. Think about it."

As old friends do, they went on to discuss less weighty topics and did not hang up for another half-hour. When they finally did, Scott kept replaying what his buddy had said. Maybe Collin O'Brien, the big goof who once filled his new Jordans with shaving cream and laughed his ass off when he'd tried to get them on, had a point.

The next morning, Scott woke up still considering the conversation he'd had with his buddy the night before. With his friends enduring their final day of school before Christmas break, he threw on some Under Armour compression leggings, a pair of shorts over them, and a hoodie and laced up his sneakers for a run. Thirty minutes and five miles later he'd come to a decision.

Scott arrived at the rink at about the same time his friends at Eastport High School were getting dismissed for the day. They'd be bouncing off the walls with excitement, saying goodbye to the hallways of high school for the next 11 days. They'd be making the final plans for tomorrow's shopping trip, and then late night Xbox sessions, trips to the movies and all the stuff they'd been waiting to do over vacation. For those guys, life was about as good as it gets.

At the Eastport Ice Arena, Scott was trying to settle the butterflies in his stomach. They were bouncing around his insides, laying body checks on his gut.

When he saw Coach Scadorski enter the building, they jumped right up his esophagus. Taking a deep breath, he put a smile on his face and made his way over to the coach's office.

"Hey Scotty, I see some things never change. Couldn't wait to get on the ice, eh?"

"Yeah, Coach. Umm, I was wondering, can we talk for a sec?"

"Sure thing, buddy, let's go in the office."

Scott sat down opposite his former coach's locker stall while the man changed into his sweats and zipped up a maroon jacket. As he sat down and eased on his left skate, Scott began to recount the conversation he'd had with Collin O'Brien the night before.

John Scadorski listened silently, nodding every now and then. He didn't comment until the young man had reached the end of his story. Then, he waited some more.

"Wow, Scott, that's a lot. I didn't know you were so miserable up there.

When you told me you were going to move on and go there, the selfish part of me was really upset. No coach wants to lose his best player before graduation, not to mention his team's leader."

"I'm sorry," Scott said, meaning it deeply.

"No, don't apologize. I get it. You and your family thought you were doing what was best for you. Heck, if you were my kid, I probably would have considered the same thing. Have you talked to your parents about this stuff?"

"That's the thing, I don't know how to. My dad thinks I'm going to be in the NHL someday. My mom thinks I can get into an Ivy League school because of Wellington. Either way, they're both going to hate the idea of me leaving. I don't know how to tell them I want to, and I don't know if they'll let me."

"Listen, buddy, you've always got a home with this team, and you know that. Your teammates love you. They'd love to have you back, but I don't know if that's a possibility even if you do leave Wellington. You'd have to re-enroll in the school and then apply for a waiver to get reinstated, which may or may not get granted. If you are reinstated, which is a big if, you'd have to wait two weeks before they'd let you play another game. By then, we're probably halfway through the season. You might get to play 10, maybe 12 games. You've got to ask yourself if it's worth going through all that for just a few games. It is a huge decision."

"I know," Scott said, leaning back in the chair with his hands interlocked behind his head. He rocked back and forth, "Am I crazy? I don't know what to do."

"Today, you're going to skate. You're going to go out there and skate with your buddies. I know I said we were going to have a full-out practice, but instead we're going to have fun, nothing but scrimmages. It's Christmas, let's celebrate.

"After that, you're going to forget about this for a few days. You don't have

131

to make any decisions right now. School doesn't start up again until after New Year's, here or at Wellington. The administration people have all gone home for the holidays, so it's not like we could get the ball rolling on any of this any time soon. Best case, if you do decide you want to come back, you can't start the process until the administration is back to work. You've got time, so relax, have some fun, drink some eggnog and eat some cookies."

"Yeah?"

"Yeah. But you should talk to your parents. They need to know where your head is at."

"Okay, I will, after Christmas."

33

Craig jumped into the passenger seat that was usually reserved for him on Friday nights and Sunday afternoons. This was the first time he'd ever ridden in the green Volkswagen bug to the hockey rink. He adjusted the seat back, strapped the seatbelt over his shoulder and tossed his backpack into the back seat.

"You sure you don't mind driving me? I can ask OB for a ride, it's no big deal."

"I don't mind at all, babe. This is nice. It's not often we get to spend time together after school. You think we have time to swing by Starbucks first? I'd love to get a cup of green tea," Emily Brown replied to her boyfriend. "We've got a half hour or so, right?"

"That should be fine, maybe I'll grab a treat."

"I could give you one tonight," Emily said with a sly smile.

"That sounds even better. It's not a school night... Netflix and chill?"

"Actually, Melissa had mentioned that she and Wesley were thinking about grabbing a pizza and watching movies at her house. She asked me if we'd like to join them."

"I don't know, I don't want to get in the way of young love," Craig said with a laugh. "Wes doesn't need me to throw the block on him if you know what I mean."

"Melissa and Wesley have only been seeing each other for a couple of weeks. We're hardly getting in the way of a bone session, no matter what your friend may have told you."

"Hey, Wes isn't the type to kiss and tell... not like me," he said, giving his girlfriend a smirk and a sideways glance. He braced for the punch to the gut that he knew was coming.

"Keep it up Craig, you'll have nothing to talk about for quite some time.

Don't make me convince your grandmother how handsome you'd look with a buzz cut."

"You play dirty," he said with a laugh as they turned into the drive-through. Emily ordered her tea with a pack of honey, and Craig opted for a bottle of water, an apple, a sandwich, and a cookie. He handed his debit card to Emily, who passed it to the barista behind the window to charge.

"You're going to eat all of that before practice? If I did that I'd be puking it up halfway through."

"This is nothing. Me and Wes get slices of pizza at 7-11 before practice all the time. Once I ate two footlongs from Subway before practice. I'm a professional, do not try this at home."

Pulling out onto the main street, Emily pointed her car in the direction of the back roads toward the rink and drove casually, enjoying her impromptu mini date with her boyfriend. She had not been kidding when she said their time together was not nearly as much as she'd like, but that was the price you paid when two of the school's best athletes ended up together. Practices, games and – unfortunately – homework had to come first.

"Do me a favor and tell Wes I'd appreciate it if he'd schedule more afterschool doctor's appointments. I like this."

"I'm not sure Wes does. He's so sick of doctors and casts and the whole thing."

"Well, maybe he'll think twice before punching a wall again."

"Probably not. He's so smart except for stuff like that."

"Will he be giving you a ride home after practice?" she asked.

"I'm gonna probably just bum a ride with one of the guys. Josh might be able to do it or Danny. At worst I'll get OB to drive me. I'll be fine. What time you want to pick me up tonight?"

"Melissa said she was heading over to Wes's house around 7:30, so why don't I pick you up around that time, and we'll get there close to 8. That way they can have some alone time before we get there."

"I don't know how much alone time they're going to get with his mom around," Craig said with a laugh. "If I know Darlene, she'll be pulling out the old photo albums. Mel will be regaled with Wesley Garrett's greatest achievements. I hope she shows the old newspaper clipping of the time we made the paper for hitting home runs against one another in Little League. That one's my favorite."

The couple continued to chit-chat about weekend plans, including the next day's big shopping trip, until pulling into the rink's parking lot. Craig opened his door and began to get out.

"Hey, I get a kiss before you leave, and close the door, it's freezing."

"You're such a pain," Craig said, meaning the opposite. With one hand still resting on the door handle, he leaned across and ran his fingers through her hair. The embrace lasted until they each needed to catch their breaths.

"Wow, that was nice," she said, a satisfied look on her face. "You sure you can't skip practice?"

"Not today, don't want to get benched. I love ya Em, see ya tonight," Craig said as he slowly backed out of the car, his gaze locking onto his girlfriend the whole time.

"Love you too, babe. Have a great practice."

Craig popped his bag over his shoulder and took off for the front door at a half-sprint. Emily watched him enter the front door and disappear around the corner.

34

Taking the last bite of his turkey sandwich, Craig balled up the wrapper and tossed it into the trash can as he walked through the lobby, waving to the people behind the counter in the concession stand before making his way over to the locker room. Scott Frazier waited outside the room. He was bouncing up and down with the nervous energy he usually saved for a big game. Collin, Danny, and Josh were there as well, and the four of them were dressed and ready to hit the ice.

"Am I late or something?" Craig asked as the Zamboni lapped the ice, turning the cut up surface into a wet, smooth sheet of perfection.

"No, you're fine, lover boy, we're just amped to get out there with Scotty. Haven't skated with our boy in a minute. This is gonna be fun," Josh said.

"You've got like 10 minutes. No worries, Mr. Assistant Captain," Collin said.

Craig hustled to change out of his jeans and t-shirt, donning the yellow practice jersey that marked him as a member of the first line. He paused at the mirror after a trip to the bathroom. He ran his hand over the scruff that had built up over the week, growing especially full around his chin. He couldn't quite grow a full-length beard yet, but it was enough to look tougher on game day. He'd have to remember to shave it off when he got home. Emily constantly reminded him she preferred him clean-shaven, and he certainly wanted to get cheek-to-cheek later tonight.

Pushing open the heavy door, Craig eased to the back of the circle of bodies waiting for the thumbs-up to open the door to take the ice. The Zamboni driver pulled off the surface, grabbed a shovel and removed the shavings that had fallen off of the long blade. He then pulled the trigger on a hose nozzle to wash away the slush before closing the big doors. He lowered the locking mechanism and then yelled out, "Have at it, boys."

Danny Stone stood by the entry door and tapped everyone on the shin pads as they went out on the ice. "Let's go, boys... get after it... hard work, hard work." Once the rest of the Cannons had taken the ice, Stone, Bishop and Cy Carpenter shared a quick whisper, exchanged fist bumps and sprinted out onto the ice themselves. Freedom and joy exploded with the first stride as they looped the full length of the rink side-by-side, starting on the right wing, circling along the far end boards and then back up the other side. They came to a hard stop in front of the bench by turning sideways and digging their blades into the ice, spraying snow all over Scott.

"Sorry Scotty, flurry came through," Bish said with a laugh. The other players joined in and even the coaches had a chuckle.

Had that happened back at Wellington, Scott Frazier likely would have gotten up, pulled someone's sweater over his head and pounded away until it got broken up. Not here, though. These were his real teammates, his brothers. Besides, he'd get even one way or another.

"Okay boys, we've got everybody here today but Garrett. We're going to choose up sides and play some 3-on-3s. With Frazier, we've got 21 skaters and 3 goalies. Keepers, you'll rotate, and I need 7 teams of 3. We're going to go all-out for 2 minutes, then the next two teams jump on, and so on. We'll keep the count."

"What are we playing for, Coach?" Stone asked.

"To win. You're playing to win. I want to see you all compete, and compete hard. Show me something, but don't be afraid to be creative. Get after it," Scadorski said. "Oh, and Coach Henry will buy the winners a slice of pizza after practice."

Coach Henry shrugged. "What the hell, it's Christmas."

For the next hour, the Eastport Cannons battled one another as if the Stanley Cup were on the line. The action stopped only when a puck went into a net or it was time to change up sides. The seniors especially attempted to play a game of 'Anything You Can Do I Can Do Better,' with Scott Frazier setting the bar. The former Cannon had been the best player in the program for years and he'd only widened the gap between himself and the rest during the interim.

Coach Scadorski attempted to make things fair by teaming Frazier with two of the younger kids on the team. It just didn't matter. Early on in the games, the youngsters caught on to the idea of getting the puck to Scott and letting him create things and did he ever create. He also got even with his friends. Knowing that there would be no penalties being called, he tripped Bishop from behind to break up a scoring chance and gave a fake apology, "Sorry Bish, didn't see ya there." He rode Stone into the boards and held him there, pinned in place, for a good five-count, saying, "Pardon me, coming through, oh I'm so sorry," as Stone attempted to wiggle himself free. Carpenter he got the best, sneaking up on him from behind to steal the puck and breaking the other way for an easy goal against an overmatched Marc Rollins. He unleashed an exaggerated celebration and exclaimed, "That's what you get!" while pointing his stick at his friend.

With eight goals to their credit, seven of which Frazier had scored himself, his team waited on the bench as the final two groups went out for their last two-minute mini-game, each knowing they had no chance to catch up. The two rookies could already taste the pizza. As the last game finished up, O'Brien skated up to Frazier and gave him a nudge.

"Dude, this is so much fun. I want you back with us," he said through a smile, in awe of what his former teammate could do on the ice. "Why'd you have to go?"

"I ask myself that same question all the time," Frazier said seriously.

"Wouldn't it be awesome if we could play together one more time? That'd be unreal. You and me on the blue line, Cy and Bill and Bish up on the first line. We'd be unstoppable."

"You never know, OB. Be careful what you wish for. You never know."

O'Brien squinted his eyes and gave his friend a sideways glance.

"You serious?"

"Time will tell, but it could happen."

"Time will tell, young man," the doctor said, looking down his glasses at Wes Garrett. The teenager's stare was to the left ear of his doctor. He could not look away from the patch of gray hair that sprouted from deep inside

138

the doc's ears. How could someone with a head so perfectly bald and shiny have that much cabbage protruding from his ears?

"Doc, no offense, but I've been hearing that for months now. Hockey season is like a quarter over already and I haven't been allowed to skate hard. I haven't been allowed to use a stick. I really want to get back out there and I need to start swinging a bat to get ready for baseball."

"I've explained to you before that you fractured the MCP, or the metacarpophalangeal joint. It's an injury that is very common in boxers. Casting it and allowing the body to heal it correctly is the best course of action. No promises, but I could see the cast coming off next week, and perhaps clearing you to start physical activities the week after that."

Wesley was not happy at this news at all. He'd Googled the injury after he had gotten hurt and had read that it took up to six weeks to heal, and another 1-3 weeks of support and rest for comfort. At worst that should have put him back in the game by the first week of November. It was now late December. Was this the most conservative doctor in America?

"Doc, why is it taking so long?"

"My best guess is that you already had an injury there that you were unaware of. You play baseball, right? Ever get hit in the hand with a ball? Or in football, you may have been stepped on, or hockey taken a slap shot to the hand? You're a very active young man, Wesley. There's no telling how you did it, but I expect it was already compromised."

Truth be told, all those things had happened to Wes at one time or another in the past few years. Patience may be a virtue, but it wasn't one he was good at using and most of his had run out. Wes decided right then and there that if the doctor did not clear him at his next appointment, he'd cut the cast off himself and play anyway.

"So when do I come back in, December 29?"

The doctor looked embarrassed and poked his glasses back up his long nose. Again, Wes stared at the voluminous ear hairs.

"My wife and I are heading to Hawaii for the holidays, a little vacation. I'm back in the office on January 2, I'm sure we can squeeze you in then."

Wes sighed. What a pain in the ass this day was turning out to be. At least he had a nice night with Melissa lined up for later. That would surely turn around this crappy day. Just thinking about her smiling at him was almost enough to put a grin on his own face. Almost.

35

"Okay boys, that's it for a few days. Remember I wear an extra-large shirt, my favorite color is blue and future playing time can be purchased," Coach Scadorski told the locker room to a combination of snickers and laughs. "In all seriousness, Merry Christmas. Enjoy the days off, but don't do anything stupid, and come back ready to rock and roll on Monday. We have a winning streak to begin."

Scott Frazier had been sitting in the corner at an empty locker. He smiled at the underclassmen seated near him, remembering he'd been just like them three years ago. He offered a fist bump to one whose name he couldn't remember and said, "Hey, good job today. Keep it up."

The little boy (well that's what he looked like to Scott even though the kid was probably 15 years old) beamed. "Hey thanks, Scott. You coming back on Monday?"

"I hope so," Frazier said.

He hoped he'd be back every day.

While Scott was boosting the morale of a fourth liner, Collin was trying to convince Craig to hurry up so they could be on their way.

"Dude, we don't have all day. I've got plans tonight with Josh. We're meeting some girls up there."

"Chill, OB. I'm almost ready. I just want to say Merry Christmas to the coaches. I've got cards that my grandmother picked up for them. After that, we're outta here."

Danny Stone sidled up to Collin with a sly smile. "Dude, you guys are heading up to that 18-plus show at The Buzzkill tonight? Got room for another?"

"I don't know, maybe. Hey Hutchinson, we got room for Stoner with us?"

Josh Hutchinson thought about busting his friend's chops and saying 'no,' but Danny was a little more sensitive than the rest of the guys. Unlike everyone else on the team, Danny had not lived in Eastport his entire life. He'd moved to town from Nova Scotia. Like most Canadians, he was nice to a fault, but he couldn't take a ribbing like some of the others.

"It's your car, but someone else to chip in on the gas sounds good to me."

"Okay Dan, I will pick you up at around 6:45. Throw in a tenner for gas and we're good. Tickets are $15 at the door," Collin said.

"Awesome," Danny said. "I'll see you then."

As Collin, Danny and Josh made their plans to go see The D-A-Z rap later in the night in the city, Craig grabbed the festive envelopes out of his backpack and entered the coach's office. His grandfather had served as the father figure in his life, but the men who had coached him over the years had taught him a lot of the life lessons he'd needed to get to where he was. Without the discipline someone like Scadorski provided on a day-to-day basis, there was certainly another life where Craig Bishop was failing out of high school and spending more time smoking weed than doing anything productive. Grandma Cookie understood that very well, so she always said "thank you" at the holidays with a card and a gift card to the coaches' favorite sports bar.

"Hey Coach, umm, me and my family just want to say Merry Christmas and thanks for everything," Craig said, clearly a bit uncomfortable. "Hope you guys have an awesome weekend."

Craig shook hands with Coach Scadorski. Coach Henry was still standing. Craig shook hands with the tall coach, then pulled him in for a somewhat awkward hug.

With a nod, Craig got ready to leave the room. "Thanks again, Merry Christmas," he said.

Craig was mostly out the door but then paused. He stuck his head around the corner of the door and said, "I love you guys," and was off again.

As Craig left the coaches' room, Collin came around the corner, threw his arm around his old friend and said, "Let's hit the skids, Bish."

In the parking lot, Collin had parked his aging Toyota under an overhang that ran alongside the building. The structure not only kept snow off the cars but had solar panels on top to help defray some of the costs of keeping an ice arena up and running year-round. The cars not parked underneath all had a light coating of snow.

Danny Stone pulled out of the lot in his blue pickup truck as Collin pressed the unlock button on his key fob. The pair opened the doors and sat back in their seats.

"A couple days off, some skirts to chase, presents to buy tomorrow. This is gonna be a fun couple of days, Craig. You sure you don't want to tag along tonight?"

"Thanks, but nah. Not my scene, and besides me and Wes are hanging with the girls. Emily is somewhat better company," Craig said.

"Have it your way," Collin said as he put the car in reverse and pulled out of his spot, the tires leaving sharp tread patterns in their wake. He rolled slowly through the quarter inch of snow on the ground as he left the parking lot and then pulled onto the side road that the rink resided on, spinning his tires and fishtailing into the lane.

Turning onto Pickerel Pond Road, Collin did not glance at the posted speed limit sign of 35 miles per hour. He'd driven this road daily and knew it like the back of his hand. The odometer reached 35 and then passed 45, settling just under 50. As the road bent slightly to the right, he spied Danny Stone about 200 yards ahead.

"Wanna screw with Danny a little bit?" Collin asked Craig, not waiting for an answer as he pressed down on the gas.

Collin's already speeding car gained ground on the little pickup truck that was puttering along. Danny's truck curved around a bend to the right a little and they temporarily lost sight of it. His rust-stained bumper came back into view as it turned back to the left.

"Dude, slow down! Not cool," Craig said, his knuckles whitening as he held on to the handle above the passenger side window.

"No worries, brother. Relax, I got you."

Danny Stone finally felt like he was starting to find his way with the hockey team. Being named captain had given him a newfound confidence that was starting to show up on and off the ice. He was tired after giving an all-out effort at practice and couldn't wait to get home, put on some jeans and a Vineyard Vines shirt and hit the city with his buddies for a night of fun. He expected the ride to the city and back home to be the best parts of the night. Josh was always a great hang, and no one made him laugh like OB.

He looked down to adjust the volume on the radio, lowering it a little bit. As his eyes came back up he noticed a car barrelling down on him fast in the rearview mirror.

"What the hell is this dickhead doing?" he said to himself, not realizing who it was that was closing the distance between the two vehicles.

That gap was closing faster and faster.

"OB, that's close enough, man. You're gonna give him a heart attack," Craig said uneasily, his voice unable to hide his growing fear. "Don't hit him."

"Easy, man. Chill, I got this," Collin said.

Collin O'Brien put his foot on the brake pedal, looking to give his friend some breathing room. Just then, his front left tire hit a small patch of black ice. The car skewed hard to the right. Collin muscled the steering wheel to no avail.

"Hold on, Bish!" he screamed.

Craig was already holding on, tense from his toes to his hairline. It didn't help."

36

The tree's diameter was 43 inches. It had probably taken root 200 years ago in what had once been a vast forest. When the road had been cleared, this one had remained on the edge. There was nothing to really differentiate it from the countless other leaf-bare oaks that littered the landscape, until that moment.

The trunk of the tree split the hood of the Toyota right down the middle. The impact pushed the engine block back. Collin and Craig screamed.

Glass exploded inwards as the boys' bodies were thrust violently forward. An explosion sounded as the car's airbag deployed, filling the car with dust. Metal groaned and twisted as the seat belts arrested the boy's forward movement.

Chaos was followed by eerie silence. The dust from the airbags settled into every crevice of the car's cockpit.

Craig turned his head slightly to the left and saw Collin hunched over, his chin aimed at the floor. He leaned over and attempted to get his friend to wake up, but he felt sleepy himself.

"OB, come one, get up. I got…"

Before he could finish the darkness overcame Craig. His arm slipped and his head leaned to the left, coming to a rest on his oldest friend's shoulder.

Steam rose from the radiator. Gasses wheezed from beneath the car. Snowflakes melted as they descended to the front of the crumpled hood, but a sheen formed on the roof.

"Holy crap!" Danny explained.

It was like a scene out of "The Fast and Furious." The silver car had been right behind him and then it just veered hard to the right into the trees. The sound of twisted metal was sickening.

145

With a hard push down with his right foot, Danny Stone stomped on his brakes and pulled off on the shoulder of the road. He jammed the car into park and fumbled for his phone to dial 9-1-1.

"9-1-1, what's your emergency?"

"Umm, a car just crashed really bad on Pickerel Pond Road. Send an ambulance right now, as fast as you can. Please... Now."

"Okay, calm down, son. What's your name and where on Pickerel Pond Road is the accident?"

"It's, uh, south, I think, of the ice rink. It's near Cumberland Road... Oh, and I'm Danny."

"How many people are in the car and are they moving?"

"I don't know, let me look."

Realization froze Danny where he stood. He knew that car. He was supposed to ride in it tonight.

"OB! Collin! Oh no, are you alright?"

Danny threw open his car's door, sprinted to Collin's door and tried to open it. He couldn't get it to budge. Smoke and steam wafted around him. He tried again, but it was seized. He kicked it and threw his body against it, but it would not budge.

Collin lay slumped in his seat, his head tilted at an angle, slightly forward and to the left, his eyes shut. Then he noticed Craig in the other seat, his head on Collin's shoulder. Neither boy moved.

"Hello, Danny, can you hear me?"

Who was talking? Was that Craig whispering? Then it donned on him, 9-1-1. He was still on the phone with them.

He put the phone to his ear. "Please send someone quick. My friends are in the car, they're not moving. This is bad, this is really bad."

It might have been five seconds, it might have been five hours, but Danny kept trying to get the door open to get his friends out. Again and again, he pulled and kicked at the door, but couldn't get it to move. Stumbling to the

146

passenger side, his fingers slipped from the handle as he pulled and pulled. "Come on, come on, open dammit."

He didn't notice that it was getting colder, nor did he hear the sirens.

"Son, it's okay, why don't you let us take over? You've done your job."

Startled, Danny shook out of the grip of the uniformed police officer. Officer Ronnie Costello had pulled up to scenes just like this far too often during the last 16 years on the beat in Eastport. In the summertime, it was usually a tourist that didn't know when to say when. In the winter it was the ice, which did not mix well with speed. He'd seen it before, but it didn't get any easier. Costello quickly inspected the cockpit of the car and then turned his attention to the stunned teenager.

"Whoa, easy buddy, settle down. Dan, right? That's what dispatch said your name is. Is that right?"

"Uhh, yes, sir."

"Dan, can you tell me who is in the car?"

"OB is driving, Bish is the passenger."

"Okay, what are their full names?"

"Oh, yeah, sorry. Collin O'Brien and Craig Bishop."

Officer Costello scribbled in a notebook.

"O'Brien and Bishop. The football players?"

"Yeah, we just left hockey practice. They were driving behind me and the next thing I knew they flew off the road."

"Were you boys messing around?"

"I honestly didn't know it was them in the car. I was just driving home. I saw the accident in the mirror and pulled over and..."

Emotion crashed over Danny Stone and he began to sob.

"It's okay, buddy. It's cold, why don't you go put the heat on in your truck and call your folks. See if they can come pick you up. You should not be driving right now."

37

John Scadorski had a little hop in his step. The players were not the only ones excited to have a few days away from the rink coming up. His three kids were all descending on Eastport over the next 48 hours, and his wife was at home making preparations for the one time all year that the entire family would be in the same area code. She was even more excited than he was.

Just like his days as a hockey player, John Scadorski made his living by hustling. He worked his tail off every day thanks to a number of revenue streams. He owned a few rental properties, as well as numerous vending machines around Cape Cod and a car dealership. Being his own boss, he'd made the executive decision that he was not going to work the next day and instead would enjoy a legitimate three day weekend with his family. Times like these were few and far between and this was a Christmas he planned to celebrate with the people that meant the most to him.

With that decision made, he allowed his ringing cell phone to go to voicemail when it began buzzing. He put it back in his pocket, but it soon began to buzz again. He ignored it again, but finally decided to answer it as he entered his pickup truck when it rang the third time.

"This is John... Whoa, whoa, slow down Danny... Oh no, where are you?"

Shaking, Coach Scadorski turned on the ignition and spun his tires as he dropped the truck into reverse. He fishtailed as he pulled onto Pickerel Pond Road, fighting his desire to drive at top speed to get there. The flashing red lights up ahead verified what Danny Stone had relayed a few minutes earlier. He slowed to a stop 50 yards behind the ambulance and watched in stunned silence as two emergency medical techs leapt out of the vehicle with large bags over their shoulders.

What was this nightmare he'd arrived at? This couldn't be real.

After turning off his truck, John made his way over to Danny's little pickup, putting as much space between himself and the crashed car as possible. The professionals were trying to pry the door open. Scadorski overheard the EMTs that were waiting to attend to the two boys he'd been coaching just a half hour earlier. What they said wasn't good, not in the least bit.

John tapped on the window of Stone's pickup truck, but his team's new co-captain did not react. He tapped again and then finally the window lowered.

Danny showed no reaction at all until his coach reached out and touched his shoulder. The already pale young man looked ghostly as he looked his coach in the eyes.

"I'm sorry, Coach."

"Danny, are you okay? What happened?"

"I don't know, I was driving home. OB's car came up from behind and the next thing I knew..."

"It's going to be okay, Dan, it's going to be okay," Scadorski said, knowing that it wasn't. How could it be?

"Are they going to be okay, Coach? They're going to be fine, right?"

"I hope so, Dan. I'm going to call your parents to come get you, just hang tight."

John stared up into the dark sky, asking God what he should do next. As his gaze came back to Earth, he saw a fireman working a machine that forced open the driver's side door of Collin O'Brien's unrecognizable Toyota. The EMTs then eased him out of the car and onto a gurney, wrapping some protective contraption around his neck and head. Craig Bishop still lay in the passenger seat, slumped over and motionless.

Tears welled in the coach's eyes, but he forced them back in. Now was not the time for mourning. He had to act on behalf of those two boys. He had to make some tough phone calls.

John first called Danny Stone's mother, Leigh, and assured her that Danny was fine, but that she needed to come get him. Then he made the hardest two phone calls of his life.

"Cookie, Craig's been in an accident with Collin... It's not good... The police said that they're taking him to Eastport Hospital soon... Yeah, I'd get down there quickly."

He then called Joanie O'Brien and said almost the exact same things as an ambulance carrying her son pulled out and began the six-mile trip to the local medical center. Scadorski stood vigil as EMT's pulled Craig Bishop from the wreckage then watched silently as another ambulance pulled away, the sound of the sirens fading.

38

"Dammit Craig, answer your phone," Wes Garrett said before finally texting his friend.

"WTF Bish, where are you? Gotta figure out 2nite. CALL ME."

Wes sat shotgun in his mother's minivan as the two of them made their way down Route 25 toward Cape Cod. He wondered what movie he and Melissa, Craig and Emily should watch that night. They'd just gone to see Star Wars, so maybe one of those old movies for fun, or maybe something scary so the girls would want to cuddle. Maybe a comedy for fun's sake. And should they order pizza, or maybe get some Chinese food? So many decisions. He watched out the window contemplating.

"What you thinking about buddy?" his mom asked while turning down the radio.

"Nothing," he replied in typical teenage fashion.

Just as she was about to dig deeper with her next question, Wes's cell phone rang.

"It's Emily," he said to his mother. "I'm gonna see what she wants."

"Hey, Em, what's...Whoa, slow down, slow down... Shoot... Are they okay?.... What? I'm on the highway with Mom, I'll meet you at the hospital... Em, take it easy, it's going to be fine... Okay, I will see you there."

"Hospital?" Darlene Garrett repeated with concern, "Who's in the hospital?"

"Craig and Collin, Emily said they were in a bad accident after practice."

"Oh honey, I'm sure they're going to be okay."

"I hope so, it doesn't sound good, though. Em is a mess right now. I'm scared."

Darlene pushed down on the accelerator, crossed the bridge and did not say another word. Her worry was palpable. Craig Bishop was not only her son's best friend but her surrogate second son and third child. Her heart went out to Cookie and her husband Carl. They had to be losing their minds. They'd had enough tragedy in their lives. That was the whole reason that Craig had grown up in their home.

Darlene didn't spend a lot of time in church – she couldn't remember the last time she'd been in one – but at that moment she began to pray.

39

Nearly a quarter of the Eastport High School athletic community had found its way to the waiting room on the sixth floor at Providence Medical Center, where the boys had been med-flighted after Eastport Hospital deemed they needed special attention. Each of the 20 available seats was taken by either a teenager or a coach. The entire boys' hockey coaching staff and most of the players waited impatiently for news to trickle out. Football, baseball, basketball players, and several female athletes were also there. A 32-inch TV in the corner was tuned to a random football game that was being ignored.

Joan and Harold O'Brien and Cookie and Carl Foley sat in an isolated room together, away from the crowd. Collin's parents and Craig's grandparents all stared at the linoleum floor, afraid to speak the horrors that filled their minds.

The O'Briens had been readying for dinner when the worst phone call of their lives had come. Harold had just walked in the door, sat at the kitchen table and popped the cap off of a Sam Adams. He hadn't yet changed out of his grease-stained jeans after a day of replacing brakes on a car that was worth more than his annual salary.

Cookie and Carl Foley had just finished making dinner plans. Since Craig was planning on entertaining his friends, they had decided to get themselves something easy and fun from their favorite Chinese takeout place. Carl had just placed their order and called in another for Craig's pizzas. The menu for Golden Kingdom still lay on the kitchen table. The food had never been picked up.

A tall man in a white lab coat over light blue scrubs underneath knocked once before opening the door. He had a sad look on his face.

"Mr. and Mrs. O'Brien?"

Joan and Harold leapt to their feet.

"Yes, doctor?" Harold managed.

"Mr. and Mrs. O'Brien, I'm sorry. We did everything we could to revive Collin but the trauma was quite extensive."

The doctor continued to speak, but the O'Briens did not hear a word. Joan sobbed, Harold cried quietly. A hard man, who ruled his home with an iron fist, he squeezed his wife close before the two collapsed back into the chair.

Cookie Foley stood up and placed her right hand on Joan's shoulder. The two women had helped raise one another's boys for the past dozen years.

As she released her hold on her friend's arm, she turned to the doctor and asked if there was any update on Craig.

"He is still in surgery, I'm sure his doctor will be in to see you as soon as he can."

The O'Briens left the room together and were escorted to the chapel where they prayed with a clergyman. The pastor attempted to ease the parents' fears and assured them that their son was with the Lord and that he was rejoicing while they mourned. "Jesus said for the children to be brought to him, and today, though we cry, Collin is rejoicing in paradise with the Lord."

Comforting as the words were, they did nothing to halt the pain coursing through the O'Briens' hearts. Joan stared at her phone at a photograph that she'd taken with Collin a month earlier. Her tall, handsome son towered over her, his arm wrapped tightly around her maroon jacket. He wore shoulder pads and eye black and was still covered in sweat from the game he'd just played at Gillette Stadium. The smile was expansive. She could not take her eyes away from the sight of her son in the happiest moment of his life, his far too short life.

"Dammit," Harold said. "Dammit all to hell. Why?"

40

"Dear Lord in heaven, please be with Craig right now as he fights. Give him strength to survive, to come back to us, please Lord. He's got this, right? He's strong enough. You once gave him the strength to score from second on a single with a sprained ankle.

"He's been my best friend for as long as I can remember. Him, and Collin, and Josh, Danny and Scott. We go together, God, and now you've taken Collin. It doesn't make sense, Lord. I know he could be stupid – we didn't always get along that great the last couple of years – but I love him, and I love Craig, and I can't do this without them.

"God, this isn't fair. Come on. Collin was supposed to play college football. He was supposed to make it to the NFL. This sucks, this really sucks.

"I know they say you work in mysterious ways, but I don't get this one. Who am I to call out God, but what the heck. They're 18 years old. Craig hasn't even gotten to see Roger Waters play live yet.

"God, I don't know what I'd do without Craig. He's not just my friend. He's my brother, Lord. You put us together for a reason, I know you did. I haven't gone more than two days without talking to him since the fourth grade.

"Please, God, please."

Wes Garrett could feel the warm tears run down his face. He felt helpless and alone. His best friend lay in a bed somewhere in the same building clinging to life. His other lifelong buddy was gone. Maybe, just maybe, though, Craig could pull through.

Coach Scadorski whispered with someone Wes did not know, some hospital guy obviously, and then moved to the middle of the collected Eastport kids. He took a deep breath.

"Guys, the hospital would like us to clear out of here. There's nothing that we can do for Collin or Craig in this room. Your parents want you back home anyway. I'll stick around here, and I'll let you know if anything changes. Make sure you grab some coffee or soda or something so no one falls asleep behind the wheel. Be careful."

The clock had already ticked past 10 PM and the kids were clearly drained. Slowly they gathered their things and emptied out. Darlene Garrett sat next to her son and whispered that they should head out.

"I'm not going anywhere," he said.

"But the hospital wants..."

"I don't care what the hospital wants. That's my brother in there. If that was me getting operated on, do you think Craig would leave? Do you think they could drag him out of here? No way, he'd never leave, and I'm not either. I'm going to be here when he wakes up. I'm going to tell him he's an asshole for putting us through this. I'm not going anywhere."

"Okay, honey, okay. We'll stay a little longer, but if Cookie asks you to leave we're going to have to," she gently said.

"Mom, Cookie's a mess."

He was right. Cookie Foley was indeed a mess. She'd had too much tragedy in her life already. She'd buried her daughter far too young and raised her son as if he were her own. She'd seen to it that the boy was taken care of every day she walked the earth and beyond that. Craig owned a special place in her heart. He meant everything to her.

Another hour passed, and still, no word had come from the operating room. The silence was deafening. Wes kept telling himself that the longer it took the better it was. He figured that the doctors weren't going to waste time on a lost cause. Obviously, Craig was hanging in there, grinding like he always did in sports. If the ball was on the ground, you knew that Craig was coming out of the bottom of the pile with it. If the puck was in the corner, Craig dug it out. With his life on the line, you knew Craig would figure a way to get healthy.

"He'll be flirting with the cute nurses in the morning," Wes said to Darlene.

"He probably will," Darlene laughed.

41

Cookie Foley could not stop shaking as she signed on a straight line. Her nerves were shot, she'd never been this tired before, and grief had sapped her of every ounce of energy that her 73-year-old bones held.

"Thank you, Mrs. Foley," a plump woman in cartoon-covered scrubs said. The nurse left the room, waddling up a brightly lit corridor.

Truth be told, the decision had been easier than she thought it would. The doctors had explained the situation and it made sense. Yes, Craig's heart was still beating with the aid of a machine, but the tubes and wires were the only things keeping him alive. He could remain this way for a long, long time, but he would never recover.

Her grandson was not going to play another game. He was not going to kiss another girl. He would not study for another test, or listen to another song. As long as he was connected to the life support system he would lay in limbo, not dead, but not really alive either.

Cookie wasn't sure what she believed in terms of religion. She believed there was a God, though that had been put to the test today, and that there was an afterlife, a Heaven. If that place truly existed that was where she wanted Craig to be now. She was just being selfish if she didn't allow him to go there.

She and Carl held hands as they entered the room. Wes and Darlene were the only other people in the room. Cookie had told the hospital staff that they were family and they had every right to be here as well. The staff probably knew she was stretching the truth a bit but did not concern themselves with the details considering the situation.

"We need to say goodbye to Craig. He's going to go to Heaven now, and we need to let him leave," Cookie whispered.

The other three in the hospital room already knew this. Craig was unresponsive, they called him "brain dead." Nothing could wake him up. He was already gone, his heart just didn't know it and it kept beating.

"I don't want to say goodbye," Carl said with his eyes on his grandson.

Wes tiptoed toward his friend and looked down at his ashen face. Craig's hair had slipped out from beneath the surgical cap, and several strands covered his left eye. Wes had seen Craig look exactly that way hundreds of times before, except the hair had fallen from a faded Boston Red Sox cap.

Lightly, Wes touched his friend's arm.

"For as long as I've known you, you have been my best friend. I already miss you."

Darlene hugged her son and then bent down and kissed Craig on the forehead. "I love you, buddy," she said. Mother and son then hugged everyone in the room and left.

Wes made it 20 feet. He leaned his back on the wall in the hallway and the emotion overcame him. Darlene sat down next to him, wrapped her arm around her son and they sobbed. Time stood still.

42

A rustling across the room caught his attention and his head craned toward the noise. Since the accident, his hearing had improved dramatically, which was a blessing and a curse. Without the ability to see for the past two years, Alex Maloney had relied heavily on the data provided to him by his ears to navigate the world on a day to day basis. The downfall of that was he didn't sleep well because his hearing had become so good that his brain responded to every little thing. The night that a squirrel had decided to nest on the roof had been hell for him.

"Hey, Alex, your parents are just outside the room. Are you ready?"

"Oh, hey Doc. Yeah, they can come in."

"Are you nervous?"

"Not really. Nothing ventured, nothing gained. That's what my dad always says."

The squeak of a sneaker on the linoleum floor alerted Alex to his father's presence. He could tell that his mother had entered the room from the swishing sound that her long skirt made.

The doctor explained what he was about to do to the three members of the Maloney family, then lowered the lights in the room and began unwrapping Alex's head. The 16-year-old could not get over the feeling that his noggin was like a present coming out from under the tree. He prayed his Christmas wish was about to come true.

After the wrapping was removed the patches were peeled off. Alex's world changed.

He tried to play it cool. "It's really bright in here."

The Maloneys embraced one another tightly.

"What can you see, Alex?"

"Everything's a little fuzzy, but I can see that my father still has really bad taste in shirts."

Alex Maloney had lost his sight in a hiking accident three years earlier. He'd slipped while trekking up Mt. Washington and hit face first into a pine tree, which had torn through both of his eyes. He'd required plastic surgery and his face looked close to perfect now.

Because another teenager had died the day before in a car accident Alex could now see. That kid – he'd heard he'd been an athlete, just like Alex had been before his spill – had been the donor of Alex's new eyes. Having brown eyes would take some getting used to, but that boy had just given Alex his greatest Christmas gift ever.

In another hospital in New England, a 35-year-old man was celebrating the arrival of a new liver that would soon be his delivery from dialysis. A 20-year-old with a bad heart valve was about to have his life changed, too.

43

Scott Frazier didn't hear the horn beeping in his driveway. He sat on the couch in his parents' home and continued to stare into the nether. He had been in the same spot for the past two hours and still wore the clothes he'd had on yesterday.

Frazier's father came around the corner, looked out the front window and saw Wes Garrett's Jeep waiting there. Josh Hutchinson strode up the front walkway. Mr. Frazier opened the door, nodded to Hutchinson and then in his son's direction.

"Let's go, Fraze," Hutchinson said.

No reply.

Josh placed his hand on his friend's shoulder and lightly shook it.

"Dude, come on. We're going."

Scott startled and looked at his friend blankly.

"What, what's happening?"

"Just get in the car. Wes is waiting for us."

"Okay, whatever."

Frazier walked outside and opened the back door. Josh came out a moment later, clutching a winter jacket in his hands. He hopped into the front seat and tossed the jacket back to Scott.

"You'll probably want this buddy, it's pretty cold."

As they traveled the only sound was the hum of the V6 engine and that of the tires gripping the wet road.

Fifteen minutes later the Jeep pulled into the parking lot at the Eastport Ice Arena. Several other cars were parked in the lot behind the locker room. The three boys found almost all of their teammates either in the locker room or just outside of it, milling about. Bear hugs were exchanged and tears wiped away.

Coach Scadorski came out of the coach's room with his skates on, a stick in one hand and a bucket full of pucks in the other. He stepped onto the ice, dumped the pucks and slowly slid around the perimeter of the rink, working a puck back and forth the whole way. He finally stopped in front of the far net and began to rifle slap shots at the net, one after the other after the other.

Soon after the players began to file out on the ice as well. Some skated hard, others just glided back and forth.

Scott slowly looped around the perimeter of the boards. He passed the benches and came back around to the corner and stopped, sitting down with his back resting on an advertisement for a local bank. Cyrus Carpenter and Josh Hutchinson slid over and plopped down next to their friend.

Cyrus broke the silence.

"Last year, we were getting ready to play Lakeville one night and me and OB got into it in the locker room. I don't even remember what we were fighting about, I think he said something that pissed me off, and I called him out on it, and you know how he is, wasn't going to back down, and you guys know how I am...

"Anyways, we're sitting on the bench, still ticked at one another. Just two friends worked up about stupid crap...

"So the game's tied and it's the third period. We're all pretty gassed – you remember how fast those guys were – and I'm chasing the puck into this corner we're sitting in right here. I pinned it with my skates and was gonna try to kick it behind the net to Billy."

As if on cue, Walker joined the three teammates and plopped down on the ice with them. "Dude, I remember this story. I was coming in from the right side and beat my man. You kicked it down to me and I got it out to the slot for Gossard and he one-timed it in... too bad it didn't count. I think that was the only goal he had all year."

"Yeah," Cyrus continued. "Definitely sucked that it didn't count, but the reason why it didn't count is my favorite thing about OB...

162

"As I was kicking the puck down to you, some dude from Lakeville took a run at me and just stapled me into the glass, face first. Absolutely rang my bell. I rolled over on the ice, trying to figure out what the heck just happened to me. Then I see Collin on top of that kid, just whaling away at him. He destroyed that dude."

Frazier, who had not said a word to that point, laughed to himself before sharing his side of things.

"I was on the ice for that. OB was the left D and I had the right. As soon as you got hit, he flew down to the corner and spun that kid and put an elbow right into his side, and then pulled him to the ice and just worked him over. It was so smart, though. The way he did it, it looked like the other guy was fighting back. Ref must have seen the cheap shot against you, Cy, because he just gave them each double minors for roughing. Collin didn't even get a suspension. They could have dropped the hammer on him for that one."

The boys laughed about their friend's audacity. Collin O'Brien had certainly gotten away with one that night.

"The penalties ran through to the end of the game, so he was in the box until the game was over," Cyrus continued. "Now remember, we were ready to tear each other's heads off before the game. I get back to the locker room, and he follows me in and puts his arm on my shoulder and says, 'Cy, you alright?' And I'm like, 'Yeah, I'll be fine, a little sore tomorrow, but fine. Thanks for getting my back out there.'"

"Next thing I know, he wraps me in a hug and says, 'Hey, no one messes with the Boys. They want to throw cheap shots, that's what they're gonna get.' And that was that. Whatever it was that we were arguing about before the game, never mentioned again. That's OB in a nutshell, no matter what, he's got your back."

"You should have seen him on the field at the Super Bowl," Hutchinson said with a laugh. "Somebody on Swampscott made the mistake of hitting Bish after the whistle. Wouldn't have mattered who it had been, but Craig's like his brother, right. OB waits until the next play, and wouldn't you know it that kid got the ball on a toss. Someone makes the tackle and puts him down and here comes OB flying into the pile and he just annihilated the dude. OB grabs the dude's facemask and uses it to help himself back up off the turf, then looks down and says, 'See what happens if you cheap shot another one of my boys.'"

While his friends shared stories on the ice, Wes sat by himself on the bench, resting his arms along the ledge with his head propped up on his hands.

Danny Stone sat down next to his friend. He hadn't changed into his hockey gear. He still had on jeans, a jacket and work boots.

Dan put his arm around Wes.

"This sucks," he whispered.

Wes just nodded.

44

Christmas came and went. There wasn't much celebration in town. Families with little ones went through the motions, but the most joyful time of the year didn't feel that way.

A memorial grew at the site of the accident. A cross made of flowers appeared the morning after. Soon after Eastport T-shirts and hats circled the flowers, along with notes from friends and classmates. Some Pink Floyd CDs, a six-pack of beer, and dozens of teddy bears were added.

On the morning of December 26th Wes pulled his Jeep up to the site. He sat behind the wheel for 20 minutes, trying to work up the courage to do what he'd come to do. Tears streamed down his face. It had been just three days, but it felt like he'd been in mourning forever.

He picked up his phone and hit the speed dial and put the phone on speaker. It rang twice and went to voicemail.

"It's your boy, OB. Don't leave a message, I'll never listen to it. Text me, peace."

Wes laughed. "Collin, I'm leaving a message. I miss you, man."

Ending the call with a push of a button, he connected with his other friend's cell number and it went right to voicemail.

"Hey, it's Craig. I'm either busy or ducking you. Leave a message."

How many times had he heard that recording before? Maybe a thousand times. Craig didn't include that he also probably wasn't answering because he'd misplaced his phone. He was always looking for it, and it was almost always stuck in the couch cushions in his living room, or on the floor in Wes's Jeep.

Wes couldn't think of the right words. Who was he leaving a message for anyway? It wasn't like his best friend would ever hear it. What the hell was he doing? Obviously, he was losing his mind.

He grabbed a piece of paper off the seat and a tack he'd grabbed out of the junk drawer in the kitchen and walked toward the tree the car had hit. Stepping over the collection of mementos and flowers that littered the ground, he stuck the paper to the tree and jogged back to the Jeep. Dead leaves and dirty snow spun under his tires as he drove off with no destination in mind.

A half-hour before sunset a group of teenage girls stopped at the site to leave a card and a bouquet.

"What's that on the tree?" one asked. She'd sat next to Collin in English class the year before. He had made her laugh so hard once during a discussion of a story they'd read that she peed her pants a little.

"It looks like a note," another said. She looked closer, turned her phone's camera on and took a picture of the note.

When they got back into the car she read it out loud.

"It says, 'Boys, I miss you. You were and will always be my brothers. We're just lost souls swimming in a fish bowl."

"Huh, what does that mean?"

The girl that had taken the photo shook her head. "Hell if I know."

45

Emily didn't hear Wes knock on the door the first time. His second made her jump and poke herself with a needle in the middle of her left hand.

"Ouch... What the?"

Wes sheepishly stuck his head into the room and apologized for scaring her.

"You okay?" he asked.

She shrugged. That question could be taken so many different ways at the moment. Her hand hurt, but she'd get over that. Her heart, her head, her psyche, those things would take a while longer.

You don't earn a captaincy in lacrosse without having seen your own blood a few times, though. Emily sucked at the pinprick out of instinct and then wiped it off on her jeans. She then set back to what she had been doing.

Wes looked around the room he'd been in so many times. Almost everything was in its proper place. The glow-in-the-dark Pink Floyd poster was over the bed. The legs of a pair of jeans hung out of a hamper, along with a T-shirt from a long-ago concert. A half-drunk bottle of water sat on a nightstand next to the bed. The laptop computer was on the desk, as were piles of papers that were either completed or pending homework assignments. Wes realized that the pending ones weren't going to be finished.

Emily sat on the bed and stitched. Wes walked to the desk and turned on the computer. He eased out the chair and sat backward. He leaned toward Emily and watched her work for a few minutes. Carefully she poked the needle through the fabric, pulled it taut and then went down and through the fabric, repeating over and over. He had to hand it to her, she was pretty good at sewing. Who knew?

"How's it coming along?" he finally asked, breaking the silence.

Blowing the hair out of her eyes, she stopped her task. She let out a long sigh before replying. "Slow, but it's almost done."

"Good," Wes answered. He had no idea what else to say.

"I've got to admit, this seems like a sick joke. It's the day after Christmas and instead of eating turkey sandwiches and returning stuff that doesn't fit, I'm here sewing an assistant captain's letter on my boyfriend's jersey that he'll never get to wear. Seems pretty screwed up."

"Yes, it is," Wes replied. "You're doing a good job, though. Looks better than the hockey tape job that Craig did. I still can't believe he played with it like that. Oh man, only Bish."

Wes shifted the chair toward the desk and began to click icons on the computer until he found what he wanted. He entered Craig's email address into Gmail and paused at the password prompt.

"Craig didn't change his password, did he?" Wes asked Emily.

She almost smiled.

"I don't think so."

Wes typed in, "3mily8rown."

"I've got to admit, I'm a little jealous. I've known him a lot longer than you," Wes said.

Wes navigated through the icons to Craig's cloud space where all his phone's photographs had been stored. He opened a new folder and began moving over his favorites to be printed up for a display at the upcoming funeral. After tying off the final loop in her sewing job, Emily stood over her friend's shoulder and watched as snapshots of her boyfriend's last few years flashed on the screen.

There were plenty of silly selfies starring Emily and Craig, Wes and Craig, Collin and Craig, and teammates and acquaintances galore. Wes stopped on one, shot at the beach, and laughed. "Your dad has to know how that happened, right?" Wes asked Emily as they stared at the screen. She nodded as a tear streamed down her face.

After looking through pictures for close to an hour, Wes backed out of the cloud. Craig's email page popped up. There was a new email from East

Carolina University waiting in his inbox.

"I wonder what that is?" Wes said as he clicked to open it.

46

"Should we be opening Craig's emails?" Emily asked with a protective tone in her voice.

"Em, come on," Wes said. "He and I shared just about everything, and I don't think he'd get mad at me for looking at an email from a college. Besides, what if it says he got in? Wouldn't Cookie want to know that? I mean, maybe not now, but eventually I think she'd want to know. Right?"

Emily scrunched up her brow. Finally, she agreed. "Okay, I guess it couldn't hurt to look."

Wes opened the email with a click of the mouse and read out loud what was on the screen. The email was from the admissions center at ECU.

"Dear Craig," it read, "Thank you for your application and essay submission. This email is confirmation that we have received your paperwork. We receive many applications but look forward to reviewing yours soon. Thank you for your submission to East Carolina University. Go, Pirates!"

"Just a form letter, nothing to get too excited about," Wes said with a shrug.

Emily took a different meaning from the email, though. She had a real grin on her face.

"What?" Wes asked.

"He did it. Good for him. He said he couldn't, but I kept telling him he could. I knew he could."

Confused, Wes asked, "Could do what?"

"Craig almost didn't apply because part of the application was writing an essay about the biggest adversity he had overcome, and what he learned from it," Emily explained. "For him, there was only one real answer to that... Losing his mom."

"Oh," Wes said.

"Yeah," Emily continued. "You were closer to him than anyone, even me. You know that he didn't like to talk about that subject at all. It was too hard for him. He told me he was going to apply somewhere else instead just because of that. The baseball stuff must have changed his mind."

"So, you didn't read it, then?" Wes asked.

"No, I would have loved to. There were times when we'd sit out on the beach at night and look at the stars and I could tell he was sad. I figured he was thinking about her. She was so young when she died."

As Emily spoke, Wes moved the mouse around the computer and clicked into the "Sent Mail" folder. He then found an email addressed to East Carolina University. Without asking Emily what she thought, he continued to click until he found what he wanted.

Emily read it out loud as Wes followed along on the screen.

Life is too short to frown. I believe that with all of my heart. Like Christmas gifts, smiles are better to give. If you make someone else smile then you've had a good day. That's what I think, anyway.

The person I loved to make smile the most was my mom. No matter how difficult her life was, she always put me first. I only spent the first 10 years of my life with her, and the last two were very hard. Her smiles were forced most of the time. She did her best to pretend they weren't, but I knew. The cancer was eating away at her insides, but on the outside, she did her best to make me feel like it would all be fine in the end.

Two weeks before the day I saw her smile for the last time I saw her best smile ever, or at least the best one I'd ever seen. Mom hadn't gotten to see any of my games because she was either in the hospital or bed. I was playing in Little League with the big kids, the 11 and 12-year-olds. They were bigger and stronger, and I had a hard time for the first few weeks. I looked into the stands that Saturday afternoon, and there she was. It was awesome. She waved to me, and I waved back. My coach didn't know what was going on, and he yelled at me in right field to "keep my head in the game."

My coach might have been clueless about my family life, but he knew a lot about baseball. With mom watching, I finally put my coach's advice to work. He loved to say, "Swing like you mean it." I swung with everything my 85 pounds had and lined one straight over the pitcher's head. It skipped by the outfielders to the fence. My first hit was a legitimate double. It might have been a triple if I hadn't been so shocked when I hit the ball that I stood in place in the batter's box to admire it. The best part was hearing my mom, who whispered almost all the time now, yell, "Yay, Craig!" at the top of her lungs from the crowd.

After the game, I ran up the hill to where she was watching. My grandmother had brought her a beach chair so she could be comfortable. Her smile was the best I've ever seen. She opened her arms so wide and I ran into them. She squeezed me as hard as she could and told me she was proud. I don't think I'll ever be that happy again. I hit the ball, and my mom saw. It made her smile.

Two weeks later my smile went away for a long time. My beautiful mom was taken from me. The sadness is still with me a lot of the time. I miss her so much. It was "us against the world," she liked to say. She might not be in the stands anymore, but it's still me and her against the world, forever.

Life goes on. Knowing that the person you love won't be in your life is a hard thing to accept, but it makes the memories even better.

The memories make you smile.

47

At Wellington, Scott Frazier had worn a suit and tie to every road trip the team had gone on. It was a team rule, they had to "dress the part for a business trip" the coach had said. That made sense in theory, but it made for pretty uncomfortable bus rides across New England. The trip to Orono Prep in Maine had especially sucked, having to ride five hours in a bus in the least comfortable clothes he owned.

Scott's mother had recently returned from the dry cleaners and handed him his travel suit. He tore off the plastic bag and hung the newly pressed blue blazer and pants on the hook in the bathroom, took a quick shower and got dressed. His black hair still dripped, leaving wet spots on the jacket's shoulders and collar, as he came downstairs to see his friends. Wes Garrett and Josh Hutchinson were in the living room waiting for him, and dressed similarly.

"You ready?" Josh asked.

"No, but let's get this over with," Scott said.

The three boys drove in silence to the local funeral home for the first of four straight days of mourning. Collin's wake was set for tonight, then his funeral would be the next morning. On Thursday a wake for Craig was scheduled, and he would be buried on Friday.

This was not the way the Boys had planned on spending their week off from school. Wes and Josh were supposed to be playing in a mini-tournament with the high school team this week at the rink and had planned to drive to Braintree to see their friends on the basketball team play as well. An announcement had been made that all Eastport High School athletic events had been canceled for the week. The school hoped to return to its regularly scheduled games after New Year's Day. In the meantime, the teams were allowed to practice if they wanted to. Sports didn't seem nearly as important to anyone involved as it had before.

Wes pulled into a parking spot and they entered through the back door, as they'd been instructed to in an email from Coach Scadorski. Most of the team was already there. Having spent time together at the rink over the past few days, the immediate shock had worn off and now the group felt a responsibility to their friends' families. They had to support them right now.

Scott took in the scene in the sanctuary. Collin's parents sat next to an open casket. There was a huge picture of OB next to the shiny wood box. The picture was the one that had been taken for this year's hockey program, and he wore his famous smirk, the one that always made it look like he'd gotten one over on you. Girls loved that smirk. Most guys hated it. Man, did he look happy in that picture, though.

The expression in the photograph was a stark contrast to Collin's parents, neither of whom looked like they'd be able to stand on their own. Collin's older brother, Roman, came over to shake hands with all of the boys, leaving their younger sister, Samantha, with a cousin on a couch.

It was obvious why Roman was one of the best athletes Eastport had ever produced. He looked like if he tore his suit jacket and button-up shirt away, there'd be blue tights with a big yellow 'S' underneath. Roman O'Brien was huge and made the collection of high school athletes around him look small in comparison.

Roman's monstrous hand reached out to Wes first, and he pulled him in for a hug. The now 24-year-old did the same with all of the boys that he'd known from back in the day. The others he acknowledged with a fist bump or a nod. Then he spoke to the entire group.

"Guys, thanks for coming out. Obviously, this is tough for my family, but I know it's tough for you too because Collin, and Craig, were part of your hockey family, too. When this thing officially starts, they're going to say a prayer and then everyone is going to approach the casket, say a prayer, and then go through the greeting line.

"My folks are kind of out of it, so if they forget to tell you, let me say that you all made Collin happy. Going to practice and playing games with you guys were his absolute favorite things in the world. He loved you guys, and we love you too."

Promptly at 4 PM, the proceedings began the way that Roman had laid out. Mrs. O'Brien sobbed as she hugged each of her son's teammates and friends. Mr. O'Brien, who smelled faintly of bourbon, rocked back and forth on unsteady feet as he shook each of their hands. Roman and Samantha offered thanks and hugs to them all.

As Josh and Scott finished their way through the hugs and shakes, they decided to grab some fresh air outside. What they saw shocked them. The line to enter through the front door stretched down the sidewalk, through the parking lot and snaked back toward the street.

"Holy crap, how many people are here?" Josh wondered.

"Gotta be over 1,000, maybe 2,000," Scott guessed.

That's when they noticed the red jerseys, and the green ones, and the blue ones, and the white ones. Dozens of kids from high schools from around the state stood in front of the funeral home with their hockey jerseys over their jackets.

Scott recognized the coach from Hyannis and went over to ask him what was going on.

"Hey Coach Jones, what's all of this?" Frazier asked.

Louis Jones had once told a referee that Scott Frazier deserved jail time instead of a minor penalty after a roughing call against the Eastport defenseman two years ago. When he was in high school he'd once challenged an entire bench of players to step on the ice and fight him. They all declined. When it came to ice hockey, the man was crazy.

Away from the ice, Louis Jones was one of the most kind-hearted people that walked the earth. The day before Thanksgiving he had his hockey players over to his home to put together care packages that were later delivered to local families in need. On weeknights, he'd convinced the Hyannis Athletic Department to allow canned food to be payment for tickets, and that food was given to a local pantry for distribution. He was one of the good guys.

Coach Jones threw his arms around each of the Eastport players and hugged them tight.

175

"Boys, I'm so sorry. We are really going to miss O'Brien and Bishop, great competitors, tough kids, good hockey players. They were Cannons through and through."

"Thanks, Coach," Josh said, "but what's with all of the guys out here?"

"Well, me and some of the coaches were talking. Hockey around here is one big family. When one of us loses someone, we all do. This is an honor guard for Craig and Collin. There will be teams here every night this week, out here, standing guard for those boys, and for all of the Cannons. It's just a way we can support you all. You are not alone in this."

The boys were stunned. What can you say to something like that, other than, "Thank you."

"Scotty, hold up a second. I'll be right back," and Josh jogged back into the funeral home. He came back with all of his teammates, who were equally impressed and surprised by the show of love they were seeing.

As the team's captain, Cyrus Carpenter stepped forward and shook Coach Jones' hand. "Coach, this is awesome. I don't know what to say."

"You don't have to say anything, son. If it had been us, you and your teammates would be out there right now."

Carpenter patted Frazier and Hutchinson on the back and asked them to get the team lined up single file. Cyrus then led the way as they walked down all of the lines of hockey players and shook all of their hands, thanking them for coming out to support their team, and more importantly, Collin and Craig.

"Cy, this is crazy. There's like eight different teams here," Frazier said as they finished the line.

"I know, and Coach Jones said it'd be like this every night this week. It's pretty amazing."

48

An hour drive away a hockey game was about to begin. Boston Baptist High School and Arlington Regional were about to play a game that everyone that cared even a little bit about high school hockey in the state of Massachusetts knew was a huge game. At least nine of the players on the ice that night were going to play at a Division 1 college somewhere in the next few years. Scouts lined the areas behind each goal, notepads and cell phones at the ready. The talk of the day, of course, was the situation in Eastport. Things like, "Such a shame," and, "Could've happened anywhere," were bandied about.

The Bears and Airmen skated on to the ice promptly at 6:55 for a 7 PM drop of the puck. The teams were amped. Ryan O'Sullivan, the captain for Baptist, and Johnny Fordham, his counterpart from Regional, were the first ones on the ice for their teams that night. Typically they'd each high-five and tap each of their teammates as they hit the surface with words of encouragement for each boy. Not tonight. It was each team's first game since the tragedy on Cape Cod.

O'Sullivan was wearing number 32 tonight, a leftover jersey that had been put aside for some lucky sophomore or freshman that would get a late-season call-up to the varsity to fill in for an injured guy. His usual number 10 jersey was on a hanger in his hand, as was another jersey, the 19 shirt. A teammate had given up his shirt for the night and was wearing another unissued jersey, the 40 jersey.

Holding the shirts up high, O'Sullivan skated once around the entirety of the rink with the two gold and blue jerseys held high at his sides. From the other end of the ice Airmen Captain Johnny Fordham did the same thing with the white and crimson 10 and 19 jerseys. The captains met at center ice and bumped fists before heading to their respective benches. They handed the shirts over to a coach from each side, who hung the jerseys high above their benches.

That same ceremony was repeated hundreds of times over the next week.

No one from the state of Massachusetts wore a number 10 – Collin O'Brien's digit – or a 19 – the number worn by Craig Bishop over the next two weeks out of respect. The numbers were taken out of circulation statewide.

Each member of the Baptist Bears had taped their sticks with white, with the same message repeated 22 times across the blades "RIP CO/CB" written in maroon Sharpie. The Airmen had chosen to wear eye black tape for the game with "CO 10" written in white Sharpie under one eye, and "CB 19" on the other.

A moment of silence was held before the drop of the puck. Then the National Anthem played. By the end of the song, a number of the Airmen had to remove their tributes from their faces. The tape was soaked from tears and wouldn't stick properly.

49

Collin O'Brien's funeral was held the next day. Danny Stone had been able to detach himself emotionally for the entire ceremony. Sitting with his teammates in the third row of St. Xavier's Church, he picked a spot on the wall behind the altar and stared at it for almost the entire hour. When his teammates kneeled, he kneeled. When they stood, he stood, but he robotically went through the motions.

The hardest part was being a pallbearer. Danny avoided looking at the casket as much as he could. He stood behind Wes as they rolled the casket down the aisle. Helping place the casket inside the hearse was the hardest thing he'd ever done. Once it was inside he peeled off from the group and headed straight for his parents' car. He rode with his parents to the cemetery and did not utter a word. The stoicism ended when the casket was lowered. The priest grabbed a handful of dirt and dropped it onto the box.

The feelings Danny had been ignoring bubbled to the surface. He did his best to remain still as the box went lower and flowers were thrown in after.

"Screw this," Danny muttered, turning on his heel and walking back to his car. "Screw this."

Danny's father, Richard Stone, followed his son. Placing a hand on his shoulder, he turned his boy back toward him. Before he could offer a word, Danny threw his arms around him and sobbed.

"It's all my fault," Danny said. "If I'd slowed down earlier they wouldn't have tried to pass me on that corner. If I'd left the rink later none of this would have happened. I could have changed this a million different ways, but I didn't, and now my friends are dead."

Richard's heart broke.

"Buddy, there's nothing I can say that will make this any better. You need to know that it isn't your fault, though. Collin made a bad decision, a horrible one, but it was his, not yours. I'm just thankful that they didn't hit your car," Rich said with tears streaking down his face. "I'm just glad I'm not having to go through what the O'Briens are right now, that it isn't you in that box."

With his arm around his son, Richard Stone walked his son back to the family's minivan and got behind the wheel. The two sat in silence until Leigh, Rich's wife and Danny's mom, got into the car after spending a few minutes shaking hands and hugging the other mothers. Their conversations all revolved around how beautiful the ceremony was, how thankful they were that it wasn't their own child and their sorrow for the O'Brien and Bishop families. Leigh had volunteered to bring meals over to both families homes later in the week as part of a schedule that the hockey moms had put together to make sure that the two families were cared for.

Gently taking her seat in the passenger side of the vehicle, Leigh turned toward her son and asked how he was.

"Not good," he answered truthfully. "This hurts. I just wish someone would tell me what I'm supposed to do. I have no idea what to do. Christmas vacation is usually my favorite time of the year. Now I'm going to funerals, there's no hockey, no practice, no school, just ... nothing. There's just nothing."

50

As people found their way into the church for Craig's funeral two days later they passed posterboard after posterboard covered with photographs that starred Craig, Collin and all of their friends. Stuffing their faces with fried dough at the Little League field, dancing at the prom, flexing like pro wrestlers, trying to look tough, trying to look smart. Memories spanned from the days they were born to just a few days ago.

For the majority of those attending, the images were something to look at as they waited their turn to say how sorry they were, just a glimpse at two young men who were done making memories. For those closest to Craig and Collin, they were reminders of much better times that had been had and how much they'd lost.

Emily Brown had been near the very front of the line of thousands. She had helped assemble the posterboards and found herself staring blankly at them when given a rare moment to herself. The pair had met in middle school, gotten close in eighth grade, and started dating early in their junior year. Their friends all had the same reaction to the news that they were together: "Well it's about time."

Emily absently scanned the anthology of images, coming back to one in particular. It had been taken at the beach, on a Sunday afternoon last August. Her smile was radiant. Her cheek was so close to Craig's that the only way you could tell where one began and the other ended was that she had a golden summer tan and his skin was more the color of a boiled crustacean. Black Ray Bans nearly obscured the large shiner under his left eye, the one closest to her.

Craig had scribbled in blue marker on the bottom of the picture, "The things I do for you."

Walter Brown laughed inside at the note on the photo, because he felt the same way.

The day before the photo had been taken was Emily's 18th birthday. A month prior she'd asked him if she could have a lavish birthday party since she'd missed out on a genuine Sweet 16, or 17 for that matter. Every year at that time Emily attended one of the nation's most elite lacrosse camps. It had made all the difference in her game and was a big reason that she had a pile of recruiting letters on the desk in her bedroom. With birthday number 18 falling on the weekend, it worked out perfectly that she'd be home in time.

Emily's father loved all of his kids very much and his successes in the world of plastic recycling had allowed him to give them the types of things his parents had not been able to afford. Mr. Brown's work ethic had not skipped a generation. His kids didn't have to worry about whether or not Mom and Dad would make the rent payment as he had. They enjoyed nice clothes and things, but they repaid their blessings with hard work in class and in sports.

Linda Brown went all out helping her daughter plan the party. They rented a soda fountain, cotton candy machine and paid $300 to one of Emily's friends to DJ the event from 8 to midnight. Emily was allowed to have her girlfriends spend the night, but the boys were informed of two rules in particular. One, they would all wear appropriate clothing – including jackets and ties – and two, they would all hit the road no later than 12:30 AM. Those were Walter Brown's rules and they would be heeded.

Emily and her mother had found an elegant black, backless dress that made Walter's little girl look very grown up. Her father knew it had cost him more than his parents had spent on his school clothes for four years of high school back in the day, but he chose not to make a fuss with Linda over that expense, or the swipe of the credit card that had been run at the hair salon. His daughter looked pretty amazing, and the expense was hardly worth bickering over with Linda. She seemed even happier with how Emily looked than Emily did.

The basement was turned into a pseudo nightclub and the kids certainly had fun. The parents spent most of the night out on their deck, getting as far away as possible from the persistent pounding of the bass-heavy music emanating from downstairs. Brown's ears perked up when a few of the boys had come up to grab some air and offered up that, "a bunch of them were spending the night at Cy's house." Cyrus Carpenter lived just two streets away.

What Emily didn't realize was that her father had once been a teenage boy and had a pretty good idea of what would happen later that night. A man of action, he put a defensive plan together to spoil the fun. The last thing he needed was to be a grandfather prematurely. He'd already lost enough of his once-thick black hair. He liked to tell Emily that he'd had a full head of hair before she got to high school and its retreat was tied directly to her going through puberty.

Promptly at midnight he turned on the basement lights and barked down the stairs that "the clock is ticking" on the party's completion. The DJ began packing up, and the young men gathered their discarded jackets, ties and dress shirts. All of that dancing had made the basement smell like a mash of perspiration and cotton candy. It would take the Browns weeks to air the room out properly.

With Emily's parents waiting by the door, the gentlemen placed pecks on the cheeks of their dates and thanked the Browns for allowing them over. Craig, Collin and the rest of the Boys that had come over shuffled out the door, hopped into cars and vacated the premises.

Within 20 minutes the five girls that were spending the night as guests of Emily had all shed their gowns in favor of T-shirts and gym shorts. They had gone from looking like they were headed for a stroll down the catwalk to a jog on the beach. Emily thanked her mom and dad for "an amazing evening" and promised that the girls were headed back downstairs to "watch chick flicks and talk."

Walter nodded his head, kissed his daughter goodnight and headed upstairs.

While serving in the Army out of high school as part of the GI Bill, Walter had pulled night watch duty on numerous occasions. Every two weeks or so it was his turn to stand outside the barracks and walk a circuit, making sure all was safe and sound.

On this night he knew exactly where the enemy would be attempting its infiltration. He grabbed his hunting binoculars and scanned the perimeter, focusing on the front of his home. The lavish estate was surrounded on three sides by a stone wall, with twin boulders marking the entrance to the 200-foot driveway. He expected he'd spot the invaders sometime within the next two hours.

It had been 75 minutes when he observed their approach. Five single LED lights, undoubtedly emanating from smartphones, twinkled up the road and stopped in unison just short of the boulders. They were going for a frontal assault, he determined as the lights were extinguished. The young men had gone through no training when it came to stealth approaches and their attempt to infiltrate the area quietly was absurd.

Walter slowly shook his head and laughed to himself. There were few things as predictable as the motivations of teenage boys. If he was 30 years younger he'd have been leading the charge for the offense, but tonight he was the captain of the defense and his game plan was foolproof.

Having informed Linda of his intention, he whispered into the bedroom for her to come over and to watch what was about to unfold. She whispered in her husband's ear, "Be nice, Walter. Remember, you snuck into my dormitory quite a few times." His response was simple.

"Why do you think I'm doing this?"

The slow process of placing one foot gently in front of the other was stopped dead when they heard the noise. There is no mistaking the sound of a shotgun being pumped and loaded.

"I don't know who the hell is in my yard, but you've got exactly two seconds to turn around and get out of here before I use this thing and call the cops to pick up the pieces."

Craig was in the middle of the group which had been led by Collin. Having spent a weekend hunting with his uncle last Christmas, Collin O'Brien not only knew the sound but had witnessed the damage that a shotgun could wreak first hand. He shouted, "Crap!" spun 180 degrees and bolted back the way he'd come. Both Craig and Wesley Garrett were in his way. Wes, the thicker of the two boys, was only knocked to his knees, but his forward momentum had resulted in a chop block at the back of Craig's legs.

184

Walter Brown heard the thump against his stone wall and hoped that no one had been seriously hurt. He laughed despite himself the next night when Emily had shown her father the photo on her cell phone she'd taken with her boyfriend.

"How'd he get the shiner?" he nonchalantly asked his daughter.

Emily certainly knew the truth. She and her girlfriends had conspired to get the boys to come back for some late night shenanigans. They were disappointed when the secret knock never came. Craig had texted Emily a message informing her of her father's actions.

Trying to save face, Emily claimed Craig had gotten the black eye from playing beach football with his friends earlier that day. Walter hadn't disputed the explanation. He'd made his point the night before. Craig and his friends would think twice before trying that kind of stunt at his house again.

Emily was snapped back to the here and now when Walter Brown came over to his daughter and put his arm around her. He squeezed her tightly, then noticed which picture she'd been staring at for the past few minutes.

"Amazing a kid that good at football, a state champion and everything, could get a black eye just playing on the beach with his friends like that," he said with a knowing smile.

Emily just hugged her father a little tighter.

51

Four days of mourning had taken its toll on everyone. Wes felt exhausted as he headed to the final family gathering, a buffet dinner at a restaurant owned by Cookie Foley's friends. He hadn't eaten much over the past few days, and now all he wanted to do was eat himself to sleep.

Leaning back against the wall in a corner booth, he loosened his tie and eyeballed the spread of food coming out of the kitchen at Palmer's Pub. Roast beef, mashed potatoes, peas and carrots, salad and cold cuts. He grabbed a plate and made his way to the buffet line, hoping to avoid conversation at all costs. He simply could not accept another moment of condolences from one of Collin's long-lost cousins or Craig's aunt on his mother's side twice removed. He'd run out of things to say. All he could do was nod his head and say, "Thank you," at this point. It was all so numbing.

Wes forked two nice pieces of roast beef onto his plate, heaped some mashed potatoes next to them and drowned it all in gravy. His mother would tell him he needed salad and some veggies, but she was on the other side of the room and he wasn't in the mood for her input on his diet at the moment.

He hurried back to the booth he'd claimed earlier and scooted all the way to the inside, trying to hide his identity in hopes of eating in peace. If anyone other than his girlfriend Melissa sat down next to him right now he would be pretty perturbed.

As he shoveled a forkful of gravy-soaked potatoes into his mouth, he was interrupted by Melissa, who had Emily and a mystery girl in tow. Emily's eyes were red and puffy. She'd obviously been crying all week. She and Craig had not only been boyfriend and girlfriend, they'd been friends, too. They were each other's last conversation each night and often the first the next morning. She was lost without him.

Melissa had held up really well. She'd given Wes plenty of space when he needed it, understanding that he had to be with his teammates and family

186

more than her right now. Emily needed her more than he did now, anyways. Her appearance brought a rare smile to Wes's face. She wore a classy sleeveless black dress, with some tiny gold stud earrings and a simple cross around her neck. Wes made a mental note to tell her later how good she looked.

"Hey, girls, who's your friend?" Wes asked.

"Babe, this is Jennifer, she's from Plymouth. She has a story that might make you laugh," Melissa said.

"It made me laugh," Emily added, which was certainly saying something right now.

"I don't know if I'm in the mood for funny stories," Wes said. "But, okay, give it a shot. Make me laugh."

Jennifer gave a half grin and explained that she was a freshman at UMass-Boston and was living with some friends in Braintree. She felt awful for what was going on here in Eastport and her heart hurt for all of them.

"Jen, that's really sweet of you, but you promised me funny," Wes said. "No offense, but if someone else tells me how sorry they are for me right now I might explode."

"Okay, let me cut to the chase. So, it was a Saturday night in early October and me and my girls headed out into the city to hit some clubs, have some guys buy us some drinks, just blow off some steam," she started. "We were at, I think it was Molly's Chamber – down near Fenway – dancing and having a good time. I was at the bar and this really cute, tall, blonde guy dropped a horribly cheesy pickup line. He asked me if I got hurt when I fell from heaven."

The girls giggled and said in unison, "Collin."

"Yup, Collin. We chatted a bit and he was pouring it on really thick. I think I believed about 50 percent of what he was saying. He told me how nice I looked, and how he'd love to talk somewhere more quiet, and that he was some big deal football player that was trying to decide which D1 offer to take. Of course, that was how I figured out he was still in high school, and normally I'd have walked away right then and there."

187

The girls nodded along.

"Okay, go on," Wes prompted.

"Well, like I said, the girls and I had plans to bar hop that night and they came over to tell me it was time to move on. A part of me really wanted to stay, because he was charming even if he was pretty cheesy. I told him to text me and maybe we could hang some other time. He smiled, pulled me in and gave me a little kiss on the cheek, and said, 'I'd like that,' and then he puts a business card in my hand."

"A business card?" Wes asked quizzically.

"Yup," the newcomer said and she slid it across the table for Wes to look at.

Wes eased his fingernails under the edge of the card and lifted it into the palm of his hand. He read the words on the card and laughed out loud.

The top line had Collin's name spelled out in a fancy font and his cell number and email addresses were in the corner. Underneath his name read two words, "Noted Expert."

"Son of a bitch, he actually did it."

"I asked him what that was all about, but he just told me that I'd have to find out in person. If he'd asked me out I probably would have gone, and he'd have told me, but we never got the chance. What's the story?"

Wes hadn't been this amused since before his life had changed forever. Leave it to Collin to crack him up from beyond the grave.

"Yeah, I can explain it. I don't know if the payoff is going to be what you were hoping for, but it does sum up OB pretty great," Wes started.

"It was probably late June, we'd just gotten out of school, and it was Sunday night. Me, OB, Scotty, Danny and Cy were over at Bish's house watching TV."

"So it was like any other night, pretty much," Emily said with a grin.

"Yeah, pretty much... So, we were watching TV and one of those stupid talking head shows came up while we were flipping channels. They were talking about some disaster somewhere in Africa or something, and some old guy shows up on the screen and the graphic flashes with his name, and next to it says "Noted Expert." I didn't think Collin was even paying attention. He was trying to figure out something on his guitar, and he looks up at the TV and says, 'That's it, boys, that's what I want to be when I grow up.'

"We all looked at him kinda funny. Craig, says something like, 'You want to be an old wrinkly white dude in a bad suit?'

"Now you girls knew Collin well and you know he loved to be the center of attention. He stands up, and says, 'No, I want to be a noted expert, that way I get paid to go on TV and talk about whatever, and everyone will just believe whatever the hell it is I'm saying. What a life, to get paid to BS about stuff without ever having to actually do anything. My goal in life, going forward, is to be Collin O'Brien, Noted Expert. Well, that'll be my second career after NFL superstar. Everyone has to have something to fall back on."

The girls all giggled.

"That's Collin," Emily said, shaking her head. "That's Collin to a T."

Wes laughed to himself and agreed. "Yes, it was. One-hundred percent."

52

Scott stared at a photograph of the 2004 Red Sox winning the World Series on the wall. The joy in the pitcher's face as he leaped toward his catcher said everything that needed to be said about that moment. His father noticed his interest.

"That was a hell of a couple of weeks. You were like three years old, your brother was four. The Sox had just come back from down three games to beat New York the week before and then steamrolled St. Louis in the Series. Everyone in the state was walking on air, it was huge," he remembered. "I went to work the next day still smelling like beer and champagne. I barely slept the night before. Amazing, loved that team."

Looking away from the photograph on the wall, Scott noticed Wes on the other side of the restaurant laughing with Melissa, Emily and some other girl he'd never seen before. He wondered what could actually be funny right now. He'd have to ask his friend later on.

His mother, sitting next to him, recaptured his attention with a simple question. He wasn't quite ready to have the conversation here and now.

"Scott, I know it's been a tough week. Are you ready to go back to school on Monday, or do you think you're going to need an extra day or two to pack? I could call the dean and let him know what's going on and that you're going to be late, I'm sure the coach will understand."

"Um, about that Mom. I'm not going back."

"Scott, we've talked about this. You can't turn your back on this opportunity. This is your future we're talking about."

For the past several months Scott had spent nearly every day miserable. The deaths of his two close friends had left him numb. The only thing that had stemmed his downward spiral had been getting back on the ice with his old friends in Eastport.

"You know how dad said he loved that Red Sox team. I love my team here even more. I miss these guys horribly," Scott admitted. "I feel lost at Wellington. Yeah, I'm doing good for the team, but I don't think of myself as part of the team. The guys are okay, but they're not family like they are here. After everything that's happened the last few weeks I've realized that I need to be here, with these guys on this team playing at home, going to school at home."

His mother paused. Before she could answer, his father spoke up.

"Okay," he said. "I get it."

"Hold on a second," Dottie Frazier said. "Do you realize what he's giving up here, Mark? The opportunity..."

"Yes, I do. I also know that Scott is really good at hockey and the college coaches aren't going to stop calling. Really, though, why does that matter if he's miserable? The kid needs a break from that and it's not like his heart is in it up there. If his heart isn't in it he's not going to play very well and that's going to put off the colleges. Coming home would be better, staying home I guess."

Scott was dumbfounded. He'd expected this to turn into World War III.

"I don't know. Will they even let him play in high school now that he's already moved on to private? How does that work?"

Scott had researched the topic. It's amazing what you can find on the internet. "The governing body has an amendment to their rules that allows for the immediate reinstatement of a transferring student for "extraordinary circumstances." If nothing else my situation has been that. Coach said he can put in the paperwork, but he wasn't going to do anything until we'd discussed it and you guys were on board. I have to be enrolled for 10 days before they'll let me play a game, but I can start practicing immediately. I kind of already have."

Dottie inhaled deeply, then acquiesced. "Okay, tell him to put in the paperwork. We will enroll you back at EHS on Monday."

Mark Frazier sat up a little taller in his chair and looked his son right in the eyes.

"One condition," Scott's dad said. "You don't just play for the team. You play for you and you play for Collin and Craig. That team lost two good players and a big piece of their identity. You make up for it. You go out there and be the best player on the ice every night, not because you can, but because you owe it to yourself, and to OB and Bish. Do you understand me?"

"Yessir, absolutely. I will," Scott promised.

"Alright then, let's get you back in a Cannons uniform. There's one problem, though," his father said.

"What's that, Dad?"

"I'm pretty sure that they gave your number to Moxon."

"They can put me in a JV shirt at this point, I don't care. Mox can have it, I'll find another one.

53

John Scadorski stood in the corner of the pub accepting thanks for the speech he'd given at the funeral. It was similar to the one he'd had to give earlier in the week. He'd talked about the character and vitality of his two players, how much heart they'd brought to the teams that they played on every day and the gaping hole that had been left in the hearts of – not just his team – but the entire community.

Television crews from all of the Boston TV stations had broadcast the funeral services. Scadorski was surrounded by reporters asking him questions outside the church, but he'd walked right by them. He'd said enough this week and just couldn't put up with another idiotic query.

He had had to mute his cell phone and screen his incoming calls since the accident. The phone just wouldn't stop ringing, and the majority of the calls were coming from reporters looking for him to give an insightful quote regarding the tragedy, or to tell him how he planned on having his team move on.

The truth of the matter was that the coach had no idea how the Cannons were going to move forward. It wasn't like he could simply ask Google, "How do you lead an emotionally devastated group of young men through an unimaginable tragedy?" They didn't make "An Idiot's Guide to Dealing with the Worst Possible Scenario for a Coach." Maybe he'd write that book when this was all over.

As Scads contemplated what was next, Mark Frazier came over and handed him a pint of Guinness. The coach accepted with a nod and weak smile.

"You look like you could use about a dozen of these," the burly man said to the lanky coach.

"At least," the coach said with a laugh. "Unfortunately, I don't think I'm going to be able to drink my way through the rest of the season."

"Well, I might have a sliver of good news for you," Frazier said.

"That would be nice, but unless you're going to tell me how to fast forward to June so I can just escape out on the water with a fishing pole and some peace and quiet, I don't think it's going to help all that much."

"Well, how about a defenseman?" Frazier said.

"That'd be nice, you know any?" Scadorski said.

"How about the one that lives at my house?"

"That'd be nice. Wait, are you serious?" Scadorski said, his mood turning and his voice rising a bit.

"He's homesick and he misses his family – his hockey family. Truth be told, I'm sure he could get by fine without me and Dottie being in his ear all the time, but he's hurting like they all are. He's lost up there at Wellington, and his grades are nothing to write home about. Being back in Eastport is the right move for him right now, I think," Frazier said.

Scadorski nodded toward Dottie Frazier. "What about her?"

Frazier shrugged.

"She's fine with it, or at least she says she is. The bottom line is that if Scott's miserable he's not going to play his best up there and the whole reason he went there was to show he could play at that level against those kids. He proved he could. Now, he wants to finish things up with his friends," Mark Frazier said. "Before we sign on, though, can you make this happen? Scott said that there's a waiver process and a board review or something. To me, that hardly sounds like this is a done deal."

"I wish I could tell you it's a guarantee, but I can't. Do I think that the board will vote for him? Probably. We've been through a lot, and the circumstances are certainly out of the ordinary. I will do everything I can to fast-track the process," Scadorski said. "Best case scenario, he's back out on the ice with us by January 12. You have to be enrolled for 10 days at the school before you can play, so get him enrolled on Monday morning. He can practice with us that day. Heck, he's been practicing with us since Wellington let out anyways."

"What's the worst case scenario?" Frazier's dad asked.

"Worst case is the Eastport Cannons have the oldest puck boy in the Coastal Atlantic League."

Mark Frazier laughed at the joke, but on the inside, he just hoped that he was making the right decision for his son. If this did not work out for Scott it could be a disaster.

54

The wakes and funerals were over, but as Melissa Johnson stared up at the stars through the moonroof of her father's SUV the pain did not feel any further away. Mel and Emily couldn't escape from the grief, no matter where they went.

If they were going to be sad, they might as well be sad together at a place they both adored. Melissa picked up Em and drove to the quietest spot in Eastport in the winter. She shut off the engine and reclined. Emily, in the passenger seat, put her hands behind her head and looked into outer space.

Outside the wind blew strongly. Sand stung at the truck's exterior and 30 yards away the waves crashed on the beach.

"If it were about 50 degrees warmer I'd say we should go jump in and play in the surf. Those waves have got to be pretty big right about now," Melissa said.

Emily sighed.

"Me and Craig did that back in September, right after school started, but at the beach over by his grandmother's house. I got a bunch of water in my ear and couldn't get it out. When we got back to the house he ran upstairs and got me a towel and I dried off my hair. I was so irritated by the water in my ear," she said.

"Craig told me the best way to get rid of it was to tilt my head and jump up and down on one foot. He said that eventually, the water would drain out that way. So that's what I did, but I couldn't get it out," she continued. "Craig being Craig, he decided he'd show me. So he's standing there in his bathing suit and no shirt and he starts hopping up on one foot to show me the right way. I'm there in jean shorts and a bikini top, and I'm doing the same thing next to him, with my wet hair flapping around and getting everything soaked."

"That must have been quite the sight," Melissa said.

"Oh, it gets better."

"Do tell."

"So I'm bouncing around, and my boobs have got to be flopping like crazy, and he's doing the same thing. We must've looked like crazy people. Just as the water finally starts to drain out for me – I could feel that weird, warm sensation of it leaving the ear canal – his grandmother walks in and sees us there bouncing like a couple of idiots."

Melissa started to laugh, slowly at first, and then harder and harder. Emily caught the giggle bug from her confidante and followed suit.

Fighting for air, Melissa said, "I would have loved to have seen that. What did she do?"

Emily forced herself to stop laughing. Taking a couple of deep breaths, she steadied herself. "Cookie was so funny. She just looked at us and said, 'Is that what you kids call dancing nowadays? Don't you need music?'"

The girls caught their breath as the giggles faded. Silence overtook the car again for a few minutes before Emily broke it.

"Thanks, Mel, I needed that," Emily said. "I've got to be honest, I don't know if I can handle any more crying. My emotions are spent. I just feel numb and empty most of the time."

"I know what you mean," Melissa whispered.

"Hey Melissa, I've got a question."

"Yeah, what?" she replied.

"You know I grew up Catholic, so I guess that means that the boys are probably in purgatory right now if you believe all of that stuff. I've heard that the rules are different for kids, though, and that they get a fastpass – kind of like at an amusement park – straight to Heaven. I've got a lot of friends, though, that claim that they're atheists and that there's no God, no Heaven, no Hell."

"Like a John Lennon song," Melissa quipped.

"Yeah, imagine that. Anyways, my question is, are the boys in Heaven? I mean, I think that they are. They'd have to be. They were good people. They never hurt anybody, at least not maliciously. I just can't imagine it all just fades to black and that's that."

"When I was in grade school I used to spend a week at Vacation Bible School over at Eastport Baptist, down near the ferry to the island. It was a lot of fun, we played games, and everything tied into Jesus and Heaven and all of that," Melissa said as she drew a smiley face into the condensation on the window to her right. "They said you had to accept Jesus into your heart and I did when I was there. I really did."

"I just figured your parents got you into church," Emily said.

"Nope, actually it was kind of the other way around. After that I asked them to take me on Sundays, and they did, and we've been going ever since," Melissa said. "I'd love it if you came with me one of these weekends. You can help me teach the third graders Sunday School. They're so sweet, and it makes me feel good. I always walk out of there feeling happy."

"I'm not sure. I don't think I'd be much help?" Emily said.

"You don't have to do much. I'll teach the class, you just make sure none of them try to escape. Some of them are pretty sneaky," Melissa said.

"I will think about it. It does sound nice," Emily said.

Melissa reached over, grabbed her friend's hand and squeezed it tightly. The friends held hands and focused on the sounds of the wind circling the car and the waves beating the shore just beyond the sand dune.

Emily broke the silence, barely, to whisper a question.

"But what about Collin and Craig, what do you think?"

"What do you mean?"

Emily was almost afraid to ask, but she found it in herself to blurt it out. "Do you think that they're in heaven?"

"I do and I can't wait to see them. Whenever that day comes, I have a feeling that they'll be there to greet us."

Emily thought about that for a second.

"I hope so."

55

Grabbing his cell phone, Wes checked the time and announced that he was running late. "See you after practice tonight," he said to his mom before kissing her on the cheek and leaving the warmth of their home behind.

Wes tossed on his winter jacket, zipped it up and then got into his cold Jeep. The engine roared to life and he quickly turned the heat all the way up before plugging his phone into the stereo and turning on some tunes. Chewing on a bagel his mom had toasted for him, he realized just how alien this morning felt in comparison to all of the others during the school year.

The classic rock streaming station he had his phone set to was playing a Pearl Jam song.

"I"ll ride the wave where it takes me... I'll hold the pain... Release me," Eddie Vedder boomed.

Wes grabbed the wheel harder. He'd been holding the pain in for days. It was his first day back to school and he wasn't really running late. He didn't have to make his usual daily morning stop over at Craig's house.

With a deep breath, Wes settled himself.

"I can do this," he said to the mirror. "I can do this. I'm going to do this."

Wes pulled away from his home as a new song came on. It was the Presidents of the United States of America. They were singing about peaches. It was a silly, inane tune. That was just what the doctor ordered as he drove past the street where he would have turned to pick up his best friend. A cup of coffee or orange juice would have been waiting. He kept driving toward the school, riding by himself. He looked over at the empty passenger seat.

"I miss you, man," Wes said aloud.

He then began singing to himself, "Millions of peaches, peaches for free."

While Wes rode solo to school, Cyrus Carpenter honked his horn from the

Frazier family's driveway and eyeballed the digital clock readout. It was 7:33. School officially began in exactly 17 minutes. They'd make it on time if they didn't hit any red lights and if Scott left his house anytime soon.

As the clock ticked from 33 minutes past the hour to 34 the re-enrolling senior pushed open his front door, waved, and then went back inside. After another minute had passed he returned, with his coat half-on, a backpack slung over his left shoulder and a plate and travel mug precariously balanced in his right-hand. He placed the food and drink on the roof, opened the door and tossed the bag onto the floor and then finished pulling on his parka.

Before he could finish buckling his seat belt Cyrus had the car in reverse and onto the road. Scott nearly choked on his breakfast sandwich as he was tossed back in his seat.

"Cutting it a little close, brother," Cyrus said, trying to keep the irritation out of his voice. "You might not get marked tardy since you haven't officially enrolled yet, but that doesn't mean that I won't. If I get two more this quarter I get a detention, and that means I'll miss a practice, which means I'll miss at least a period of a game and get reamed out by Coach Scads."

"Sorry dude, I couldn't figure out what to wear, or what to eat. My brain isn't working."

"Scott Frazier, are you nervous for your first day of school?" Cyrus asked with a laugh. "You've never been nervous about anything like that before."

"Nah, not nervous, more like anxious. I can't screw this up," he said.

"Dude, it's fine. It's Eastport High. They throw diplomas at people as they walk by the building. You'll be okay."

Knowing that Cyrus was running late, Scott offered to park the car and get the keys back to his buddy later in the day. Carpenter put the car in park, grabbed his stuff and jogged to the entrance, slowed by the ice on the sidewalks.

Scott then circled to the far reaches of the student parking lot and found a space about as far from the school as could be, out near the girls' field hockey field and the tennis courts. He put the car in park, grabbed his stuff and then just stopped in his tracks.

"No big deal Frazier, this is just high school. You've got this," he said before exhaling and zipping up his coat.

Because the school day had already officially begun, Scott could not enter the same side door Cyrus had. He had to walk all the way around to the front of the building, adding an extra three minutes to his journey through the cold. It was a typical Eastport January morning, 25 degrees with a windchill that made it feel like seven. By the time he reached the entrance and pushed the buzzer to be allowed in, his eyes were tearing and his cheeks stung.

The electronic release on the security doors clicked, then buzzed. He pulled on the handle and walked into the front lobby where it felt at least 65 degrees warmer.

A new lady was at the reception desk. She looked over the top of her reading glasses and asked him who he was and what his business was.

"Umm, I'm Scott Frazier. I'm re-enrolling today," he said.

Scott was told to have a seat in a hard wooden chair along a wall that had motivational posters that dared students to "achieve greatness" and "work hard."

As time slowly moved forward, Scott grabbed his phone and pushed the button for Instagram. Nothing loaded. He then attempted to check his SnapChat feed and again was thwarted by a spinning icon and no images.

"That won't work too well in here," the receptionist said. "All social media is blocked by a firewall on the wifi."

"Oh, okay," Scott replied. He disconnected from the school's internet connection and tried to use his phone's connection, but discovered that the thick cinder block walls were killing his reception.

Before he'd lost his patience he was finally told to go to the guidance counselor's office. He told the lady at the desk that he knew where it was and headed up a flight of stairs and down a hall to meet with Mrs. Buckingham. She stood up and reached out her hand to Scott as he entered her office. *The pixie-ish 30-something must have been something extra special to look at when she was in high school, Scott thought, because she was still pretty amazing now.*

"Welcome back, Scott," she said. "Let's see about getting you up to speed and into class. I'm going to assume that you won't need a guide to take you from class to class."

"Umm, yeah. I know my way around," he said, confusion written on his face. "Umm, how'd you know who I was and why I'm here."

"The receptionist relayed your name to me, and your mother left me a voicemail this morning saying you'd be by to re-enroll. I already got the paperwork started. We just need to go through a list of electives for you and finish up your schedule. You should be all set to go by the start of the second period," she said with a smile. "I am sorry to hear about the circumstances that led to your transfer back here. There are grief counselors available to all students for the next two weeks in case you feel the need to talk to someone about how you're feeling. It's never easy to lose a friend, let alone two of them."

With the hustle and bustle of getting himself prepared for the day, he hadn't thought about Craig or Collin all morning. Did that make him a bad person? His shoulders slumped at the mention of his departed friends.

"Thanks, I'll keep that in mind," he said. "I don't know if I'll need to talk to anyone else. I've got my friends, but thank you for mentioning it."

"No need to thank me. Of course, you aren't obligated at all to visit them, but they are available and more than happy to speak with you. All of their teammates are being given a bit of leeway for the next few weeks. If you are not able to concentrate on your classes you will be allowed to sign out of class, no questions asked by the teachers, and report to either the counselors or the library," she said.

Scott thumbed through a program of studies booklet and decided upon a media arts elective and a drawing class. Along with his required classes, he'd have a pretty full day every day, but that was fine. After Wellington, he had a feeling this stuff would be pretty easy in comparison.

"You're all set Scott, you are free to wait here until the next period begins in 10 minutes, or you can go check out your locker," she said with a smile as she passed along a piece of paper with a locker assignment and a combination. He smiled back and thought that if she was a grief counselor rather than one for guidance that he'd make every effort to skip class to look at her legs several times per week. Rising and gathering his things, he said he was going to go put his coat in the locker and thanked her.

Roaming the familiar hallways, he found locker number 508. He spun the dial on the lock, opened it up and hung his thick winter coat on the hook. He put the piece of paper back in his pocket so he would be able to retrieve his things at the end of the day. Spinning on his heel, he accessed his schedule on his phone to see where his first class would be. Third period meant he'd be in United States History, Post World War II.

The irony was not lost on him that his new chapter in life would start by studying the past. "Learn from the past or repeat it," he said to himself. It was time to make some new history.

56

"Are you sure this is worth the trouble, Coach?"

John Scadorski attempted to keep a friendly smile plastered to his face as he conversed with his boss, Harry Burnette, the athletic director at Eastport High School. Looking around the small office, Scadorski could not help but notice how blank the walls and the desk were. There were no family photographs, or team pictures, or even those clueless motivational posters that all of the liberal bureaucrats seemed to love. No personal effects around at all. A whiteboard with the schedule for all the winter athletic teams at the school hung on the wall opposite Burnette's desk, with each sport color coded. Other than that, and some random paperwork, it would be hard to tell that anyone actually used the room.

"Harry, you know how difficult it's been. Scott is a kid who needs hockey in his life, and he needs his teammates. Educators are supposed to help kids grow on every level these days, right? We'll be helping him to do that and to heal. I don't see what the problem is, this should be a slam dunk," the coach said.

"I'm not sure it will be. If you were just adding a random kid to your team, I couldn't imagine anyone at the governing board would balk," Burnette said. "But, let's be honest, we all know this isn't just another player. He's a star, and that is going to raise some uncomfortable questions. I hope you're prepared to answer them and to be put on the hot seat."

Scadorski was not surprised his AD believed there could be potential problems. Burnette was a bureaucrat and concerned himself with politics first. He also believed the AD was wrong.

"This stuff can be pretty political, I get that. At the end of the day, these guys are all former coaches and sports parents. They're sports people. They're not going to vote against Scott. They're going to do what's right," the coach said, his eyes never leaving Burnette's.

"And if they don't?" the AD queried.

"If they don't we've got one of the best high school players in the state videotaping our games and serving as a quasi-assistant coach. It's not like he can go back to Wellington now, he's pushed his chips to the middle of the table," Scadorski said.

"I've got to be honest with you, I'm not a big fan of this. I don't like kids being able to jump away from a commitment on a whim. It sends the wrong message, but I'll support you guys at the hearing."

"Thank you, Harry. I appreciate that. Scott starts officially practicing with the team today. Next Thursday will be his tenth day back, which means he'll be back for our game that Saturday up at South Yarmouth."

"If the board votes for him," Burnette said ominously.

"They will."

He hoped he was right.

57

Cyrus Carpenter tugged on his laces and then went to work on taping up his long black practice socks. The shirtless captain of the Eastport Cannons looked around the locker room and was taken aback by how normal things felt in that moment... until he spotted the empty lockers of his friends Bish and OB.

"Let's get after it today, boys," the captain of the Cannons bellowed. "Practice like you want to play."

Billy Walker, the ex-captain who had made a truce with his longtime friend, walked over to Carpenter's locker and sat down next to him.

"Hey buddy, have you seen Danny? I don't think he came to school."

Carpenter paused to think if he'd seen his friend that day. "You know what, I think you're right. Usually, we have lunch together. I guess it didn't register that he wasn't there. Is he sick?"

"Anybody see Stoner today?" Walker asked the room.

Heads shook in the negative, followed by several "nopes" and "not today."

"It's too late to worry about it right now. You want to head over and check up on him with me after practice?"

"I can do that," Carpenter agreed.

Practice went by in a flash, with barely a mention of Bish or OB. Everyone knew it was the first official practice without their friends, but no one wanted to bring it up. Since the Cannons had not been out on the ice in an official capacity since the accident, Coach kept it simple. Conditioning was the emphasis for the day. The team skated sprints and worked on breakouts and passing, but no lines were assembled. Scadorski had not figured out how he was going to shuffle things around yet. With everything they'd been through, he hadn't yet concerned himself with X's and O's. Frazier would slot in where OB had been, but figuring out what to do with the forward lines was something the coaches had not yet addressed.

After an hour the horn buzzed and the Zamboni doors opened. The boys skated off the ice to the locker room to shower up and head out.

Cyrus had decided he would be the last one out of the room after practices and games going forward. He encouraged his teammates with "attaboys" and "good job today" as they left for the evening. Billy caught on and joined in, patting his teammates on the shoulder and fist-bumping them.

Scott waited outside for them to finish up and they all left the rink together. Frazier rode with Carpenter and Walker followed behind. Ten minutes later they pulled up to Stone's house. Nearly every light in the two-story cream-colored ranch home was ablaze, except for the one on the top right side. That was Danny's room.

The boys strode up the walkway and up the steps to the front door, their hands buried deep in their winter coats. Carpenter pressed the doorbell and the three waited silently, hopping back and forth on the balls of their feet to keep warm.

They heard shuffling, the front door slowly opened and a tiny head popped around the edge of the door. A big smile broke out and then an excited shriek followed.

"Cy-wus, you came to see me!" Danny's four-year-old sister said with excitement.

"Hey Lily, how's my favorite girl?"

"I'm gweat, howayou?"

"Cold, can we come in?" Cyrus asked with a smile. Everyone loved Lily Stone. Danny's little sister pressed her face to the glass at every home game, rooting on her brother and his friends.

"Mommy, Danny's fwiends are here, can they come in?" Lily yelled in the direction of the kitchen.

Leigh Stone came bustling around the corner and waved the boys in. "Lily, you don't have to make the boys stand in the cold. Boys, I'm sorry, please come on in," she said.

"Hi Mrs. Stone, we were wondering if Danny was here. He didn't come to school or practice, and we just kind of wanted to check up on him," Cyrus said.

"I think he's sleeping. He wasn't feeling very well this morning so I let him stay home... How are you boys doing?"

"Good," all three said half-heartedly.

"You mind if we go up and talk to him?" Billy asked, already turning to head up the stairs.

"I guess that's okay, but if he's asleep wake him up gently. He's a deep sleeper," Mrs. Stone pleaded.

The boys agreed and bounded up the stairs.

"How you want to do this?" Scott whispered to the other two.

"Let's scare the crap out of him, that's always fun," Billy said.

"Let's go," Cyrus agreed.

The three flung the door open and in unison hopped on the end of the bed, bouncing mercilessly. "Wake up, time to wake up sleepy head," Billy said while doing his best Mrs. Stone impersonation. "Rise and shine."

Groggily Danny Stone rolled over, looked at his three friends and scowled.

"What the hell is wrong with you? I'm sleeping, you jerks."

"You skipped school, practice, didn't text anyone," Billy said, sniffing the air. "Dude, are you hammered?"

"No, I just took a couple of shots to fall asleep," Danny said.

"A couple of shots of what?" Frazier asked.

Grabbing something from under Danny's bed, Billy said, "I think I know." He then pulled out a pint of Jack Daniels.

"Whiskey, really? I always took you for more of a wine cooler girl," Scott said.

Billy unscrewed the cap, threw back a swig and nearly choked as it went down. "Oh yeah, that's the stuff... smooth," he said, trying his best not to spit it out.

"Dude, none of us have heard from you in days, and we come over here and find you sloshed. I'm not trying to turn this into a very special visit from your friends, but it doesn't look good, brother," Cyrus said. "Remember the stuff about captains being leaders and all that, the only thing this is leading you to is a really nasty hangover tomorrow."

"Screw you. It was just a couple of shots, I've been stressed out. I didn't want to deal with school today, so I stayed home. Sue me," Danny said defensively.

None of the boys were buying what Danny was selling. Of the group, he was more likely to volunteer to be a designated driver than the one pounding down drinks. For him to drink alone seemed very out of character and worrisome.

"Dan, you alright, man? I mean, this isn't your style," Cyrus said.

"No, I'm not alright. I'm absolutely not close to alright. I'm a million miles from alright," Danny said, staring daggers at his friends. "I can't stop reliving that day. I keep seeing them flying up at me and hitting the tree. If I'd slowed down, left earlier, left later, gone home another way, whatever, they'd still be here. I watched our friends die. I saw OB just sitting there, and he was dead, and I couldn't do anything about it, and I still can't, and I miss them, man. Every day I want to text OB and say 'what's up.' I want to go watch a game at Bish's house and then I remember that I can't. I actually started to text Bish last night, and then I remembered."

None of them spoke for several minutes.

"I miss them too," Billy finally said. "Collin and Craig, the C & C Dufus Factory."

The boys snorted out half-laughs.

"Danny, you can't just get drunk, though. Brown liquor makes people mean. You need to get back into life with the rest of us," Cyrus offered.

"They're gone, we're not, and we're still your friends, man. You need to talk, or whatever, we are here."

"Thanks, but I've got to deal with this on my own."

"That's bull, man. You can't, none of us can," Scott said while he thumbed through an old yearbook. "Look at this, JV hockey picture from ninth grade. You guys were so frickin' young."

"You were too, you were just a baby on the varsity," Cyrus said, taking the book. "Look at that, we're all there. We had no idea how good we had it."

"Yup, all that mattered was sports and girls," Scott said.

"So what exactly has changed?" Billy said with a smile.

"Danny, I'm confiscating this bottle for your own good," Billy said, giving his friends a look that said he was keeping it for a later time. "You've got to get back to school and practice tomorrow. We need you on this ride, man. We're back at it on Saturday."

"Whatever, fine. I'll be at school tomorrow," Danny said.

"Yup, you will, because I'm sending Wes to pick you up," Cyrus said. "He told me at school today that it was weird driving in by himself. He needs a passenger, and we need someone to get you there, at least this week. I'll tell him to be here at 7:30, be ready."

"Fine, now can I get some sleep?" Danny said, pulling the covers over his head.

"Yeah, but make sure you get something to eat. Drink some water and take some Advil," Scott said. "School sucks enough without a hangover, and you really don't want one at practice. You missed out on a lot of conditioning stuff today. I nearly puked, and I was sober."

Danny rolled over and buried his head in his pillow as his friends left. He wanted nothing more than to sleep and forget. He knew that sleep would not come easily, though. It came in moments, not hours, these days. Another restless night awaited.

58

John Scadorski, Harry Burnette and Scott Frazier sat on a bench, side by side, outside a meeting room at the Massachusetts Scholastic Athletic Association's headquarters in Wrentham. Scadorski looked over some paperwork, Burnette answered an email on his phone and Scott stared straight ahead at the wall, tapping his heel and wishing that the meeting would just start already.

"Hey Scott, calm your nerves, this is just a formality. It's all going to be fine," Scadorski said cheerfully, patting the player on his shoulder.

"I don't know, Coach. What if they vote against me? What do I do then?" the 18-year old said, fear in his voice.

"They're going to vote however they vote. This fulfills the process," Burnette said.

"All due respect Mr. Burnette, but this is not a process to me. This team is my family. I hated that my parents sent me away from them, and now my family needs me back. I need to be back. If I can't play, I don't know what I'll do."

Burnette looked like he was about to say something to Scott, but stopped when the door they'd been waiting in front of abruptly opened. A gray-haired man in a fancy black pinstriped suit waved them in and told them to take a seat at the far end of a long conference table that reminded him of the one from "The Last Supper." He hoped this would end better for him than it did for the guest of honor at that party.

The gray-haired guy introduced himself as Joe Rogers. "This is Carol Wright," he said nodding to the woman on his left, "and this is Benjamin Lewis. We have been selected to hear your waiver case and to rule whether or not you will be reinstated for immediate play for the Eastport hockey program."

Mrs. Wright chimed in, "First off, I think I speak for all of us when I offer my deepest condolences for everything that your team and town has gone through over the last few weeks. Losing someone is never easy, but it is truly heartbreaking when two outstanding people are taken so young. We feel for you."

Lewis, maybe feeling left out, jumped in, "Yes, we certainly offer our thoughts and prayers, but with that said, this is a very extraordinary case and not a decision that the MSAA should make hastily or emotionally. As a former baseball coach, I know that if one of my rivals were to add one of the best players in the state to his team because that player had decided to leave a private school during the season that I would balk at his reinstatement. It is clearly stated that student-athletes that transfer to a school cannot join a team in-season and must wait until the beginning of the following season to do so. In my eyes, this rule is pretty straightforward and above reproach. It was set in place to prevent an unfair playing field, and I do believe that the addition of Mr. Frazier to the Eastport hockey team would give them an unfair advantage over their opponents this season. I understand that you also play baseball son, I have no problem with you playing in the spring, but as for hockey, I don't see how I could in good conscience vote for this waiver."

Scott grimaced. Scadorski tried to put on a poker face. Burnette nodded once.

"I certainly appreciate and understand your stance, Mr. Lewis. Until recently I would have agreed with you wholeheartedly. I wonder, though, will we be able to state our case, or will this be voted upon based on our written appeal? The bylaws seemed a bit unclear on that," Burnette said.

Mrs. Wright, who looked like she'd be more comfortable with knitting needles and a blanket in her lap than at a game, spoke up, "I think that'd be fine. I for one would like to hear Scott's side of the story."

"I think we can hear Eastport's request," Mr. Rogers said. "It might be more appropriate though if the school's official representative, Mr. Burnette, spoke on the record."

Harry Burnette pushed back his chair and faced the two men and one woman that had the power in the room. "As I said earlier, I understand Mr. Lewis's stance. Until recently I think it would have been quite easy for me to walk out the door with the vote having gone against Eastport, for a variety of reasons. As the official representative from Eastport, I would like to cede my position and grant it to Scott Frazier, who will be representing both himself and Eastport High School in this matter today."

Lewis leaned forward and pointed at Burnette.

"This is both inappropriate and unacceptable. Is this some sort of a joke to you?" Lewis sneered.

"No sir, quite the opposite. Scott can tell his story far better than I can. I believe it will carry far more weight with the committee to hear it straight from him," Burnette said.

"I think that would be just fine," Mrs. Wright said.

Rogers, who had not said a word since making the introductions, sat quietly in the middle of the other two board members. His pause seemed to go on too long, at least to Scott.

"Okay, let's hear what you've got to say, Mr. Frazier."

59

Both Scadorski and Frazier looked at one another with questions in their eyes. This was not a scenario they'd envisioned, or planned for. Scadorski shrugged and whispered, "You got this."

Scott inhaled deeply and stood. He tried to smooth the wrinkles that had appeared in his button-up shirt and felt like the tie around his neck was suffocating him. He wanted to loosen it up but feared that Mr. Lewis would see that as disrespectful, and not only kick him out of the room, but maybe out of sports for the rest of his life.

"Umm, thank you," he began, searching for the words that he needed to make this happen.

"I made a mistake, maybe the biggest one I've ever made. I let my parents make a decision for me based on what they thought was in my best interest and didn't tell them that I hated it and did not want to leave Eastport. I really wanted to stay. I should have stayed. When I got to Wellington, all I wanted was to come home. I watched my friends win a state championship in football and wished I'd been on the team. They celebrated that night. I was alone in a dormitory.

"When hockey season started, I thought maybe everything would improve. It didn't. I missed my friends at home and playing with them. I put on a strong front, but being away was the worst. It really sucked. Oh, sorry, I mean, it was awful.

"When OB and Bish passed away a part of me died that day. I'd known those guys for as long as I can remember. We played house mites together, Little League, Pop Warner, went to school together. You name it. Now they're gone and they can't finish their senior years. They left a big hole in our team, and our team is a family.

"I can't fill that hole. No one can, but I can finish for them what they started. If you allow me to play you need to know that I'm not playing just for Scott Frazier. I could probably sit out the year and still play in college next year. I could go play juniors this year to get ready. I don't care about that, I don't want to play for me," he said.

Scott turned to Coach Scadorski. "Can I see that for a second, Coach?" he said.

Scadorski handed over a pile of papers that he had with him. Scott almost immediately found what he was looking for. He handed the pile back to his coach and then slid the piece of paper he'd found across the table to the committee members.

"That's our roster. Those are the names and numbers of my brothers, every one of them. That's why I want a waiver. Craig and Collin are still listed on that piece of paper. Collin was number 10. He had your back no matter what and hit like a truck. Craig was number 19, biggest heart you've ever seen. They can't be there for the other guys anymore. I can. That's all I wanted to say."

Joe Rogers stood up in his pinstriped suit. "Thank you for that, Scott. Gentlemen, if you'd give us some privacy, we need to formally discuss the matter."

"Should we stick around?" Scadorski asked.

"No. We've kept Scott out of school long enough today and you men away from your responsibilities. Thank you for your time, I will call you with our decision this afternoon," Rogers said, waving his right arm toward the door.

Scott, Scadorski, and Burnette left the room and walked in a straight line down the hallway to the exit. Burnette pushed a button on his key fob that unlocked the doors to his Cadillac. Scadorski got in the passenger's side and put his papers down on the floorboard in front of him. Scott buckled his seatbelt and stared out the window.

Scadorski spoke first.

"You did a nice job, Scotty. Win or lose, you laid it on the line for them," the coach said.

"Thanks," Scott muttered.

"The way I see it, you walked in with the vote tied at 1-1," Burnette said. "Obviously Mr. Lewis is going to vote against you. I'd be surprised if he doesn't start a motion to make sure another student-athlete never speaks, unless questioned, at one of those hearings again."

Scadorski chimed in. "Yeah, but I think Mrs. Wright not only is voting yes for you, but she may send Scott a care package in the mail with some cookies."

"That leaves it up to Mr. Rogers. He played his cards pretty close to the vest," Burnette said. "I have no feel for which way he was leaning. We will know soon, I'm sure."

Scott turned toward the window and watched the trees blur by him again. After a minute he spoke up.

"Hey Mr. Burnette, why did you want me to talk?"

"Because I didn't realize how important it was that you get reinstated until we spoke while waiting for the hearing to start. You convinced me. I thought you had a better chance of being successful than I would have," he said. "Besides, Coach tells me you are the guy he wants to have the puck on his stick with the game on the line. I figured that this was one of those situations. Win or lose, you took your shot."

Scott considered that for a moment. He smiled.

"I hope I didn't miss the net," he said.

60

Joe Rogers had never played hockey growing up. The son of a Somerville cop, Rogers' game had been baseball. He actually had preferred stickball with the neighborhood kids in the alley behind St. Anne's Church. Enough light seeped into the alley from the streetlights to allow them to play deep into the night. At least twice a week the priest would kindly ask them to make it their last inning so that he could get some sleep before the next morning's mass.

He'd taken his skills from those games to the diamond and starred for Somerville High, lettering as a sophomore and making All-City twice. Northeastern had offered him a scholarship, and he happily accepted. College ball hadn't landed him a coveted pro contract, but it had allowed him to get a degree and a job in finance. He'd run the rat race in Manhattan for almost 20 years. A month after his bank account crested his magic number for retirement, he kept good on a promise he'd made to his high school sweetheart and moved his family back to Massachusetts.

Rogers' wealth allowed them to find a great place in Winchester, before the town's property prices had gone through the roof. They'd paid a little over $175,000 for the place back in 1988. The last valuation report said it was worth $1.1 million, but Rogers would never part with the place. There were too many memories. He'd let his two kids cash in on that investment someday after he was gone.

Too young to fully retire at 45, he'd started looking for a job that was more interesting than anything else. He saw a posting for a job at a place called the Massachusetts Scholastic Athletic Association. They needed a treasurer and his resumé got him the job that paid him annually what he made in about six weeks on Wall Street. He'd worn numerous hats at the MSAA since that first job, though his job description still included the treasury. He also directed tournaments, advised athletic departments, administered discipline and oversaw hearings, such as Scott Frazier and the Eastport Cannons and their desire for a waiver that would allow him to play this year despite starting the school year, and the hockey season, at a private school.

Rogers entered the hearing room that day pretty sure he'd be the deciding vote. He'd worked with Benjamin Lewis and Carol Wright for years and their personalities always factored into how they voted.

Lewis was a hardliner. Rules were rules and they were to be adhered to. Changes to them should only be made after lengthy discussion, dissection and proper paperwork. There was no way he was going to vote for the waiver. He'd never voted in favor of one before, and if nothing else, Benjamin Lewis was consistent.

Wright was even easier to read. An advocate for children's rights, she wanted to hug every kid that had ever come through their door for a meeting of any kind. She'd once argued against suspending a player that had been caught with both opiates and alcohol in his high school locker, despite video evidence of him placing it there. She had voted in favor of Scott Frazier before he'd walked in the door.

Looking to his left at Carol Wright and right at Benjamin Lewis, Joe Rogers smiled to himself. He found himself back in the middle of another vote. Many times his decisions were easy. He'd wished this one was.

On the face of the matter, he wanted to vote against the waiver. The rules were clear that a student-athlete could not transfer during the school year and play with a team during the season that was currently in play, barring extraordinary circumstances. It was to prevent high school coaches from recruiting players who felt disenfranchised at private schools and loading up their teams for playoff runs. It was a good rule, quite valid. It kept the playing field even.

Allowing Eastport to add Scott Frazier to its roster in-season would not keep the playing field even for the other teams in the state, Rogers was sure of that. He'd never seen Frazier play in person, but he'd heard stories about some of his exploits from the hockey tournament director. The man in charge of hockey for the MSAA for the past 12 years had seen Eastport lose in the playoffs the year before. He came back to work Monday recalling a magical goal that a defenseman had scored for Eastport. He'd called it a "million dollar move from a kid that might make a million dollars someday on the ice."

Voting against the waiver should have been easy to do, but as he stared down at the form that would decide the fate of Frazier and the Eastport Cannons, he could not mark an X on the "No" box.

Joe Rogers' years on Wall Street had taught him many lessons, but none of those were as important as the ones he'd learned back in the day playing stickball behind that Catholic church in Somerville. His older brother had served in Vietnam and paid the ultimate price for his country. Joe had been 12 at the time, and the only thing that had gotten him through that painful time were those stickball games. If he hadn't had that outlet he didn't know how he could have managed through that year.

Scott Frazier's impassioned speech had resonated with Rogers. He understood what the kid was going through. If he voted the way he knew he should – according to the letter of the law – he wouldn't be able to live with himself.

Rogers had wrestled with his decision long enough. With two quick strokes of the pen, he voted. He looked up from the form and said, "Would you mind if I called the Eastport people and let them know of our ruling personally?"

61

Route 25 curved to the right and the sign appeared, "Welcome to Cape Cod." Scott Frazier laughed to himself when he thought about all of the arguments he'd had with Collin O'Brien about how the Cape didn't really begin until you'd crossed the Bourne Bridge.

Collin had said, "You're not on the Cape until you've crossed the bridge." Scott argued that the landmass of the actual Cape began right about at the welcome sign, so if you'd passed it, you were technically on Cape Cod. Most people who lived across the bridges sided with Collin, but Scott figured that had more to do with being a little bit snobby than anything else.

Scott was about to pose the age-old question to the two adults sitting in front of him when he was taken out of his daydream by the ringing of a cell phone. Mr. Burnette fished into his back pocket, looked at the screen and turned down the radio.

"This is Harry Burnette... Hello Mr. Rogers, how are you?... Yes, he's sitting right here, hold on."

"This is it," Coach Scadorski whispered.

Scott's stomach tightened and he felt like he needed to take off his jacket and open a window. He accepted the phone from the athletic director, swallowed and spoke.

"Hello Mr. Rogers, this is Scott... Thank you, sir... Yes, sir... No, sir... Yes, sir... I will, thanks."

Scott handed the phone back to Harry Burnette, looked back out the window and smiled.

"Well?" Burnette and Scadorski asked in unison.

"I'm a Cannon again!" he screamed. "Let's go!"

Scadorski pumped his fist. Burnette laughed, and said, "Your speech did the trick, kid."

"I think so," Scott agreed. "He said he was moved by my words and then he asked me if I was sure that I'd finish the school year. He wanted to make sure I wasn't going to bail after the season, and then he said he wanted me to make the most out of my opportunity."

Scadorski could not stop smiling. After the past two weeks of losses, it finally felt as if Eastport had gotten a break.

As they drove across the Bridge and came around a rotary, Scott looked to the front seat where his coach and athletic director sat. "Hey, if you hurry I can still make it to History class."

"You'll make it in plenty of time," the coach said. "How do you want to tell the team?"

"I'm not sure, but can I do it at practice?"

"Absolutely, but you know that they're going to hound you the second you walk in the door," Scadorski said.

"Yeah, but the only people in Eastport that know are the three that are in this car. I think we can keep a secret until 3:30. I know I can."

62

Wes had once fallen down a Youtube rabbit hole about space and time in which a monk had said that time only existed in your head and that it didn't exist physically, only mentally. Obviously, the dude in the red and gold robes had never sat through one of Mr. Cory's Chemistry classes. The clock on the wall did physically exist and the second hand was moving in slow motion.

The teacher droned on about covalent bonds as time seemed to stand still. Wes picked at the cast on his wrist absently and tried to pay attention to the action in the front of the room.

A buzzing in his pocket jarred him out of his semi-slumber. Knowing that Mr. Cory enjoyed taking cell phones hostage, Wes slyly grabbed his phone from his pocket and placed it horizontally in front of his textbook, then moved his notebook on top of that in order to shield the device from the teacher's field of vision. He nonchalantly swiped the message icon and, while keeping his head and posture lined up with the teacher, gazed down at the words on the screen.

The group message had also been sent to Josh, Danny, Cy, and Billy. It was from Scott.

"Back from meeting. Need a ride to the rink after school."

Every fiber of Wes's being wanted to respond to the obvious question. What had happened? Did he get the waiver? Could he play? Wes couldn't afford to lose his phone until Mr. Cory saw fit to return it so he completely covered it and waited out the final 20 minutes of the class, cursing that stupid monk the whole way.

Josh Hutchinson was staring at a digital clock countdown at the same time, needing another 10 minutes to tick down so that he could remove his blueberry muffins from the oven and present them to the Home Economics teacher for grading. With AP classes filling most of his schedule, Josh had signed up for Home Ec his senior year to have at least one easy class and to learn how to cook. His mother said it was an important life skill to have and he usually enjoyed the end result of his work.

His phone buzzed, he eyed the screen and immediately responded.

"Did U get da waiver?"

The three little flashing dots that meant someone else was typing immediately appeared.

"Don't know, they haven't said yet. Waiting sucks."

Josh sighed. The phone buzzed again.

"WTF, did they say when?" came from Danny.

"When did they say you'd know?" popped up from Cy.

"Anyone want to grab McDonald's after school?" was Billy's addition.

The stove's timer sounded and Josh slipped the phone into his back pocket. He slipped his right hand into an oven mitt, opened the door and was pushed back by the out-rushing heat. He then reached into the stove and pulled out the pan to find six perfectly formed blueberry muffins.

The teacher allowed her students to take half of what they baked home with them and the rest was donated to the Eastport Food Pantry to be distributed to needy families. Josh figured some kid was going to enjoy his breakfast in a day or two and smiled as he grabbed a large zip lock bag to put his share of the goodies in. He then brought the half-full pan over to the teacher and handed them over with pride. She smiled and thanked him. Josh returned to his station in the kitchen to wait out the last few minutes of class.

He opened the phone to see that Wes had offered Scott a ride to the rink and that Cyrus agreed to go to McDonald's with Billy. He considered joining his friends for fast food but decided against it. He was supposed to stick to a healthier diet to prepare for college baseball and a Big Mac was not going to help with that.

Later on, as the school day ended, Danny Stone grabbed the books he needed for homework out of his locker, put the rest away and grabbed his coat. He turned around to see Wes standing behind him.

"You good to go?" Wes asked cheerfully.

"I guess so," he responded, tossing the bag over his shoulder.

The duo walked through the hall, out the exit and to the parking lot where Wes's SUV awaited. Scott Frazier was sitting on the rear bumper as he waited for his friends to arrive. The three boys saddled up and Wes headed in the direction of the Eastport Ice Arena. He took a pull on a bottle of water and then looked into the back seat to query his friend.

"You hear anything about the vote yet?" he asked.

"Nah, nothing yet. Shouldn't be long, though," Scott said, not wanting to let the cat out of the bag just yet.

Wes asked about the meeting, and Scott told his friends about the three board members, the way that Coach and Mr. Burnette had backed him up and the speech he had given.

"Sounds pretty intense," Wes said.

Scott agreed and turned to Danny.

"You're talkative," he said sarcastically.

"Just thinking."

"That's new for you," Wes said with a laugh. "What about?"

"Nothing," Danny said. "Everything, I guess. I don't know. I'm just kind of a mess right now."

"I get it, buddy, I do. Bish was my best friend ever. Collin was my boy and he cracked me up. I miss them too, man. I miss them all the time. It's okay to miss them, ya know. Nothing wrong with that."

Danny sighed.

"I know. I just can't stop thinking that I could have done something, that I could have stopped it from happening. I mean, I guess I know it's not my fault, really, but it feels like it kind of is," Danny said.

"Dude, it's not, and I get it," Wes said. "You don't think I feel guilty? If I hadn't had to get this stupid wrist looked at, if I had never punched that stupid wall, I would have driven Bish to practice that day. Collin wouldn't have driven like a douchebag – well, maybe he wouldn't have. All of that stuff is going to drive us nuts forever if we let it. No matter how much we want to change what happened, we can't. It sucks, but we can't."

"Yeah, but... " Danny tried to intervene.

Scott spoke up.

"Yeah, but nothing. Dude, it's over. We can't change it. No amount of wishing is going to bring them back. Beating yourself up about it isn't going to change anything."

"I know, you're right. I just can't get over feeling like I could have done something," Danny whispered.

"You'll get there," Wes said as he pulled into a parking spot at the rink.

The boys headed into the locker room. Danny began to suit up for practice as Wes sat at his locker stall and stared at Craig Bishop's empty spot. He began to bob his head up and down, making a decision in the moment.

A few minutes later all 22 players were on the ice. Wes was the last one out and for the first time all year, he was fully dressed. He'd spent the last few minutes loosening up his right glove as much as possible and pulled it snugly over the cast on his right hand. He wondered how long it would take for Coach Scads to realize he was out there.

Coach Scadorski stepped onto the ice and took several long strides toward the blue line, spun around and grabbed a puck with his stick blade. With one quick motion, he scooped the puck into the air and began to bounce it on the end of his stick like a hacky-sack. After about six straight knocks, he caught it flat on the blade of his stick and swept it through the air, delivering the puck into the net.

The players gave a little cheer. They knew that their coach had once been one of the best players in the state, but it was little acts like that that reminded them just how good he actually had been.

"Fancy stuff is fun," Scadorski said with a smile. "You know how many games stuff like that ever won for me, though? Zero. Zilch. You can have all the silly moves in the world, but if you're not willing to move your feet, grind in the corners, find the open man, move the puck, it all amounts to a hill of beans."

"We've got two days before we get back on the ice for real. No matter how bad South Yarmouth might feel for us, they're coming in here looking to get a win. Make no mistake, there isn't a team in the state that's going to roll over for poor Eastport. They'll shake your hands, they'll tell you that they hope you're okay, but they're coming in here to tear you a new one on the ice if you let them," Scadorski said. "And the reality of it all is this, guys, we didn't just lose two friends, we lost two of our better hockey players. There isn't one of you here that can play your game and also replace who we lost. The sum of the parts will have to make up a better whole and it's on all of you to give everything you've got. That all starts on the practice ice. Today I need all you've got and tomorrow too. Saturday we play for real."

With the day's point of emphasis explained, the coach began to line the boys up for drills. He sent the usual pairings to their usual spots, and when they'd all gone where they were supposed to, standing alone by the bench was Wes Garrett.

The senior spoke up sheepishly.

"Umm, Coach, where do you want me?" he asked.

"Garrett, you didn't tell me you were cleared. That's good news. Let's get you with the forwards, left wing. You can switch in and out with the third line for now," the coach said.

"Yessir," Wes said as he started to skate over to where the forwards were working on making a diagonal pass to lead a breakout to the right side.

Scadorski smiled to himself, happy to have one of his seniors back. He watched Garrett skate over to his teammates and noticed the cast on the senior's right hand jutting out of his glove. Rather than throw Garrett out of the lineup, he decided to see how the kid looked playing again. If he clearly wasn't ready, the coach knew he had a reason loaded up that would make sitting him down justifiable. If Garrett looked ready, they could figure something out.

A right-handed shot, Garrett's right hand gripped midway down the shaft of his graphite stick. The tool had cost him $275 in the pro shop. It was painted black, and the lettering was all dark red, close enough to the Cannon's maroon colors that it almost looked like it was a part of the uniform.

The drill was simple enough. The initial pass was to come from halfway between the defensive blue line and the red line. On the coach's signal, the skater on the right side flew up his side and accepted a pass from the guy in the middle, whose job was to send a pass and streak up the middle himself, accepting a return pass and then firing at the net. The goalies were supposed to try to save whatever came their way.

Wes was fourth in line to throw a pass. After watching two of his teammates succeed, and one fail miserably, he was up. Billy Walker was the guy on the right wing streaking toward the blue line and Wes snapped off a decent enough offering, one that led Walker a little too much, but the skilled senior was so good that he made it look better than it was. Walker rocked the puck back onto his forehand and returned a horizontal pass to Garrett. The returning senior had not handled a hard pass in many months. He accepted it, but not without popping it around on his stick a little. His quick shot to the net was off the mark, flying far to the left beyond the goalie's outstretched glove and to the glass behind.

Garrett circled back to the line on the right side to do that job. He was sure to avoid eye contact with either of the coaches. If they weren't going to call him out for missing the net he wasn't going to draw any attention to himself either. Wes did not want them to sit him down or notice he still had the cast on.

"Gotta be better," he told himself.

His second play was a little better. He easily handled the first connection as he moved up the wing, and relayed the puck to where he wanted it, though not as quickly as it needed to be. Feeling better about that try, he noticed the speed of the drill picking up the second time through. With each repetition, the Cannons got a little crisper and played with more purpose.

Wes put a hard pass on Walker's stick, in just the right place with the correct speed, and was in the right spot to get it back. Walker put the comeback pass right on the tape and Wes let one fly. It beat the goalie but hit the pipe.

"Dammit," he said as he spun back to the line.

Scadorski had been watching the drills intently, especially when Garrett's turn came up. He blew his whistle and signaled that the senior come to see him.

"Not too bad, Wes," he said.

"Thanks, Coach."

"We've got one problem, though. You and I both know that the refs won't let you play with a cast on. It's seen as a hazard, not to mention that opponents will take a run at it if they know it's bothering you," Scadorski said.

"Oh, I know," Garrett said, searching for the right thing to say to keep him in the practice and hopefully into the game on Saturday. "It's coming off tomorrow. I just didn't want to wait to practice."

"How's it feel?" Scadorski asked.

"Not bad. It's a little stiff, but other than that it's fine," Garrett said truthfully.

"Alright, no more today for you. Why don't you watch the rest of the practice from the bench and then go peel your glove off that thing? Tomorrow you can go all-out, but make sure to tape it up good. You'll have to if you're planning to play on Saturday," the coach said.

"Yes, sir," Garrett said as the realization that his coach was going to play him in the return game hit him. It had been at least two weeks since Wes experienced anything resembling joy, but in that moment he got that old familiar feeling of happiness back. Then he realized he had a problem, the doctor had once again rescheduled the removal on him and wasn't supposed to remove the cast for another week. He was going to have to figure out how to get it off on his own.

63

Over the next 45 minutes, the Cannons worked on forechecking and penalty killing. Those two parts of the game, at least under Scadorski's system, went hand in hand. Every mistake resulted in push-ups as the coach hammered home the need for perfection. The boys hadn't worked that hard in weeks, but during that hour on the ice, their minds did not drift to the overwhelming sadness that had dominated their every waking moment for the past few weeks. They were just hockey players again. Their only care in the world was playing well and pleasing their coach.

The scoreboard buzzed at the end of practice, signaling to Scadorski that he had to have his team clear of the ice in five minutes so that the Zamboni could clean the ice in preparation for the girls' team's practice that was to follow.

"Good job today boys, don't anyone leave. I need to talk to you all in the locker room," Scadorski announced.

The players filed off the ice and into their locker room. Each grabbed a seat in front of his locker. Most removed their practice jerseys and shoulder pads. Fingers combed sweat-soaked hair out of eyes and towels wiped away the hard work from faces. Scadorski entered the room and stood just at the edge of the large "E" logo that decorated the locker room floor, the spot that designated the exact middle of the room. No one walked on the "E" without punishment, which was apologizing profusely to it and getting down on all fours to kiss it. Stepping over it with a large stride was okay, but no one's foot was permitted to ever touch the "E." It had been that way ever since the building had been erected, and the first senior class that year had implemented the rule that had been adhered to ever since.

"Not bad, boys, not too bad at all today. Wes, good to have you back. Tomorrow, full-speed for you. If you survive the hour you're playing on Saturday. Stoney, you're looking better, you too, Gaudreau. You guys are starting to look like a hockey team," the coach said with a smile. "Speaking of which, there's a member of the team who wanted to say something before we finish up."

Scott stood up at his locker stall, which was in the back of the room. He'd had to take one of the leftover stalls since he joined late. He was surrounded by the freshmen and the sophomores. He didn't mind being with the younger kids, and since they all looked up to him, it certainly didn't hurt his ego to have them asking him questions all of the time. Usually, those questions were about hockey, but sometimes it was about how to deal with a teacher or a girl. He felt like their big brother.

Scott wanted to blurt out his good news but knew that he had an opportunity to mess with his friends a little bit, and he couldn't let it go to waste.

"Yeah, so you all know I went up to have my hearing today. So, I've actually known for a while and I didn't want to ruin practice, but… " he let his words trail off, looked down at the floor and did his best to pretend he was about to cry.

"What'd they say, Scott?" Carpenter asked breathlessly, fearing the worst. The team had all moved to the front of their seats. Every eye in the room was sharply focused on the top of Scott's down-turned head.

"They said… Umm, they ruled that under the circumstances that," he stopped again, pausing for effect, and to raise the tension just a little higher.

"What, under the circumstances what?" Danny shouted. "Just say it, man."

"That under the circumstances, that I'm… freakin' back baby!" Scott shouted.

The room erupted as a cheer went up that could be heard out on the ice by the girls' team, which stopped and stared at the boys' locker room door wondering what the heck those crazy boys were doing now. Scott was wrapped up in a team-wide hug. He struggled to catch his breath as they crushed in on him.

"Hey, hey, give me a little space. You guys are going to kill me before I get to play a game," he said.

"You jerk, you had me going," Walker said as he punched his teammate in the arm.

"Me too," Moxon said. "Had me worried, man."

"I am officially returning to the team for our game next Saturday. That's the tenth day and that's when I can play. You guys have one game without me and then I get back out with you. I can't freaking wait," Scott said.

Scadorski smiled and calmed the troops down. He had one last thing that he wanted to address.

"Guys this is a new day for us," he said. "I'm excited and it feels a little like we're starting the season over in a lot of ways. With that said, I cannot look at those two empty lockers side-by-side all year long without tearing up. Anyone have a solution?"

Wes didn't think, he just spoke.

"I want Craig's locker," he said.

"I'll gladly take Collin's," Josh added.

Scadorski could not have asked for that situation to have gone better.

"Are you guys all good with that?" the coach asked.

It was settled, and best of all it had gone down the way he'd hoped it would. Maybe things were starting to get slightly better.

64

Wes had lied, and he knew he'd lied, and he really didn't care. He'd been in the cast for his wrist for too long. He knew it was healed. His mom knew it was healed. The doctors knew it was healed. It would have been removed by now if the doctor hadn't gone on vacation. He had promised that it would come off right after the New Year, then the office had rescheduled that to the third week of January. He'd asked his mom to see a different doctor, but she insisted she stick with the specialist because he was "the best in the business" and had overseen the entire process.

"Screw it," he said to himself. Life was a risk. The thing was coming off today, one way or another.

As Wes and Danny started for home, Wes asked his friend a question.

"Dan, your dad has some tools and stuff, right?" he asked.

Danny thought about it for a moment. His father was an accountant, but he did take on the occasional weekend project. Danny and his dad had nailed together a decent little tree house for Lily the previous summer and his dad had put in a patio the year before that.

"He's got some basic stuff, I think," Danny offered. "Why?"

"Because the cast needs to come off, like yesterday," Wes said.

"Won't they just do that at the doctor's office? It'll take them like two minutes to get it off. That's what they do."

"You're right, but the problem is that I can't get in to see the doctor for another couple weeks. I don't have that kind of time. We have a game Saturday night, and I'm playing, but they won't let me play as long as this thing is still on. Coach said once it was off, I was good to go, but it's gotta come off, and so I'm going to have to do it," he said.

"Won't your mom get pissed?" Danny asked.

"Don't know, don't care," Wes retorted quickly. "It's healed. We've got a game, and I'm playing. You know that OB would have just ripped it off for me if I asked him to. We are two smart guys, I think we can figure out how to take off a cast," Wes said.

"Alright, I'll help you, but you're falling on the sword if we get in trouble for this," Stone said.

It turned out that it was more difficult to get a cast off than either thought it would be. Mr. Stone had an impressive amount of power tools, but neither boy wanted to try to use an electric saw. They certainly would not only remove the cast, but also the arm beneath. They attempted to snip it off with a pair of gardening shears but were unable to get the blades in under the cast far enough to split it. After looking around the garage for 10 more minutes to no avail, Danny had an idea.

"Hey, did you check YouTube? There's got to be videos of guys doing exactly what you're looking to do. Everything under the sun is online," Stone offered.

A quick search of the online video housing site did indeed return numerous options on how to safely take one off and a few that didn't seem too safe. Finally, they settled on a doable option.

Danny ventured into the kitchen and retrieved a pair of regular scissors with sturdy blades and a bright orange grip, as well as a butter knife. He reached into the cabinets for a large bowl but decided that it wasn't going to be large enough for their needs. He headed to the upstairs bathroom that he shared with his little sister and called Wesley to follow.

Wes exited Dan's bedroom and headed to the bathroom. Following closely behind was Danny's younger sister, Lily, who was wearing a pink cape, a tiara and carrying a magic wand.

"Whatcha doin?" she asked quizzically.

"We're going to take my cast off, Lily," Wes said to the adorable little girl.

"Isn't a doctah s'posed to do dat?"

"Sometimes, but sometimes big boys take their own casts off," Wes said.

"Yeah, Silly Lily," Danny said, trying to make the situation seem as normal as he could.

She scrunched her face up, clearly trying to process whether or not her big brother and his friend were being honest or trying to put one over on her. After a second, she conceded that maybe this was how things worked for big boys.

Lily waved her wand overhead with a flurry. She then tapped it to Wes's right arm and said "Allacabam, abracadabra wiggily woo. Okay, now it should work."

The boys smiled and proceeded with their task. Danny lifted the stopper in the bathtub and filled the tub nearly to the top with cool water.

"Is Wes takin' a tubby?" Lily wondered out loud.

"No, we have to soak the cast in cool water to get the wrappings and glue loose," Danny told his sister.

"Ahh, that makes perfect sense," she said, mimicking something she'd heard her mother say.

Both boys giggled.

"Dang, this is cold," Wes complained as he sat parallel to the bathtub, "And it sure ain't comfortable."

"I'm sorry that the amenities are not up to your high standards," Danny said mockingly.

After five minutes, Wes stood up and Dan grabbed a towel to put under the arm. They searched the perimeter of the cast until they found a seam and worked the edge of the butter knife under the edge. Once they'd lifted enough of it off the surface, Danny grabbed the edge and pulled. Slowly but surely the inch-wide wrapping began to unravel a bit. He handed the wet remains to Lily to throw in the trash.

"This stuff stinks, Weswee," the little one said as she stuffed it in the rubbish. "You do need a bath."

Carefully Dan grabbed the scissors and had Wes lay his arm out flat on the bathroom sink, palm up.

"Hold still," he instructed his friend before working the scissors through the gap at the top of the thumb hole. He squeezed until he felt the cast begin to give, readjusted his grip and then sheared through.

"Okay, now take the butter knife and get a sliver going for me," Danny said to Wes, who did as he was told and tediously sawed through the edge closest to his elbow, in line with the thumb. After a few minutes, he'd opened up about a half inch long slice.

Danny took over from there. Slowly he was able to cut through the length of the cast. Each squeeze dissected a quarter to a half of an inch. In just a few minutes they'd gotten through to the end.

"Okay, you grab one end and I'll grab the other," Wes said.

Danny took the side nearest him and Wes worked his fingers under the other side. The duo counted to three and then pulled hard. It did not snap, as they'd hoped, but they were able to pull it far enough apart that Wes wiggled free of the cast that had kept him captive since the summer.

Wesley gazed at his naked arm and smiled.

"Finally," he said, the relief heartfelt. "You have no idea how good that feels."

"I don't think you have any idea how bad it stinks," Lily said. "Peeeeee-youuuu. You really need that bath soon."

Danny put his hand on his sister's shoulder and laughed. "Yup, he does," Danny said. "Showtime's over Lily, thanks for the help."

Danny went to his room, and after scrubbing his arm clean, Wes joined him.

"Okay, so it's off, what's the plan now?" Danny asked as Wes entered the room.

"Well, I'm going to wear long sleeves at home tonight and hope my mom doesn't notice. In a perfect world, she won't know until she sees me on the ice on Saturday. Since that's unlikely, I'm just going to put off telling her as long as I can," he said. "As for hockey, I'm going to tape it up tomorrow and wear one of those protective sleeves over it. I picked one up at the sporting goods store last month when I thought it was coming off then. It does feel pretty stiff, so I'm going to just try to loosen it up as much as possible."

"You should ask Coach for the trainer's number. Give him a call and find out if he's got any physical therapy exercises you can start. Don't mess around with it. You don't want to end up back on the disabled list," Danny offered.

"Not a bad idea," Wes said. "I'm gonna get out of here. Thanks a million for the help buddy, I really appreciate it."

"Not a problem. Hey, Wes, that was fun, I mean riding to school and practice together this week... Can we make that a regular thing?"

Wes didn't hesitate and agreed immediately. He missed driving Craig to school every day. Hanging with Danny was not nearly as entertaining as chilling with Bish had been, but he liked Dan's company and hated seeing the passenger seat empty. It would be weird having someone else sitting in that seat on a regular basis, but that was better than it being empty.

65

The yellow bus rumbled outside the Kelley Rink as the South Yarmouth boys' ice hockey team removed their canvas gear bags from their shoulders and lofted them through the rear emergency exit. Some of the junior varsity players pulled the bags up into the back of the bus, placing them one on top of the other. By the time they'd completed their task the entire back three rows of the vehicle were filled with bags piled nearly to the ceiling.

Earbuds dangled down the fronts of nearly every player's jacket. They'd all plug themselves into their pump-up music of choice once the bus was underway, but they knew better than to do so before they'd been given the go-ahead from Coach Manny Zahn. In a matter of just two minutes, all 24 of the Yanks had taken their seat on the bus with their traveling uniform of khaki pants, dress shirt, and tie. Only the matching green varsity jackets with white leather sleeves gave away that this was a sports team heading to a game. That and the smell from the mountain of hockey bags.

Coach Zahn looked up and down the aisles and assessed the mood of his players. They seemed pretty laid back, all things considered. They had no clue what they were driving toward in Eastport. The coach never liked taking his team on the road to face the Cannons because it never seemed to go well. They had not won a game in that building since he'd taken over the reins three years earlier. The coach before him had been there for four years and never won there. In fact, the Yanks had lost in Eastport 11 straight years. During that time they'd defeated the Cape's top hockey program just three times, all at home, and each time by a single goal. Last year they'd lost 6-2 at the Eastport Ice Arena.

Zahn would do everything he could to convince the Yanks that this was the year. He'd tell them that they were just as good. He'd tell them that if they worked hard that everything was going to go their way and they were going to buck history.

He wasn't sure even he'd believe what he was saying. Zahn wondered how it had been that his team was the unlucky one that had to play Eastport first after the tragedy. His heart ached for John Scadorski and his team. It was the worst kind of break, not one he'd wish on anyone. Zahn knew that the Cannons were going to play with a level of emotion that an NHL team would not be able to match, not on this night, not under these circumstances. Selfishly he hoped that the opposition would be mistake-prone because of that emotion. The chance of that was low, though, and Zahn knew it.

As Zahn sat down to take his seat at the front, the big diesel engine growled as the bus pulled away. Earbuds were inserted by his players and they lost themselves to a variety of hip-hop and classic rock while the coach stared out the window wishing the day would go by quickly.

While the Yanks drove toward the Eastport Ice Arena, Danny Stone snapped the scissors across the white tape and then stuck the end to the rest of the wrapping on Wes Garrett's right hand, deeming the job he'd done exemplary. "This is the last time I perform a procedure on you for free," Danny said to his friend.

"Yeah, until next game," Garrett replied.

Wes flexed his hand, twisted it clockwise and then counterclockwise and made a fist. The arm was not 100 percent yet, he'd lost a lot of strength while the cast clung to his arm the past few months. This was not the time to worry about that.

It was game day, finally.

Glancing around the locker room he could tell his teammates were a bit tense. Jimmy Martinage was bent at the waist, rocking slowly from left to right, his long black hair waving back and forth like overgrown field grass on a windy day. J-Mart was a goalie, they were weird to begin with. Moxon sat back in front of his locker, listening to music, Eminem no doubt. He liked angry hip-hop. Maybe it was Wu-Tang Clan. Whatever it was it had an edge. Davey Gaudreau was juggling three golf balls, reversing the direction every so often. Cy Carpenter was talking up Alex Gossard, going over some power play ideas or something. Josh Hutchinson listened in, nibbling on a Power Bar. Billy Walker was napping at his locker. You could say whatever you wanted about Walker, but you had to hand it to him, the kid sure was calm under pressure.

Coach Scadorski walked into the room, surveyed his players, and smiled. Finally, the time had come for the Cannons to return to doing what they were supposed to. There was certainly more tension than a normal game would have had, and it wasn't the same type of nerves that went with a playoff game. This was uncharted territory altogether.

Scadorski had waited until the Zamboni was out to clean the ice to come into the room to speak to his players. He knew what he wanted to say to them, and it was going to be simple.

"Collin O'Brien would have had you all laughing right now. Craig Bishop would have been ready to smash South Yarmouth's best players on the first shift. They were leaders on this team. I miss them. You miss them. They're not here, but you all are," he started.

"Guys, this has been the hardest thing I've ever had to go through as a coach. I know it's the hardest thing that you've ever had to go through. Tonight, though? Tonight we play. For the next three periods, no one is sad. For the next three periods, you're a hockey player playing for your brothers. That's it. It's that simple. Every shift, every check, every shot, it's not for just you. It's for them and everyone in this room. You see that board? That's staying up there the rest of the year."

Every head turned toward the dry erase board that had last been written on by Craig Bishop. The coach pulled a marker out of his pocket and handed it Danny Stone, who got the idea. Careful not to touch where Bish had written, in meticulous lettering the native Canadian added a word underneath Bish's final message to the team, which had been "H-E-A-R-T."

His mantra was simple as well, one word, "Together."

Scadorski grinned.

"Perfect, couldn't have thought of a better message myself. We get through this thing together, and we win this game together... Now go do it."

Together, the Cannons moved to the center of the room, circling the "E" in the middle of the floor. Cy nodded to Josh, the town's star quarterback and pretty good winger, who did what is usually frowned upon. He entered the middle of the circle and stood squarely upon that capital letter. Josh took a deep breath and recalled the words that his teammate, Ryan, had bellowed all football season long, the last time at Gillette Stadium.

"Boys, repeat after me."

"Dear Lord above, as we go through life..."

The Cannons shouted their echo.

"We ask in our prayer for strength and health..."

"If we should win, let it be by the code with faith and heads held high..."

"If we should lose, let us stand by the road and cheer as the winners go by..."

"It's game time..."

"We can't be beat... " Hutchinson said, emphasizing each syllable.

"Won't... Be... Beat!"

"Eastport Cannons rule the day!"

As the boys cheered, Josh got down on his hands and knees. He kissed the "E" and took a deep breath. With a look at the blackboard, he whispered to himself, "I got you."

66

As the players waited for the signal to hit the ice the crowd began to announce itself. The student body at Eastport High School had gone through the motions at school since it reopened. They were still mourning and shell-shocked by the horror they had lived through, but on this night they were intent on blowing off some steam. The best way they could think of to do that was to be loud, like rock concert loud. As the Zamboni began a final lap around the ice, hundreds of high school kids began to chant, repeating their mantra over and over.

"Let's go Cannons! Let's Go Cannons!"

Inside the Eastport locker room, the boys heard the cheers. They lined up to take the ice, bouncing on their skates as the nervous energy percolated.

"Okay, Wes, Josh, you're taking us out onto the ice," Cy said as he opened the door to the noise outside before quickly shutting it. "You hear that boys? That's for us. That's for OB and Bish. Let's give them something to cheer for, so loud they hear it in heaven."

Cy waited until he heard the intro to "Thunderstruck" over the public address and threw the door open. He scooted out to the right, opened the door to the ice and Danny went out to the opposite side. Scott Frazier, still sidelined by the mandatory waiting period, joined the team's captains as they all prepared to fist-bump each Cannon as he skated out onto the ice.

Wes was out first and Josh was right behind him. Each carried a jersey on a coat hanger in their hands. Wes lifted Craig Bishop's No. 19 toward the silvery insulated ceiling, and Josh raised Collin O'Brien's No. 10.

It seemed impossible, but the roar from the crowd rose a couple of decibels as Wes and Josh skated side-by-side around the rink. After looping their way around for all to see the shirts of their departed friends, they stopped at their bench and handed the jerseys over to Coach Scadorski, who hung the sweaters, number sides out, on the wall. On the other bench the same sweater numbers, but in green and gray, were also hung with respect.

Wes handed over Craig's jersey as tears rolled down his face. He noticed Josh too could not keep the emotions in check. The teammates bumped fists and made their way over to stretch with the rest of the team, trying hard to get centered. Danny Stone looked over at Wes and nodded. Wes nodded back.

After taking their warm-ups, the Cannons and Yanks lined up on their respective blue lines for the National Anthem to play. Eastport's players stood just in front of the rink's newest addition: over the past week, a new logo was painted under the ice to memorialize OB and Bish. A black ribbon with a 10 on one side and a 19 on the other filled the area on the near side boards between the blue and red line.

The South Yarmouth players stood still, overwhelmed by the scene. The stands were packed and hardly anyone wanted to see them win. Heck, people in their hometown were probably rooting against them tonight. They were deer staring at an oncoming 18-wheeler, frozen with fear. On the other side, the Cannons swayed back and forth, all eyes focused directly on the new logo.

The song could not finish fast enough for them. They were a bottle of soda, shaken and waiting for someone to unscrew the top.

When the anthem finally concluded the teams skated to their respective benches. The messages from the two coaches were very different.

"They're going to come at you hard, you've got to match that intensity," Coach Zahn warned his players. "Just play your game. They're going to blow through that adrenaline eventually, and that's when we jump all over them. Weather the storm, they're going to come at you hard early."

Scadorski had a simpler approach.

"Let's go, boys," he said. "It's time to play some hockey."

67

Cyrus Carpenter bent at the waist, his stick resting on his knees, looped back toward his teammates and then looked to each of his wingers. This was not a line he'd ever skated with before, and it wasn't one he expected, but it was the one Coach had put on the board as the starting line for tonight. Carpenter in the middle, Stone on the left, Garrett on the right. He'd played with both players separately before, but never together. Stranger still, Hutchinson was back on defense, with Walker, another forward, playing the other D spot. Josh Hutchinson had not played defense since the fifth grade, but he was out on the ice to start the game tonight. Walker had never been back there.

Obviously, Coach knew this was big for his seniors, so he put them out there together.

Slowly Cyrus entered the faceoff circle where he eyeballed his counterpart from South Yarmouth, a kid he'd played against numerous times over the last two years. The kid was a good faceoff guy and Cy decided he'd play it safe and try to win the puck back to his defense.

The ref offered a quick, "Good luck guys," and then dropped the puck. Just as it connected with the ice it was on Cyrus's backhand and zipped back and to the right where Hutchinson got it and snapped it up to Wes. With a quick snap of the wrists, Wes Garrett flung the puck down the boards into the corner and the game was on. He chased it but lost the race, and South Yarmouth worked it out. A whistle blew quickly, just 25 seconds into the game, as the puck went over the glass, and Scadorski changed the lines.

Carpenter stayed on, with Stone and Billy Walker up front. Moxon jumped on to play D and Gossard replaced Hutchinson. It was back to business as usual.

That business was going the way South Yarmouth's coach had feared it might. Over the first few shifts, it was apparent the Cannons were on a mission, but the Yanks were weathering the storm, thanks mostly to their sophomore goalie Charlie Baynard, who took up half of the net just by standing near it. Baynard's size was his biggest asset, and he'd needed every bit of it as Carpenter and Walker each had early bids to get the Cannons on the board. Gaudreau nearly broke the seal with a wraparound try, and a blast by Moxon from the point had hit the crossbar.

On the South Yarmouth bench, Coach Zahn tried to keep his players believing they had a chance, and with Baynard stopping six shots in the first five minutes, it seemed he might have been on to something. Martinage had faced just one shot during the first five minutes and it hit him square in the chest. That came two minutes into the action, and he'd spent the rest of the time squinting down the far end of the ice watching his teammates dominate.

Despite controlling the action, the Cannons were starting to get frustrated. They wanted, needed, to score. The tension in the building rose with each save that Baynard made as the fans held their collective breath on each windup and sighed out a disappointed "ahh" with each stop.

Baynard was playing great, but the ice was tilted and there was no way he could hold on forever. He'd stopped 88 percent of the shots he'd faced this season, but his team was giving up an average of 34 shots per outing. Statistically speaking, that meant he was allowing a tad over four goals per game, and his weakness was obvious if you knew what you were looking for.

Goalies are taught to keep their catching gloves above their waist. Ideally, the top of the glove should be at least a tad higher than their shoulder. That way they can take away the top shelf. Baynard must not have hit the weight room too hard, because as each game wore on, that glove got lower and lower.

"Bar south, glove side boys," Assistant Coach Tom Henry repeated over and over on the Eastport bench. "We saw it on the video from last year, high glove side."

Despite his roller coaster of a start to the season, Billy Walker had been putting up decent statistics before the accident. One of Walker's biggest strengths on the ice also tended to be his biggest problem. With the puck on his stick, he was creative, like an artist with a blank canvas. He could make the thing dance, but he could also look like a dad on the floor at a wedding reception when he tried too hard.

With a little more than four minutes to go in the first period, Walker had his chance to show his stuff. He flew the zone after a tipped shot and got the puck on his stick. With a swirling motion, he worked the puck off of his backhand to a perfect shooting position and heeded his coach's words, firing for the glove side, upstairs.

Baynard stopped it but did not catch the puck. The shot hit off the hard padded part of the glove that protects a goalie's wrist and bounced back to the ice, on the far side of the net where little Davey Gaudreau was doing his job. The 15-year-old crashed the net and tipped it, lightly, for the inside of the far post. Baynard almost recovered, sliding his right leg back to the post quickly enough to get the edge of his skate on the shot.

It was the back of his skate. The puck crossed the goal line. The referee, who had circled behind the net to be in position to see the play unfold, pointed toward the puck in the net, signaling an Eastport goal.

A jet fighter could have flown over the Eastport Ice Arena roof and been unnoticed at that moment. More than 2,000 arms shot straight upward. Two weeks of emotion and tension were screamed out.

Gaudreau raised his stick in his right hand and pointed toward the sky before being enveloped in a hug by the other four skaters on the ice.

"Attaboy, Baby G," Cyrus shouted.

"Hell yeah, Davey," Walker followed.

As the boys released their grips on one another, Davey led a line to the bench but took a circular route. Five boys in a row skated around the new logo, tapped it with their sticks as they passed, then went over to the bench where they high-fived each teammate.

"Eastport goal scored by number 25, Dave Gaudreau, assisted by number 5, Billy Walker. Time of the goal 10:33 of the first period. That's Gaudreau from Walker at 10:33," the public address announcer shouted. No one heard him over the still deafening roar.

68

The floodgates opened in the two periods that followed. Carpenter wowed the crowd with a gorgeous goal, followed by an ugly one from Hutchinson that bounced off of his skate. Alex Gossard slapped one in from the point in the third period, glove side high, and the Cannons began their new season with a 4-1 victory. Martinage had given up a goal early in the third period, which made the game seem a lot closer than it actually was at that time, but Gossard's bomb sealed it. South Yarmouth had just 11 shots in the game and left the ice feeling shell-shocked.

A mob of reporters from media outlets statewide surrounded Scadorski outside of his coach's room after the game. The coach stuck his hand up in the air and collected himself as reporters tried to shout over one another to get the first question in. "Give me a second," the coach pleaded. Scadorski examined the crowd of reporters before him and chose the one he knew. "Mac, I believe you had a question."

Richardson grinned.

"Scads, you and your team have been through a lot. How did it feel to get out there and play hockey again, and how do you feel about the way they responded?" he asked, lifting his iPhone up to record the question every other reporter would have asked.

"We feel pretty great, to be honest. It's been a long road for these guys, and it's not over. This was the first step toward healing, I think, but it's going to be a long, long time before any of us feels normal again," Scadorski said. "Winning is nice, but our team won just by stepping onto the ice. Those guys didn't just lose two teammates, they lost two brothers, two friends, two family members. They'll never be the same again, none of us will. How could you be? There's no road map for what we're going through. I wish someone would tell me all of the right things to say, all of the right things to do. To be honest, we're all playing this by ear, learning as we go. Playing hockey doesn't make anyone forget about what happened, but it is a helpful distraction."

Another reporter, from the Cape's daily paper, was the only reporter not recording the conversation. He was quickly scribbling in a notebook, doing his best to keep up with the coach's stream of consciousness. Looking over the top of his eyeglasses, he asked, "It took awhile for that first one to go in. What was the feeling like on the bench when Gaudreau put in that rebound?"

"Can't describe it, really. Time kind of stood still for a second there. He got to the spot, had his stick on the ice like he's supposed to and the littlest guy we've got scored the biggest goal of our year, at least so far. The reaction, on the bench, in the crowd, well, you were here, I'd say it was amazing – and a relief. We needed that one. After that, it felt like we could just play hockey again," the coach said.

Scadorski answered a few more questions, each of which was basically a repeat of the first one. Richardson, knowing that Scadorski would play the game with the TV guys as long as he had to, faded back from the throng and watched the door to the locker room. When he saw Gaudreau leave the room, walking out with Moxon and Gossard, he waved the sophomore over.

"Davey, great game buddy, mind if I ask a quick question?" he asked.

"Oh, yeah, sure Mr. Richardson, whatever you need," Gaudreau, who was obviously straight out of a postgame shower, said as he ran his fingers through his still dripping hair.

"Can you tell me about the goal and what you were thinking about when you scored it?" he queried.

"Coach Henry had been telling us to go high to his glove, and that's what Billy tried to do. I saw him break to the net, and my job is to get there on the other side. I got to the spot, and the puck was just there and I kind of poked at it," Gaudreau said sheepishly. "Hardly the prettiest one I've ever scored, but I guess it was kind of a big one. I've never heard a roar like that before, it gave me chills."

"That's awesome," Richardson said. "Anything go through your mind in the

250

moment?"

"Umm, not really in the moment, but on the bench, I thought of something kind of funny."

"What was that?"

"Last year, I got called up to play varsity – you knew that – anyway, my first goal was kind of similar, but I tipped in a shot on the fly. It was a bomb by Bish, from the right side, and I had my stick down and it just hit the blade and bounced off and into the goal. The guys all congratulated me and patted me on the back and all of that," Gaudreau recounted. "Anyways, we're sitting on the bench, and Craig reaches over and hands me the puck – he had fished it out of the net for me – and said, 'Nice job, rookie. Next time don't steal my goal, though, okay. I don't get many of them.' He patted me on the head and laughed... so, yeah, I thought about that. He would have kidded me about this one, told me I do a good job of stealing goals from the older guys. Tonight's goal, that was for Bish, and OB too."

Richardson thanked the kid and shook his hand. In the next paper, Richardson recounted the story under the headline, 'Gaudreau Steals Another Goal.'

69

After congratulating her friends after their big win, Emily whispered in Melissa's ear that she was leaving and disappeared from the crowd. Tonight had been a lot of fun. She hadn't yelled so loud in ages, and some of the weight that had pressed down on her chest lately seemed to wane – just a bit. It was fun to experience positive emotion after all of the negative ones.

But Craig wasn't on the ice. She'd seen every home game he'd played for Eastport varsity hockey, and most of the away games, too. After every game, they'd spend time on the phone talking. They weren't just the conversations of two kids in love. They were game breakdowns.

One of the best parts of their relationship was the ability to have those post-game talks. She watched him intently on the ice and had opinions for him. If he didn't play well, she'd tell him he was standing around too much, or not getting back fast enough. Last year she'd noticed he was allowing his man to get an inside position when he was playing defense. That turned around in the next game.

Craig had respected those opinions. Emily knew her stuff. She might not ever have been a hockey player, but as one of the best lacrosse players around, she knew about being in the right spots. Emily didn't just watch the puck, she watched the players. She loved how the spacing in hockey and lacrosse were so similar. The boys hit the puck with their sticks, she threw and shot a ball with hers. They were different games, but similar in many ways.

He did the same for her in the spring when his baseball schedule allowed him to get to the lacrosse field. One day he asked her why every time she shot she delivered the ball from the same spot, over her right shoulder. "You're letting the goalie see the ball too well," he noted. "Try mixing it up, drag the stick low, shoot from the hip." Emily went out and tried that the next game and scored seven goals.

As she headed away from the rink she stopped at the roadside memorial that had been set up in honor of Craig and Collin. The flowers had all wilted and frozen, the teddy bears iced over.

Emily left the car running with the lights on and walked over to the white cross someone had stuck in the ground. She reached into her pocket and left the game day roster next to it.

"Wow, great game tonight. You would have loved every second. Wow, this is hard. I promised myself I wasn't going to cry," Emily said as she wiped at her eyes.

"They left you and Collin on the roster," she said. "The Boys played great tonight, all things considered. Davey got the first one, and Billy and Josh scored, too. Danny just missed on another. Martinage gave up a soft goal, but he was okay. It was only one, but you know how inconsistent he can be. You guys won, 4-1. The team was really nervous in the first period, you could feel the tension. Once that first goal went in everything started to roll.

"Wes came back. He said there was no way he was going to miss it. He's not all the way back, you can tell his shot's not all there yet. It's just good to see him back on the ice. He's lost off the ice without you. I mean, we all are, but he's doing his best. Him and Mel are getting on great, though, so he's got that, and he's driving Danny around a lot. They're trying to cope together.

"Oh my gosh, I almost forgot, Scotty's back. He's back on the team and in school. He plays this weekend. He said he couldn't stay up there anymore, he missed you guys too much. After the accident, he refused to go back. His mom must've been pissed. Somehow they got him a waiver. I would have loved to see you play with him again. It'll be fun to see him back out there.

Drawing a deep breath, Emily continued.

"I'm going to get back in the gym this week. I need to get my cardio back and get stronger. I'll be playing on Sunday nights up in Plymouth starting in a month and I can't go back weak. I've got a lot of goals to score this year. I'll point up at you after every one. Wave back, okay."

The tears stung her face as they froze in the winter air.

"I miss you, Craig. I love ya, babe. I'll be back to chat soon."

70

Scott had been counting down the days, and he double-checked with Athletic Director Burnette and the guidance department during his lunch period on Friday afternoon to make sure his math was correct. His first day back to school had been January 2. It was now January 13. Five school days attended last week, five this week. His 10-day wait was over.

The Cannons had a game scheduled for the next day, Saturday, at Forestdale High School. Barring an act of God – and that's what it would take to keep Scott Frazier from getting to the rink – he would be back where he belonged, on the ice in an Eastport Cannons jersey.

The school day went by in an uninteresting fashion. Hockey practice consisted of a simple walkthrough and skate around. Knowing a big game was on tap the next day, Coach Scadorski had eased up. He wanted his players to have all the energy they could for the next night.

"No letdowns, no hangovers," Scadorski said to the boys in the locker room before they exited the locker room for the night. "And for God's sake, no one do anything stupid tonight. No drinking, no drugging, no partying. Curfew is 10:30, no exceptions. I will be calling your houses. If any of you are having sleepovers, let me know ahead of time – I'll check in on all of you."

Scadorski clung to the idea that most kids got into trouble after 10. If curfew was 10:30 they'd have to be out the door before most bad things had a chance to escalate. Since taking over the team his rule had worked, for the most part. He had lost just one player in-season to a drinking violation. Unfortunately, he could not legislate what happened the rest of the year and had a couple of kids get into trouble before hockey season had begun, costing them the first five games of their season. Johnny Moxon had been caught the year before and had sat out a quarter of the season, mandated by the MSAA when a picture of him at a party had been posted on Instagram. He was holding a bottle of Captain Morgan's rum in his hand.

It wasn't until January that he'd been able to hold a hockey stick for the team.

Scott had no plans to do anything that could jeopardize his chance to get back out on his skates. Most of the team was planning to go to Milliani's Wing House for their all-you-can-eat boneless wing feast, a monthly event that every true carnivore in town attended on the second Friday of every month. The wing house was owned by an ex-NHL player who played parts of four seasons with the Toronto Maple Leafs and Detroit Red Wings.

The owner had not grown up in Eastport but had bought a summer home there after chasing girls and downing beers in the summertime during his playing days. The now 49-year-old had been born north of Boston and had attended Bellingham High School before playing in college at the University of Vermont. He'd gone on to have more fights than goals in the NHL but made enough money to open up his restaurant. The food was great, the décor was cool, and the man with the crooked nose and scar on his left cheek – a reminder of a fight that was a favorite on YouTube – liked to chat up the patrons and regale them with war stories.

Scott ate more than his $11.99's worth at the buffet and beat the curfew call from Coach by an hour. After playing Call of Duty for a few hours he was in bed by midnight and slept well, waking up at 8:30 the next morning. With a coating of fresh snow out on the lawn and roads, he decided against a jog and did a few sets of crunches and push-ups before pouring half a box of raisin bran into an enormous bowl. He ate breakfast while the highlights of the previous night's basketball and hockey games played on ESPN.

He was scooping up the last few milk-covered raisins when his phone beeped with a text message from Coach Scadorski asking him to show up to the rink early.

He tapped in, "No problem." The Cannons were visiting Forestdale High's rink in Sagamore Beach. Since it was a half-hour drive to the rink the Cannons were told to meet up at their home arena at 2:30 for a 3 PM bus ride over. They'd get to the arena around 3:30 and have plenty of time to get dressed and ready.

Scott asked his mom to drive him to the rink at 2 PM. She wished him luck as he slung his hockey bag over his shoulder and headed inside. He dropped the oversized bag in the corner of the lobby and headed over to the coaches' room where he found Scadorski talking on the phone, apparently with a coach from another town. He tried not to listen to the conversation but knew right away that his coach was getting some tips on how Forestdale played from a coach whose team had already faced them.

"Thanks, buddy, I appreciate that. I'll let you know how it goes. I owe you one," Scadorski said before ending the call.

Turning his attention to his best player, Scadorski smiled. "Scotty, big decision time for you. You've got to pick a jersey number and the pickings are kind of slim."

Once tryouts had ended everyone on the team had picked out their jersey numbers. Every returning player kept the number they had before unless they requested a change. Hardly anyone ever changed their jersey numbers. The players tended to feel a kinship to the digits they wore on their back, an unexplainable devotion to represent that particular number during their high school career. Everyone wanted to build a legacy that the next guy who got the shirt would have to live up to.

Scadorski rolled over a cart on which hung all of the remaining jerseys. He had not been kidding. All of the best numbers were gone. There were no single digit shirts left. In the teens, 11 and 13 were the only ones available. There were three shirts in the 20s, and two in the 30s. Players typically shied away from the high numbers in high school. Everything higher than 28 was usually reserved for goalies.

The hangers screeched on the metal rod as Scott moved them from the left to right, eyeing the back of each one. Nothing grabbed him until the sixth sweater. There was something about the number that spoke to him. At first, he didn't know what it was, and then the realization smacked him upside the head. His mind was made up.

"This one, no doubt," Frazier said to his coach. "I'm number 29."

"Okay, kind of an odd choice. I figured you'd take 11, or maybe 13 since

Moxon has your old number 12. How come 29?"

"Do the math, Coach. What's 10 plus 19? If you'd told me I could wear one of the boys' sweaters in their honor, I wouldn't have been able to choose. This way they're both out there on my back."

Scott grabbed the sweater off the rack and carried it over his shoulder. He could not wait to wear it on the ice later that night.

71

Over the next two weeks, the Cannons could do no wrong on the ice. Frazier led the charge, and the reinvigorated team won four straight games. The win streak had them right back in the thick of the race for the league championship. It was like clockwork, Wes and Josh skated the jerseys out onto the ice, handed them to Coach Scads and then the team would go out and lay their foes to waste. They beat Forestdale 6-1 on Scott's first night back and he scored twice. Eastham was next and they toppled them 4-0. Chatham didn't stand a chance and lost 8-2, and then it was Plymouth High's turn to be Cannon fodder. EHS rolled to a 5-2 win that night.

Danny Stone should have been feeling great. He'd been playing better, had scored two goals during those four games, and was finally playing without fear of getting hurt again. When the puck went into the corners, the dirty area as the coaches called it, he wasn't hesitating anymore. He'd bang around guys that had 30 pounds on him without thinking twice.

Off the ice, though, Dan still hurt. One of his teachers emailed his mother to say she was worried about his lack of focus. Wes, who had become like a brother to Danny over the last four weeks, constantly seemed to be poking him during their car rides to and from practice, asking him, "Are you still with me buddy?"

Finally, he reluctantly succumbed to his mother's prodding to "talk to someone about what he was going through." Leaving school early on a Monday afternoon, right after lunch, he'd ridden with his mother across town and now sat in a waiting room, terrified by the words on the fogged over glass door before him.

"Dr. Cheryl Watkinson, Psychologist."

The school had offered grief counselors in the weeks following the accident, but Danny had eschewed that. None of the other players had gone to talk to them, as far as he knew, and he didn't want it to get out that he had. Why load their barrels for teasing him?

His friends' mini-intervention had convinced him not to continue to look for answers in a bottle, not to mention that he didn't really care for the taste of the bourbon his dad had in the liquor cabinet. And the hangovers had really sucked. The booze hadn't dulled the pain as much as he'd thought that it might anyway. Instead, it had made him mentally travel down some dark paths. Now, a month removed, the pain had waned some, but he still ached in his head. He couldn't kick the feeling that he was responsible.

The door cracked open and a smiling face appeared behind a set of red eyeglasses. "Come on in, Daniel," the doctor said.

He rose to his feet and entered, pausing to glance over his shoulder at his mother. She smiled. "I'll be here when you're done."

Two comfortable chairs faced one another with a round table between them. An empty notepad sat on the table. Sunlight spilled in through half-closed Venetian blinds, casting a pattern of shady lines on top of a large desk with a laptop on it. The walls were painted a soft sky blue. *If deep dark secrets weren't spilled inside this room, it might be a comfortable place to relax,* Danny thought.

"Have a seat, Daniel."

"Danny."

"I'm sorry, Danny. Go ahead and get comfortable and let's have a talk. I'm here for you. I'm a psychologist, which means I try to help people cope with life issues that they're having," she explained. "Nothing you say will leave the confines of this room. It is a safe space."

"Okay, I get that," Danny said.

"So I understand that you're a pretty good hockey player and that you were friends and teammates with Collin and Craig. I'm sorry for your loss."

Danny thanked her. He'd had to thank lots of people for the same sentiment since the accident.

"From my conversation with your mother, I understand that you were close with Craig and Collin. Do you mind telling me a little about them?"

"I've known them ever since we moved here. We got to know each other playing hockey, and we played baseball together, too."

Holding a ballpoint pen between two fingers, she looked over the top of her red glasses and smiled. "Okay, they were athletes. That's part of what they were, but not who they were. Who were they to you?"

"Friends, teammates. Craig was cool, he was always nice to people. He loved music, he introduced me to a lot of the stuff I listen to. He taught me how to talk to girls without coming off as creepy. He was one of the best people I've ever known. I miss him all the time. Collin, he was kind of larger than life, if you know what I mean. When he walked into the room he kind of ran the show, and he was funny, really funny, and a little tapped, too."

"Tapped, how so?"

"He was a little bit crazy. He took risks he didn't have to. When we were 12 he filled up like 20 water balloons and threw them at a police car that always came through his neighborhood around the same time. He didn't really get into any trouble, the cop thought it was funny."

"They sound like two good guys," she said. "It must have been traumatic to see their accident. Do you mind telling me about it?"

"I was driving, Collin was driving his car and flew up on my back. He sped up on my car and he lost control. He hit a tree."

"That's awful. Were you speeding as well?"

"No, I was just driving. Actually, I was really excited, we were supposed to go out that night to Boston. I was trying to figure out what I was going to wear."

"Did he attempt to pass you? Did you start to goof around with him in his game?"

"No, I was kind of scared when he sped up on me, and I didn't know it was him at the time. All of a sudden there was this car coming up on me really fast, and the next thing I know it swerved off the road into the trees. I

261

replay it in my mind all the time, and I just wish I could have done something, anything, differently. If I'd pulled over and just let him pass, or if I'd left earlier, or later... They'd still be here."

The doctor wrote something on her notepad. Danny thought she must be a great poker player because her face didn't give anything away.

"How's school going? I hear you're a pretty good student?"

The change of topic caught Danny a little off-guard. Happy to be talking about something else, he answered quickly. "It's fine. I'm okay, mostly B's, a couple of A's. Trying to get my C-plus in chemistry up to a B for honor roll. Mr. Cory used to play sports, I think I'll be able to talk him up to a B if I get close."

"Is it hard to concentrate at school?" she queried.

"Sometimes."

"I remember high school. There were times I fell asleep in math class," she admitted with a grin. "Since the accident, is it harder than before?"

"At times. It's like I can go along all day without thinking about what happened, and then something will remind me of the guys, or what happened, and I sort of tune everything out. That's when I get thinking about them."

"Can you give me an example?"

"Well, the other day I was sitting in English class, and we were talking about this play our class is going to go see in Boston. Collin was in that class with me, and I remembered that he'd joked about us ditching the group when we were up there to go see this girl he knew who is going to school at Emerson," Danny said, laughing through the end before pausing. "He said that she was going to hook me up with her roommate."

"Did that make you sad?"

"Sort of, yeah."

"What in particular made you sad?"

"I realized that I don't get to go on any more of Collin's crazy adventures.

262

The girl is probably hideous looking – the roommate that is. I've seen pics of the girl he was visiting, she's amazing – but even that would have made it funny. Whenever I did stuff with Collin we always had a story to tell afterward. Like half of the best things I've ever done seem to be because of one of Collin's ideas," Danny's voice grew thick. "I miss him. It's like I didn't just lose my two friends. I lost a part of who I am, and I don't know what I'm supposed to do."

"You did lose that, I'm sorry," she said. "There's nothing wrong with realizing that you associated part of your identity with your group of friends. Lots of people do that. The key is figuring out where you exist outside of them."

"Does your family go to church?" the doctor asked, throwing Danny off a bit with her abrupt change of subject.

"Well, not often. We go on the big holidays, and every now and again, I guess."

"A lot of people find solace and peace from faith," she said.

"I don't know about that. God seems to have forgotten about Eastport if you ask me," he said, the anger rising in his voice.

"That's understandable. I've been through situations in my life where I felt the same. Our conversation reminded me of something my pastor said recently that applies to what you're going through. I don't know if I will do it justice, but if you're open to hearing it, I think it might strike a chord."

"Why not," he said, more than a little sarcastically.

"He started by saying how Paul, one of Jesus's disciples, said that 'in this life, you will have trouble.' Just a statement of fact, I think we can all agree with that. The pastor went on to explain that suffering, hurt and pain aren't picky. They don't search out only people who deserve it. We don't go through hard times because we deserve it. Hurt does not discriminate, it happens to all of us. Paul basically told us that you can't opt out of difficulties, hardship or suffering. It's something we all go through."

"That doesn't make it any easier, does it," Danny spat.

"Certainly not," Dr. Watkinson said, brushing her bangs out of her eyes. "Let me ask you something. Have you ever been injured playing hockey?"

"Yes. I missed all of last year because of a collarbone break. It sucked."

"Ouch. That must have been very painful."

"It was, the bone protruded against my skin when it busted. That was the worst pain I'd ever felt."

"But it felt better, eventually, right?"

"Yes, but it took a long time. I had to rehab my upper body and they wouldn't let me play for months. The waiting sucked and it took forever."

Dr. Watkinson shifted in her chair and leaned closer.

"Your heart, your feelings, are just like your bones. They won't heal immediately. It takes time, and it leaves a scar. Just like your collarbone, your heart was broken. That doesn't heal right away, but it will get better. Right now it's all new, and the pain is fresh. When you think of your friends there is so much hurt. Over time when you think of them, you'll laugh, or smile, or maybe cry, but the hurt will lessen. It may never go entirely away, but you will heal."

Danny nodded along as she spoke. He didn't have a scar, he had an open wound. He wasn't sure it would ever heal, no matter how much talking about it he did.

72

Billy Walker stared down into Cyrus Carpenter's eyes, trying to hide a smile.

"Come on sweetheart, three more... two... one... down," Walker growled. "There you go. Nice set, way to finish."

Carpenter exhaled sharply, sat up slowly and then toweled off the bench. Ten reps of 150 pounds might not be the best on the team, but the captain didn't want to overdo it during the season. He'd lived in the gym up until late November, spending six days a week prepping for the hockey season. During the season he only went on the days after games, as maintenance.

The season had already taken a toll on Cy's body. Back in December, when the year was just beginning, the six foot, one inch 18-year-old was in the best physical condition he'd ever been in. He could run a 10K in his sleep and bench sets of 180-pounds easily. Trying not to look too much like a Schwarzenegger wannabe, he flexed his shoulders and triceps and inspected his physique in the gym's mirror. Anyone off the street would say he looked great, but he knew he'd lost 12 pounds since opening day. He'd celebrated when he got to 205 pounds. He'd finally reached the playing weight he'd wanted for two years. It was heavy enough to win fights for the puck, but not so heavy it'd slow him down chasing it.

"Would you stop staring at yourself, you megalomaniac?" Walker said to his teammate.

"I prefer to think of it as narcissistic," Cyrus retorted.

That the two were together in the gym, pushing one another to get better and sharing lighthearted jabs was a big step forward. It hadn't been that long since Walker was ready to leave the team altogether. His antics had driven Cyrus nuts. The accident had certainly brought them closer together, though neither would admit it. That would mean acknowledging the rift had existed in the first place.

"Just seeing what I've got loaded up for Hyannis on Saturday night," Cyrus said, trying to sound menacing but instead coming off like a caricature of a tough guy.

"Gonna be fun. They've been playing pretty well lately. I think they're like 8-5 right now. They won the other night. Always fun to beat H-town, especially in their barn."

While the Eastport boys were working out, Hyannis High's Bubby Seaver snapped one of his mother's nice bath towels on the dining room chair and declared his one-day-only barbershop was open for business.

"Step on up boys, don't be shy," the winger for the Red Hawks shouted from his home's spacious kitchen. The room smelled of piping hot pizza and potato chips as the team assembled to honor an old tradition.

For as long as anyone could remember every hockey player at Hyannis High shaved his hair into a mohawk prior to the Eastport game. It was a custom that was held in high regard in H-Town. It also was something that the school's athletic department tried very hard to ignore, as it had potential bullying and hazing ramifications. No one was forced to cut their hair, but as a member of the team, you just did it. Every boy signed a waiver that a lawyer, whose son was on the team, had drawn up a few years earlier, deeming that every haircut had been agreed to willingly.

Gunnar Ellison signed on the dotted line when the paper had been handed to him but really did not want to be shorn by Seaver's shears. Gunnar prided himself on his perfectly coiffed mane, which paired perfectly with his go-to look of khakis, button-up shirt and loafers. Ellison dressed like he was the cover model for Young Republicans Illustrated. As a sophomore the year before he had avoided the cutting because he'd been on the junior varsity team. This year he'd made the big team and had exceeded expectations. Gunnar Ellison was a big reason that the Hawks were rising.

"Gunnar, why don't you go first," Bubby said, his eyes dancing with excitement at taking off the flashy locks of the resident pretty boy.

With a deep breath, Gunnar agreed. "Okay," he whispered.

Seaver wrapped a polka-dotted bed sheet around his teammate like a backward cape and then clicked on the clippers. The room sounded like it was infested with angry bees.

Starting above Ellison's left eyebrow, Bubby slowly cut through the haircut that had cost $45 just three weeks earlier. The room erupted with cheers as the first strands fell away. With a couple more swipes, the entire left side of Gunnar's head was naked, and the floor was littered with locks.

"Spiky hawk or short hawk?" Seaver asked his client.

Figuring that if he was going to do this he might as well go all-in, Gunnar said, "Let's spike it up. Why not?"

"Hell, yeah," Seaver agreed. "The pretty boy's going punk rock, I love it. Someone grab me the hair gel."

Moments later it was done. In minutes Gunnar Ellison went from looking like the boy that every parent dreams will show up with flowers at their front door to date their daughter to one that those same parents would chase away.

"Give the boy a leather jacket and a guitar and he'd be a Ramone," Seaver said as he admired his handiwork. "What do you think, Guns?"

Ellison looked at himself in a mirror and smiled. He felt different, in a good way, a cool way. He certainly looked tougher, which was a great thing.

"It looks badass," Ellison said.

"Hell yeah it does," Seaver said. "Eastport doesn't know what's coming for them. Punk Rock Ellison is gonna get them."

"Hell, yeah," Gunnar said with an ear-to-ear smile. "The Hawks are coming for ya Eastport!"

73

Forty-eight hours later Walker and Carpenter sat next to one another in the visitors' locker room readying for the biggest game of the year so far. The Cannons had not lost since the accident and were now sitting pretty at 10-3 on the season. They had already wrapped up a spot in the state tournament, where the state championship game was played at the TD Garden in Boston, the home of the NHL's Bruins.

Walker had just gone through his pregame ritual, one he'd adopted when the season restarted. For the first game back he'd bought a white headband and drawn in big black letters, 'OB 10—BISH 19' on the front and "Heart" on the back. Initially, he'd hoped to wear the same headband for every game under his helmet, but the sweat from his brow had smudged the lettering nearly beyond recognition during that first game.

Going forward he'd made it a routine to stop in the pro shop and buy a new one before each game. The owner made sure to keep the shelves stocked up for him, and the price - just $4 - wasn't bad. He'd had to be more precise in his lettering than usual because the floor seemed to be shaking. As he finished, he realized why it felt Hyannis was being rattled by a small earthquake.

"Carp, calm down, man. You shake that leg any more you're going to crack the blades in your skates. It's just a game. We've played them like 50 times since we were little kids. They never beat us. We've got this," Walker said.

Billy wasn't completely right. They had played many, many games against Hyannis since the Boys were old enough to skate, but Hyannis had won against Eastport in the somewhat recent past. When Walker and Carpenter were freshmen, riding the bench for the varsity team quite a bit, they had lost to Hyannis in fantastic fashion, 5-4.

That night Eastport's goalie, Kostas Pappadoras, had allowed a goal on a clear-in from the far blue line. Pappadoras dealt with anxiety issues throughout his high school days and liked to smoke half of a joint before big games. He said it calmed his nerves and helped him deal with the stress of his job. Before that particular Hyannis game, his nerves must have been especially haywire because he'd finished off a full joint and started a second one just an hour before game time. He didn't make it out of the first period, allowing four goals in the first 15 minutes, including one from way down the other end of the ice.

In the time between that loss and the current night, the teams had played six times. Eastport had won three of those games and the other three had ended in ties. People liked to say that you could take two groups of toddlers, one from each town, and throw a ball into the room and the teams would play a game worth watching. The rivalry dated back to the late 1800s, starting on the football field. Literally, thousands of games had been waged between the high school teams, across dozens of sports. If familiarity breeds contempt, it was safe to say there was a deep dislike for the opponents on each side.

"It's our last game against those guys, ya know," Carpenter said. "As soon as the schedule came out I looked to see when we were playing here. You know how big a deal this is. We're seniors, Bill. This is is."

"Yup, but we got this. Our boys upstairs aren't going to let us lose tonight," Walker said with a smile, patting his teammate on the shoulder. "We got this. Chill, take a deep breath. You're the captain, at least pretend you're cool and calm. You lead the way, we'll follow. It's going to be awesome."

Across the locker room, Scott Frazier felt like the energy from his teammates was way too nervous. If someone opened the door the pressure change might make everyone fall down.

Since rejoining the team, he'd done his best to be just one of the boys. He knew he was the team's best player, but he'd also left them behind. In doing so he vacated his potential captaincy and right to lead. He'd sat back and let Cyrus and Danny handle the heavy lifting to this point. Rather than be the vocal guy, he'd tried to set the tone on the ice, or by taking the younger guys under his wing with some encouragement and pointers.

The time for staying in the background had ended, though. This was

Hyannis, and this was the last time he and his friends would ever line up against those jerks - even if it was hard to think of them that way after they'd shown up for the wakes and funerals and said all of those nice things. Screw it, he thought. "Tonight they're the enemy," he said to himself. That's how it had to be.

Coach Scadorski had gone over his game plan earlier and waited by the door for the players to come out. Having played in this game himself as a kid, he knew there wasn't anything he could say that would matter. This was Hyannis, and the motivation had to come from inside the room. His leaders had to lead, and he was going to let them do just that. With five minutes left before the team was supposed to enter the arena, it was time for the captains to pump up the boys before they went out to warm up.

Scott caught the eyes of Danny and Cy and waved them over.

"Guys, I don't want to overstep my bounds here, but can I talk to the team tonight before we go out there?" he asked quietly.

Danny had been visualizing his personal game plan for the last 15 minutes and had forgotten to think of something to say. He was fine with it. Cyrus felt a little relieved. He knew how important this game was to him, to everyone, but wasn't sure he could spit out the words in a cohesive manner.

"Sounds good to me," Danny said. "Cy?"

"Yeah, sure Scotty, make it good."

Cyrus moved to the middle of the room and whistled between his fingers to grab everyone's attention. The background noise ceased.

"Big game, boys, big game. Scotty's got some stuff he wants to say before we head out there," Cyrus said.

Scott Frazier straightened his back and took a deep breath.

"I was nine years old the first time I played a game against Hyannis, back in Mites. Carp was on that team, Billy and Wes and Bish and OB all were too. We won that game, 2-1. I remember it like it was yesterday, Wes and Bish scored our goals. Carp missed an empty net at the end and we teased him about it at McDonald's after the game. We were all so happy. We beat Hyannis. We didn't know why it mattered so much, but we knew that it did.

"That was nine years ago, boys. A lot has changed. I left and came back. Wes has a girlfriend, who'd have thought that would ever happen," he continued as giggles broke the silence.

"OB and Bish aren't in the room anymore, but they're here tonight, boys. They wouldn't miss this for the world. OB loved to play Hyannis. He wanted to see how many guys he could wreck. Bish always showed up. Remember he scored against them last year? It was beautiful.

"We know they're here with us, but you've got to be here too. In this moment, the next three periods, you have to be at your best. Hyannis doesn't care at all what we've been through, not tonight they don't. They're going to see that big cannon the front of your shirt and they're going to try to run right through it."

Scott paused.

"Are you going to let them do that?" he asked quietly.

"No," they all responded.

"I said, are you going to let them do that?"

The response was louder this time.

"Who are we?"

"Eastport!" they boomed.

"Who's better?"

"No one!" the Cannons roared.

"Prove it," Scott said as he turned toward the door and held it open. The Cannons grabbed their sticks and sprinted out the exit toward the ice.

Dan stopped on his way out and lightly head-butted Scott. "Good speech," he said, smiling wide.

Cyrus did the same, but just said, "Thanks man, that was perfect."

271

74

Most Saturday nights hockey fans in Hyannis can walk right up to the box office and buy a ticket just as the game is about to start and sit wherever they want. Once a year, though, they have to show up pretty early just to make sure they get into the building. When Eastport comes to town the place is packed.

Connor Donaldson had made a mint at school in the days leading up to the game. A senior at HHS who was determined to be a millionaire before his 30th birthday, he knew money was to be made exploiting the big hockey game, and he'd found a way. He offered a friend in his graphics class, who was very good at that artsy stuff, fifty bucks to draw up a logo of a cannon with a big screw blocking the barrel and a hawk perched on top.

He then took the logo to a local print shop and ordered up 250 red t-shirts in a variety of sizes with the logo screened in white, along with the words "Screw Eastport" scrawled on the front, and "Hit 'Em Up Hyannis" on the back. The cost of the shirts were $5.75 each. It cost him $1,437.50 out of pocket. He'd covered the investment at lunch on Wednesday and was in the black on Thursday. By Friday afternoon he'd sold out of the run of shirts. He kept one for himself and gave freebies and $20 bucks each to his friends who had helped sell them.

In less than a week he had a profit of around $3,400. Nearly every one of the shirts was on display in the student section, which was filled to capacity across from the home team's bench. As the Cannons skated out onto the ice they were greeted by a repetitive chant from those Hyannis students.

"Screw you Eastport," followed by a clap, clap, clap-clap-clap. "Screw you Eastport!"

Along with their new T-shirts, several fans had brought signs either supporting the home team or berating the visitors. The same kid from Connor Donaldson's graphics class had used the heavy-duty printer at the school to produce a three-foot reproduction of Cyrus Carpenter's face.

Normally, Cyrus would have gotten a laugh out of seeing his face at billboard size, but the photo they'd chosen was the worst representation of him in existence. The Hyannis kids had dug deep into Cy's Instagram account and found a picture of him from his freshman year at the end of the hockey season. He had enough pimples in the picture to play connect-the-dots, along with a stupid grin. It was not his finest moment.

As the Cannons warmed up, it did not take long for them to notice their captain's visage in the crowd.

"Oh crap, Cy, did you see that?" Josh Hutchinson asked, trying not to laugh at his friend's oversized face in the stands. "That's brutal, man."

Cyrus spotted the sign and it caught him off-guard. Not wanting to show his teammates it bothered him, he shrugged nonchalantly. "Whatever. It's gonna take more than a bad picture to rattle me."

75

Cyrus was right, it did take more than just a picture to rattle him. It also took the entire Hyannis student section chanting his name for five minutes straight before the drop of the puck.

Over and over and over, they repeated in a sing-song fashion, "Cy-rus, Cy-rus, Cy-rus."

As the puck dropped at center ice, Carpenter won the puck back to Scott Frazier and hit the first thing he saw, which just happened to be the face of Gunnar Ellison. The referees, in an effort to take control of what they knew was going to be an emotional game, whistled Carpenter for an interference penalty and tossed him into the penalty box.

Ellison had his revenge. He scored on a rebound 30 seconds later to put the Hawks on top, 1-0, just 50 seconds into the game.

Carpenter sat on the bench waiting for his next turn and felt a hand grab his shoulder from behind.

Coach Scadorski had a clear message and barked it in Cyrus's direction.

"Hey, be smarter than that. Don't be taking stupid penalties. We're chasing a goal already because you lost your head. Be a leader or sit on the bench... that goes for all of you. Don't get caught up in that cheap shot BS. Play our game, be physical, not stupid. Let them take the bad penalties."

Neither team was called for another infraction in the first period or added to the score before the first intermission. Hyannis took a 1-0 lead into the break. The surplus of adrenaline the squads felt had led to a lot of mistakes and general sloppiness.

In the second period, Billy Walker had an epiphany. It helped change the mood for the Cannons.

"Carp, talk a little trash to them at the next whistle. Get under their skin some more," Walker said to his linemate.

"More? They're already all over me," Cyrus said with exasperation.

"They're overplaying you. Let's get them to really sell out to stop you, then get it to me. We'll get this turned around quick."

The next time out Carpenter lined up to take the faceoff outside the Hyannis zone with Walker on his right side and Wes Garrett on his left. Garrett had been moved up to team with his friends in an effort to get things going. Cyrus won the draw, but the Hawks tipped it onto a bench and another faceoff was to come.

Hyannis's Seaver chopped at Carpenter's skates and blew him a kiss. "You look really pretty in your picture," the agitator said.

"Funny, your mom blows the same way. Did she teach you her technique?" Carpenter said.

Seaver brought his stick around and slashed at Carpenter's ankles before closing the space between the players and jabbing a left hand at his adversary. Cyrus, heeding his coach's warning about penalties, threw his hands into the air in mock surrender and played up the role of Mr. Innocent.

"Whoa, whoa, whoa. What's that all about? Come on, man," Cyrus shouted, trying his best not to crack a smile.

The referee stepped between the two players and pointed Seaver toward the penalty box. "Number 16 in red, two minutes for roughing."

Walker slid over to Carpenter and patted him on the back. "That was even better than my plan," Walker said through a grin. "Now let's use this power play to turn this thing around."

It took Eastport just 44 seconds to tie the game at 1-1. Carpenter won the faceoff, Frazier slapped a shot from the blue line and Walker tipped that shot past the goalie. Neither team scored again in the second period, but Eastport had clearly taken over the momentum.

During the second intermission, the disposition of the Eastport locker room had relaxed considerably from earlier.

Walker, Carpenter, and Garrett huddled together and discussed their attack plan. Carpenter, who'd found his mojo after drawing the penalty on Seaver, did most of the talking.

"Billy, I want to get you the puck at the top of the circle. Their goalie is super weak on the stick side. If I can pass it to you from the top of the zone that'll get him moving to his left, and you'll have half a net to shoot at. Even you can hit that," Cyrus said with a laugh. "Wes, you keep grinding. We're going to try to pound that stick side, that'll leave plenty of garbage for you to put away. Get to the rebounds, get a goal, maybe Melissa will give you a kiss later."

"I'll get that either way," Wes said smoothly.

Scott, Josh, and Danny came over to join their friends before the end of the break. Josh spoke up.

"Fifteen minutes of perfect hockey. We've got this. For OB and Bish, we owe it to them. They were seniors and they're out there with us, let's go," Hutchinson urged.

As Josh spoke to his close group of friends, the rest of the team joined them. Josh looked around and realized that the speech he'd just made to the Boys needed to be shared with everyone.

"Seniors, this is the last time we get to play these jerks in this building, ever," Josh said, voice rising. "I don't care what it takes, but we are not leaving here with a loss. Everything we've got for 15 more minutes!"

76

The chant was deafening as the Cannons came out for the third period, and it was aimed once again at Cyrus Carpenter. The Red Hawks fans were determined to rattle the Eastport captain.

"Cy-ruuuuussss, Cy-ruuuuuussss, YOU SUCK!" over and over they repeated.

Carpenter egged them on. He waved his hand back and forth in rhythm with their chant, like a conductor leading his orchestra.

When the puck dropped, the Eastport captain was shot out of a cannon. He nearly scored the go-ahead goal just 30 seconds into the third period, and then set up Garrett two minutes later for another bid that almost lit the red light.

The third shift was the charm for Carpenter.

The play he'd envisioned with his friends between periods materialized perfectly. Frazier dumped the puck around the boards to the corner and Garrett won the footrace to it and muscled it to his stick for a pass to Carpenter high in the zone.

Cyrus received the biscuit a few feet above the left circle. With his eyes on the goal, he took a stride to his right, which got the Hyannis goaltender to move that way. A perfect pass to Walker found him open at the right faceoff dot. Walker whistled a wrister for the far side that the goalie just got a piece of. Both Carpenter and Garrett were in position to chop at the rebound. Garrett's first shot hit the pipe, but Carpenter slid his stick at the puck like he was playing shuffleboard and pushed it over the goal line to make it 2-1 Eastport.

Cyrus Carpenter had scored hundreds of goals since taking up the game of hockey. He'd once scored six times in one game as an 11-year-old. He'd potted dozens against Hyannis teams over the years. Scoring goals was something he'd been doing for as long as he could remember.

No goal had ever felt so satisfying. After every goal a Cannon scored, the players on the ice ritualistically skated back to their bench in line, with the goal scorer leading the way. Cyrus sprinted to the bench, hitting each high-five with bliss.

This time he continued right past the bench to the section with the Hyannis High students that had held his picture high in the air earlier. He stopped dead in front of them, arms held high in a 'V' and then brought down a single finger in front of his face, hushing them.

77

Cyrus's moment of joy was glorious, but there was far too much time left on the clock for the Cannons to start celebrating. Nine-and-a-half minutes can be a lifetime in any sporting event, and no lead is harder to protect than a one-goal advantage on the road.

Scadorski encouraged his players to be smart and make good decisions. "It's not over, don't let up," he insisted. "We need another one."

Eastport did not stop, but neither did Hyannis. Bubby Seaver was known around the Cape Cod Athletic League for being an instigator who wasn't afraid to play dirty. What was overlooked because of that reputation was how good he actually was at the game of hockey.

Seaver was the guy you hated if he was on the other team and adored if he was on yours. His team trailing, he took matters into his own hands and made the play of the game, with just two minutes to go, to tie things up. In the process, he made the worst winter of Wes Garrett's life even worse.

Little Phillip Charles started the play that tied the game for the Red Hawks and earned the only assist on Seaver's goal. Charles had grown up in Eastport and had played with many of the kids that he was now playing against. His parents had moved to Hyannis because of his dad's job when he was 13. "Chucky," as he'd been called for years, had to make new friends and learn a new system on the ice. He couldn't imagine being a Cannon now. His maroon blood had transformed red for good.

Charles was simply trying to be smart with the puck. His team needed to get fresh legs on the ice. He came up with the puck near his own blue line and was going to just chip it out to get a line change. Before he could dump it, he saw Bubby breaking free. Phil saucered the puck off the right wing boards brilliantly, hitting Seaver in stride. Alex Gossard was out of position to stop the streaking Red Hawk, and Seaver went right at Jimmy Martinage in the goal.

The Eastport goalie had played very well, but he was a man on a deserted island against an incoming hurricane. Seaver faked a shot to his left and brought it back to his right, flipping the puck out of the reach of Jim's glove. The red light came on behind the net and the game was tied with just one minute and 57 seconds left.

Whilst dancing on the ice, Seaver tried to reach into the net to grab the puck as a memento. The Cannons took offense at that. Wes Garrett shoved at Seaver to get him away from his goalie. Seaver swung his stick in Garrett's direction and chopped right under Wes's skate blades.

Wes knew the second he hit the ice that his season was over. His shoulder hit first and a half-second later he heard the snap. It was gross.

Martinage took a swing at Seaver. Ellison threw a punch at Gossard. Everyone on the ice found himself in a tornado of flailing punches. It took a good two minutes for the referees to sort things out. The refs, understanding the emotion of the game, did not throw anyone out. The players would have all been suspended for two games had the stripes followed the letter of the law.

Instead, everyone on the ice was cited for roughing and unsportsmanlike conduct penalties. The double minors were for four minutes each. Their games were over.

Wes Garrett was included on the score sheet for those same penalties. He did not pile into the overcrowded penalty box with his teammates though. He was quickly escorted off the ice.

Coach Tom Henry supported Wes as he winced along the ice and out to the locker room. Darlene Garrett put on a strong face for her son. "Oh Wesley, another trip to the emergency room. I hope you brought your punch card, the sixth visit is free."

The joke didn't help. Tears streamed down Wesley's face as the final horn of a 2-2 tie echoed in the background. Darlene untied Wes's skates and helped him out of his hockey pants. He gingerly slipped on his dress pants that he'd worn to the rink and she assisted him into his boat shoes.

The Garretts opened the door to leave the locker room as the Cannons came down the hall to enter it.

"Wes, hold up," Danny Stone shouted.

The Garretts stopped and Stone, along with Hutchinson and Carpenter, walked over to their friend.

"Hey man, you okay?" Danny asked.

"Shoulder, heard something break. I'm done," Wes stated blandly.

"You're fine, big guy," Hutchinson said. "Probably not as bad as you think. Go get an X-ray, you'll see."

"No man, I'm done. I heard it crack."

The teammates did not know how to respond. Every player knew the real chance that every game they played might be their last. It was a fear that hid in the corner of everyone's mind, one they did their best to ignore.

"We'll make sure your stuff gets back to the rink," Stone said.

"Danny, my keys are in my locker. Can you take the Jeep home and throw my gear in it?" Wes asked.

"Sure buddy, no problem. Whatever you need."

Another trip to another hospital. With his mother beside him, Wes began the slow walk toward the exit. The door opened to the parking lot and icy wind burned his cheeks. Harsher than the cold was the realization that hit him.

Wes Garrett had skated his last shift for the Eastport Cannons. His hockey career was over.

78

"Does your father use this to strip furniture? It's harsh," Scott said, wincing as he put back a shot of the brown liquor Danny Stone had procured from his parents' cabinet, which later had been confiscated by Billy Walker.

"That's the smoother stuff. You should try the stuff he usually drinks. The last time I tried it I was hungover for two days," Stone said, giggling as he sipped on a light beer.

Following the tie against Hyannis, which felt like a loss, the Boys assembled at the old abandoned parking lot in the technology park near the rink. The usual suspects were all there to commiserate. Danny had driven Wes's Jeep back to his own house and rode to the spot with Cyrus, who'd followed him over. They picked up Josh, Scott and Billy, who were all spending the night at Josh's house and made their way to the place no one else seemed to know about. It was rare to have a private hangout place in this town, where every secret was broadcast immediately.

The Boys, though, had kept it their own for the past two years. Collin O'Brien had discovered it while working his part-time job as a packager at one of the science outfits in the tech park. After a shift during the summer between his sophomore and junior years, he'd decided to go for a run on a rare cool August evening. He'd stumbled upon the abandoned lot and then told his friends about it. The seven of them had kept its location classified ever since. They hadn't even told any girls about it. Well, Collin had brought a couple of girls there on his own, but his friends were none the wiser to that, and he'd been pretty sure that they'd have been unable to find it on their own anyway.

"It feels weird to be here without Craig and Collin," Cyrus said as he stared up at the sky from the hood of his car. The night's designated driver, he sat up to take a pull on a Gatorade and looked around at his friends, who nodded their agreement.

"Death is weird. I have had to stop myself from calling one of those guys so many times the last few weeks," Josh said. "It's like, I'll be sitting around and I'll think 'what's Bish doing?' and I'll grab my phone to hit him up and then all of a sudden, I remember he won't be there to answer."

"It's messed up," Scott agreed. "Tell you what, though. OB would have loved that scrap tonight. He'd have been right in the middle of it all."

The Boys laughed and agreed before silence overtook the group. The leaves on the trees surrounding the park rustled and a brown rabbit spied on the humans from the edge of the woods before scurrying back into the darkness. The quiet was broken by the sound of a can careening after the bunny.

"Get out of here rabbit, you weren't invited," Billy said, giggling as he reached for another sip.

"This sucks. We're here, Wes is at the freakin' emergency room and Craig and Collin..." Scott didn't finish his sentence. He didn't have to.

"Screw this. Listen up boys," Cyrus demanded.

The only sober one in the group pushed himself off of the car's hood and stood in front of his friends. They stared back, waiting for his proclamation.

"I screwed up tonight and cost us that game. If I didn't take that stupid penalty early, they don't score there and then we win the game, plain and simple. I was selfish. I admit it. Just dumb," he began.

"We all know what we've been playing for, and now you can add Wes to that list, along with Craig and Collin. At least they don't have to suffer by watching and not playing. Wes has to sit in the press box – again – and just friggin' watch us.

"We're going to put on a show for him, and for Bish and OB. This group, right here, is going to win the whole damn thing. We're taking it to the Garden, and we're going to hang those 10 and 19 jerseys behind the bench and we're going to win the championship and then we're going to skate around the ice with the jerseys and the trophy and it's going to be the best damn moment of our entire lives."

"Sounds good, but you're forgetting something," Scott said.

"Whatever it is, it doesn't matter. I'm telling you, we're winning this thing," Cyrus demanded.

"Dude, our goalie kind of sucks," Billy said quietly.

"We'll score more than they do, we'll block shots, whatever it takes, we're going to do it. Winning this is the only way we can justify the crap we've been through," Cyrus said, choking back tears that were catching him by surprise.

"Alrighty then," Danny said, stumbling over to his friend and putting an arm around him. "We're going to be state champs. Cyrus said so, that's how so it's going to be. I'm in."

"I'm in, that's why I came home," Scott agreed.

"Makes sense to me," Josh added. "We won one state championship this year, might as well win them all."

79

Melissa told the room to "settle down please." Using the same tone she'd use to get the attention of her teammates on the field hockey field, it was enough to momentarily halt the chattering mouths of the six third-graders seated at the round table in one of Eastport Baptist Church's auxiliary rooms.

That was Emily's cue to begin handing out plastic cups full of Goldfish crackers. Each little one reached excitedly for their snacks.

There were about 15 minutes left before the end of Sunday School. Melissa had led the group through a story about Jesus and forgiveness, and the kids had filled in their worksheets and done a craft. Today they created necklaces with twine and little wooden crosses. The the little ones munched away as the end of the session neared.

"So, does anyone have any questions about the lesson?" Melissa asked the group.

"My dog died," shouted Brandon from the far end of the table. "We buried him yesterday."

Emily cringed. Melissa went with the flow.

"That's so sad, I'm sorry to hear that. What was your dog's name?"

"His name was Dewey. He was the best dog ever," Brandon said with a sniffle. "I miss him."

One thing that Melissa had learned since taking over this class was that her little students had real feelings and that they wanted to be heard. She remembered being that age and thinking that grown-ups had all of the answers. Now she was the "grown-up" in the room, and this little guy was going through one of the hardest things he'd ever dealt with. She understood profoundly.

"He sounds amazing," Melissa said. "I bet he's going to love being in

Heaven, though."

"Dewey's in Heaven?" Brandon asked, his eyes big and excited.

"I think so," Melissa said. "Jesus loves all the children, and their pets, too. He can help you with your sadness, and part of that is taking care of the ones that we love that pass away. It's hard not having Dewey with you every day. I bet he was a great friend. Me and Emily lost good friends recently, too. Now Jesus gets to take care of them, and Dewey. We will get to see them all again someday when we're in Heaven."

"Really?"

"Really, and I bet you my friend Craig is throwing Dewey a tennis ball right now."

Brandon smiled and went back to his crackers. Melissa glanced over at Emily, who smiled and nodded. She mouthed "thank you" and began to pour little cups of apple juice.

"Shhh, we don't want to wake him up," Melissa gently whispered.

"We don't? Then how will he know we are here visiting him, Melissa?"

"I mean, we will wake him up – eventually – but let's let him rest for a while more, Emily, besides, he looks so cute and peaceful."

"He looks like he got worked over by those doctors, but he's your boyfriend. To you, he might look like a cross between Ryan Reynolds and Chris Hemsworth, but all I see is a serious case of bed head and someone that really should consider using the tanning bed every now and again."

Melissa couldn't help but laugh, which stirred Wes Garrett. Groggily he surveyed the room and figured he must still be dreaming when he saw Melissa and Emily at the foot of his bed. He closed his eyes in hopes that the dream would pick up and head down a very particular path.

"Mel, I feel like a stalker right now," Emily whispered. "This is kind of weird."

"Okay, okay, I'll wake him up," Melissa said.

Melissa leaned over her boyfriend, planted a kiss on his cheek and carefully shook his thigh in hopes of stirring Wes from his slumber. His eyes fluttered but shut tight again.

"Wake up!" Emily yelled, grabbing Wes's toes through his bedding.

"Whoa, what... Ouch, what the hell?" Wes shook his head and saw the same vision he'd seen earlier, though this time Emily looked sheepish and Melissa looked pissed off.

"Hey, it worked," Emily said with a shrug.

"What is going on?" Wes asked. "Am I dreaming, or are you two really in my room right now, decked out in your Sunday best?"

"That we are, Mr. Emergency Room, that we are," Emily said with a smile. "Aren't you glad to see us?"

"We came over after church to see how you're doing. Your mom said she would put aside her no girls in the bedroom rule for today so that we could check on you. We brought you some presents," Melissa cheerfully said while helping Wes to sit up comfortably.

"What time is it? I feel like I've been out for days," Wes said, adjusting the pillows to push up his arm.

"It's almost three o'clock. We've already had breakfast, taught Sunday School at church, went out for lunch and then came here. You've been sleeping since you got home around midnight, according to your mom. Fifteen hours straight, that's pretty damn impressive," Emily said.

"I feel like I got hit by a truck. My shoulder is so stiff, I've got a headache that won't quit and I've got to pee like you wouldn't believe," Wes announced. "Can you help me up Mel, please?"

Using his good arm, Wes grabbed his girlfriend's arm and spun himself to the right, planting his feet on the floor. She pulled him up, and he stood and stretched. The girls laughed.

"That's quite the look you've got going, Garrett," Emily said. "Sexy."

Normally Wes would have felt embarrassed for the girls to see him in his plaid boxers, tattered Pearl Jam concert shirt and matted hair. Today, he just didn't care.

He shuffled off to the bathroom and the girls tried to contain their giggles.

While Wes heeded nature's call, Melissa and Emily looked around the room. It was everything that they expected it to be. There were band posters and pretty girls in bathing suits on the walls, a small flat screen TV hooked up to an XBox and a shelf filled with baseball and hockey trophies that dated back nearly a decade. There was also a photograph in a frame on that shelf of the Boys all together, with Wes right between Craig and Collin. They were all shirtless at the beach behind Bish's grandmother's house. Craig's smile was electric, Wes looked content and Collin was making eyes with whichever girl they'd asked to take the picture.

"I love that photograph," Emily said with a sad smile forming. "That was such a great day."

She picked up the frame and ran her fingers over her departed boyfriend's face. Just then, Wes reentered the room. He'd managed to find a pair of sweatpants on his way back and had thrown them on.

"Boo, I liked the boxers," joked Melissa.

"Um, yeah, thanks. I just didn't want to make Emily, or either of you, uncomfortable," Wes said. "Mom's downstairs, gotta keep it PG."

"I didn't mind the boxers," Emily said while putting the picture back on the shelf. "You pulled it off."

"You said something about presents," Wes said in an effort to change the subject. "That sounds fun, and something smells amazing now that I'm awake."

"That would be the cheeseburger sub we picked up for you from Ehrhardt's. Extra mushrooms, extra pickles, just like you like it. Mitch's dad wouldn't let me pay for it when I told him it was for you. He was at the game last night, said you did the right thing sticking up for your goalie," Melissa said.

Wes couldn't get the paper off of the sub quick enough. Crumbs exploded onto his comforter as he took a shark-sized bite.

"Mmmm, so good," he growled before taking another. "This is amazing."

"Don't talk with your mouth full young man, that's gross," Emily scolded light-heartedly. "And chew before you swallow. I'm not taking you back to the hospital."

"We also stopped at the Redbox and got you a couple of movies, 'Miracle' and 'The Avengers.' I would be happy to come back later to watch them with you if you want the company. I've got to drop Emily off at home, and study for an English test, but I can be back around 6 if you're interested in snuggling and watching movies," Melissa said with a smile.

"I'm chaperoning, by the way," Emily added.

"Sounds good to me," Wes said. "Man, I need to get hurt more often. I like being spoiled."

"And one more thing," Melissa said. "At Sunday school we made cross necklaces with all of the third and fourth graders. The cross is my favorite symbol because of the price Jesus paid on it and because it's forever. We also had all of the kids pray that you'd get better quick."

Wes bent forward and Melissa placed the necklace of the little wooden cross on a leather strand around his neck. She kissed his cheek again.

"I love it," he said, admiring her handy work. "I love you."

Melissa blushed. He'd never said that before to her. Her face lit up.

"I love you too, Wes," she said. "Very, very much."

"Gross, did I just witness a moment?" Emily said. "Get another room."

80

Over the next two weeks, the Cannons lived up to the high standard that Cyrus demanded of them. They had five games left to play on their schedule and won four of them. The only loss came in the last game of the regular season against a Super-8 competitor, Holy Cross High School. The four wins put them at 13-6-3 to end the regular season.

All in all, Coach Scadorski felt very good about how the team had finished the regular season. After their poor start, and then the tragedy, no one would have thrown blame his way if Eastport had missed the playoffs altogether. The fact that they'd rallied and won as many games as they had was a borderline miracle.

Having Scott Frazier certainly hadn't hurt. Frazier made the most of the 12 games he was able to play and finished third on the team in goals – behind Carpenter and Walker – with 11 goals and 14 assists. Walker, who was ready to walk away from the team early on, led the way with 22 goals and 13 assists. Carpenter had a strong season as well, with 18 goals and 18 assists.

There was little doubt that the Cannons would have a real chance to win the south region and go to play for the state championship at the Garden. To get that done, though, it would take four wins in a row against increasingly better and better teams. No team from Eastport had been to the finals since 1999, and the last time they'd won one was 1997, exactly 20 years earlier.

Based on his team's record, John Scadorski had a pretty good idea where his team would be when the brackets were released. He'd scoured the internet all week to get a handle on the numbers and it seemed a safe bet that Eastport was looking at the third position.

With the tournament spots set to be released online around 2 o'clock on Saturday afternoon, he and his assistant coach met at the rink with a laptop and hot beverages. Scadorski opted for tea, having already downed a pot of coffee earlier in the morning. Tom Henry sat at the round table with a medium cup of black java.

Scadorski hit refresh on the browser and sighed as the page remained blank and the clock ticked five minutes past the expected release time.

"Would it kill the association to actually get these things out on time?" the coach muttered. "Just once, it'd be refreshing."

Henry nodded in agreement. They'd lived this same scenario and conversation each year he'd served under Scadorski. Adding fuel to the fire would only fire up the boss more, so he kept his mouth closed.

Of course this year the tournament meant so much more. This year's team actually had a chance to make some noise. They'd been labeled fan favorites, the feelgood story, and the team no one else wants to play, by all of the media outlets covering high school hockey in the state.

At 2:08 Scadorski hit the F5 button again. The bracket appeared magically where a blank page had been before. He scanned the right side and saw Eastport, a spot higher than he'd figured. Eastport was ranked second overall, behind just Braintree Catholic. The Cannons first game would be against 15th ranked John Quincy Adams Regional, which barely got into the tournament with a 9-9 record.

The coaches exchanged high-fives. The field had been set and the road to the finals for Eastport looked manageable. With Hyannis on the other side, the only way they'd face their rivals was in the championship game, which would be a dream match-up, but unlikely.

"How'd we get the two?" Henry asked. "I thought Onset Regional was locked into the spot?"

"Apparently they used an ineligible player early in the season and had to vacate four wins. They dropped from 14 wins to 10, and they're the 11 seed now. We could play them in the semis, which is what would have happened if they'd been the two and we were the three. It just makes it a little easier for us up to that point. I'll take it," Scadorski said.

Tom Henry leaned back in his chair and crossed his arms. His eyes picked a spot on the ceiling and stayed there for a moment before he spoke.

"If we play like we did the last few weeks we can beat anyone. If we play like we did at the start of the year anyone can beat us," he said. "It's all about us. We're going to go as far as our goaltending will take us. If Martinage is on his game, we've got a chance to win it all. If he craps all over himself, we're screwed. It's really that simple."

Scadorski mulled over what his assistant had said, but did not respond immediately. Typically he'd be leading the conversation, but the year had taken its toll on the coach, and he was not immediately forthcoming. He sat in his chair, analyzing the bracket, playing the likely scenarios in his head.

After 10 minutes of silence, Scadorski spoke.

"We're winning the whole damn thing. We're going to the Garden Tommy, I can feel it," he said while grinning ear-to-ear.

"Yeah?" Henry said. "Ya think?"

"Absolutely. These kids want it more than any team we've ever had. They're on a mission. I can't imagine it ending any other way."

Henry's gave his boss a look that said "really?"

"Maybe I'm just being overly optimistic," Scardorski conceded. "This team's been through the wringer, and so have you and I. Some days I'll be sitting at my desk at work and just wonder how I even got there. I'm spent. Maura and I are going to book a flight somewhere warm the day the season ends, and I'm going to spend a week drinking fruity things with umbrellas in them and trying to forget about real life."

Henry grinned.

"That sounds pretty great. Mind if I come too?" Henry said.

"No offense, but no way."

81

The final practice before the start of the state tournament was a lot like the ones that had come before. The difference was that it had the potential to be the last one of the year. If the Cannons lost their next game, they'd be cleaning out their lockers when they got back to the rink.

Those high stakes did not factor into the team's preparation at all. The group was loose and confident. They knew that they were supposed to win, and they acted like it. It didn't hurt that Martinage had one of his best practices all year, stopping shot after shot in 2-on-1 drills. If he was going to play like that in the tourney, it wasn't going to be easy to top Eastport.

At 4 PM the next day at the Liberty Memorial Arena, the Cannons would open up the postseason. To a man, they were ready to go. The night before, though, Billy Walker had planned something special.

Walker's year had been a weird one. He had been ready to bail on everyone at the start of the season. Looking back, he recognized how selfish he'd been. It had taken the horrible deaths of two of his oldest friends for him to really see what was important, and near the top of that list were his friends and teammates. With the big tournament about to begin, Bill wanted to revisit an institution that the boys used to hold dear, a meal together before a big game. Billy had invited Wes, Danny, Scott, Josh, and Cyrus to come over at 6:30 for video games and grub.

Two cars pulled in simultaneously. Danny and Wes were in one ride, and the other boys were in Josh's car. Scott led the way to the front door and didn't bother to knock, he simply let everyone in.

"Honey, we're home," Cyrus shouted as the kids walked through the breezeway into the vast living room.

"Hey boys," Bill said, coming around the corner with his mother's red and white heart-dotted apron around his neck.

The laughs filled the room. Billy had hoped for that exact reaction. It had been a while since that kind of laughter had filled the house.

"I'm going to fire up the grill on the deck and have a couple of boxes of frozen burgers ready to go. All the fixings are out on the table. In about 15 minutes you can all make your own plates."

"Wow, you went all out. What's up?" Wes queried.

The boys crowded around the island counter in the middle of the Walker's expansive kitchen. Every surface was either granite or steel. His mother spared no expense when she decorated, going for state-of-the-art everything. It was ironic that most nights the meals came out of the microwave, with Billy cooking for himself.

"My mom's out at a dinner party. She'll be out late... if she comes home at all," Billy said, his irritation obvious. "I figured it's been months since we all got together for a meal, just the Boys. The last one I can remember was breakfast at Bish's house before the Super Bowl. That's too long. We used to feast on breakfast at his place before every big game."

"I already had breakfast, about 11 hours ago. Big bowl of cereal, some avocado toast, and scrambled eggs. It was good," Scott said.

"Me, too," Josh added. "Man, Scotty, I need to come to your house in the morning."

"Alright, alright, I know," Billy said, trying to regain control of the conversation. "My point is, us having a meal together before a big game has been our tradition, something we've all done together for a long time. Since the accident, we haven't done it. Maybe it was just scheduling, maybe it was something else, I don't know. We have to do this. It's who we are, not to mention I'm pretty hungry."

Heads nodded in agreement, and that was that.

"You guys can fire up the XBox and I'm going to grill up these burgers," Bill said.

Billy's plan was a great one, except there was one thing he'd forgotten to take into consideration: it was still winter. The deck was one big sheet of ice. He tiptoed over to the grill only to find the cover frozen down. After a couple of failed attempts to lift it, he realized he was going to have to cook inside.

"Too cold out there?" Wes asked as Bill came back inside.

"Yeah, I just loved the idea of a cookout in February. It seemed awesome."

"Agreed, but kind of tough to cook out when you can't get the cover off the grill," Wes said with a laugh.

"Well aren't you Mr. Chipper," Bill retorted. "I figured we'd all have to be delicate with you tonight, what with the injury and all."

"I'm not gonna lie, this sucks… a lot," Wes said. "I got to thinking, though. I was having an okay season, but it's not like you guys can't win it without me. The doctor said it wasn't as bad as it could have been, and that I should be ready to go when baseball season opens. I won't get to practice before the start of the year, but I should be ready for the first week, second at worst."

"That's great, gonna need that bat in the middle of the lineup," Bill said.

"Yeah, so I've got that to look forward to. I wish I was going to be out there with you guys, but you'll get by."

The boys chowed down on their burgers and fries, spending their time when they weren't chewing busting on their friends. For the first time in a long time, life seemed very normal.

"Who's my next victim in NHL?" Scott asked as he shoveled his last handful of fries into his mouth.

"Wish I could knock you down a peg or two, but can't play with my arm in a sling," Wes said. "Consider yourself lucky."

"Danny, why don't you step up and take a beating?" Scott said.

"Nah, I'm good. Not in the mood."

"Come on man, it'll be fun."

"I said, no!" Danny exclaimed. "Give me a break, I don't want to play the stupid game."

The room grew uncomfortably quiet.

"I'll play with ya, Scott," Josh said. "I need some payback."

Danny buried his head in his cell phone and began aimlessly surfing the internet, paying no mind to anyone else in the room. He could feel the eyes of his friends bearing down on him but tried to ignore them.

Josh and Scott began to play their game, and Billy and Cyrus settled in around them to watch, cheering on Josh to unseat the room champion. Wes poured two glasses of soda and brought one over to Danny.

"Hey, you want to talk?" Wes asked.

"Not really," Danny sniped.

"Alright, that's cool," Wes said.

Danny continued to surf on the internet and finally handed over his phone to Wes. He had been reading through old Tweets by Bish.

"Breakfast with the boys is the best," was the tweet, accompanied by a silly group photograph.

Wes smiled at the photo and handed the phone back.

"How can you do that?" Danny queried.

"Do what?"

"See that photograph and not start crying, or get mad, or throw something. You were Bish's best friend, Wes. Doesn't that tear you apart? It's freaking killing me," Danny said, standing up and addressing all of his friends. "How can we just act like everything is normal? They're gone. I don't know if you noticed, but there were two empty seats at the table for dinner. I wake up in the morning and they're usually the first thing I think about. I dream and I see that car twisted around the tree and Craig and Collin just lying there.

"And look at all of us, trying to pretend everything is okay. I can't pretend anymore, it's not okay. It's wrecking me."

"Calm down Dan, just chill. We all deal in our own way, buddy. We're in this together, man. We all got you," Cyrus said. He approached his friend, placing his hands on his shoulders. "You need to talk, let it out."

Danny seethed for a moment. He'd been to the psychologist two more times since his initial visit. He remembered something she'd said. "Close your eyes, take a deep breath and quiet your mind for a second." She said it wouldn't fix anything, but it might help with the anger. He tried it and it did help, a little bit.

"Okay, here it is, I've been seeing a shrink. Sometimes I think it helps, and other times I feel like I'm just talking in circles. I keep talking about my feelings, but it doesn't change them," he said, tears running down his face. "I just want to wake up and find out this has been a nightmare. It has to be, but it just won't end."

A heavy silence seized the room. None of Danny's friends knew what to say.

"I get it Danny, I get it," Wes said, finally breaking the silence that followed the outburst. "I miss them every day. I can't tell you how often I think about hanging out with Craig or having Collin send me a text that makes me laugh. We didn't just lose two friends, we lost two brothers, and it hurts. I thought about going to talk to a shrink myself, but I just couldn't stomach any more doctor appointments."

Scott rubbed his eyes and spoke up next.

"Yes, our brothers are gone. The only way to honor them is to carry on for them. You think Collin and Craig would want us to be this messed up? No way. They'd both tell us to suck it up and move on. You know they would. OB would never sit back and waste a chance to make us laugh, or gross us out."

"So that's it. That's your answer, just suck it up. Just move on?" Danny said, challenging his friend.

"Yeah, it kind of is," Scott answered quietly. "I hate to say it, but there's no magic button to press that is going to make it all okay. Look at Wes, he got hurt again. No matter what he does, it's going to take time to get better. His shoulder is no different than our hearts, man. They got ripped up, they're not going to be okay, just like that. At some point, we're all going to heal. You will too Danny, you just will. It might take a while, and it's going to leave a big scar, but you'll heal."

82

The boys eventually returned to their video games, tried to lighten the mood with jokes and talked about the next day's playoff game. Around 10:30 the phone rang. Coach Scadorski was calling to make sure all the players were adhering to curfew. Billy put the phone on speaker and each player spoke up, informing the coach where they were. He said he was happy they'd all behaved and stayed out of trouble, and then ordered everyone to head to their homes for a good night's sleep.

"I need you guys fresh and ready to go tomorrow," the coach said to them over the speaker.

Five minutes later the friends began to disperse. Scott, Josh, and Cyrus left together, thanking Billy on their way out the door, giving bro hugs to all as they departed.

As Wes gingerly put on his parka, Danny apologized to Billy for the drama.

"Man, I'm sorry. I didn't mean to bring the room down with my messed up head," Danny said. "You did a good thing here tonight. We needed this."

Billy nodded and pulled Danny in for a hug. As the boys separated, Bill spoke.

"Don't apologize. You needed to get that stuff off of your chest, and we're family. No one's going to judge you for still being messed up, we all are one way or another. Just remember one thing."

"What's that?" Danny asked.

"You're not alone. You might feel that way sometimes, but you've got us, all of us, in your corner. You need someone to talk to, just call me. I got you."

Danny thanked his friend and walked out the front door into the freezing evening air. Wes followed, walking carefully to make sure he didn't lose his footing and worsen his situation.

Danny's car roared to life. He flicked on the headlights and cranked the heat up to its max. As he drove away from the Walker home, the falling snow made it seem like they were driving through a Star Wars movie. Wes plugged his phone into the USB port in the radio and turned the volume on the music up, bobbing his head to the rhythm as he pretended everything was totally normal.

Danny stared out the windshield as he drove. The snow and his melancholy lulled him into a bit of a trance until he hit a hidden pothole that jarred him back to the here and now.

"Since when do you listen to Drake?" Danny asked, bewildered to be hearing hip-hop on his friend's playlist. "I didn't think you knew that they actually made music that came out after we were born."

"Umm, Melissa really likes this stuff. I guess he dropped this track last week, and she's listening to it non-stop."

"Wow, you must really like her. I wish OB were here to see this. He'd be laughing his ass off at you. I can hear him now, 'Wes has gone street on us.'"

The friends started laughing. Giggles escalated to raucous hilarity. Danny pulled over to the shoulder, worried he might run off the road.

"Oh man, my diaphragm hurts," Danny said, holding onto his stomach.

"I know, mine too. Why is that so funny?" Wes asked, laughing out every word.

It took another two minutes, but finally, the boys caught their breath. Danny let out an audible sigh and then patted his friend on the back.

"That might be the first time I've been able to think about either of those guys and not get depressed," Danny said. "That feels better."

"I know what ya mean."

83

With a clipboard under his arm, Wes hustled up the flight of stairs from ice level. He jogged behind the bleachers, around to the snack bar and slid through the back door to the press box at Liberty Ice Arena just as the canned recording of the National Anthem was about to begin. He grabbed an empty seat next to Mr. Richardson, pulled off his pen cap with his teeth and used the fingers on his slung arm to steady the shot chart. As Wes got comfortable, he watched the puck drop, with Cyrus at center ice for the Cannons. The state playoffs were underway as John Quincy Adams Regional looked to upset the boys from Eastport.

Eastport got off the first shot on goal, a flick from high in the zone by Gaudreau, and then JQAR got the next one. Wes notched each one on the chart, noting where they'd been taken and by which player. His assignment from Coach Henry enabled him to focus on every little thing happening out on the ice.

As the puck popped off the ice and into the stands, Mac Richardson turned to greet Wes. After pleasantries, he asked the senior what his prediction was.

"Oh, we've got these guys. Coach Scadorski said if we didn't score at least six goals there was something wrong with us," Wes told the reporter.

An assistant coach from John Quincy Adams, who was standing in the back of the press box to get the high view of the action for between-period adjustments, sarcastically laughed. "Six goals? I wouldn't count on that," he said. "Our boys are pumped up for this one. It'll be a lot closer than you think."

Wes shrugged.

"You're probably right," the senior said to the other team's coach. "I mean, I'm not playing today, so you've got a better chance right there."

Garrett's joke broke the tension and all eyes were back out on the playoff game. It didn't take long for the presumed outcome from the Eastport coaching staff to take shape. Frazier bombed one away for the first goal and then got another to make it 2-0 before John Quincy Adams answered with an ugly rebound goal late in the first.

Walker made it 3-1 on a pretty move early in the second period. Danny made it a three-goal lead with one of his best plays of the season. He sniped a wrist shot between the goalie's catching glove and hip. In the third period, the Cannons poured it on. Gaudreau and Hutchinson popped in one each and in the waning seconds, one of the rookies scored his first-ever goal for a 7-1 final.

Wes counted up the final shots as the final horn sounded. The Cannons had 38, the Senators only 12. As he stuck his clipboard under his arm the assistant coach from JQAR locked eyes with the injured player. Wes just gave a half a shrug.

Three nights later, back at the Liberty Rink, the second game of the tournament unfolded. This time seventh-seeded Bass River stood in the Cannons' way. The Strikers were certainly a step above their first-round foe, but Jimmy Martinage picked a great time to play like a hero.

Martinage stopped everything thrown his way and made it look easy. He used his pads, his gloves and even his mask at one point to stop all 23 shots on goal that Bass River produced.

After 15 scoreless minutes, the Cannons gave Martinage a little breathing room in the second period. Cy Carpenter froze a defender with a pump-fake and in the same motion got the goalie moving. With a flick of a wrist, he rung the bottom of the crossbar and lifted his hands in celebration as the Cannons broke the ice. Later in the period, Danny Stone got one for Eastport to double the lead. The celebration on the ice was exuberant for that one. An empty-netter by Walker with less than a minute to play iced the victory for the Cannons and put them into the regional semifinals the following weekend.

Martinage was the first one off the ice and could not get the smile off his face as his teammates patted him on the head in the locker room after the

3-0 win.

"Attaboy, Four Eyes," and, "Great job, Specs," poured down on the goalie. He'd waited all year to play like that. The satisfaction oozed from his pores.

Coach Scadorski moved to the center of the room and clapped his hands, spinning slowly in a circle to make eye contact with each of them.

"I know I'm not always the easiest guy to please. I demand a lot from all of you. What you did today was outstanding, gentlemen. I'm sure I could nitpick and find mistakes when I watch the tape later, but I'm going to be honest with you," he said, pausing for effect. "That was about the most perfect game you guys could have played. I'm so proud right now. That was great, hats off."

Anyone still in the rink heard the roar that emanated from the locker room after that statement.

"But, and this is a big but, it's not over. All that this means is that you have the opportunity to do it again. We've got another game – a bigger game – Friday night right back here against Humarock. Win that one, and it'll probably be Braintree Catholic on Sunday. You win and it gets harder, that's how the tournament works. That means you've got to work harder in practice this week, you've got to stay focused.

"I know none of you guys wants this thing to end any time soon. You know what we're playing for, you know who we're playing for. Let's keep it going."

84

With a towel wrapped around his waist and another resting on his shoulders, Scott Frazier walked from the showers to his locker stall. He gingerly sat on the bench and took inventory of his bumps and bruises.

A check in the first period had come at a strange angle and reopened a cut on his chin that had been bothering him. A red and purple bruise had begun forming on his left bicep from a particularly hard hit he'd administered to knock someone away from the puck. That one would need a bag of ice later, and the chin would need a bandage. Everything else seemed to be holding up pretty well, which was a win by itself at this point of the season.

"Hey Scotty, when you get dressed there's someone out here who would like to talk to you," Coach Henry informed the team's best player.

Frazier said he'd be just a minute. He dried off his body, pulled on khakis and then his dress shirt. He'd been careful to just loosen the tie and undo the top two buttons before hanging it in his locker earlier, which made redressing much quicker and easier. After tucking the shirt in, he buttoned one of the undone buttons and pulled the tie tight enough that it was clear he had one on, but not so tight it suffocated him. Next, his letterman jacket went on and he stepped into his loafers. He looked good but hated the team's dress code all the same. He was a hockey player, not a lawyer.

Hoisting his hockey bag over his shoulder, Scott left the locker room and tossed the bag against the boards before heading in the direction of the team's assistant coach. Tom Henry was talking about the game with someone in a dark blue warm-up jacket who had a roster sheet rolled up in his left hand. The stranger emphasized something he was saying by tapping Henry on the shoulder with the piece of paper. Both men laughed.

"Hey, Coach, someone wanted to talk to me?" Frazier asked politely, knowing that it had to be the guy in the blue jacket. He also guessed the man was probably a scout for a college team that wanted to tell him why he should be attending the college that wore that particular shade of blue.

"Scott Frazier, I'd like you to meet Martin Valdez. He's the scouting coordinator at Merrimack."

With that, Henry slipped away, leaving recruit and recruiter to converse.

"Great to meet you, Scott. You played a heck of a game out there today."

"Thank you, sir. The boys were great today. Our goalie really stepped it up."

Frazier had passed the first test every recruiter gives and with flying colors. Valdez always wanted to know if the player would deflect praise onto his teammates, proving he saw the big picture, or talk about themselves. Praise deflectors tended to be leaders, and Valdez liked what he heard because it sounded genuine.

"I've been following your team's story pretty closely and I'd be rooting for you and your team even if I wasn't looking for a defenseman for the future. I'm sorry for your loss, and I know it can't be easy. I also know about your experience at Wellington. I've talked to the coaching staff there, and even though they clearly were not happy to lose you, they had nothing but praise for you as a player and a kid," the coach said.

Scott nodded and the coach continued.

"We'd love to have you up to the campus for an official visit after your season ends. Having seen a couple of your games and talking to your coaches, I really think you'd be a great fit with what we're trying to do, which is build a team that is capable of going to the Frozen Four. You might have to put in a year of junior hockey next year, but I think you've got the potential to be a very good college hockey player."

"Wow, um, thank you, that's really nice to hear," Scott said, trying to play it cool. Inside he was both excited and nervous. Finally, a big-time school was showing some interest. "I think that would be an amazing opportunity. Thank you."

"Don't thank me, son. I'm just glad Coach Scads reached out to us last year.

We've had you on our radar for a while. I'll be honest, there were some doubters when you left Wellington. Commitment is the number one thing at the D1 level. If you want to go to Merrimack or any school at that level, it is a complete commitment from day one."

"I understand that, sir. To be honest, I never wanted to go to Wellington in the first place. I went because other people told me it was the right move and I was trying to do the right thing by my parents," he said. "It was not the right move for me, personally, though. Wherever I go to college to play, I want to make sure I don't make that same mistake again. I want to go to the right place."

Once again Valdez was impressed by what he was hearing. Scott Frazier was not only a leader and a good teammate, but he had a good head on his shoulders, too.

"That's great to hear," Valdez said. "Making the right call for Scott Frazier is the most important thing. I hope we can convince you that Merrimack is the place you're looking for. I'd love to get you on campus in a couple of weeks for that visit. Here's my card. Just call or email me and we'll set up the visit for you and your parents."

Scott shook the coach's hand and began to walk away until a thought occurred to him.

"Coach, are you looking for other players too?"

"We're always looking for talent."

"You should talk to Walker. He can play at that level, no doubt in my mind."

Valdez nodded his head and drafted a note to himself on his phone. "Thanks for the heads up," he said as the two parted ways.

Scott walked away satisfied. Merrimack had not made an offer right then and there, but it sure sounded like they were ready to. If they were after him, there were surely more to follow.

Valdez shook hands with the Eastport coaches as Frazier picked up his bag and made his way for the team bus. The Merrimack coach waved as he passed the bus and waited until he sat in his car to pick up his phone.

"You should have let me offer him today," Valdez said to the Merrimack Head Coach on the other end of the line. "We want this kid in the program. I don't want anyone else to scoop him up on us. Oh, and there's another kid we might want to check up on, too."

85

Driving home after a win was always a lot more fun. Danny Stone sat behind the wheel, bobbing his head. Wes mirrored him in the passenger seat. As the track reached its crescendo, Danny hit pause on the touchscreen.

"I'm starving, wanna grab a burger or pizza or something?" he asked.

"Does Walker smell horrible after a game?" Wes answered. "Let's head to The Nines, I want the bottomless bucket of fries and the Guac Burger. Oh my gosh, now I'm starving just talking about it. Punch it, dude, get me to food."

The friends got to the restaurant and found a booth with a great view of the big screen TV, which was playing the Boston Bruins game against Montreal. They placed their orders and snacked on free popcorn while the Bruins killed off a penalty.

"Think you'll be able to see a game up in Montreal next year when you're in college?" Wes asked as he tossed a handful of popcorn into his mouth. "That would be awesome, to see one up there. They love that team, those crazy frogs."

"I think so if I can score affordable tickets. McGill's campus isn't that far from where they play."

"Man, you're so lucky having dual citizenship. I wish I could get that kind of a break on tuition. I'm going to be paying off Bryant for the rest of my life, and I don't even know what I want to major in yet," Wes said.

Momentarily the boys' attention was captured by two girls entering the restaurant. The pair dressed like they were were trying to get some attention. It was working. Danny raised his eyebrows and Wes giggled.

"Man, now this is a situation where OB would come in very handy," Danny said.

"What, I'm not a good wingman?" Wes deadpanned.

"You're tied down, so you're like the worst wingman right now. I talk to girls about as well as I do to my shrink," he said with a laugh. "OB would scoot up next to one of them, introduce himself and have them sitting in our booth within two minutes."

"Yup, and then he'd tell us he was driving home with them, and call us 20 minutes later when they kick him out of the car for being inappropriate," Wes tacked on. "I miss that dude."

They lifted their cups and toasted their friend.

"This is not how I pictured senior year at all," Danny said between french fries. "I knew we'd be winning hockey games, that was a given in my mind. But, I figured we'd be partying and counting the days until graduation. Strange as it sounds, I'm dreading the end of the year. I don't want it to end because I don't know how I'm going to survive without you guys at my side next year."

"You'll be fine. The drinking age in Montreal is 18, so you can go out any time you want. You'll meet a nice French-Canadian girl, learn to speak the language, settle down, move into an igloo. It'll be awesome."

"I'm being serious, Wes. I'm considering putting off leaving, I just don't know if I can handle it on my own. No one up there knows what this has been like. I won't have anyone to talk to, anyone to have these kinds of conversations with."

"Last time I checked the Canadians have discovered Wi-Fi. We can Facetime and email and SnapChat and all of that. You worry too much," Wes said. "If you ask me, you've got the perfect set-up. Getting away from here is the best thing you could ask for. You won't have the daily reminders of what happened. You won't have to drive down that road or past one of their houses. You won't think of what happened because of something one of us says. It's a fresh start. I'm envious.

"I already know what's going to happen to me. Every time I meet someone new and they ask where I'm from they'll say, 'oh yeah, that's where those hockey players died. Did you know them?' It's going to suck. No one wants to hear about how they were my best friends and that I can't go an hour without being reminded they're not here anymore. People don't want to be brought down by those things."

"I never thought of it that way," Danny said.

"No one in Montreal has ever heard of Eastport, Massachusetts. They'll just ask you if it's near Boston and then give you a hard time for being a Bruins fan. And, they invented poutine – freakin' poutine – you've got it made."

86

Scott sat on the ground with his back against the wall in the lobby of the rink as his teammates slowly began to fill the room. He noticed the crowd growing as he doodled on his iPad, fiddling with the design he'd started in his media arts class earlier in the week. He'd never been a particularly artsy kid, but he'd been hit with inspiration and wanted to get this one right.

Josh Hutchinson's shoulder rubbing up against his own as his friend plopped down next to him pulled his attention from the digital screen.

"Drawing up some plays for the game?" Josh asked.

"No, just a design for graphics class."

Josh reached over to take the iPad so he could take a look. The guy with the quickest hands on the team denied the attempt, flicking the cover closed and pulling it back.

"Ouch, that was my hand," Josh said. "Can't I take a look? I want to see what you're working on."

"It's nothing, a logo I guess," Frazier said as he tucked the iPad into his backpack. "Come on, we've got a game to go win."

Josh persisted. "Come on Scotty, you've piqued my interest. What is it a logo for?"

"It's just a design, I guess. I was thinking about getting a tattoo to honor the boys, and I was working on it."

"That sounds awesome," Josh said loudly.

"What sounds awesome?" asked Wes as he walked over, trailed by Danny.

"Scott is designing a tattoo for Bish and OB," Josh enthusiastically offered.

"Dude, that's perfect. I'm in," Wes said without hesitation. "Sign me up, what's it look like?"

"It's not done," Scott said sheepishly.

"I'm not getting a tattoo, I hate needles, but I want to see it. Show us, Scott," Danny said.

Knowing his friends would not stop pestering him until he agreed to unveil his concept, Scott reached into his bag and pulled out the tablet. He touched the screen a couple of times and then spun it around and held it close to his chest for them to view.

"Whoa, that's good. We are so doing this," Wes said. "I love it. I mean, I love love love it!"

The design was simple. He'd borrowed from "The Dark Side Of The Moon," the album that they'd listened to together countless times, and drawn a black triangle. The line on the left and rainbow on the right were there, but they were accompanied by a 10 and a 19 below the triangle. Above them were the words "Bish" and "OB."

"I was thinking about putting the Cannon logo in the middle, but that might make it a little too busy," Scott said.

"I wouldn't touch it, that's it," Josh said. "I'd go right now if I could. Can you send me that?"

"Let me finish it up at school and then I will," Scott said. "You guys serious? Are we doing this?"

Wes and Josh both nodded enthusiastically. Danny smirked and shook his head in the negative direction. "Nope," he said. "But I definitely will watch you guys get it done. I'm gonna video it for posterity and blackmail."

87

The Karson Field House at Eastport High School was designed in the 1970s and the architects thought it'd be a great idea to put a huge sectioned skylight in the center of the pyramid-like roof. For over 40 years it had done nothing but cause headaches. Volleyball games in the early fall got super hot from the ambient sunlight. In the winter, the cold air made those panes of plexiglass contract, which led to leaking. The going joke was that Eastport High School was the only place in New England where basketball games could get rained out.

Wes Garrett, Josh Hutchinson, Scott Frazier and Danny Stone felt their way through the dark as they entered the gym. Finally, Scott thought to turn on his cell phone light and found the switch that turned on all of the overhead lights.

"Does anyone besides the coach know we're in here?" Frazier asked. "It'd be pretty embarrassing for the cops to show up and drag us out of here."

"Stop worrying so much," Josh said. "Coach gave me the key last summer and said we could throw in here whenever we wanted as long as we put everything back the way we found it."

Josh had been gifted the key so that he could hone his prodigious talent during his rare free time. The Eastport baseball team had gone deep in the tournament the year before. They had a chance to win it all if everything played out the right way in the spring. Not having OB and Bish was going to really hurt, so a lot hinged on the right arm of Josh Hutchinson being healthy and in tune. Hutchinson had already accepted a scholarship to Boston College to pitch there after high school and had dreams of one day pitching in the big leagues. Eastport had produced one Major League pitcher, who was working as a reliever for the San Diego Padres at a cool $4 million per season. Josh had thrown a session last winter with him and learned a nice slider grip.

"I don't want to throw too hard, I just need to get the arm loosened up a bit. After some long toss we can take some swings in the cage if you want," Hutchinson told his friends.

"Why am I here?" Garrett asked, pointing at his bum left shoulder. "I'm pretty sure I'm not going to get much out of this."

"Because we needed someone to laugh at," Frazier said.

Danny grabbed his glove out of his bag, stretched his legs and his arms for a minute and then lobbed a baseball 60 feet in the air to Hutchinson, who followed suit. The ace of the Cannons pitching staff threw even higher and lazier than his friend as he tried to awaken the muscles he hadn't used in a few weeks.

"Hard to believe we'll be doing this for real in just a couple of weeks. There's still six inches of snow on the ground and we've got our first practice on the 15th," Danny said.

Frazier stepped in front of a throw intended for Stone and stole the ball away. He took two big steps to his right and spun the ball to Danny, aiming the ball right at chest level.

"I'm looking forward to it. Baseball is just fun for me," Scott said. "No one expects me to hit a lot of home runs or pitch no-hitters. I can just play third base, pitch a little relief and smack a couple of singles. It's a nice change of pace."

For the next 20 minutes, the intensity of the throwing picked up. Both Scott and Danny were relieved when the timer they'd set began to announce the end of their throwing session. Their hands hurt. Josh didn't have to ramp things up very high to throw more than 85 miles per hour. He was capable of throwing in the 90s when he wanted to and would be doing just that in a couple of weeks when he took the mound for the first game of the season.

Scott tossed his glove toward his gym bag and retrieved a bottle of water. He drank half of it in a gulp.

"So, are we gonna win this game on Friday or what?" Frazier asked, switching the group's focus back to the ice. "We have to, right?"

"If Martinage stops the puck we'll be just fine," Garrett said, juggling a couple of baseballs in his right hand. "They're not that good."

"I don't know," Josh said. He wiped off his brow with a towel. "They have good players up and down the lineup, and their goalie is pretty freakin' good. It's not going to be easy."

Danny lay on the ground with his arms tucked behind his head, looking like he was thinking about taking a nap right in the middle of the gym. His focus was on the championship banners in the rafters. Every team that had won a league, sectional or state championship for the past 70 years had a flag that hung in the field house. The hockey banner had plenty of league championships on it. The last state championship added to the mix had come a little more than two decades earlier.

"It sure would be nice to have one of those that was ours," Danny said. "Those things last forever, ya know. Win one, you're immortal. Let's go be legends, boys!"

88

Cyrus Carpenter and Billy Walker arrived together early at the rink on Thursday to work out in the gym. The duo then suited up for hockey practice, grabbed their sticks and passed a golf ball around as their teammates entered the rink.

Each boy who passed by them got a nod and words of encouragement: "Get after it today," "Go hard," and, "Everything you've got." By the time the coaches had laced up their skates every one of the Cannons was ready to go. The Zamboni began its final lap of the ice and Walker opened the door, hopping up and down as the energy in the rink built.

Coach Scadorski followed his players onto the ice and caught his assistant's eyes. He gave Tom a look that said, "Can you believe this?" Without a puck having hit the ice yet the coach knew his team was about to have its best practice of the season. The timing could not have been better. Humarock High School, tomorrow night's opponent in the semifinals, would stay home if they could have seen the team that was ready to face them today.

Once the pucks came out, the team was sharp as a knife. Every pass was exact, every shot on target, every play crisp. Time seemed to be running in fast forward as the doors opened up and the Zamboni inched out and beeped at the players, signaling them to exit the ice.

One by one the Cannons filed into the locker room. Carpenter and Walker tapped each of their teammates on the head as they went past. The 22 individuals who composed the roster were in synch and ready.

Scadorski followed the players into the room, trailed by his assistant. Over the past few weeks, the coach who stood so tall on the ice had seemed to shrink down to a normal height. His posture had slumped, his shoulders sagged. His salt and pepper hair had far less pepper and a lot more salt. The weight of leading this team through turmoil had taken its toll on him, manifesting itself physically.

The practice had rejuvenated him. He stood straighter and looked a decade younger than he had an hour earlier.

The buzz of the room died down as he perked up to speak. All eyes were forward and attentive.

"There's a word I don't use lightly because it is a word that is nearly unachievable. We strive for it, reach for it, grasp for it, but few people in life ever achieve it," he started.

"I don't know if we achieved it today. Truthfully, I don't know if you can ever truly get to it. It's like a mountain's peak that you can't see. You climb, higher and higher, but that summit might not be reachable," he paused and looked from locker to locker.

"I'm talking about perfection. You hear it all the time, 'nobody's perfect.' That's true. But, boys, today, for that practice, you were about as close to perfect as I've seen in a while. I've been coaching this game since before you were all born. Hockey's been in my life since I could walk. I'm not kidding you when I say that today was the best practice I've ever seen. I don't know what you all had for breakfast or lunch, but eat it again tomorrow," he continued.

The players laughed.

"You're two wins away from the south championship. That hasn't been done here in 20 years. You're two wins away from a trip to the Garden. Again, no one here has done that in 20 years. It's not going to be easy, I think you all know that. In fact, it's going to be damn hard. Humarock High School deserves to be in the semifinals. They're really good and they've played like it. They want to beat you more than anything else in the world. No one in the state is giving them a chance, they're an afterthought. They'll have a chip on their shoulder the size of the Bourne Bridge. They're going to come at you every single shift tomorrow like it's the Stanley Cup Finals. For them, it is. That school has never gotten this far and they want it. They can taste it."

The coach walked over to the whiteboard. The green marker had faded a little bit, but the word that was printed on it all those weeks ago by Craig

Bishop was still readable. Pointing with the blade of a hockey stick, he carefully tapped the board right next to the word 'H-E-A-R-T.'

"Bish left you that message. He knew, I don't know how, but he knew. There were times that I wondered if this team had one. Back in December, I wasn't sure. If you're honest with yourselves, you know that at times we didn't," Scadorski said.

"I wish Craig and Collin were here. Those guys had hearts the size of oxes. They were fighters. They were leaders and they wanted this chance. After that practice, I have no doubt in my mind you all are on that same level. We're not perfect, boys. Today we were freakin' close, but we play tomorrow, not today. Tomorrow, as crazy as this might sound, you've got to be better than today. That's what it's going to take. When you get into the rink, before we go out on the ice, I want everyone to look inside their heart and see what's there. Then I want you to take that heart and wear it on your sleeve for three periods. Leave it all on the ice, every bit of heart you've got... Think you can do that?"

"Yes, Coach!" they hollered as one.

"Bus leaves at 4:30 tomorrow, bring your hearts."

89

Every player has his own ritual and superstitions that must be adhered to before a game and Scott Frazier was no exception. The left skate always went on first, then the right. He tied the skates, always the left first then the right. Next, he grabbed a marker and touched up the '10' and the '19' he'd written on each of the blade holders, followed by a new tape job on the stick. On the toe of the blade, he wrote "OB" and on the face "Bish."

Once his day's artwork was done, Scott checked all his gear one more time and then stood up and made an announcement. "Everybody on my back and enjoy the ride to the finals."

That drew plenty of cheers and whoops from the team. The Cannons' best player had just taken responsibility for the outcome, something he'd never done before. Everyone knew he was capable of winning a game by himself. Heck, he'd done it so many times in the past. He'd never implied that he was going to do that. Scott Frazier was known for letting his play do his talking, but today he wanted everyone in maroon and white to know that losing was not an option.

Frazier took the leadership role even further. As warm-ups progressed before the start of the game, the head referee called over the teams' captains for final instructions. As Cyrus and Danny made their way over, Scott skated up next to them and asked if he could join them.

The ref welcomed over the lone player with a 'C' on his red sweater from Humarock and then nodded at the three from Eastport. His gaze lingered on Frazier.

"Captains only, son," he said.

"He's one of the captains," Cyrus said as Danny nodded his agreement.

The ref shrugged and then gave his spiel.

"What was that all about?" Danny asked Scott as they made their way across the ice to their bench.

"Hey, I told you guys I'm putting the team on my back. I just felt like I should be over there with you two. Is that cool with you guys?"

"It's okay with me," Cy said.

"Hell yeah, Scotty," Danny said. "Lead the way my man, lead the way."

Humarock High had adopted the mascot Hurricanes when it became a school back in the late 1970s. The village situated on the Massachusetts South Shore was a target for many tropical storms which had left their mark on the community throughout its history. In the regional semifinals, Humarock was hit by another one, Hurricane Scott.

There were more scouts than before on hand to watch Scott Frazier work his magic, and his stick might as well have been a wand. He factored in all four goals the Cannons scored. In the first period, he set up young Davey Gaudreau for a gorgeous backdoor shot. In the second period, he snapped one in from the point himself and then later made a pass that eventually led to a Cy Carpenter snipe. Finally, with the seconds counting down, he chipped a pass out of the zone for Hutchinson, who skated in alone against an empty net. The next day's newspaper showed Josh standing in front of that net, arms raised in a V while several Hurricanes lay on the ice below him.

Wes Garrett once again enjoyed the proceedings from the press box. After the game, he hustled down to greet the team as they exited the ice. Eastport was all smiles as the team hurried through the handshake line against the worn out Hurricanes. Last off the ice were the seniors: Danny, Billy, Josh, Cy and Scott.

Wes pulled the sweaty quintet in for a group hug.

"We're going to the ship baby, we're going to the ship!" Garrett joyously screamed.

Just like practice the day before, the moment was perfect.

90

Not wanting to wear the boys out with an even bigger game coming up in 24 hours, Coach Scadorkski ratcheted the intensity down a few levels for Saturday's practice. They stretched, skated and built up a light sweat. He dismissed everyone without a big speech, saving that for the next day.

"Stay out of trouble, curfew is 10:30 PM, and we will be checking in," the coach offered his troops as they left the rink.

For the first time in weeks, the Cannons were free on a Saturday night. Some of the younger kids were going to Gaudreau's house to watch movies, while the older boys were either teaming up to get dinner or going out with girlfriends. Cy, Billy and Josh were headed to the Cape Cod Mall to get new kicks; Wes promised Melissa he'd have dinner with her parents.

Scott spotted Danny leaving the locker room and told him to hold up.

"Dude, looks like just you and me are solo. Want to head out and do something?"

Danny hesitated. He and Scott hadn't really hung out together, just as a pair, in ages. That wasn't the issue that made him hedge on agreeing, though.

"I kind of had something I wanted to do tonight. It shouldn't take long, but I've got to get it done."

Scott, seeing that something about his friend seemed curious, quickly came up with a plan. "How about this. Let's swing by my house so I can bum some money off of my mother and change, then we can head out to whatever it is you need to get done, and then we can check out the mall and catch up with Cy and Bill. Maybe we can steal some of the Hyannis guys' girlfriends while we're there."

Danny was still a bit reluctant but doubted Scott was going to take no for an answer. He agreed to his friend's plan and they left the rink and drove out to the Frazier abode so that Scott could ready himself for the night.

Danny stood by in the car for 15 minutes while Scott procured two $20 bills from his mother and put on a clean pair of jeans and a hoodie. Finally, he jogged out the door and to the sedan, pulling a baseball cap on as he hopped in on the passenger's side.

Initially, Scott had no idea where they were going as Dan left his house and turned the car back toward the downtown area. With Danny pensive, he didn't prod him for any information. Scott sat back and watched the leafless trees zip by. As they came around a corner and turned onto a familiar road, he understood where Danny was headed.

"You don't have to come if you don't want to. Actually, if it's all the same to you, I'd kind of like to go by myself," Danny said.

Scott nodded his head.

"Hey man, do what you gotta do. I'll be right here if ya need me."

With that, Danny opened his door, stepped out of the car and began the slow walk over a pathway that was still moist from a recent snow melt. Spring hadn't quite arrived, but the air was warming, leaving a bit of fog hanging over the brown grass. Passing name after name that belonged to strangers, he came to the plot where his two friends rested side by side. Collin was on the left and Craig on the right.

The last time Danny had been here, he'd left in tears, unable to get to the end of Collin's funeral service.

He stared straight ahead at the two headstones until his eyes lost their focus. He stood as still as the residents of the graveyard, lost in his thoughts.

After a deep breath, Danny did something he had not done in a long time. He prayed.

"I know I haven't talked to you in a while God, but can you help me? I still feel lost. I'm sorry, but I was mad at you – so pissed – because you let my friends die and I saw it happen. I still see it a lot when I go to bed, but you know that...

"I was pissed at them too, especially Collin. If he'd just driven like a normal

322

person, he and Craig would be playing with us tomorrow. It feels weird for the team to be doing this well without them, and every time I look over to where they should be sitting in the locker room, it feels empty, I feel empty.

"Please help me get my head together, God, please. When I'm not distracted by my friends or school, I just feel lost and alone, and sad. I'm sad all the time, and I get mad at myself when I do feel happy, which is just weird. I guess... I guess I just feel broken and I need fixing and I don't know how to do it on my own."

There was no holding back the tears anymore. They came freely. This time, though, Danny did not run from the cemetery. Rocking back and forth on his feet, he continued.

"I don't want to be mad at Collin anymore. He was my friend and I want to forgive him. I wish we could just rewind life and I could make him slow down, I wish that more than anything, God. I know we can't, so can you help me figure out how to accept it all? I need to get it together. Please help me get it back together. Thanks for listening."

Slowly, Danny took two steps forward. Like back in Pee Wee hockey, he was the center with Collin on his left and Craig on his right. Stretching his arms out, he placed a hand on each headstone.

"I miss you guys so much. I hope you're there tomorrow watching us play. Thanks for helping us get this far."

With that, Danny walked back down the path to his car. His motion scared a couple of crows off their perches in a maple tree. When he reached the parking lot Scott was staring at the screen of his cell phone.

"Did you say 'hi' for me?" Scott asked his friend.

Danny sighed before responding.

"I just had to see them before tomorrow, ya know?"

"That's cool," Scott said. "Let's put a show on for them."

91

A yawn escaped John Scadorski's mouth as he waited for the barista at The Coffee Experience to pass over his drink. He'd ordered what they called a "red eye," a large dark coffee with two shots of espresso mixed in.

Scadorski was dragging because he'd spent the majority of the night in front of his 65-inch flat screen, which was tethered to his laptop, breaking down game tape of Braintree Catholic. The Cougars were going to be the best team the Cannons had faced all year long — of that he was positive. The forwards were so talented. BC's third liners would be on the Eastport first line, Scadorski figured. They played great defense and liked to push you around. Topping it off, the top team in the region had an agile gorilla between the pipes who never allowed a bad goal.

He'd known when the tournament began that if Eastport was lucky enough to get this far, they'd probably be playing Braintree Catholic. In theory that was going to be difficult enough. Braintree Catholic had it all and Eastport was a clear underdog. He'd thought long and hard about having the team watch the other team's footage so that they'd know what they were up against, but had decided against it because he did not want to undermine the confidence they'd gained. After watching a video of each of the Cougars' playoff games all night, he believed he'd made the right decision.

Assistant Coach Tom Henry had spent his evening in the same manner. Once he and his wife had gotten the kids to bed, he poured a dark beer into a glass and sat down with a notebook. By the end of the first game, he'd stopped taking notes and poured a larger glass. He didn't bother turning on the third game, but did down a third beer. He'd needed it.

Coach Scadorski sat at a corner in the back of the coffee shop with the business section of the newspaper spread out in front of him. Henry grabbed a cup of coffee and joined him.

"So what did you think, Tommy Boy?"

"Honestly, unless Martinage has the game of his life – which he's already done this postseason – I don't know if we stand a chance."

"Under normal circumstances, I'd totally agree with you. They are good enough to blow us out, no doubt about it. We could come home with our tails between our legs, 10-0 losers, and it wouldn't surprise me. They're that good."

"Why do I think there's a but on the way?" Henry asked.

"But – of course, there's a but – but, our team is not going to let that happen. I think we're winning this game. I don't know how, I mean I really don't know how, but somehow they're going to find a way to get it done. They've come too far, been through too much to let it end short of a trip to the Garden. And, if we get there, we're winning the whole thing, no doubt in my mind."

"From your mouth to God's ears."

"Oh, trust me, if we're going to win this game, God's definitely going to have to play a role. He might have to be our best player."

92

Pulling at the headset to adjust the fit, Mac Richardson poured over his game notes and tightened his tie. He wiped his glasses clean and sipped on a throat coat tea in preparation for the south regional championship game. For the playoffs, Richardson made extra money serving as a color commentator for the High School Internet Sports Network, a company that streamed the big games online. He'd been doing it for two years and loved it, especially the extra paychecks.

During that time, he'd become tight with the play-by-play guy, Jake Cabral. The affable recent college grad had big league career goals, and the voice to match. Best of all, Cabral did not take himself too seriously on the air, which made the duo's give-and-take something they both enjoyed.

With time running down quickly before the puck dropped, they exchanged pleasantries before the producer counted down their time to go live.

"Welcome ladies and gentlemen to Liberty Ice Arena in the shadow of the Sagamore Bridge on Cape Cod where we bring you today's Massachusetts Scholastic Athletic Association Division 1 South Regional Championship game. I'm Jake Cabral alongside Mac Richardson to bring you three periods of hockey, with the winner punching their ticket to the state title game at the TD Garden in Boston.

"This is the match-up that everyone predicted two weeks ago when the tournament began, the number one seed, the Braintree Catholic Cougars, and the number two seed, the Eastport Cannons. Mac, BC is running on all cylinders and has blown out everyone they've faced to this point, you've got to figure that they're the big favorites," Cabral said, turning it over to his partner.

"Let me tell you, Jake, this Braintree Catholic team is one of the most loaded teams I have seen in a while. They live by the old adage, forecheck, backcheck, paycheck. They are in your face at all times, and they've got five or six guys that can put the puck in the net at any moment. Top to bottom, they might be the most complete team in the state," Richardson told the audience at home.

"On the other side, we have the team that everyone who isn't related to a player from Braintree Catholic is rooting for, the Eastport Cannons. Mac, you might know more about that team than anyone else, so why don't you fill in the folks at home."

"I think everyone knows what Eastport, as a community, has been through this season. The losses of Collin O'Brien and Craig Bishop tore a hole in the heart of Eastport that still hasn't healed. They were stars on the football team that won the state title and were senior stars for this hockey team. Losing them hurt emotionally and functionally on the ice," Richardson said.

"But they've played really well, despite that tragedy, haven't they, Mac?"

"Yes, Jake, they have indeed. The Cannons are on a roll. Scott Frazier might be the best defenseman in all of New England and he's led this team on a fantastic run of storybook proportions. Cy Carpenter and Billy Walker have exceeded expectations and the role players, like Josh Hutchinson, Danny Stone and Davey Gaudreau have all stepped up. If Jimmy Martinage can play like he has in the net recently, the Cannons could deliver the upset and continue this amazing story with a trip to the Garden."

With that, the duo was given the cut sign from the producer and the microphones were cut off while a couple of commercial messages were announced.

"Mac, I'm rooting for your boys. With everything your town has gone through, they deserve a happy ending today," Cabral said, patting his friend on the back.

"I hope so too, but something tells me that Braintree Catholic doesn't share those sentiments."

93

Surveying his locker room, Raymond Nilan liked what he saw. Under his watch, the Cougars of Braintree Catholic had spent the last decade as the power in the state of Massachusetts. Other coaches liked to tell him he took the ice with a 1-0 lead already because of the fear his team generated. Today, though, he did not expect his opponents to have that same feeling of dread so many defeated opponents had experienced before.

His hockey machine was bigger, stronger and faster than most everyone he faced. That was the advantage you had a private high school where you were gifted the best players from the area's public ranks each and every year. Catholic schools were not allowed to openly recruit players away from other programs, as that would be considered cheating. Rules could be circumvented, though.

Coach Nilan had a network that clued him in to which towns had the top junior high talent. All it took was making an appearance at a rink to bump into the head coach of a player. Nilan would shake hands and say something like, "He sure would look good in a Catholic uniform, wouldn't he?" and that would get back to the player's parents. Within a couple of days, he'd get a phone call or email from the family asking if their son was good enough to play at that level. Nilan would respond that he'd happened to see that kid play, and he sure liked what he saw. He'd then offer a scholarship for an upcoming camp he was running, and the wheels were in motion just like that.

If Nilan wanted a player, most of the time he got that player. Technically, it was all fair and square according to the rules. In reality, the gray areas were being exploited to the fullest, and that kept his winning wheels turning.

Another trip to the Garden would be the Cougars' sixth in the last nine years. His team practiced in shirts that had a picture of the pro palace on the front, with the words "At Catholic, we play one home game per season." They were three periods away from making it seven out of 10 years.

Nilan had thought long and hard how to approach his pregame speech. Typically he simply told the boys what the points of emphasis were and kept the rah-rah stuff for the other team. Tonight, he decided he needed to change things up a bit.

"Gentlemen, you all know exactly what is at stake tonight, a trip home for us. Back to the Garden with a chance to win another trophy. That's what we play for around here, championships. Nothing less.

Over there, though, those kids don't care about a championship. They're playing for something bigger, something far more important to them. They're playing for their fallen brothers. They're playing for family. You want to win, they have to win. Think about that for a second."

Nilan counted to 20 in his head, allowing the message to take seed.

Other than your classmates and your families, there will not be one person in this rink today rooting for you. You're the evil Empire, the Cobra Kai and Judas rolled up into one. There will be boos and jeers. I want you to embrace that. You're the bad guys, fine. If you have to be the bad guys to get where we want to be, then put on that black hat and wave it around in the air.

"Eastport has had a helluva year after a really bad break. No one wants to be the team to knock them out, nobody. Personally, I hoped we'd be playing someone else so we didn't have to do it, but that's what we have to do. My heart goes out to everyone in that locker room. If it had been any of you boys in that car I would have been devastated. But,, none of that matters for three periods. For three periods they are just hockey players and so are you. You're the better hockey players, and it is your job to show it. Let them play with emotion, you play with skill and precision and speed. If you do that, you'll win, and that's why we came down here today. We didn't drive all the way to the Cape to lose. We came all this was to get back home to the Garden."

The Cougars joined in a circle in the middle of their locker room. The captain counted to three and in unison, they yelled, "Win!"

94

In the Eastport locker room, the mood was amped up. The music was loud and the players were ready. Coach Scadorski liked what he saw as he cracked the door and entered. Everything that had happened this year had led up to this moment. This was what it was all about, one team with one goal.

He tapped Cyrus on the shoulder, and the team's captain shouted for quiet. It took a second, but the noise halted, replaced by the rhythm of heaving chests and pumping hearts.

"Boys, I'll keep it brief. The team we're playing is really, really good: in fact, they're better than you from top to bottom on the roster. They've got kids going to play at big-time colleges and some who might play for a paycheck some day. That's just a fact.

"We've only really got a couple of things going in our favor. One, every time you do something good, this crowd is going to explode. Use that energy, feed off it. Tap into it and exploit it. Secondly, and more importantly, you all know who we're playing for. Out of the worst thing that could have ever happened was born a mission for you guys. You have done everything we've asked of you. You've climbed every rung on the ladder, and shocked people – shocked them.

"Today, we're going to shock Braintree Catholic, not because we're better, but because we have to. Collin and Craig will be with you today, I believe that to my core. Everyone in the stands will be behind you. You are capable of doing this. It's the same game you've been playing your whole lives, today you play it better than you ever have and if you need a jolt of energy turn around and look at those two jerseys hanging behind our bench. Touch them if you have to, whatever it takes, just know that you can find that extra gear and you make that play you have to make.

"Three periods, one mission, one team. That's it, boys, let's go."

The Cannons came together and bounced up and down on their skates. Cyrus shouted, "You know what to say, 1-2-3..."

As one, 22 voices yelled, "Heart!"

95

A representative from the tournament committee stood outside the locker room trying to eavesdrop as best he could on the final instructions being given to the local squad. Once he knew the coaches had finished, he cracked the door open and caught Scadorski's eyes. "One minute, Coach," he announced.

Jimmy Martinage started the march to the door and gave it a headbutt as Cyrus Carpenter stood next to him and grabbed the handle. Danny took his spot and Wes, still out of the lineup, stood behind him. The rest of the squad fell into line, with Billy, Josh and Scott bringing up the rear.

"Okay boys, good luck," the committee member said, giving them the okay to head out to the field of battle.

Cyrus went through first and then opened the door to the ice, with Danny and Wes opposite him to high-five everyone through. Each player got a tap on his shins, a pat on the back and words of encouragement. When everyone else had gone through the doors, the six seniors were left together. Five helmets and one bare head came together.

Scott spoke for all six of them.

"We've got this, boys. Let's do this, for Bish, for OB, for us. I love you guys, let's go!"

Josh and Danny - filling in for Wes - carried Collin's and Craig's jerseys to the bench. As they stepped onto the ice they were met by screaming guitars over the public address system as the team lapped their half of the ice. For the first time in the playoffs, the Cannons were decked out in their maroon road jerseys, with white detailing and commemorative patches sewn on the chest in honor of O'Brien and Bishop.

Danny handed over the jersey, did a few laps and then returned to the bench where he lifted first his right and then his left leg up on the boards, stretching his hamstrings. He then touched his toes, like he had a million times before, and then looked up to the stands at all of the maroon and white varsity jackets and t-shirts. Familiar faces everywhere shouted encouragement and twirled towels in the air.

Looking higher up, he focused on a ceiling tile and spoke quietly to himself.

"God, give us a hand today, please," he prayed.

Scott skated by and put his hand on his friend's shoulder.

"Don't worry, my man, God's a big Cannons fan today. We've got this brother, we've got this."

96

It wasn't long after the puck dropped that Josh Hutchinson was reminded of his experience at the Super Bowl back in early December. This time he knew how the other team must have felt when the Cannons had put those quick touchdowns up on the board. It was a sucky feeling.

Eastport had all the energy in the world to start the game and was flying. They were quickly grounded by two fast goals by Braintree Catholic. Just two minutes into the game the Cougars took the lead 1-0 when Eastport was slow changing its lines. Frazier got off the ice when he was supposed to, but Joey Moxon was late getting onto the ice in his place. That allowed a 2-on-1 break for Braintree and Jimmy Martinage was hung out to dry. Bing-bang-boom and BC was up a goal.

Three minutes later some old fashioned buzzard's luck bit the Cannons. Eastport was enjoying its best offensive possession of the game thus far. Cy Carpenter put a shot on that got stopped, leading to a faceoff. Carpenter won the draw back to Frazier, and the big defenseman wound up high to put all of his 220-pounds into a slapshot. Unfortunately, all of that torque was too much for his stick, and it exploded. A microfracture that had formed at some point during the life of the stick split in half as the blade came down on the ice. The front half of the stick went over the goalie's head, but the puck stayed exactly where it was, at Scott's feet.

Frazier had been taught at a young age to follow his shot, and he lived by the adage. As he came through the blast, he continued on forward. That left the puck behind him by a stride, served up on a platter for Braintree Catholic's best forward Frankie Hollins, who was off to the races.

In the time that it took Scott and his teammates to realize what had happened, Hollins was already at center ice and zeroing in on Martinage. All five of the Eastport skaters reversed their direction and tried to get back, but it was all for naught. Hollins was long gone and made Martinage look like he was drunk in the net. The goalie fell over himself when the sniper shrugged his shoulders to the left and then snapped off a shot to the upper right corner.

Just like that the Cougars were up a pair and looking to put the game away early. Eastport was reeling.

"It's only two, get the next one before the period ends," Scadorski urged the players on the bench. "Nobody panic, there's still a lot of hockey to be played."

The message was clear, but easier said than done. Throughout the postseason the Cannons had been the aggressors in every game. It seemed like ages since they'd had to play from behind, and when Walker was called for a tripping penalty with two minutes left to play in the period, Eastport was on the verge of letting it all slip away.

With a chance to ice the game early, Coach Nilan put his best players out on the ice with simple instructions. "I want someone in front of that keeper, screening him at all times. Don't let him see the puck."

Braintree Catholic had plenty of options when it came to blocking Martinage's sight of the puck. The Cougars were one of the biggest teams going, and all three of their top forwards stood at least six feet, one inch tall. They didn't compare, though, to junior defenseman Evgeny Machkov. The Russian-born defenseman had dressed up as "The Rock" for Halloween because he had the proportions to pull it off. He was six feet, four inches and 240-pounds of Siberian sirloin, and his specialty was parking in front of the net on a power play and being a human blindfold.

Eastport recognized what it was up against, but couldn't do much about it. Frazier tried to win a pushing battle to get Machkov off of his spot, but it was like the monster's skates were frozen in place. Moxon attempted to help in that cause, but his 165-pounds bounced off harmlessly.

Braintree's point men worked the puck back and forth methodically, waiting for a window to deposit the goal that would all but guarantee them another Garden party. After five movements up high, it was slid to the right for a slapper by Frankie Hollins.

If Hollings had taken 100 more shots he would not have struck a better one. It spun off his stick at 90 miles per hour and had the back of the net written all over it.

It didn't go in, though.

The presence of Machkov in front had certainly blinded Martinage, and there was no way that he was ever going to get in position to stop the puck. It was labeled. However, Machkov – while battling the Eastport defense – got his stick caught up under Moxon's right arm. While trying to shake the 16-year-old free from his grasp, he shoved the Eastport junior directly in the path of the shot. The puck deflected off of Moxon's left bicep and jumped out of play. The Cannon screamed, and not from joy, as the shot caromed off of his body and over the glass.

Carpenter won the next faceoff for Eastport and Frazier iced the puck down the length of the ice as time expired on the period. The Cannons got to the room down by just two. They'd survived the first 15 minutes of the game, barely.

97

"Mox, I don't know how to tell you this, but your bicep muscle looks like there's something trying to burrow out of your body. Can gangrene set in this quickly?" Walker said to his shirtless teammate during the first intermission. "That is nasty."

"Thanks, Bill. Maybe if you stayed out of the penalty box I wouldn't have to worry about getting an amputation after the game," Moxon said spitefully.

Tempers flared in the Eastport locker room. The Cannons hardly resembled the confident group that had been eager to hit the ice just a half hour earlier. Their swagger had waned, and instead, they were bickering with one another and unraveling.

When Coach Scadorski first took over the job at Eastport he'd promised himself he would not fall into the old school coaching trap of calling out his players and questioning their desire. In the long run, it did more harm than good. What good was a temporarily motivated player at the cost of lifelong resentment and bitterness?

There were plenty of potential targets. Walker's penalty had put the team in a bad spot. Martinage had given up two goals. The defense had allowed too many breaks the other way. The offense managed just four shots on goal. There was enough blame to go around for the deficit, that was for sure.

Something he'd heard at a coaching clinic a few years back had resonated with him then and stayed with him to this day. The head coach at one of the top colleges in the country had done a session on coaching winners. "Great coaches don't point fingers, they point the way."

Leaning on that teaching, he quieted the room and laid things out.

"Are you guys done? If you are I can just go sit my butt on the bench and watch the season go up in flames," Scadorski started.

Through clenched teeth, the players glared at their coach.

"We are down two goals. So what? Big deal. You've been behind before and you've come back before. I know those guys are really good, but let's look at what happened. They got one on a mistake and another on a bad break. Is that enough to make you quit? If so, I greatly underestimated the heart of this team."

He put a little extra emphasis on the word heart.

"Did I?"

Scott spoke up.

"We're not done Coach, not by a long shot."

"Well then, if you want to have a chance to win this game you have to score next. Have any of you ever heard about the 1980 Olympic hockey team? The Miracle on Ice?"

Every player in the room had seen the Disney movie about those events multiple times. They could all recite Coach Herb Brooks speech verbatim. Heads nodded and stone faces cracked.

"What happened when the Russians found themselves having to play in a close game? Anybody?"

"Umm, they panicked and the US guys outworked them," Walker said, perking up.

"That's what you've got to do, outwork them and put a little panic in their minds. They haven't had to play a close game this whole tournament. Did you see how much they threw into that power play at the end of the period? They were trying to finish you off. They don't want to let you hang around because they know what this place will be like if you have a chance in the end. That building is packed with your fans, but you haven't given them a reason to get loud. Give them a reason, make them loud and it will give you a lift, and maybe rattle those guys. Gentlemen, I promise you this, if you score the next goal this becomes a hockey game you'll always remember. If they get the next one it's a game you'll want to forget."

98

In the stands, the Eastport fans had been raucous before they'd even seen a maroon jersey on the ice. The place had sounded like a rock concert the moment EHS exited the locker room up until the first goal was scored by Braintree Catholic. Once the top-seeded team had made it 2-0 they'd shut up like a scared clam.

Walking back up from the locker room to his perch in the press box, Wes spotted Melissa, Emily and a host of their friends from school. He mouthed, "Get louder," toward them, and the Cannons faithful took notice. The entire town had been through hell the last few months. The hockey team had been a rallying point, and they showed their appreciation for that as the horn sounded for the teams to take the ice.

The cheers of "Let's Go Cannons" reverberated off of the silver roof of the Liberty Arena. On the ice, the players took notice and perked up. As they gathered in front of the bench, Scadorski's final message before the frame began was simple, "Give them a reason to get even louder."

It wasn't a goal that took the fans to another level. It was a good old-fashioned, bone-crunching check from an unlikely source.

Hardly known for his physical toughness, Danny Stone's mental state post-accident was hardly a secret around the school. The slumped shoulders and the slow gait were noticed and whispered about. A lot of his classmates wondered when Danny would "snap out of it." Rumors of a mental breakdown ran rampant. Kids talked, and the stories got wilder with each retelling.

When the senior hit the ice for his first shift of the second period he did not go out intent on wrecking someone. He just wanted to get the puck, and there it was loose along the left wing boards, near the red line. With every bit of speed he had, Stone pushed off his skate blades ferociously to get there first. One of the Cougars had the same idea, and won the race, but not the battle.

Braintree Catholic's forward reached with his stick and pulled the puck toward him. He made the mistake of keeping his head down to make sure he had possession of the vulcanized rubber. Danny recognized he wasn't going to get there first. That left him just one option, to make a hit.

Pulling his hands in close to his chest and squeezing his shoulders in close to his torso, Danny skated directly through the opposing player. The impact sent both boys flying, but it was clear the round had gone to Stone. He quickly picked himself up off the ice and looked down at the destruction he had wrought. A whistle stopped play because the opposing player had lost not only his stick and gloves, but his helmet had gone spinning through the air and landed 10 feet behind him.

Shaking the cobwebs out after the check, Danny was called over to the bench for a line change and greeted like a conquering hero. The back slaps and pats on the head felt great, as did the new cheer that erupted out of the Eastport section.

"Danny Stone!" Clap-clap, clap-clap-clap. "Danny Stone!"

Adrenaline coursed through every Cannon's veins after that check. Braintree Catholic was still able to control the puck for most of the first seven minutes of the stanza, but the tide was turning. The Cougars shied away from the corners and were content with dumping the puck down into the Eastport end without charging hard after it.

Exactly midway through the second period one such play supercharged Eastport's chances. At the end of a shift, the Cougars spun the puck off the boards, looking to get five fresh sets of legs on the ice. The shot from just inside the red line had been a half-hearted rap on Scott Frazier's side. The Cannons best player charged to the short wall and was able to stop the puck with his right thigh and collect it all in one motion.

While Frazier was getting control, Josh Hutchinson saw open space appear in front of him on the left wing. The man that was supposed to be marking him had not yet gotten onto the ice, and Josh screamed, "Scott, wing," to give his teammate a heads-up.

So many of Scott's attributes on the ice had garnered him the interest of all of those college coaches. At the top of that list was his ability to move the puck, and he added another amazing pass to his prolific highlight reel by snapping it to the edge of the far blue line for the streaking Hutchinson. The hero of the football season had nothing but open ice between himself and the goaltender.

Josh did not possess the dynamic set of fake-out moves that his friends Cyrus and Billy had, but he did have a go-to maneuver in these situations. He flew up the wing and cut across the zone at the left faceoff circle, which got the big goalie moving to his left. As the keeper's feet slid that way, Josh bode his time until he saw the left knee bend. Once it had, he knew the goal was as good as scored.

Josh used a quick flick of the wrists, then converted his shot to a backhand motion. With an audible "ting" the puck hit off the inside of the post and bounced over the goal line.

Josh's hands shot up and he crashed into the rear boards, having cut the deficit in half. His teammates engulfed him, leaping high into the air in celebration and landing on top of him for a celebratory hug. His right hand pointed towards the sky out of the pile of bodies.

Eastport was very much alive. It was a brand new hockey game.

99

"Mac, those were two great periods of hockey here at Liberty Arena. What can we expect to see in the third?" Jake Cabral shouted into the microphone to be heard over the crowd noise that was filtering through his headset.

"Braintree Catholic dominated that first period and were one bounce away from going up by three goals. The second period was a lot more even, and that amazing pass by Frazier to free Hutchinson has Eastport right back in this thing. If you're Braintree Catholic you're looking to push that tempo back to where it was earlier in the game. Eastport's good, but they cannot skate with the Cougars up and down the ice. They need to make this a grinding contest, but find ways to get the puck to the net. Eastport only has one goal so far, and that was on a breakaway. You can't bank on another one of those coming your way."

"So who wins?"

"Good question. My head still says it is Braintree Catholic, they're the best team in the tournament. My heart says the Cannons, though. They've got one goal in mind and they're so close right now they can taste it. Look for them to try to get Cyrus Carpenter and Billy Walker involved early in the third period. That dynamic duo has been kept off the scoresheet so far tonight, and they don't win if one of those two can't get something done."

As they rested between periods Cyrus and Billy were thinking the exact same things that the color commentator was. They had been shut down by Braintree Catholic so far. It was evident that their numbers had been written in large numerals on the chalkboard during the week by Coach Nilan as the guys to worry about. Between them, they'd managed just three shots on goal and had not been able to get comfortable at all.

"This is our time B-dub, our time," Cyrus said to the former team captain as they circled around the faceoff dot before the opening draw for the third period. "Time to go win this game."

Before Billy could respond, Frankie Hollins smirked and spoke up on behalf of the Cougars.

"Not today kid, sorry," he said. "Enjoy this period, it's your last."

Walker and Carpenter gave one another a knowing look. The pair had played hundreds of games together. They might not always get along off of the ice, but the chemistry that they had on it was spectacular. They reached their gloves up for a fist bump and then pointed at Hollins. The Cougar responded with a smirk. Billy and Cyrus wanted nothing more than to wipe it off his stupid face.

The puck dropped on the third period and Walker and Carpenter were dead-set on getting the score evened up. Their first shift saw Carpenter put one on net that was just kicked aside with a skate. Walker then nearly tied it on a wrist shot from the hashes that painfully rung the crossbar.

The scales were tipping more and more in favor of the underdogs, and Braintree Catholic was beginning to waver. Finally, the Cougars made a big mistake that presented a golden opportunity for the Cannons. Machkov had been throwing his weight around throughout the first two periods without repercussions. With each bullying tactic that was not called, he grew more and more confident that he could get away with pretty much anything. While trying to clear out the space in front of his net, he swung an elbow that caught Carpenter on his facemask.

Compared to a lot of the stuff that the Cougars defenseman had done so far, this one was hardly egregious. However, the referee happened to be looking right down the slot at the beefy blueliner and Cyrus sold the heck out of it. As soon as the elbow grazed him, he went down to the ice as if a sniper had taken him out from the rafters.

The ref's arm went up and his whistle blew. The elbowing call drew a two minute penalty, and for the first time all game long, Eastport was going on a power play. With just nine minutes left the opportunity was enormous.

Scadorski called his power play unit over and drew up a play. He instructed Cyrus to win the puck back to Scott, who would then look for the best option in terms of shooting or moving the puck.

"Coach, that's what they're expecting. Can we try this instead?" Cyrus pleaded, quickly marking up the paper with X's and O's.

"I like it," the coach said. "You only get one chance, run it."

The referee prepared to drop the puck to the right of the BC goalie. Cyrus set up to take the draw, and Danny Stone took the right side, as opposed to his usual spot on the opposite wing. Stone angled himself behind Carpenter, and three steps to the right while Billy took the left side, in the usual spot for the winger.

Danny knew what was supposed to happen next. He looked skyward to the deity he'd reopened communication with and said a quick prayer. "Please, now's the time," he whispered.

The puck was dropped and Cyrus won it cleanly on his backhand right to Danny. As his stick went back in an exaggerated fashion, one of the Braintree defensemen dove to the ice in an effort to block the oncoming shot. The goalie tensed and squared up to the shooter. Another Cougar reached with his stick to try to tip the puck away.

Danny never shot it. He wasn't supposed to. The slap shot motion had done exactly what it was intended to do, cause Braintree to sell out to stop him, and allow Billy to creep down to the side of the net by himself. The slap pass Danny struck was right on the money and all Billy had to do was put his stick on the ice for the ricochet. Clapping off of his stick blade the puck bounced into the wide-open nearside corner.

Game tied 2-2.

"And just like that, Eastport has come back to tie the game," Cabral shouted to the audience watching the game at home. "What a play by the Cannons! Danny Stone makes the play of the game to find Billy Walker and the score is tied at 2-2 with just 8 minutes and 51 seconds remaining in regulation time. Unbelievable!"

Billy was mobbed by teammates and Danny led the charge. The stadium shook, the Eastport fans making the building sound like a tarmac at takeoff as their score changed from a one to a two on the scoreboard.

Coach Nilan did something he had not had do throughout the entire playoff run as the players came back up the ice. The Cougars' leader formed a straight line with his right hand and crossed it into a T with his left, calling for a timeout.

100

The celebration was raucous but didn't last long for the Cannons.

Coach Nilan ordered his top line out on the ice after the goal, while Eastport was forced to go with its third line following the power play. Eastport's forwards got beat to the other end of the ice and Alex Gossard was left in a tough spot on defense. He tried staying between the guy with the puck and the wing flying up the right side. That left the junior exposed to the forward trailing the play, who had also beaten the rest of the Eastport skaters up the ice.

The pass was dropped back for a big bomb. Gossard tried to block it, but his sliding body missed the puck and did not get any part of it. Martinage flung his glove in the general direction of the shot in vain.

The volume at the Liberty Arena plummeted. Only the smattering of Catholic fans and their players could be heard cheering.

After all of that work to come back, the Cannons were right back where they'd been to start the period, chasing a goal. The difference between then and now, though, was that just eight minutes and 16 seconds remained on the clock. It wasn't time to panic. Yet.

As the clock neared the five-minute mark, Scadorski shortened up his bench, going with just two lines the rest of the way so the best players were out on the ice at all times. The first line was Cyrus with Billy and Davey Gaudreau on the wings, and the second line was Josh in the middle with Danny and Cam Roget, who had moved into Wes's spot after his most recent injury. Looking on from the press box, it pained Wes not to be out on the ice.

Eastport's focus was getting the puck to the goal by any means necessary. Coach Scadorski urged his team to shoot from everywhere in the zone. "Can't score if you don't shoot," he'd said time and again over the course of the year. "Shoot the puck and good things happen."

And shoot it they did. Roget, who had just two goals all year long, had an effort that went just a little wide. Gaudreau and Walker both put bids on goal that were covered up. Eastport had the edge in play, but the clock seemed to be running in fast forward.

With two minutes to go, Walker nearly tipped in a shot by Gossard. The wrister flew true, right at the goalie, and Billy raised his stick and deflected it. The puck bounced like a basketball, just past the goalie but wide of the net and into the corner.

Braintree Catholic needed a breather with the relentless pressure on their defense adding up and iced the puck down the rink. Scadorski called for a timeout with 101 seconds to go and laid out his instructions.

"Martinage you're off," the coach told his goalie, informing the team that it would be pulling the keeper so that it could have six attackers on the ice for their last-ditch effort at tying the score. He then lined up his players, with Cyrus, Billy, Danny, Josh, Scott and Joey Moxon responsible for finding a way.

"I don't want anything fancy, just shoot the puck and crash the rebounds. Get an ugly goal. And do not let them get the puck out. If they fill that empty cage the game's over. You've got almost two whole minutes, no need to panic. Fire pucks on goal and get this game tied up."

The team counted down a quick 1-2-3 followed by, "Heart!"

Carpenter slowly wove his way to the faceoff circle to square off with his nemesis, Frankie Hollins. The Catholic centerman had reveled in running his mouth all game and was not about to stop now.

"Told ya this was your last game. See that empty net, I'm about to put one in it and end your season. Hope it was fun," Hollins sneered.

Carpenter responded with a grin as he devised a plan that would both win him the draw and be enjoyable to implement. Throughout the game, he'd used a backhanded stick lift whenever the faceoff had come in the spot it was in now, on the left wing offensive dot. Every one of the Cougars was expecting him to do that again. Cy decided it was time to try something different.

The referee flashed the puck between the players and slowly raised his right hand before dropping it down. Hollins, who was holding his stick in a backhand grip, reached forward with his hands to try to snap the puck back into the corner. His hands came forward as the puck approached the hard ice, but his body went backward.

Just as the ref was about to reach up his hands, Cyrus had given a nod to Walker and then dragged his eyes to the dot. That informed his friend that the puck was his to take because he was about to run straight through Hollins. With the puck nearing the ice, Carpenter lowered his shoulder and skated right at the logo on his opponent's chest, pushing him straight back toward the rear boards.

Billy had loved his friend's idea the second he realized what he was up to. He pounced toward the dot, measured the puck and lined up for a wrist shot. He saw his opening, zeroed in and let it rip.

The crowd groaned at the sound of rubber meeting iron. Billy had the goalie beat but hit the pipe.

Braintree's defense stopped the puck in the corner and ate up precious seconds by boxing the puck between their skates. Danny came in with his stick blade and poked and poked and poked, finally freeing it and snapping it back around to Moxon, who immediately let one go from the right point. The puck floated over the net and wide to the other corner.

Walker crashed into the rounded boards and was met by two bodies blasting into him. They were then hammered by Hutchinson, who threw himself into the fray. Chopping away like lumberjacks, all four players battled ferociously. Finally, Walker kicked it back to Frazier, but the puck was on edge and bounced out of the zone. All six Eastport players had to clear out of the zone and get back onside while time continued to descend.

Now just 50 clock ticks remained as Eastport cleared out and then back in to chase a slap shot around the boards by Frazier. Stone got to the puck first and whistled it to the front for a cutting Hutchinson. The multi-sport star swung his stick and tapped it on net, but the goalie kicked it aside. Again the Cougars iced it all the way down.

Slowly the pellet kicked up snow as it headed straight toward the vacant Eastport net. Someone yelled "get it" from the Cannons bench. Scott Frazier sprinted back as hard as he could. He dove face first and reached with his stick to just narrowly push it offline and into the corner, saving a goal and the Cannons hopes.

Moxon, who also flew down the ice, got to it and took a brief glance at the scoreboard. Now just 28 seconds remained. Hastily he flung a pass up the left wing for Walker, who swiveled by a BC player and went straight to the goal. Billy had some daylight, and another chance to be the hero. This time his shot was exactly where he wanted to put it.

Billy's eyes widened with excitement until a flash of leather exploded out of nowhere and knocked the shot wide.

There was no time to be stunned. Just 12 seconds remained.

Cyrus scurried to the puck and spun it to the goal, firing wildly. Once again it was on net but saved by the goalie.

Eight seconds to go.

Stone secured it next and spotted a wide-open Frazier. He found the team's de facto leader and best player with a perfect pass.

The guy that everyone wanted to have the puck with the game on the line reared back for a one-timer and hit it as hard as he could. The goalie moved laterally to his right and the puck hit his shoulder. A rebound presented itself. Danny Stone desperately lunged at it, but the goalie's big glove covered it just as the horrific sound of a foghorn bellowed through the arena.

Game over: Braintree Catholic 3, Eastport 2.

101

Blue and gold gloves and helmets rained over the ice. The BC goalie found himself at the bottom of a pile of bodies, gleefully gasping for air.

On the Cannons bench, the players all slumped on the boards, blankly witnessing the celebration unfold in front of them as they attempted to compute what had just happened. Eastport's six skaters each collapsed, exhausted mentally, physically and emotionally.

It was over.

Stunned, the Cannons eventually lined up on their blue line and were greeted by an enormous ovation as they were awarded the runner-up trophy. Cyrus and Danny, along with Coach Scadorski, posed for a grim photograph with the hardware that they did not want.

Braintree Catholic then partied as they accepted the regional championship trophy. Their captains and coaches wore monstrous grins in their acceptance photo and even bigger ones as the team lined up for a group shot at center ice.

While BC hammed it up for the cameras, the Cannons slowly retreated off the ice toward their locker room, resembling felons making their final stroll down Death Row. Heads were low and tears rolled under their facemasks. They were oblivious to the continued standing ovation from their fans. The coaches carried the jerseys of OB and Bish over the ice back to the locker room for the final time.

Inside the locker room, the mood was grim. No one removed any equipment for some time. All 22 players, whether they'd played a ton or rode the pine, slumped at their stalls. Some wept openly, others in silence. They all sobbed.

Cyrus smashed his helmet onto the ground, severing the facemask from the housing. "That was our title, dammit," he wallowed as the cage from his helmet bounced off the floor. "Ours!"

Wes, slumping through the door to console his brothers, wrapped his arms around his friend. They cried together.

Outside Scadorski tried to give thoughtful answers to questions from the media that he could barely process.

"We gave it everything we had... I'm so proud of these guys... Braintree Catholic is a heck of a team... We didn't lose, we ran out of time... We've been through a lot, but this is a character building moment," and on and on the rote answers went.

Finally, as the questions became repetitive, he tapped out. "Guys, that's all I've got. I have to go talk to my team. They're hurting in there."

Scadorski, who was also hurting, knew what to expect when he walked through the doors but still wasn't prepared for it. The sadness strangled the air out of the room. He reached for his tie and loosened it, then gulped half a bottle of water before speaking.

He knew what he was about to say was very important, but he had no idea what it was going to be. Closing his eyes, the words came from his heart.

"No one thought you'd be here today, no one. There were people who thought we should just cancel the rest of our season, mourn and try to recover. Not one of you, not a single one, ever told me you wanted to do that. You wanted to play, to honor Craig and Collin. I wanted that, too," he started.

"Boys, mission accomplished. You didn't need to win the state championship to honor those guys, you didn't need to get a trophy to stand up for them. You needed to play, finish the season, do your best. I've coached a long time, and I hope I never have to deal with what we all dealt with this year ever again. That's too much to ask anyone, let alone a group of kids, but you guys figured it out. You survived it. I know you're hurting right now, nobody can blame you for that. Losing sucks, especially when you're so close you can taste it.

"Someday, not today, but someday you're going to realize just what it is that you guys accomplished this season. As a team, as a family, you got to the finish line. You left every ounce of effort and hustle you had on the ice.

You emptied the tank," the words came slowly, but he continued.

"Life is hard, I don't need to tell any of you that. Unfortunately, you don't always win. What matters, though, is how you move forward, how you respond. Life is about bouncing back, advancing from one day to the next. Get knocked down, get back up. Some days are hard – like this one – and some days are amazing. Every single one of you has what it takes to be great in life. You're Cannons, and I'm proud to be your coach. I love you guys, thank you for crossing the finish line with me."

102

A week had passed since the end of the season. The team had cleaned out its locker room at the Arena on Tuesday afternoon and hugged their coaches one last time. Scadorski thanked all of the seniors for their tenure, offered to help where he could for their futures and hugged them tightly. Everyone cried some more, but they laughed a lot too.

Wednesday was weird, with nowhere to go after school for the players, as were Thursday and Friday. On Saturday, Wes sent out a few texts and rounded up the Boys for a road trip to Providence. Josh loved the idea, and so did Scott. Danny balked but eventually agreed to go. With room for two more on the trip, they invited Emily and Melissa to join in, too. They said they wouldn't miss it for the world. Cyrus and Billy said they'd drive down together and meet them at the place.

Driving one-handed, Wes took the Jeep over to Danny's house to pick him up and turned the driving duties over to his friend.

"You know that you guys are nuts, right?" Danny said as he hopped into the front seat.

Wes shrugged an agreement as they began their adventure by whipping over to Josh's, then Scott's house and finally the Brown estate where both girls were waiting. With the Cherokee packed, they made their way down Route 195 toward the Ocean State.

"I can't believe we're going to do this," Josh said.

"Believe it," Scott said.

"I think you're all crazy," Danny said.

"No, crazy is that we have baseball practice on Monday. Talk about moving on from one thing to the next," Josh said.

"Yup, I get to go watch another practice. I'm an expert on observing other people practice sports," Wes said snarkily.

"Calm down, you'll be back out there with us in a week. Then you're going to be complaining about all of the running and how tired you are," Scott countered. "Enjoy the time off while you can."

"Lax for me and Mel," Emily chimed in. "I can't wait."

"I don't know, I could use another week to get ready. It's not warm enough for lacrosse yet," Melissa said.

The conversation continued for the next 45 minutes about school sports, classes and college plans as they drove over the state line and into Providence. Danny suggested stopping for some of the amazing burritos down off Gano Street, but the group decided that they'd put off eating until after.

With one more left turn, they found the right street. They then marched down the sidewalk, two by two, and opened the door to the shop they were looking for. Wes had called ahead to set up an appointment and had worked out a group rate. Scott reached into the back pocket of his jeans and unfolded a piece of white computer paper, handing it over to be inspected.

"That's pretty straight-forward. It'll take about 45 minutes each," the owner and head artist at Ink Better said. "You'll have to come back to get them colored in later."

Realizing that they'd be there for the bulk of the day, Danny took burrito orders and collected money. He'd stuck to his guns and refused to get the artwork done on himself. The rest of the friends had tried to convince him, but he claimed his parents were dead set against it. In reality, he just didn't think he could handle a daily reminder of seeing his friends die. It was just too much.

Josh volunteered to go first and lifted his shirt off. The future D1 baseball pitcher said he'd like the work done right over his heart.

Wes and Danny walked out the door just as the buzzing of the needle began. They couldn't help but laugh at the sound of Josh yelping while Emily teased their friend as they left. "Suck it up, buttercup," she giggled as he squirmed.

"Keep chirping, Em. You're next," Josh rebutted.

By the time they returned back to the shop, Josh, Emily, and Scott were recovering from their sessions and admiring the artist's handiwork. Cyrus was doing his best not to clench up each time the bearded man touched his skin. Billy then clenched his teeth through his session.

As Wes's turn approached he urged the group to head over to the mall so that they didn't have to sit through another.

"It's no big deal, we can wait," Melissa said, while the rest were already heading out the door.

Wes persisted, and Danny agreed to sit with him while the others went to roam the stores at the Providence Place Mall. They planned to meet up for fast food and a movie to end the day before driving back to the Cape.

Wes endured his time under the needle, sweating through the whole thing. He admired the new tattoo in a mirror and then handed a scribbling to the artist asking what it would cost for one more. The artist read it to himself, helped Wes pick out a font and informed the two boys it would be another hour to get this one finished. Danny sighed, leaned back in his chair and tried to catch a nap. Sleeping was hard to do while his friend made all of the associated noises one makes when being mildly tortured.

Finally, it was done. Wes winced as he stood up and looked at the mirror. The artist was about to cover it up with protective plastic when Danny asked if he could see the tattoo that had cost them another hour of their lives.

He saw the writing and asked what it meant.

"Craig had to write an essay for his application to East Carolina. They wanted to know what the biggest obstacle he'd ever had to overcome was. He wrote it the day he got back from that trip, which was just a couple of days before the accident," Wes said. "He told Emily about it, and I found the essay while I was looking for some pictures in his room for the funeral. I took this straight from his essay. It was one of the last things he ever wrote."

"Wow, that's crazy," Danny said.

Danny drove with Wes to the mall and they found everyone milling about the food court sucking down chocolate shakes. Wes and Dan had made it with plenty of time to spare before their movie began. Danny got into line to order himself and Wes their own cold, thick concoctions to sip on while Wes sat at a table with the rest of their friends.

"What took you guys so long?" Billy asked before stealing a french fry from Cyrus. "You took forever."

"Yeah, we could have driven to Eastport and back again," Cyrus said, placing his hands over his order of curly fries to protect the rest.

"Sorry about that," Wes said. "I had the artist do two."

First, he showed them the one that looked just like the ones they'd gotten. The Boys had all had it cut into their chests, while Emily's adorned her shoulder. Underneath, though, he'd added the phrase, "I got you."

Josh grinned when he saw the phrase.

"I guess I've gotta go back now," he said. "I need that added to mine."

"So, are you going to show us the other one or what?" Scott asked.

Wes agreed and told them the same thing he'd explained to Danny earlier.

"Craig had to write about the biggest obstacle he'd overcome in life. He'd written about losing his mother as a young kid," Wes explained.

Danny came over just as Wes lifted his shirt.

"I've got to admit, I'm kind of jealous of that one," he said.

As Wes pulled the fabric up, they saw the phrase framed by a baseball bat on top and a hockey stick below. They all read the words that were inked in cursive on Wes's rib cage aloud in unison.

"Knowing that the person you love won't be in your life is a hard thing to accept, but it makes the memories even better. The memories make you smile."

Acknowledgements

This novel never would have happened without the help and support of so many fantastic people. I know that this list will end up being incomplete. I wish I could mention every single person that offered me a word of encouragement or said that they were looking forward to reading the book when it was done. Every kind word helped me get to the finish line. I've been blessed. With that said, I would like to thank...

My rock, my world, my life, my wife. Lyra, somehow, some way, we get to the next day. As Eddie sang, *"I am lost, I'm no guide, but I'm by your side. I am right by your side."* I always will be, thank you for being by mine.

Rye and Leanna, my kids. They named many of the characters in this book and always lent a willing ear when Dad had an idea he needed to think out loud. You two make me proud each day.

Mom and Dad. Whenever I camped myself in the studio for some peace and quiet, you were very cool about it. One day I will finish reading those letters, Dad.

Nicole LeBoeuf. What can I say, and how can I say it without needing to remove a comma? The first draft wasn't bad, but this project took off when we met. You made me – and this book – so much better, and for that I will be forever grateful. God bless you and your wonderful family.

All of my friends that dove into this world to help me make it better, especially Amy (Sawyer) McDonald, Lannan O'Brien, Kirstin (Simpson) Pimental and Debbie Huff. Your insights and notes were so helpful.

My beta readers, some of whom revisited a tough time in their life to make this better. A heartfelt thank you to Cooper Rogers (great catch btw Coop), Kellie Matthews, Cate Brodie, Melissa Hamilton, Emily Wheeler, Ben Kennedy, Chris Parkinson, Victoria Little and Tommy Brennan.

Leslie Smith, you thought I'd forgotten you. No way, you were the first one to finish it and one of my biggest fans before you'd even read page one. You're a great friend.

The Lavins, Higgins and O'Reillys. I don't know if you'll ever be able to sit down and read this from cover to cover, but I just hope that I was able to do justice to the memories of James and Owen with "Season On the Brink." While this novel is a work of fiction, the inspirations were real, and they were great kids.

The Fellowship. "The Boys" are also inspired by real life people, and they know who they are. You guys inspire me with your dedication to, and love for, one another. I'd especially like to thank Brandon Woodward and Nick Couhig for taking time to sit down with me and hash up some tough memories to assist me with this process.

Paul Moore. Moorzy, getting your team through that season is the most impressive thing I've ever seen a coach do. With that said, you're an even better friend than you are a coach, and that's saying something.

Ted "T.M" Murphy, my Yoda. I can't tell you how helpful it has been to have your wisdom at my disposal. Who else would take time to sit down and be a friend while they were trying to get a movie made? Can't wait to see you accepting awards for "The Running Waves" after its theatrical run.

Michael Bailey. Writing books is something that real people do, and you proved that to me. I miss our daily nerd sessions so much.

Steve Maclone. Who knew what you were starting when you bought me that subscription to Sports Illustrated when I was 12. This is all your fault, and I thank you for that.

Sargent Matthew Croteau. Thanks for the tickets to those game sixes.

The town of Falmouth, Massachusetts. If Eastport seems a little familiar, it might be because it's a lot like my hometown. Since I started talking about this project the town has given me wonderful support. The people here hurt a whole lot when that accident occurred just before Christmas of 2016. I hope that this book has helped some process and deal with some of the grief that remained.

God. Every time this project needed something to get to the next step, it was provided. I don't deserve the blessings I have received, but I am grateful. Thank You for all things.

About the Author

Rich Maclone has been writing about sports on Cape Cod for more than two decades. An award-winning reporter, Rich's love for the sports and people he covers is evident in his prose. "Season On the Brink" is his debut novel, and inspired by true events. Rich lives next to a cranberry bog on Cape Cod with his wife, Lyra, their children, Rye and Leanna, and their two dogs, Mo and Murphy. When he's not working as a reporter, or professional photographer, he can be found at his secret fishing spot scaring the bass away.

Visit RichMaclone.com and sign up for the newsletter to keep up with all the goings on in Eastport, including updates on the sequel to

"Season On the Brink," planned for 2020.

Made in the USA
Middletown, DE
20 June 2019